Dedication and Thank You

I dedicate this book, which has been the culmination of several years of work and whatever success may come from it, to those in my life who have helped support me throughout this journey.

To my mother and father for all of their love and support, and to my biggest supporter, Olivia, who's always encouraged me to keep moving forward and have confidence in myself.

I want to thank all the people who have helped, including my beta readers, Cathy, Rhonda, and Lisa. I also want to thank Peggy, who came along later in this journey but has helped to provide a renewed sense of hope that I am on the right path with this writing thing.

Last but most importantly, thank you to all of you who've purchased the book. I hope you will enjoy the story that follows as much as I have enjoyed creating it.

PROLOGUE

WASHINGTON, DC

Agent Troy Sanders burst from his chair, sending it careening backward as it ricocheted off the desk behind his.

"Holy shit," he exclaimed with his eyes wide, his mind struggling to comprehend what he'd just read.

He waited for the email to finish printing. "Come on, come on," he muttered under his breath, snapping his fingers and discerning that the inanimate object was useless, but he continued to snap at it anyway.

"Thank you," he blurted sarcastically to the printer, snatching the paper from its tray as soon as it finished.

Quickly, Agent Sanders shoved the still-warm paper into a manila envelope and rushed out of his office. He needed to alert his bosses and fast. Throwing open the office doors, he slid into a long-tiled hallway and broke into a sprint.

Rounding a corner at full speed, he crashed hard into the adjacent wall, driving his left shoulder into the drywall. "OW!" The collision hurt like hell, but the agent kept running, knowing what he held could cost many people their lives.

He continued to race down the hall, rubbing his shoulder as he went, ensuring the envelope was still intact in his hand and checking behind him to make sure he didn't lose anything.

Agent Sanders pumped the brakes, pulling up to slow himself as he rounded another corner of the empty corridor. He slowed down, but his worn dress shoes caused him to skid around the bend, just barely tapping the wall.

He pushed off, course-corrected, and barreled into an unsuspecting janitor cleaning the floor, knocking him to the ground.

"Sorry!" Agent Sanders shouted at the startled man, who was glowering at him as he looked for his glasses. Unfortunately, there was no time to help him up. The secretary needed to hear this information as soon as possible.

Turning the last corner, he finally screeched to a halt outside the Secretary's office. Agent Sanders could tell that someone was still inside through the frosted glass. There was a light on inside. The secretary was his boss's boss's boss. However, thankfully, he was the only high-ranking official still in the building.

Henry Smith, the Secretary of the Department of Homeland Security. Agent Sanders fixed his jacket and hair before knocking.

"Enter," came a gravelly voice. Agent Sanders timidly opened the door, peeking inside. "Well, enter." The man behind the desk gave off an intimidating vibe. He was a veteran of multiple wars and recipient of two Distinguished Service Crosses. He had only just been appointed Secretary of DHS three weeks prior.

"Sir, I… I"

"Son, collect yourself," Smith said, seeing that the young agent was clearly out of breath. "Who are you?"

"Agent Sanders. Troy Sanders, sir," he said, calming himself as he approached the desk. "I know I'm breaking the chain of command here," he apologized, bringing the folder up between wheezes.

The senior official glanced at the young agent over his laptop; his eyes flashed to the prop.

Well, then, that must be very important, judging by the haste in which you've brought it to me," Secretary Smith responded, indicating the file. "Hand it over then." Agent Sanders handed the folder of documents over. "What exactly am I looking at here, son?" he asked, putting on a pair of spectacles.

"Well, sir, I believe that there is a terrorist attack coming, eminently."

"Coming where?"

"Here."

Secretary Smith looked up from the documents, his face suggesting a mixture of disbelief and concern. "What makes you say that, son?"

"That top page." He pointed out, referring to the email he'd printed. "That is directly from the Canadian Security Intelligence Service, stating they believe there is a high probability that a terrorist cell may have entered their country last week."

"How does that lead to a terrorist attack on U.S. soil?"

"Turn to page three," the agent insisted. "The CIA has been monitoring several terrorist organizations. One of which has been making some noise in Yemen, with some of the chatter suggesting they have been planning something big. Real big, like 9/11 big, sir."

Secretary Smith skimmed the documents. "When is this happening?"

"Not sure, sir, but my guess is soon. With July 4th approaching, I would say we're looking at it real soon."

He handed over the documents and gave the young agent a long, silent gaze in reply, making Agent Sanders slightly uncomfortable.

The silence dragged on.

"Okay, we're going to need to verify and reverify all of this as soon as possible," Smith said, handing the folder back to a relieved Agent Sanders before picking up the phone. "Then, we must disseminate this information to all law enforcement agencies. Start with the FBI field offices in the northern states and work your way down from there."

"Yes, sir," Sanders said, taking the folder back and heading for the door.

"Oh, and Sanders, call everyone in now." His tone suggested that he believed the Intel was solid enough for his concern to outweigh his last disbelieving look.

"I'm on it."

CHAPTER ONE

Fred Jones let the warm water cascade down his body as steam engulfed the bathroom, turning it into his private sauna. Steadily and meticulously, he worked his joints out top to bottom, trying to loosen himself up. He arched his back to hear the satisfying crack of his vertebrae.

The release of synovial fluid and pressure brought a faint smile to his face.

Satisfied and ready to go, he turned the water off and stepped out of the shower. He snapped a towel off the rack and wrapped it around his waist as he made his way to the sink.

He wiped the fog from the mirror, exposing his reflection. He stared pensively at himself, examining every inch of his face.

He didn't feel his age, and his body didn't seem to reflect it either. Sure, his hair had a little more grey mixed with the black, as did the three-day-old stubble on his face. But that meant he was more refined, sophisticated, and educated by life, right?

Forty-five is practically the new thirty-five. At least, that's how he felt.

Still, he promised his wife, Sherry, last year that he would hand in his retirement paperwork after hitting the big 45. Unfortunately, it happened a little sooner than he wanted. Now that the day had arrived, he couldn't help but second-guess the decision. He still had so much more to give.

For the first time, he didn't want to honor the agreement he had made with his wife. But these thoughts would have to wait because he needed to finish getting ready. Shaving off the stubble made him look even younger, further affirming his doubt.

Putting on his familiar and comfortable black suit, white shirt, and black tie, he was ready to go. But he took another glance in the mirror for good measure, fixed his tie, and gave himself a slight nod as he snapped up his badge before heading to the kitchen.

As he drew closer, the aroma of fresh blueberry pancakes tickled his nose, followed by the scent of freshly brewed coffee.

Sherry had prepared his favorite breakfast. He expected that would be the case, as it was his birthday. He hoped she wouldn't remind him of his promise, but having been married to her for fifteen years, he knew it was only wishful thinking.

Crossing through the archway, he walked into their newly remodeled kitchen. He had spent the entire last month redoing it, complete with everything his wife wanted. Brand-new appliances, countertops, cabinets, and even an island. He made sure she got it all. He couldn't help but survey his handiwork, drawing a bit of pride in himself. He spotted Sherry sitting at the table.

She set the paper down when she heard him enter, smiling at him. Her combination of fiery red hair and blue eyes was the rarest in the world. Even after fifteen years of marriage, he still found himself amazed by it. He grabbed his plate and sat down.

"Happy birthday, honey. Did you sleep well?" she asked, still smiling at him.

Fred saw the question coming at him from a mile away. Her facial expression gave it away. He answered hesitantly, "Yes, I did. Thank you for asking."

"So… do you remember what you promised last year?" Somehow, her smile grew wider.

Bam, and there it was. Even before taking his first sip of coffee

"Yes, dear, I remember," he begrudgingly admitted. "I will start the process today." His face fell flat, as did his smile.

Sherry sensed something was wrong right away. "You promised Fred. You're not having second thoughts, are you?"

"Well, to be honest, I sort of am," Fred conceded. "You know what being an FBI agent means to me. I don't feel ready to give that up right now. I still love doing what I do," he explained. He didn't want to start a fight, but he had to be honest. He was always honest and truthful with his wife.

Sherry's smile dissipated, turning into more of a glare. "Ok, I hear you. But don't you love me more?"

"That's not fair," Fred objected.

She was trying to make it a competition between her and the FBI. "Of course, I love you more. But it's not just my job or career. It's…" Fred paused. He didn't want to go further on the subject because he didn't want to hurt her, but he also didn't want to retire because the job gave him a sense of belonging. A purpose, almost. Allowing him to mentor the younger agents who saw him as a father figure. Something he had always missed in his life.

The young couple discovered early on that Sherry would never be able to have children. The news had almost broken their relationship. It was mainly a gut punch for Fred. He grew up in a large family and always wanted kids. Knowing they couldn't have them, they managed to work through the tough times early on.

Fred realized there was another way he could fulfill that fatherly role. He would work with the young incoming agents out of Quantico as their trainer and mentor. It was a task he took pride in, and now Sherry was asking him to give that up, too.

Sherry knew exactly what Fred meant and why he had stopped talking. Her glare softened. "Look, I know what your job means to you. So, if you're not ready, I understand. I want my husband to myself for once and not have to share him with anyone. I want to go on those vacations we always dreamed about."

He reached across the table, taking her hands in his. "I know, I know. I'm not ready, and I don't think I will ever be ready. That said, I do love you and made you a promise. "So… as I said, I will start the process today, okay?" Fred assured her as he kissed her hands.

Sherry jumped up, hugging and kissing her husband. "Thank you, thank you," she said happily.

He picked up his plate and dropped the dishes in the sink as he heard his wife say, "Well, you better get going, or you'll be late."

****

Fred didn't know how he would break the news to his boss. That's the only thing he thought about as he drove to the Milwaukee FBI field office. For now, he had decided to keep the decision to himself. He hoped this would give him an out in case he changed his mind and somehow convinced Sherry to let him continue working. But wouldn't it be better to rip it off like a Band-Aid and just come out and say it? He still couldn't decide as he walked into the building.

Waiting for the elevator doors to close, he heard a voice yell, "Fred, wait for me."

A young, fresh-faced agent rushed through the doors before they closed. Agent William Finch slid in beside Fred.

William had been Fred's new partner and protégé for six months. As he always did with new agents, Fred had taken William in from the moment he arrived after graduating from Quantico at the top of his class. Fred had seen something in William that reminded him much of himself at that age, which convinced him to take the kid under his wing and mentor him.

William also took very kindly to Fred and made every effort to ingratiate himself with the senior agent. The kid listened intently to Fred, soaking it all up like a sponge. Although William had one trait that Fred found hard to change, his need always to be the first at everything. It made him impulsive at times, which is never good for an agent. It got him through Quantico, but that stuff wouldn't work in the real world.

"I see you got a haircut," Fred said, glancing over at the kid.

"Of course, sir. As you say, look the part, be the part. Right?" William fired back in a nearly military tone.

"That's right, kid. You look good-"

"You feel good, sir," William boasted, cutting Fred off, knowing exactly what he was about to say.

"Keep this up. You'll have your own division someday; hell, you might even have your own field office."

The elevator doors opened, and William smiled at the compliment. They stepped off the elevator, and the entire floor buzzed with activity, too much activity for 9 a.m. Fred looked around, his interest instantly piqued.

"What's going on?" he asked William as another female agent rushed up to him.

"Fred, good morning. Tobias needs to see you right away in his office." Her tone, combined with the jitteriness, suggested something big was happening.

"Good morning to you, too, Michelle. Do you know what it's about?" Agent Michelle Ramirez had worked under Fred in his

Counter Intelligence division for the past two years. He had never seen the dark-haired, tech-savvy agent so flustered.

"I'm not sure, but I think it's something important. There's been a lot of buzz around here this morning."

"I can see that," Fred answered, turning to William. "Go ahead, get settled in, but I want you in my office as soon as I'm done with Tobias."

"Roger that, sir," William replied, heading for his desk.

Fred made his way to Tobias Stevens' office. Tobias was the Special Agent in Charge of the Milwaukee field office and a good friend. He had tried to get Fred to take the Assistant Special Agent in Charge job multiple times, but he always turned him down. Fred loved doing fieldwork and didn't want to get stuck behind a desk. It would also deprive him of the opportunity to mentor the younger agents.

Fred knocked on the glass door to Tobias's office when he didn't see Jill, Tobias's administrator, at her desk. The senior agent waved him in but indicated for him to be quiet. He was in the middle of a phone conversation.

He hung up a few minutes later and stood up. The two men shook hands. "Fred, good morning," he said. "Please sit."

Despite having known each other for seven years, Fred still had no clue how someone as big as Tobias made it through training. The man would have stood out like a sore thumb at six feet six, easily weighing two hundred and fifty pounds of mostly solid muscle. He would have been the easiest target ever to pick out. His shiny bald head would've also given him away at night.

"So what's so pressing that you needed to see me immediately?" Fred asked, taking a seat.

"We have information that between today and July 4th, there will be a terrorist attack somewhere in the continental United States."

Fred couldn't believe what he had just heard. How could that be possible? But the sternness of Tobias' face said it was.

"So, sometime in the next two days. Somewhere here in America. Is it 9/11 big or something like the recent attacks in London?"

"Don't know. That's all the info we've gotten so far from our friends at DHS. They believe that a terrorist cell has entered the country via the Canadian border and that an attack is imminent."

"Where did they get their information?"

"You know, I didn't really ask that. I'm guessing NSA or CIA. Who cares where it came from? We need to be ready. Have you heard anything?"

"No, nothing at all. Everything's been really quiet. No chatter," Fred answered.

"Ok, but I want your entire division to be working on this. You know the drill. I don't want us to get caught with our pants down. I want a list of all the events in the area that could potentially be targeted. I don't care how small, even if it's a minimal risk target, I want us investigating it."

"We'll get right on it."

Fred had his marching orders in hand.

Leaving Tobias' office, shocked that another attack could happen, he was taken aback on the way to his office. Reaching the door, he turned and waved at William, getting the young agent's attention and signaling for him to come.

Waiting for William, Fred took his time to process what his good friend and boss had laid on him. Standing by the window, he gazed out across Lake Michigan, quietly watching as the waves slapped against the breakwater, the sun glinting off the ripples on the surface.

Another attack on U.S. soil. How could this happen?

A few moments later, William knocked on the door. "You wanted to see me, boss?" he asked, poking his head in.

"Yes, come in." Fred sat in his chair behind his mahogany desk, inviting the young agent in. He entered, gliding across the room to take a seat across from the desk and settle in. "I have just been informed of a potential terror attack here in the United States sometime in the next two days," Fred said bluntly, not knowing any other way to say it.

William's eyes grew larger as he leaned forward. "Oh my god. Do we know the target?"

"No, unfortunately, we have no idea at this time. I want you to gather the team in the conference room. We need to go over every event from now until the Fourth of July celebrations throughout the state. Create a risk assessment on each immediately."

"Sure thing-" William paused, noticing his boss wasn't listening. Something else had grabbed his attention. William glanced over his shoulder to see agents darting across the office. The commotion was followed by a cacophony of oohs, ahhs, and frightened gasps.

Fred stood, making his way to the small terrace at the back of the room where the main offices were located, slightly elevated above the main floor. They called it the dugout. William followed.

The dugout was where most of the agent's desks were located. Fred, Tobias, and the Assistant Special Agent in Charge's offices were up a small flight of stairs at the back. Several smaller offices and conference rooms flanked the dugout on each side of the room. Everyone had gathered near the break room.

A crowd of agents had assembled around the TV, intently watching a special news report. Fred couldn't exactly tell what the reporter was saying from the back of the room. He descended the stairs, making his way through the throng of agents, pushing past those who were stunned. His knees grew weaker the closer he got as images of some explosion flashed across the screen.

Drawing closer, he caught a glimpse of what was on the screen. Across the bottom banner, the words *explosion* accompanied by *bomb* were easily discernible. Fred's heart sank. Could this be the attack Tobias had warned about?

Tobias flew out of his office. His booming voice could be heard from the terrace.

"Everyone gather around." He paused, waiting for the shocked agents to pull themselves from the television. "I just got off the phone with the city's police chief. There has been an explosion at the Harley Davidson Museum and a report of shots fired near the area. Many of you may have heard that we have been warned of a potential terrorist attack. I don't want anyone jumping to conclusions here. This may be nothing. I want everyone to continue doing their jobs. Right now, we need to be back to work. Hundreds of calls will start rolling in. I want us on top of those as they may be tips. We all know what to do right now, so let's do it. Fred, now." Tobias motioned for him to follow.

The two entered Tobias' office. The senior agent took out a set of keys, unlocking the top drawer of his desk. Fred watched his friend fish out his badge and gun. "Look, I know you've been thinking about retirement, and today was supposed to be the day you submitted your request. This may be nothing but-"

"Tobias, save it. How long have you known me? Have you ever known me to leave anything unfinished or leave my friends out to dry?" he stated, ignoring the fact that Tobias was aware of his impending retirement.

"No, I can't say I do," Tobias replied.

"Ok, then why would I start now? I'm with you on this to the end."

"Great," his friend said, relieved. "Gather whatever resources you need and prepare a team. We're headed to the scene to find out what's happening."

Fred left Tobias's office, stopping by Agent Ramirez's and Agent David Franks' desks to inform them that they were coming with him. He also told William to gear up as he went to his office. There, he grabbed his badge and gun before walking to the elevator. The other four assembled with him while waiting for the car to arrive. They clustered silently inside, each with their own thoughts. William pushed the G button.

The ride down was silent, but it was time for Fred to take charge once free from the metal box and show the kid how to lead. "Ramirez and Franks, I want you to bring the mobile command unit. Even if this isn't what I think it is—I hope it isn't. The Police can still use it on-site. Fred and William, you're with me," Tobias ordered. The three agents climbed into a Cadillac Escalade and headed for the scene, not knowing what to expect.

CHAPTER TWO

Since leaving the parking structure, no one inside the Cadillac had spoken a word. The only sound permeating the car's interior emanated from the police scanner. The three occupants were cloaked in their thoughts and emotions, each contemplating what awaited them at the scene.

Fred and Tobias, having encountered similar situations numerous times, possessed the fortitude gained from extensive training and drills to confront terrorist attacks, augmented by a lifetime of experience that guided their actions.

However, William lacked the reservoir of such seasoned expertise. Though he had undergone training and attended classes on responding to such events, the classroom environment paled in comparison to the unpredictable reality. Fred had endeavored to instill this truth in the young agent, and now it was time to discern the extent to which Fred's instruction had resonated within him.

Fred gave his young protégé a side-eyed glance, worried he wasn't entirely prepared to handle the situation they were about to face. His penchant for running into things headfirst without thinking and evaluating would not serve him well here.

The young agent was a little too gung-ho, something Fred had tirelessly worked to stop over their time together. Hopefully, the lessons stuck. Either way, he would soon see the young William in action.

A radio squelch, followed by a woman's voice, brought Fred's thoughts to Sherry, hoping she was okay. Their house was clear on the other side of the city, so thankfully, she wasn't in immediate danger. However, due to the chatter over the scanner, a significant amount of misinformation and confusion arose among the first responders.

So, what was the news reporting? Usually, cellphone towers would be overloaded and shut down during a crisis like this. Getting a good connection would be nearly impossible. So, getting ahold of anyone would be out of the question.

He glanced down at his phone. No missed calls. He assured himself Sherry was smart enough to figure out that phones would be unreliable. He would call her when he was able to. She knew the drill. After all, she had been married to an FBI agent for fifteen years.

Looking over at Tobias, Fred peered into his usual stone-faced demeanor as he drove. Not a second thought in his mind that his boss was in the right headspace to lead them through what was about to come. Like him, Tobias had been involved in a high-profile terrorist attack at the London office in 2005.

He also assisted in the investigation when seven separate suicide attacks happened on the London transit system. So Tobias knew what he was doing and probably already had a plan.

Between thoughts, Fred looked back to ensure that Agents Ramirez and Franks were still following in the mobile command unit. The two vehicles tried to make their way through the traffic that had nearly ground to a halt.

As they headed towards the blast site, Tobias occasionally lay into the horn, flicking their lights, hoping to get people to move. But no matter how loud their sirens were, they were drowned out by the wailing horns of all the other emergency vehicles en route.

William broke the silence in the vehicle as he cleared his throat. "So, what are we expecting when we get there?" the novice agent asked with hesitation.

"Well, honestly, first, we will have to find out who is in charge and get whatever information they have. Depending on that, we will provide whatever assistance they need or assume full control. The rest we figure out once we get there… Fuck shit, asshole," Tobias blurted, swerving around a car that wasn't paying attention before casually continuing. "That's all we can do, kid. Stay next to Fred and learn; that's it. Got it?"

"Yes, sir, I got it," William responded.

They finally pulled up to the hastily established perimeter of the scene. Tobias murmured a half-hearted compliment that the Milwaukee Police Department had done an excellent job setting up the boundary as two cops approached them.

The Harley-Davidson Museum was situated on a promontory of land encircled by the Menomonee River on three sides. The sole means of entry to the small island were the two primary access routes via 6th Street. However, the police had promptly sealed off the area several miles away from the explosion site, including West Canal Street, where they were currently positioned.

"Feds?" one of the officers asked as they approached the Cadillac, staring at the enormous mobile command trailer behind them. "Man, we're glad to see you for once. The police chief has been expecting you. Go ahead on in. Make a left after the cement factory. That's the staging area. You'll see the command tent. I'll have someone on standby to guide you in."

"Thanks, Officer," Tobias responded, flashing his badge out of courtesy and rolling up the window. They waited while two other officers removed the makeshift barricade.

****

Fred stepped out of the vehicle and right into the chaos of the situation. Almost as if he'd been transported into a scene from the latest Hollywood disaster movie. All around, the sound of wailing sirens, people screaming and yelling. The piercing bellows of others writhing in pain and agony were unmistakable, similar to those he had heard at the World Trade Center.

The day was still young. The sun hadn't even reached its peak in the sky. Yet, the area had an ominous feel, gripping it in darkness. Black plumes of smoke billowed from what remained of the stage. Fires burned as first responders mixed with civilians and attempted to put them out. More minor explosions from propane tanks boomed, and one canister launched into the air, causing people to duck in terror.

People were still running all over the place, some with minor injuries and others with more serious ones. One woman looked to be holding her hand when she tripped, exposing that it was attached only by a flap of skin. The mass of injured pleaded with any available rescuer to help.

Another group of paramedics appeared to be setting up an emergency triage unit. Some of the survivors had already been marked with a red card. It wouldn't be long before they could no longer be called survivors.

He caught a glimpse of a man walking in shock as half his body was burned, falling into the arms of the first paramedic he saw. Another red card was handed out. The whole scene was utter chaos all around. Scenes and images Fred never wanted to see again in his life, but here he was, standing in the middle of it all again. He could not help the victims, but he could help them in another way. Catch those responsible.

Fred peered over the truck's hood, his gaze fixed on Tobias, who was engaged in a heated exchange with an unseen individual on the opposite side. Despite their proximity, their voices were drowned out by the wind. A gust swept through, carrying with it the nauseating scent of burning flames and blood, causing Fred to wrinkle his nose in revulsion. His focus was abruptly diverted as the cacophony of screams intensified, carried by the wind in hopes of reaching a compassionate soul who could provide assistance.

His gaze returned to the horrific scene unfolding in the field adjacent to them. It seemed the screams were growing louder. The stage fire grew more intense, heating the surrounding area and intensifying the already oppressive heat. In the distance, Fred could see the heat shimmer enveloping the field under its cloud. He watched as more paramedics arrived, rushing over to aid the wounded. He took a step forward, about to follow, before he heard Tobias.

"Fred, grab the kid, and let's go."

Fred turned to find William's mouth agape, his skin pale white, his eyes wide, as he absorbed the carnage before him.

The reality of life set in. It was one thing to be in a controlled training scenario where you know that the people running around were actors and not injured. This was on a whole different level. A woman ran by him, holding her child, who had been burned. All William could think about was how that family would cope with this tragic event.

"Oh my god... this... this is horrible," the young man stammered, his hand running through his hair and down his face. "I have been through training for this, but... but." The kid stumbled backward, bracing himself against the truck.

Fred pulled him along by his arm. "I know, kid. No amount of training can ever prepare you for this, though. I told you real life is different than a classroom. Look at me." Taking his protégé by the shoulders, he stared him in the eyes. "Just remember, you're an FBI agent; act accordingly. Now close your mouth, and let's do what we were trained to do. Got it?" Fred said, slapping him on the chest to pump him up. All the while, his legs had been wobbled by the devastation.

"Yeah, I can do that," William responded, arching his back and composing himself.

"Good, let's go. It appears we're getting an escort to the command post." Fred pointed up ahead a bit where Tobias was following an officer.

They were led to the command area on a grassy field just behind the museum's parking structure. Adjacent to the command post was the field where the stage had been set up for the Fourth of July concert before the bomb.

Entering the makeshift command room, which was essentially a large tent. He pushed aside the flap, lowering his head to duck in. The agents were introduced to Sheriff Randy Thomas, a grizzled veteran of the Sheriff's office. Fred had worked with him on several occasions. He was hard-nosed and no-nonsense, always looking rough behind his mustache.

"Sheriff, what information do you have for us at this time? I know things are pretty chaotic here," Tobias asked, getting straight to the point.

"First, I want to say there will be no jurisdiction pissing contest here," the Sheriff said before pausing for a second and then continued. "This was, without a doubt, a terrorist attack, and I'm handing full control over to you and the FBI. Of course, you will have my full cooperation and assistance in whatever you need." The two leaders shook hands. "I want to find the assholes who blew up my city." Anger oozed behind every word he uttered.

"That's something we both have in common, then, Sheriff. That's exactly what I intend to do here. You all know the drill. We need to work fast and smart." Tobias gave his friend a nod. Without exchanging any words, Fred knew what needed to be done.

"William," he whispered to the kid, who had been enthralled with Tobias's ability to command the room. "Come on," Fred said, pulling him outside. "Time to learn," he said, approaching agent Ramirez. "Agent, have Franks bring up the truck. It's time to set up. We're running this operation from here."

"Yes, sir," the dark-haired agent responded. "Franks, get the truck. We're-"

"Oh, and Ramirez. Call everyone in," Fred ordered. "William, stay here. I want you to park them over there," he ordered, pointing to a large blank space in the field. "I'll be right back."

Returning to the tent, Tobias pulled him aside. "Ok, you heard it; this is all ours from here on out. I don't want anything to look sloppy or half-done. We must close this out and find the people who did this."

"Yes, sir, absolutely," Fred responded. His initial shock had dissipated. "I have Agents Ramirez and Franks bringing up the truck, and William knows where to park them. Plus, every available agent is on the way over as we speak. Did he tell you what he knows?" Fred asked, hoping they had a solid lead to go on.

"He gave me a little background but wants to wait until everyone's here for one big meeting, and then he'll hand everything over to us. Officially. For now, get the truck up and running," Tobias said before walking back towards the Sheriff, who was talking to someone else near the front of the tent. Fred turned to finish getting everything set up as instructed.

✳✳✳✳

Twenty minutes later, Sheriff Thomas asked everyone to gather back in the tent once the police chiefs arrived.

"Alright, everyone," his gravelly voice commanded everyone's attention. "Ok, so this is what we know so far. Moments before the bomb went off, a security guard alerted local officers to a suspicious van parked near the concession area."

"How do we know that?" someone interrupted. "Where's this information coming from?"

"Who are you?" the Sheriff snapped, annoyance written on his face.

"Sorry, Sam Watkins, the mayor's aide. He's not here right now, but I want to give him all the correct information."

"Well, Mr. Watkins, it was radioed in to dispatch."

The Sheriff continued after the interrupter nodded, "As I was saying. Shortly after that, we got further reports *through dispatch*." Adding emphasis for the benefit of Mr. Watkins. "Several Middle Eastern men fled the van's interior when the officers approached. They began firing indiscriminately into the crowd before running away from the scene. At some point, one of them must have triggered the bomb. Right now, that's all we know. And now, I would like to hand everything over to Special Agent in Charge Tobias Harris."

"Thank you, Sheriff," Tobias said, taking the floor.

Meanwhile, Fred stood at the back of the tent, watching Tobias launch into his spiel. He'd heard it several times over the years and knew it almost verbatim.

Mid-brief, a Sheriff's deputy quietly snuck into the back, whispering something to Sheriff Thomas, who waved for Fred to step out with him.

"What is it, Sheriff?" Fred asked; judging by the look on his face, it was good news.

"We have a local factory worker reporting that he may have information on the attackers' location," Sheriff Thomas said.

"Well, shit, where is this guy? We need to find out what he knows," Fred cursed, trying to hide his annoyance.

"We have him in your command truck," the deputy responded, but he was immediately pushed out of the way by Fred.

They entered the mobile unit to find Agent Franks sitting with a man in his mid-thirties, clothes covered in concrete dust. His eyes glazed over, and his hands were trembling.

Fred placed a hand on Agent Franks' shoulder, signaling him to get up and move away. Fred took the seat across from the potential witness. "Sir, my name is Agent Jones. The deputy says you may have some information."

"Um… uh… yes, sir, I… I think I do." The man's breathing

increased as he rubbed his head and dropped it into his hands. His knees twitching up and down, he mumbled, "I've never seen anything like this before."

"Can we get this man some water?" Fred ordered, sending Agent Ramirez out. "What's your name?" he continued.

"Um, um… my name is Anthony Davis." His mouth quivered as he bit into his lower lip. "I work at the cement factory a few hundred yards north of here." He continued, "We heard the gunfire and then the explosion and our foreman ordered us to evacuate the area. I was headed to my truck when I saw two men running in this direction. It appeared they were trying to conceal weapons on their sides. One looked injured, maybe. I don't know. Another turned and saw me, so I ducked, but I lost my balance and fell down the hill, hitting my head on a rock." He instinctively rubbed the bump.

"Can we find a paramedic, too, please?" Fred asked Agent Franks. "How do you know they were trying to hide weapons?" he asked, continuing his line of questioning. "Could they have been people fleeing the scene? I mean, you said you hit your head." Fred wanted to be sure Mr. Davis saw what he saw.

"Well, sir, I'm a hunter, and when I'm out in the woods, that's how I move when I have my rifle slung over my shoulder. I know what I saw, Agent Jones." Mr. Davis's voice rose, and his leg froze, as he did not like Fred's condescending tone. "Bump or no bump, I *know* what I saw."

"Okay, Mr. Davis, thank you for the information. The deputy will take your written statement and get you all patched up."

Fred was convinced that despite the admitted head injury, what Mr. Davis had seen was indeed two of the attackers fleeing the scene. Knowing this could be a huge break, he immediately sought out Tobias, who was back by the Sheriff's tent.

"Sir, we may have something," Fred said, informing his boss. "A factory worker claims he saw two men run into the factory carrying weapons. They may still be there, as one of them appeared to be hurt. What do you want to do about it?"

Tobias seemed to linger on the information, contemplating what to do. Of course, the attackers may have already left the area by now, making this a potential wild goose chase. However, it was the only lead they had to go on.

"Ok, Fred, I want… I *need* you to take a strike team and investigate this lead. Get as many agents or police officers as you need and check out this cement factory. Hopefully, with any luck, they might still be there," Tobias ordered.

"Got it. Sheriff, I'm going to need some of your men," Fred demanded.

"Like I said, anything you need," the lawman responded, radioing several of his men back to the tent.

"Oh, and Fred, be careful. Or Sherry will never forgive me," Tobias added.

"Aren't I always?" Fred said, looking back at his friend with a smile.

CHAPTER THREE

Fred assembled a team to investigate the tip provided by the cement factory worker. True to his word, Sheriff Thomas gave three of his officers to the team. The rest of the unit consisted of five FBI agents, plus William and Fred. After checking their equipment and the layout of the grounds, they proceeded to move out on foot toward the Buzzi Unicem concrete facility. Successfully reaching the parking lot, the team took cover behind the vehicles that were left. Fred poked his head over the SUV they had gathered behind to survey the area.

"Ok, the teams are in position. We're set up in the parking lot holding," he radioed to the MCC, where Agent Ramirez and Tobias were monitoring the mission.

Agent Franks opened the side door quietly, re-entering and taking a seat beside Agent Ramirez.

"We're all set," he said, flipping a few switches. "We should be able to bring up the feed now."

Agent Ramirez checked the monitor to her left, and a video feed popped up on the screen. A drone provided an aerial view of the museum grounds. She watched images as Agent Franks took control of the flying object, rocking it back and forth to ensure he had complete control.

From above, the chaos of the blast sight took on another form. It no longer seemed real as the drone panned the site, revealing the grotesque horror. Through the monitors, it didn't feel real. As if she weren't there, but she could still hear the screams and pleas of the people outside.

"Agent Ramirez, please get it into position," Tobias directed. The SAC noticed the look on the woman's face. She had drifted into the maelstrom of emotions. However, he needed the young woman to stay on task. "Agent Ramirez?"

"Right, sorry," she blurted, snapping out of her train of thought.

"Are we clear to go?" Fred asked over the radio, growing impatient. He knew every second was crucial. If the two suspects were still inside, they might get closer to escaping.

"All set, Alpha one. The drone should be overhead in a moment." Agent Franks worked the joystick controls, bringing the UAV around the factory, flashing into view. "Okay, Alpha One, a transportation terminal is approximately 200 feet ahead of you. A small loading dock and warehouse, a couple of storehouses located to the left, and then a field behind the stacks," Ramirez informed the team.

"Thanks, Ramirez. Over and out. William, Johns, Marks, and Rodriguez, you're with me. The rest of you go right."

With a quick series of hand gestures, the two teams moved out in separate directions. Fred led Alpha team towards the storage sheds, with Bravo team heading towards the main entrance.

Fred's team approached the first shed. It wasn't actually a shed at all. Peering through the door's window, Fred spotted a pair of train tracks entering the building from beneath the massive, closed roll-up door on the front of the structure. It appeared to be some type of weighing station.

Stacking up outside the door, the team prepared to move in. Fred motioned for Marks to take point. The burly agent swung around to the front of the stack, preparing to kick in the door.

Fred paused for a moment, drawing in a deep breath. Suddenly, his conversation with Sherry from earlier that morning popped into his head. Part of her argument about wanting him to retire was an incident that happened two years ago. He had been shot in the leg while executing a raid quite like the one he was about to embark on. His hand subconsciously rubbed the spot as a tinge of fear crept into his bones. What would happen to her if he wasn't so lucky this time around?

No, I can't think like that, he said to himself, brushing aside that feeling. Fred saw William looking back at him, staring blankly. He could see the wonder in his eyes; why hadn't they gone yet?

Fred gave the signal.

Marks kicked the door in, and the team burst into the room. He remained on point as he moved in first, cutting to his left. Johns followed, moving to his right. William rushed ahead, weapon drawn, eager to shoot anything that moved. Fred followed closely behind, with Rodriguez in the rear, watching their six. The team swept through the room, checking every square inch of the building.

Nothing.

There was no one inside.

"We're clear, sir," Marks stated. "It doesn't look like anyone was ever here."

Fred nodded, keying the mic. "Command, this is Alpha one, over," he radioed.

"Go for command, over."

"First structure has been cleared. Moving to the next. Out."

"Damn, my finger was itching on that one," William groaned.

"Patience," Fred advised. "Trust me. You don't want a firefight," he said, again rubbing his thigh. "Let's move out."

The team cleared the rest of the buildings and found no signs of the terrorist. Fred began to wonder if this was a wild goose chase after all. The terrorists couldn't possibly have remained in the area for this long.

"Agent Jones, come in, over." Ramirez's voice broke Fred's train of thought.

"Go ahead, building four clear. Over."

"The drone shows a broken-down house at the back of the compound. Do you see it? Over."

Fred spun around, facing the rear of the compound, and placed a hand over his brow, squinting. The dirty façade of a wooden house shimmered in the distance.

"That's a good copy, Ramirez. I see it." It was the last of the buildings in the area to clear. "We're en route. Out." Fred motioned for the team to gather. Marks, Johns, Rodriguez, and William gathered around their team leader. "Bravo Team status report. Over."

"We're wrapping it up in here. All Clear so far. Headed back down. Over," Agent Johns answered.

"Okay, great. Finish that up, and you heard about the house? Over."

"Yes, sir, we'll meet up with you out there. Over."

"Roger. I want you to flank it from the right, just in case. Out."

Fred gazed over the terrain between the last storage building and the run-down house. Aside from a few shrubs and small hills, there wasn't much cover between them. The dilapidated single-floor house was half torn apart and appeared to be in the process of demolition from the outside.

Fred analyzed the best route to take. But, no matter which way they took, the biggest unavoidable danger would be the eight yards of flat, wide-open ground they'd cover before reaching the house. If the terrorists were inside, they would see the team coming clear as day. The only cover was in the form of a crane parked halfway in that kill zone. Despite the danger, Fred knew they had to get closer and search the house.

"Looks precarious," William said, standing beside his mentor. "No good approach points."

Fred eyed him; they were both on the same page in assessing the situation. Some of his knowledge had been rubbing off. "You're not wrong on that." Turning to the team, Fred said, "Alright, boys, we're moving. I want a wedge formation. Keep your distance, stay sharp, and, most importantly, keep your eyes open." He patted William on the shoulder. He let the young agent know that he was proud of him for recognizing the danger. "Johns, on point this time." The agent nodded, taking up the point of the formation and striding towards the house.

Meanwhile, William, Rodriguez, Marks, and Fred lined up behind the agent in a V formation and staggered out, leaving five feet of space between them. Maintaining their distance and fields of fire on their approach gives any possible shooter a harder target to hit.

As they closed in, Tobias watched the drone's camera feed, his eyes sliding to the edge of his seat. Ramirez's eyes were glued to the monitor as Franks moved the drone in for a closer look—*forty, thirty, twenty yards out.*

Ramirez shouted through the radio, "I SEE MOVEMENT. GET DOWN."

Her warning was too late. A loud, rapid succession of muzzle flashes came from the house. Johns took several rounds to the chest and felt them ripping through his Kevlar vest. Another round hit him square in the middle of his forehead, tearing through his skull, exploding out the back of his head, instantly killing him.

The rest of the team threw themselves to the ground. Fred, luckily, had been walking past a crane when the shots rang out. Hitting the deck hard, he rolled behind the steel behemoth for cover, then popped back up to a kneeling position, ready to return fire and scan for targets.

"Agents taking fire, I repeat, agents taking fire. One KIA'd. Bravo, get your asses here now," Fred screamed over the radio between intermittent bursts of fire from his M4. No target had presented itself, but he knew he needed to lay down cover fire as others were still in the open and would be easy to pick off without suppressive fire, even if it was blind and aimless.

From the drone, Tobias watched in horror as his agents started dropping like flies. He slammed his fist into the table, nearly breaking it. Ramirez saw the sheer anger in his eyes as he watched Johns's body fall. He scrambled in the truck, grabbed an M4 and a vest, and leaped out of the command unit without a second thought. "I need every available agent on me now," he shouted. "We have agents taking fire. Let's move."

He and a contingent of ten men moved out, taking off in the direction of his friend to provide support.

Fred had already emptied his first magazine. He changed clips, seeing everyone else pinned down in the open. They needed to move. "Get your asses out of there now."

Marks hopped to his feet, making a beeline in Fred's direction. Another rapid succession of gunfire hit the running man in mid-stride. His arms shot up into the air, gun flying forward, screaming in pain as the bullets ripped into his flesh. A round sizzled past his left arm, grazing him. Another struck under the vest just above his waist, puncturing a hole near his kidney. The final round sliced right through his right thigh, and blood spurted into the air. It had torn straight through his femoral artery. The agent fell to the ground, screaming in agonizing pain, frantically clutching at his leg.

Fred knew he had to get to him fast. He jumped to his feet, wildly running out into the open, shooting at the house. Unable to tell exactly where the shots were coming from, he just needed to create an opening for him to reach Marks.

Grabbing hold of the back of the young agent's vest, he started dragging him back to the crane. "Hang in there, Marks. Just hang in there."

Bullets zinged by his head as dust plumes kicked up all around him, chunks of dirt spraying Marks as Fred dragged him across the ground.

The bullets were getting closer and closer.

Fred could tell that they were using AK47s. The only good thing about that gun is that it isn't exactly known for being accurate. Still, the AK47s are formidable weapons, nearly indestructible, and with an extremely high fire rate. And, despite their inaccuracy, the shooter would eventually zero in on them before they could reach the crane.

From his right side, more gunfire filled the air. Finally, the Bravo team joined the firefight, flanking the house. William, seizing the opportunity created by the Bravo team, jumped to his feet and raced over to help Fred drag Marks back to the crane, with Rodriguez providing cover fire.

Now that Bravo team had joined the fight, the two shooters in the house knew they were outgunned and would soon be flanked, cutting off any possible escape routes. They decided to make a break for it now while they still had a chance. The two bolted out of a side door, running towards an open field.

From their advanced location, the Bravo team couldn't see their targets fleeing. They continued their course straight towards the house. William continued to help Fred as the two dragged Marks back to cover, with neither agent realizing that he had already bled out.

William, hunched over, dragging his dead comrade, caught movement from the corner of his eye. Glancing up, he spotted the two shooters making a run for it as they reached the safety of the crane.

"Fred, they're making a run for it. Let's go get them." Not waiting for a response, the impulsive agent took off in a dead sprint after them.

"William, no, wait… don't go, wait for bac-," Fred shouted, but it was useless. William was either not listening or out of earshot.

"Rodriguez, stay with Marks, and let Bravo team know where we went," he told the remaining agent as he rounded the back of the crane. "I'm going after William."

Rodriguez nodded.

****

William was gaining ground on the shooters fast. The agent had been a track star throughout high school and most of his college days. So, he was sure they would have no chance to outrun him.

Dodging and weaving in and out of construction materials, he briefly lost sight of the two fleeing men as they rounded a dumpster for a split second. Not thinking he might be running into an ambush, he blindly whipped around the corner at full speed.

A split second later, he was wide-eyed, staring down the barrel of two AKs. "Shit."

He tried to stop. But the gravel beneath his shoes made it impossible. Instead, he slid across the ground before losing his footing, falling backward into the dirt as the bullets flew over his head, embedding with a twang into the dumpster. William quickly retreated behind the object. More rounds pinged off the side of the dumpster. Breathing heavily, he quickly checked himself. No blood or searing pain. He hadn't been hit.

****

Fred had been pursuing the three and saw what had happened. He ran to the opposite side of the dumpster, hoping the terrorist would be distracted from shooting at William and that he could catch them off-guard. He drew his M4, unleashing a hailstorm of rounds. One struck a terrorist dead center mass, instantly killing him. The second gunman switched targets. Fred forced the agent to dive for cover behind the dumpster, landing beside his protégé.

"Don't you ever fucking do that again, kid, got it?" the senior agent shouted, grabbing the younger agent by the vest, yanking him closer. The two agents were nose to nose. William drew back immediately. It was the first time he'd ever seen anger in Fred's eyes. "You ALWAYS wait for backup. Get it? You hear me?" Fred screamed as he caught his breath. "Now get your ass up, and let's get this bastard."

The two reloaded and continued after the shooter, who had run off after the barrage.

Knowing he screwed up, William wanted to make it up to Fred. Trying to stand up, he got yanked back to the ground. His vest snagged something on the dumpster. He was stuck.

Fred ran after the shooter, not realizing William got hung up.

"Fred, wait!" William was struggling to break free. "Oh, fuck it!" he shouted, ripping off the vest. William joined the chase.

The shooter raced across the clearing as he headed for the overpass of the North-South Freeway. Fred knew catching up with him in the factories would be impossible. He had to catch him before then. They couldn't afford to lose the one potential lead they had on who was behind the attack.

William was much faster, but Fred still had some fight left in his legs for a 45-year-old. Adrenaline spurred him on even faster, blocking out the pain in his joints.

He lowered his head, tapping into a hidden reserve of energy, and surged forward, propelling himself with a vigor he hadn't experienced in years. His legs churned with increased intensity, driving him closer to his target. Panting heavily, Fred narrowed the gap between them, growing more confident that he could take a precise shot. His intention was not to end the man's life but merely to incapacitate him.

Stopping dead in his tracks, Fred drew his M4, peering down the sights, locking in his target. A kneecap would do just fine. The shooter had looked back to check how far ahead he was. Fred could almost see the terror in his eyes, knowing he had him dead to rights.

He squeezed the trigger.

Nothing.

Instead of the thunderous burst of expelling gas, a disheartening *chink chink,* followed each squeeze of the trigger.

Jammed.

"Shit," Fred spat, panic rising.

The terrorist, relieved he was not dead, decided to take the opportunity to eliminate his pursuer. He turned and swung around his AK, squeezing the trigger. A flash of fire from the barrel brought on a rapturous explosion, ejecting death and hurtling a storm of metal slugs flying 2,350 feet per second, barreling straight at Fred's chest.

An intense pain shot through Fred's body. His head whipped back, snapping, and his back arched as his arms flew out to his sides. He felt the sharp pain of a shoulder being driven into his lower spine as he face-planted into the grass.

William crashed bodily into his mentor, spearing him from behind. Using his momentum, he rolled straight over the top of Fred as the bullets tore over both their heads. Not stopping, the younger man continued his roll another few feet before popping up onto one knee, ready to shoot.

Glock drawn at the ready, William lined up his shot happily. The terrorist, shocked that he had missed his target, had already turned to run. William fired off three rounds. Direct hits, all three of them striking center mass, caused the man to fall sprawled out in the field, motionless.

"You ok, boss?" William asked, slightly huffing but keeping watch ahead for any movement.

"I'm good, kid," Fred wheezed before standing and arching his back to try to hide the pain. "Thanks for the save. Now go make sure he's dead," he said, panting.

Fred's body ached; his legs were sore, and he was struggling to get oxygen back into his lungs. But he was pleased that he could still draw breath, thanks to William. Fred was overcome with a sense of pride in his young trainee. He had proven his worth in a gunfight. He was very proud, although the kid had made the stupid mistake of running after a shooter alone. But they were both still alive. That's what mattered most.

Shaking off the bone-jarring tackle and catching his breath.

Fred lumbered up behind William to ensure that he checked the terrorist's body for anything that might be of use.

William was already rummaging through the dead terrorist's pockets after checking for a pulse. He paused for a second, looking up at Fred with a sly smile as he slipped a small silver object from the dead guy's pocket. "He has a phone," he handed it over to Fred with a smile.

CHAPTER FOUR

The battle-weary agents returned to the MCC, legs heavy after their chase. They plopped down in the closest chairs they could find. Letting the cool blast from the vehicle's A/C wash over their bodies.

Tobias quickly retrieved a couple of water bottles from a small fridge nearby, handing the first to William and then to Fred. The latter two swapped valuable items. Fred took the bottle and handed over the recovered cell phone. Tobias turned, handing the device to Agent Franks, who swiveled his chair around to face a computer terminal.

Fred took a swig from the bottle, watching Agent Franks plug the phone into the computer. "See what you can pull from this. Two agents lost their lives trying to recover it." He hoped their loss wouldn't be in vain. "And I already know what you're going to ask," he said, turning to Tobias. "Yes, I'm fine, thanks to the kid here," he added, pointing at William, who was gulping down his bottle.

"William, you ok?" Tobias asked the young agent.

No response.

"William, hey, earth to William," he asked again, snapping his fingers. The two veteran agents saw the look of shock on his face.

"Yes… Yes, I… I think I'm ok. I have never killed anyone before." William's voice cracked behind the revelation.

"It's ok, kid. The first time is not easy for most people. And if anyone found it easy, I wouldn't think that person was sane." Tobias attempted to reassure the kid.

"Hey, you did a fantastic job out there. Hell, you saved my ass," Fred praised, taking a long gulp.

"Yeah, but if I hadn't run off like that, your ass wouldn't have needed saving."

"Hey, we got the guys and recovered a possible lead that we can use to trace them back to their hideout. Don't beat yourself up. You did a good job. You made me proud out there." The old man managed an exhausted smile.

"Thanks." William grinned. "I… I think I just need a minute."

The young man stood, excusing himself from the MCC and stepping out.

Tobias waited for the door to close. "Fred, what happened out there?" I have two dead agents."

"You know what the fuck happened. You were watching through the drone feed," Fred snapped dismissively, waving his hand in front of the bank of monitors on the wall, rolling his eyes.

"They got the drop on us. They picked a great spot to hide and hit us in the wide open. That's that. What do you want me to say?"

Tobias could tell Fred was not in the mood for an after-action review of the incident. He decided to abandon the discussion, tabling it for later. There were much more important matters to attend to.

Laying a consoling hand on his friend's shoulder, Tobias didn't say another word but instead moved to another workstation.

The two men had worked together long enough to know neither was very good at verbally expressing emotions. Instead, they had developed a shorthand of body language to convey their feelings. In this instance, it was just a hand on a shoulder.

That was all it took for Fred to realize that Tobias meant nothing by the question. He wasn't challenging his command while in the field, and he knew just how hard it was for Fred to lose an agent under his command.

Vibrations in Fred's pocket alerted him that his phone was ringing. However, it stopped before he could reach it. The caller ID showed five missed calls and a dozen texts, all from Sherry.

Fred quietly stepped outside, walking past William, who was leaning against the side of the trailer, deep in thought. He flashed him a quick thumbs-up, making sure the kid was all right.

William nodded, returning the gesture.

"Sherry, hey, sorry I missed your calls. As you can imagine, I'm a little busy. Fred said, not wanting to let on how close he had come to death, trying to sound as normal as possible.

"I know, honey. I just needed to hear your voice. I'm watching the news report right now. Are you there? They are reporting a shootout nearby. Please tell me you weren't involved."

"Honey, you know I can't give details like that." Her anger

was clearly heard through the phone as she let out a long sigh.

"Please know that I'm fine, and yes, I'm here at the scene, working to determine what happened. Unfortunately, I can't say much else."

"Well, you better come home to me as soon as possible."

"I-" Behind him came the gagging sound of someone throwing up. He looked back just in time to see William vomit.

"What was that noise?"

Attempting to squelch his chuckle, he replied, "Nothing, dear, just the kid getting a reality check."

"Well, like I said, come home to me. And make sure William is ok, too. I wouldn't mind having him over for dinner again."

"Sure thing, gotta go. Love you." Hanging up the phone and handing William a towel from a nearby drink station. "Kid, you alright?"

"Yeah, just-"

"It's nothing like what they show on T.V. or the movies, uh?"

"No, no, it's not," William said, slightly embarrassed, checking around to make sure no one else had seen him.

"No sweat, kid, just about everyone has the same reaction. Shit, I had a tough time the first time I shot someone." Fred wanted to reassure him that these things were normal, just another opportunity to impart some wisdom to the kid.

"Hey, if you two are done out, he-" Tobias stopped, picking up on what he had interrupted, and smiled at Fred before asking William. "You okay, kid?" Shooting a glance back and forth between William and the ground where he had upchucked.

"He's fine. Aren't you?" Fred patted him on the back. William nodded.

"Ok, good, get your asses back in here then. Franks might have something."

Everyone gathered back inside, sitting in silence while Franks pounded away at his keyboard. The suspense had grown to a level where impatience had started to take over. Agent Franks swiveled around in his chair.

"Ok, unfortunately, the phone is useless," Franks informed the team. He could see the anger wash over everyone's face as he continued. "The SIM card has been removed, and there was no data. So it's essentially a burner."

"So that's it. It's a useless piece of shit. Might as well be a fucking paperweight," William fumed, having just put his life on the line for it. The emotions of the moment overcame his judgment.

"Is there anything that we can get off it, or are we completely out of leads?" Tobias asked, stepping in and cutting off the rookie before he could say anything else.

"Not exactly. We might have something on CCTV. Ramirez?" Franks turned the floor over to his colleague.

It was her moment to address the group. "I believe I may have made a discovery," she declared, a hint of a smile gracing her face. "I diligently reviewed the CCTV footage of the vicinity, tracking the movements of the assailants. We observed the two individuals who separated from the main group, the same ones you have just eliminated," she added. "As for the remaining three, I trailed them to a parked car they had commandeered. Utilizing the street cameras and citywide CCTV network, I continued to monitor their progress."

"Where did they go?" Fred quickly sat up and asked, sliding to the front of his seat. "Please tell me you got us a location."

"Yeah, I'm itching to finish the bastards off," William chimed in.

"As I was about to say," she replied, frustration at the interruption palpable in her tone. "I followed the trail. They drove into the warehouse district. Several of the buildings there have been closed for quite a while."

"Making it a perfect hideout," Fred added.

"Exactly. My best guess places them in this building." She pointed out a red-brick three-story factory on a satellite map.

"Are you a thousand percent sure on this, Ramirez?" Tobias asked. "I don't want to authorize a raid on an empty building based on a false hunch."

"Sir, I would stake my career on this. I'm positive this is their hideout." Ramirez sat resolutely, eyeing her boss.

Her confidence in the information is steadfast, making it all the easier for Tobias to make a decision. A smile grew across Tobias's face after a few moments of contemplation. He turned to Fred. "Let's go get'em."

****

The day faded away as Tobias, Fred, and William exited their vehicle, taking in the makeshift hub that served as a staging ground. They set up a few blocks from their target building, the most likely home base of the terrorists that Agent Ramirez had tracked down.

"Be right back," said Tobias, spotting Sheriff Thomas ahead. The two senior leaders had already coordinated each other's roles before arriving.

The plan entailed deploying the Sheriff's personnel to establish a blockade, effectively sealing off the surrounding region and diverting civilian traffic from imminent danger. As a precautionary measure, the U.S. Coast Guard had also been alerted, considering the district's close proximity to the waterways. Given that Lake Michigan lay just a few miles distant, there was a genuine risk that the terrorists might attempt to reach it, enabling a swift escape into Canadian waters, vanishing without a trace. Preparedness for every conceivable scenario was paramount.

Fred and William, meanwhile, met with the FBI's Special Weapons and Tactics team leader, Agent Michael Bray.

"Agent Bray," Fred said, the two men greeting each other. "Are your men ready?"

"Yes, sir, We're locked and loaded. Sorry about what happened at the cement factory," he added with a tinge of condolence. "We'll get these assholes."

"Appreciate the enthusiasm, agent. Let's ensure we don't lose any more men today," Fred replied. The two men exchanged solemn looks, each having known the burden of losing men.

"Absolutely. So, I assume you'll want to head up your team then?"

"If you don't mind, I would. We'll split into two teams," Fred continued. "According to the plans, there are two possible points of entry and egress. William and I will take the front. You will take Bravo around the back."

"Understood," the FBI agent replied, turning. "Men, let's move out."

The two teams split up to begin their assault on the target building. The main concern for Fred, aside from the three men who had fled the scene, was that they weren't sure how many other possible targets were in the warehouse. They would essentially be flying in blind. Their only advantages were that they would be going in with the element of surprise and under cover of darkness.

Fred took Alpha team, consisting of himself, William, and six other agents, and headed to the front side of the building. Agent Bray led his team around the back. The plan was simple enough: two teams executed simultaneously, hitting from both sides. With any luck, they would be able to get in and out quickly, bringing an end to the horrific day.

The teams proceeded to their staging points, reaching them around 10 pm. The cloud cover blocked out any moonlight, which concealed their movements.

A light rain began to fall, and with the orange-ish glow from the still-burning fire a few miles away, they moved in quickly on the old brick building. Traversing the field and train tracks, they kept low and out of sight until they reached the side of the building, where they quietly stacked up against the brick façade.

Fred gave Bravo an extra moment as they had a longer distance to cover. "Bravo team, are you set? Over," he radioed the other commander.

"We're all set here. Over."

"Ok. Base, Alpha, and Bravo teams are all set. Kill the power. Out."

Back at the staging ground, Tobias was monitoring the assault. He signaled to Agent Franks, who was on the phone with the power company. "Cut it," he said.

Seconds later, the streetlamps and light fixtures in and around the buildings went down.

Fred could now hear the commotion inside. The sudden

blackout startled the terrorists. Men were shouting at each other, confused, trying to figure out what had happened. Determined to use this element of surprise, Fred flashed his hand forward, and the team moved in.

Foster, running point, swung around the edge of the building, heading straight for the small steel stairs that led up to the door. Something unexpected and unplanned caused him to pause, stopping in his tracks.

The cause for the stoppage was a red Ford F-150 truck parked directly ahead, twenty yards away from the staircase, by the loading dock bay door. Visible was the silhouette of a man standing at the rear of the truck, holding a canister in his hand. He appeared to be refueling what was possibly their getaway vehicle. Another stood in the bed, loading containers. Both were shouting at each other in Arabic, while the man in the bed also seemed to be arguing with another guy inside.

The agents had not been spotted yet and remained hidden in the shadows. Foster looked back at Fred, waiting for his command. The team leader paused for a second, contemplating what to do.

He knew that if they shot the two outside, it would alert the others inside that an attack was coming. However, he didn't really see another option. They needed to get inside one way or another, but once the first shot was fired, their element of surprise would be out the window. Fred gave the all-clear to engage.

Foster pulled up his silenced MP5 with the refueling man in sight. He squeezed the trigger, unloading several rounds. The bullets quietly pierced right into his back. His body jerked forward, hitting the side of the truck before slumping to the ground. The sound of the dead man hitting the truck was loud enough to alert the man in the bed that something was wrong. Before he had time to react, Foster squeezed off another burst.

All three rounds were direct hits. Two to the chest and one to the forehead, the latter blowing the back of his skull out. His lifeless body stumbled backward and fell out of the truck, thudding to the ground.

Fred's initial worry was right. There was indeed another terrorist coming out to the loading dock when Foster shot the second man. This guy saw his brother get shot and fall out of the truck and started screaming and yelling loud enough to wake an entire city block. How many people was he alerting with his screams?

"Shit," Fred cursed. Their advantage of surprise had been blown.

A barrel of an AK47 popped out from the corner of the open bay door. It let loose a barrage of 7.62mm rounds at the strike team before they could spot it. The first few hit Foster, killing him instantly.

The team was exposed and vulnerable with no cover.

Fred ordered the agents to fall back. As they retreated, a shower of glass cascaded down from above. More AK barrels poked out from the windows and started raining down gunfire on top of them.

Pulling back, they heard gunfire inside and saw bright flashes of light followed by the echoing sounds of flash bangs going off.

Bravo team had breached the building from the back door, engaging the hostiles inside, as bullets poured down on Fred's team. Agent Meeks took a round straight through his left thigh. Agent Li, who was behind him, grabbed his vest and pulled him back to safety.

The shooters still had time to reload and continue firing on the team. One of them hit Meeks again, this time in the chest with two more rounds. Li, still dragging him, was hit from above as a round drove straight through the top of his helmet, killing him instantly.

But within the next minute, Fred saw the body of the terrorist at the loading bay door fall to the ground.

"First floor of the building secure. Over," Agent Bray reported.

At least Bravo team had been successful.

A brief lull in the fire from the second floor gave Alpha team the window it needed to enter the building now that the threat in front of them was gone.

"Move in," Fred shouted, ordering the remaining three agents and William to push forward into the warehouse.

Gunfire broke out again from above as they pushed onward to

the door. Agent Trucks was struck in the leg, causing him to drop to the ground. William rushed ahead and scooped Trucks up from underneath his arms, hauling him to his feet; the two limped inside before they could be hit.

What was left of Alpha team burst through the steel door to the first floor. "Shit, are you guys ok?" Bray asked, helping Fred up to his feet.

"Status report," Fred demanded, ignoring the question.

"We got four dead terrorists in here, more on the second floor. I have two KIA'd. Jackson and Upton."

"Shit, fuck dammit," Fred yelled, kicking a bucket across the floor and watching it clang around before hitting a pillar. "How many assholes are in here?"

Bray shrugged. "Counted maybe another four or five guns above. Recalling the separate brattles of distinct gunfire locations.

"Base, we're in," Fred said, keying the mic on his vest. "But sustained multiple casualties. We have five. I repeat, five KIA'd and one wounded. Continuing mission. We have shooters on the second floor. Out."

Tobias became incensed at the report that they had lost five more agents. He flung his coffee cup across the parking lot, smashing it into a thousand pieces.

"Bray, we still need to complete the mission. We proceed with the plan, understood? Take your team to the second stairwell, and we'll move to the other. Copy?"

"Copy that."

"Dunn, you stay here with Trucks to dress his wounds."

"Yes, sir."

Bray took Bravo team and headed toward Stairwell B. Meanwhile, Fred regrouped, taking the remaining members of the Alpha team — William, Daniels, and Skaggs — and continued to their objective, Stairwell A, at the building's southeast end.

The door flung open as they approached the stairwell entrance. Five armed men came rushing out. Caught in the open, the agents scrambled for cover as the terrorist opened fire.

Fred and William dove behind two large crates. Skaggs took cover behind a brick column, and Daniels threw himself over a desk, kicking it onto its side. The agents stayed down, enduring the barrage of fire until their assailant's guns ran empty.

Fred and William popped out from behind the crates, unloading several rounds at the group, striking two of them and downing them for good. Before their bodies could hit the floor, the remaining three ran off. Fred and William couldn't get a clear shot as they rounded the open bay door and ran outside.

"Daniels, Skaggs, you ok?" Fred bellowed, ears ringing from the firefight in the enclosed space.

"Good here," Skaggs reported.

"Yeah, fine," Daniels added, coming out from behind the column.

"Good, get your asses in gear. Let's go," Fred said as he recovered, heading for the open door.

"Base, Bravo, we've got three runners going in pursuit. Out."

Alpha team sprinted across the open factory floor, following the three escapees. William easily overtook the three older agents, having jumped out to a ten-yard lead. Fred, Daniels, and Skaggs tried to keep pace. William leaped off the loading bay, making it outside before the others could turn the corner.

Shots clanked off the steel columns as two more terrorists ran out from the stairwell door. Daniels and Skaggs spun around, opening fire, catching one in the shoulder before diving for cover.

The second guy crashed into Fred while making a blind mad dash for the door, knocking them both to the floor.

Fred and the terrorist tussled on the floor, rolling over each other several times while exchanging blows. Finally, Fred gained the upper hand, managing to push the man back far enough to deliver a forceful haymaker to his face. The blow hit so hard that his head rocked back. Daniels saw this as the perfect opportunity to put a round into his forehead.

Covered in blood, Fred tossed the corpse off, took Daniels' hand, and thanked him as he pulled him to his feet.

"No problem, sir."

"Where's William?" Fred asked, looking around, figuring he would come back to help.

"He's not here, sir," Skaggs answered. I think he'd run out

before we got stopped.

William had unknowingly continued on his own after the other three men.

Fred quickly clawed at the mic button on his vest. "William? William?" he tried to radio his protégé. "Where are you?" He inquired, jumping down from the loading dock and surveying the direction he would take.

Three shots echoed in the distance from around the corner of the building. Fred sprinted in their direction.

A small alleyway existed between the warehouse building and an adjacent office structure. The agents rounded the corner swiftly, following the narrow alleyway as they moved down the darkened passage, guns drawn.

Midway down the alley, two objects were lying on the ground. Fred could barely make them out, but as they approached, they began to take on form. His heart sank into his stomach as it became clearer with every step. They were human.

One was still moving, but only slightly. Pulling out his flashlight and shining it down, he dropped to his knees.

One of the masses was William.

"Oh god, no. William."

Fred's young protégé was one of the two bodies lying on the ground. His hands wrapped around a knife in his throat, bright red blood still flowing. The other was a dead terrorist with two gaping maws in his chest. Dead.

The kid tried to say something, but no words came out; instead, a gurgling sound was followed by frothing blood bubbles. Fred lowered his head closer to William's lips. He couldn't distinguish any words, though, only the sound of him choking on his own blood.

"William, stop trying to talk. Just hold on, kid. We're going to get you some help."

Agents Skaggs and Daniels quickly pulled bandages from their first aid packs, handing them to Fred, looking at each other in dismay.

"Base, Alpha team leader. We have an agent down in need of immediate first aid. We're in the alley behind the target building, over."

William grabbed Fred's hand, tears streaming down his face again as he struggled to find the words.

"Hang on, kid. Help's on the way. Be strong. Stay with me."

William squeezed tighter; Fred looked down into his young eyes. Fear, sadness, and terror filled the young man's once-deep blue eyes as he stared back into Fred's. The senior agent did all he could to remain calm and composed, but he could no longer continue. A stream of tears welled up in his eyes.

"I'm not losing you, kid. I have put too much work into training you. You're not going out like this," he reassured the kid. "Where is the fucking medic?" Fred screamed, turning back to the other two agents.

Daniels sprinted back to the opening to usher in the med team.

William summoned all the strength left in his body. Squeezed harder, picking his arm up and pointing down the alley in the direction the terrorist had run.

Fred followed William's eyes as he looked down the stretch of the alley, understanding what he was trying to say. "Are you sure, kid?"

William stared straight into Fred's eyes. Gone was the look of fear and sadness; instead, it was replaced with a steely stare of determination. He squeezed his mentor's hand twice more.

That was all the confirmation Fred needed.

"I'm going to get these pricks for you, kid. You got one of them. I'm going to finish them all," he said, standing up. "You stay here. Skaggs, on me." Fred ordered Daniels to stay with William while he and Skaggs continued pursuit of the remaining two terrorists.

Fred had a good hunch as to where they were headed. Based on their location, he figured the terrorist would've planned a water escape route as a backup plan. So, Lake Michigan would be their most likely destination.

The Milwaukee County Boat Launch led directly into the lake, just a few hundred yards away.

"Alpha team to base. They are headed to the marina. Alert the Coast Guard," Fred radioed, voicing his suspicion. "Come on, keep up," he shouted back to Skaggs.

The two agents were in full stride, legs churning as fast as they could. Fred's chest pounded as each foot drove into the pavement below. Energized with anger and hate, all he wanted to do was catch the men who had killed so many of his friends. Feeding off his anger and hatred, Fred easily outpaced Skaggs by a few yards. The rain had now picked up and was coming down harder.

Two gunshots rippled through the silent night. Fred knew by the sound of the shots that they were not aimed at them. They were too far away, coming in the direction of the launch. Another innocent civilian had just met their untimely demise at the hands of these murderers.

Running full speed, they approached the launch, spotting one of the terrorists as he walked out of the boathouse, oblivious to the fact that they had been followed. Fred drew his gun and fired off two shots. The first one missed, but the second hit the terrorist in the right leg, tearing straight through flesh and bone. He fell to the ground, screaming something in Arabic. Fred figured it was a curse or something to alert the second guy.

As he ran up to the downed man, Fred caught the flicker of his gun in the moonlight. Without breaking stride, he kicked the weapon, sending it skittering across the blacktop and sliding underneath a car. He then drove a swift kick to the man's gut.

A bullet snapped by his head. Instinct told him to duck. Looking back up, he spotted the second terrorist trying to lower a boat into the water. Fred returned fire but missed. The terrorist threw himself behind cover against the side of the boat.

"Skaggs stay on this piece of shit," Fred ordered, pointing at the man he had just shot. "I got that guy."

He moved in the direction of the remaining terrorist. As he got closer to the boat, he slowed down stealthily, creeping and trying to stay out of sight. *Bang,* another shot rang out in the night. It was fired directly over the boat railing, a mere ten yards in front of him. Fred quickly returned fire, launching a volley of rounds from his MP5, which sprayed the side of the boat, splintering wood chunks into the air and ripping through wood and fiberglass.

Off in the distance, he could hear the sirens from the

approaching Coast Guard patrol boats. And if he could listen to them, so could the terrorists. By now, he would have figured out his water escape was no longer an option. He would be surrounded shortly.

Fred decided to try and get the remaining terrorists to surrender. Sure, killing him would be easier and help dissipate some of the anger and hatred he felt. Getting him to pay for all the dead agents would also make Fred feel better, but there's a chance that he could have had the valuable intelligence they needed as well. This group couldn't have carried out this attack alone.

Fred called out, "Give up now. You can hear the boats coming. There is no way to escape. You must know that." Pausing for a moment, he hoped for a response.

The man said something in Arabic.

Fred couldn't make out what the terrorist was saying. The only word he could make out was ' Allah,' right at the end.

"Oh Shit," the realization dawned, sending him sprinting in the opposite direction, realizing it was a prayer.

BOOM!!

The terrorist had been wearing a suicide vest. The man and boat exploded into a thousand pieces, sending wood, fiberglass, metal shrapnel, and human parts flying everywhere.

Fred, unable to clear the blast radius fast enough, was caught in the explosive concussion blast that threw him in the air, sending him flying several yards and crashing back to the asphalt.

Hitting the ground with a thud, he continued to roll some distance before coming to a stop. Crawling away, head ringing, Fred tried to stand, only to realize he couldn't. His legs felt like Jell-O. He fell back to his knees, blacking in and out. Ears ringing, still dazed, unsure of what just happened, he caught small glimpses of Agent Skaggs lying beside the guy he had shot earlier.

From his blurred vision, Fred could see that he was alive and starting to move. Next to the unconscious agent, the wounded terrorist had already realized he wasn't being watched and began to scramble away. Fred, unable to stand, crawled to his MP5. His eyesight flickered in and out. He pawed around for his weapon, watching the last remaining terrorist limp away. Finding the cold metal object, he gripped the submachine gun and drew it up.

He managed to stabilize himself just enough to get off one shot. That was all he needed. It struck the prisoner in his other leg, dropping him back to the ground as Agent Skaggs began to stir.

Picking himself off the ground as his sight and hearing began to return, Fred glanced over his shoulder at the massive ball of fire that had once been a boat. There was no chance in hell that anyone survived that. Several SUVs ripped around the bend, screeching to a halt.

Tobias jumped out of the lead SUV, racing to Fred.

"Holy shit, are you ok?"

"WHAT!"

"I said, are you okay?" Tobias shouted directly into Fred's left ear.

It took a few seconds for the words to unjumble in his mind. "I'm good, just a little ringing still," Fred responded, tapping his ear.

"Alright then, let's get you back to ops and get you looked at."

"What about Skaggs and the prisoner?"

"They'll be taken care of. Come on, let's go," Tobias replied, pulling Fred away from the inferno and into the SUV.

****

Fred glanced around the command post while the paramedics checked him over to ensure he had no severe injuries. The ringing in his ears had finally subsided.

The harsh realities of the day set in for the rescuers, police, and agents. Many families would not see their loved ones return home tonight and some of those families he knew very well. The emotions overcame him for the first time as tears streamed down his cheeks. But this was not the time and place to break down. He wiped away his tears and started looking for answers.

He knew where he might be able to get them. A prisoner had to be interrogated, even if that meant beating the answers out of him.

As Fred pulled himself off the stretcher, Tobias called him

over to the MCC before he could ask anyone where the prisoner had been transported.

"Fred, you good? Docs clear you?"

"I'm fine," he answered, shambling over. "Where's the kid?" Fred asked.

Tobias's face fell flat, eyes dropping to the floor. Fred had seen this face only a few times but knew precisely what it meant.

"I need to hear it, Tobias. I know you don't want to say it, but I need to hear it," Fred stated curtly, fighting back the tears.

"The kid... the kid didn't make it. The injury was... too severe. He had already lost too much blood by the time the medic got to him. There was nothing you could have done," Tobias added, trying to console his friend.

"So, how many men and women did we lose today?" Fred's whole body felt numb; he didn't want to process the loss of William.

"Ten. Ten agents in all. Around fifty from the bomb and another twenty-thirty injured," Tobias responded.

"My God," Fred said, dropping into a chair beside him, burying his head in his hands and resting his elbows on his thighs. The two sat in silence for a few minutes.

"It's been a tough day. Maybe you should go home and get some rest. All that's left right now is cleanup and sifting through the debris and whatever they left at the safe house.'

"You're wrong, Tobias. I have a prisoner to interrogate." Fred fixed an intense gaze on his friend, and he meant that he wouldn't take no for an answer.

"No. No, you're not doing it. At least not right now; it's not the time for that.' Fred stood, about to protest. "Besides, they took him to the hospital to patch those bullet holes you put in him."

"Awe fuck it, whatever then," Fred spat, chucking a towel across the MCC.

Agent Franks had been sitting in the command truck the whole time, trying to ignore the conversation. He turned. "Sirs, I... I think you're going to want to see this."

Both Fred and Tobias turned towards Franks. "Well, what is it?" Tobias snapped.

"It's a video that Al-Jazeera just aired, and our national news networks are picking it up," Franks stated.

"Well, play the video, dammit," Fred replied tersely. Franks tapped a few keys, bringing it up on the monitor.

A man with a long beard, coal-black eyes, and dressed in a Thawb appeared on the screen.

"I'm Amell al-Gharsi, Leader of the Abyan Islamic Army. We're what the West will fear. We're your terror. America will feel what our people have felt for decades. Death is around every corner, down every street. You will know death. It will become your only friend. Allah spares no infidel. We're coming for YOU."

CHAPTER FIVE

Fred splashed water over his face, the cool liquid snapping him back to alertness, if only temporarily. Sleep hadn't been a priority the last couple of months.

Leaning over the bathroom sink, he tried to be as careful as he could. Now wouldn't be a good time to get his new shirt wet.

He cautiously blotted away the excess water with a paper towel. After all, he'd just spent an obscene amount of money on his new suit. Sherry's doing, of course. So, he didn't want to mess it up before the hearing started.

Fred stood and looked in the mirror, adjusting his new tie. Then he took a deep breath and closed his eyes to collect his thoughts. It was his first time on Capitol Hill professionally, and he had no idea what to expect.

His hand began to tremble as images flashed before him. Images from that fateful, horrible day two months ago that had left him indelibly scarred—not physically since he had managed to survive two firefights in a day.

No, these scars were the worst kind. The Psychological type.

Every time he closed his eyes, the same scenes would play out. William's face stared up at him, and all Fred could do was watch as the brightness in his protégé's eyes slowly faded.

Fred's eyes jutted open, hearing a distant prattle of gunfire. Making the movie-like recollection seem all too real. He swung around quickly, scanning the room. But nothing was there.

"Calm down, Fred. You're just nervous and tired," he repeated to himself, trying to shake off the feelings of failure and dread he'd been carrying around with him.

For nearly two months, he'd been haunted by the events of July 2nd. A day he'd not ever forget and one that had undoubtedly taken its toll on the agent.

He knew it was impossible, despite his desire to take it back. His only solace was knowing he got those responsible for William's death. However, there was still plenty of work to be done to catch the perpetrators of the attack.

He and Tobias had been summoned to Capitol Hill to report on their response that day and the progress of their investigation since. People wanted answers—powerful people, and they weren't going to wait any longer. The two hadn't been invited. They'd been summoned via a subpoena to brief the intelligence committee assembled by the Department of Justice on their investigation into Amell al-Gharsi and his terrorist group. The American people wanted these vile and evil monsters hunted down and forced to pay for attacking America.

Hell, Fred wanted answers and a little payback himself if he had to admit it. A burning desire to see them all pay. He didn't see the need for this hearing and didn't even want to attend. It was taking him away from finding those responsible. That's why he always let Tobias handle the politics. He never cared much about politics, nor politicians for that matter. Always viewing them as fat, lazy cats, taking whatever deal was in front of them while trying to swindle you from behind, always playing an angle to fatten their own wallets.

Another reason he'd always passed on promotions to Special Agent in Charge. That role came with far too much politics behind it.

But now it was time to face the inevitable. He'd have to talk to the politicians. He steeled himself, pushing past his tiredness from their flight to get there. He paced the restroom several times, then exited, rehearsing his words quietly like studying a movie script. His dress shoes clacked against the marble floor as he walked, practicing. The slaps echoed down the empty hallway of the building.

The Cannon House Office Building seemed deserted, with not a soul in sight. Typically, politicians prefer not to conduct business on weekends, much less before 9 am. But today was different. Unfortunately, this hearing had to take place, so they had to find a time to fit it in, and this was the best time they could.

Fred continued down the ghost town of a hallway, trying different tones as he walked until something odd struck him. Erasing his train of thought. He couldn't help but notice the extensive use of marble in the building.

He recalled a conversation he had with his brother several years ago. He remembered how Franklin was going on about using the Beaux-Arts style of architecture for the buildings in D.C., which had its roots in Roman and French designs, as well as many other styles he couldn't recall. All he could think at the time was how it was a waste of money. It was merely a venue for overpaid men to debate who could become richer first.

Busy in his newfound thoughts, no longer focused on his speech, Fred finally reached room 311. He could hear the rapid clanking of another pair of dress shoes on the marble floor. Rounding the hallway, he saw Tobias. For the first time in a long time, his friend seemed nervous. He managed a light chuckle at the sight of Tobias pacing faster as he drew nearer.

"What the hell are you laughing at? This is no time to be laughing. We're about to get hammered in there," Tobias snapped upon seeing his friend's smirk.

"Sorry, chop it up to delirium," Fred acknowledged. Knowing all too well, this was no laughing matter. "I know… I know how serious this is, but you're doing the same thing you were doing when I left ten minutes ago."

"I know. It's just that I'm anxious and tired, which makes me more nervous. I'll slip up in there, and everything we've worked on will be for nothing," Tobias confessed, sitting down for the first time. However, his right foot started tapping—another nervous twitch.

"I know… trust me, I know. We have worked our tails off these last two months tracking this terrorist group, but all we can do is our best and see where that leads."

Sighing, realizing Fred was right, he said, "I guess so. I wish we had more to give them."

Fred sat beside his friend, blowing out a sigh of his own. "Me too."

The two sat quietly for what felt like an hour. Finally, the doors to room 311 opened ten minutes later. Out came an aide. She was young, had brunette hair, and was wearing a black pantsuit. Mid-twenties, Fred guessed. She approached the two. They both stood, greeting her.

"Agents, they are ready for you."

The two men followed her in.

Fred, who had previously thought all that marble in the hallways was excessive, saw real opulence upon entering the chamber.

A huge, C-shaped, solid oak desk sat on a small platform leading to the long, rectangular room at the front. In the center of the C was a smaller, similarly shaped desk made from oak.

A few feet in front of the two desks was a smaller table with a couple of chairs. This, he figured, would be their place to sit. This is where they'll be looked down upon by those behind the exquisite furniture at the head of the room—being judged.

The aide continued to lead them past several rows of seats. Some government-looking types were sparsely affixed in the gallery. None were directly involved with the proceedings, but they caught Fred's eye. He had been told this was going to be a closed session.

His eyes darted up to the vaulted ceiling, supported by large arches denoting the Beaux-Arts design his brother had droned on about.

This was one of the fanciest rooms he had ever been in.

Leaning over to Tobias, Fred whispered, "Guess this is where all our tax dollars go. I thought it went to their pockets."

The aide overheard the comment and couldn't help but laugh a little. She looked back at him, nodding her head while pretending to tuck something into her pocket.

Fred's face flared red as his body temperature rose in embarrassment that she had overheard his joke. She seated them and then left the room through a hidden side door, camouflaged to blend in with the wall.

Fred scanned the present committee members, recalling some of their names. Others, he had no idea who they were or what they did. But one he definitely knew for sure. James Sprague, Director of the FBI.

Fred's nerves calmed slightly for a split second, knowing that at least one person on the committee would be in their corner. That was until the director looked up from the desk. His stare was like two piercing daggers splicing right through him.

He had met Director Sprague several times and knew him well enough to know he was a no-nonsense type. That stare was the only warning they would get to not fuck the hearing up.

Some other members he recognized were Mark James, Director of Homeland Security, whom he had met at an intelligence briefing a year ago, and Eva Ramirez, a Democratic Senator from California—his birth state.

As for the rest of the committee, he had never meant them, nor did he necessarily know who they were aside from their nameplates.

They were Melissa Joyce, Undersecretary of the Department of Defense. There were three other senators aside from Senator Ramirez. One was from New York, Hilary Samms, Senator Roy Stone of Oklahoma, and Marco Sanchez from Florida.

Senator Samms was seated in the middle of the curved table, making her the committee chairman. Several members silently chatted amongst themselves as everyone took their places. Finally, Senator Samms raised her hand, and the room fell silent.

"Ladies and Gentlemen of this committee, as You're all aware, we have convened this hearing to gather any and all information regarding the investigation into the Museum bombing. We ask that Agents Stevens and Jones provide truthful and forthcoming answers to all their questions. We're not here to blame, but we do want to know why and how this happened and what You're doing to bring those responsible to justice. We do not need to discuss the event or the steps taken that day. I think we have all read the after-action reports, have we?" Senator Samms looked around the table for confirmation as all the others had nodded in agreement. "Great, so let's get started then. Agent Stevens proceed."

Tobias began, "Members of the committee, as you are aware, this is still an ongoing investigation, and We're pursuing every lead we can. We already know who is responsible for the attack. We have verified that the video sent that day was authentic. The AIA is indeed responsible for the attack."

Senator Samms raised a finger to stop Tobias.

"Agent Stevens, if you know who did it, why haven't we

brought anyone to justice then?"

"It's not that simple, Senator. First, the AIA is not a country. They are a trained terrorist group that operates in other lands. And these aren't any sovereign lands we can invade or a government to place sanctions on. The major problem is that the group rose just over a year ago, and no one knows where it operates. Furthermore, information from the CIA indicates that this is not your run-of-the-mill terrorist group. Despite being new to the game, they have proven to be extremely well-trained and well-funded."

"Agent Stevens."

Another interruption mid-sentence. Fred could see Tobias starting to get upset.

This time, the interjection came from Senator Stone in his slow Oklahoma drawl. "When you say 'far more advanced than other groups, what do you necessarily mean by that? Don't we have the world's most advanced military and law enforcement?"

"To answer that, I'll invite Agent Jones to chime in. He has been my lead investigator in this matter."

Tobias gestured for Fred to step in.

Clearing his throat, Fred began, hoping it wasn't his turn to be cut off. "Senators, we mean that they have the means to purchase rather expensive and hard-to-find materials, the know-how to assemble top-of-the-line explosives as our bomb technicians uncovered after studying the device used-"

"Ok, so is that it? Do they have more money than other groups? And that made this attack possible without our intelligence agencies knowing it was coming?" Senator Stone asked, rudely interrupting again.

Now, it was Fred's turn to hide his frustration at the senator's terse tone. "No, and I was getting to that. They use a form of communication that is proving difficult to crack. The CIA, NSA, or we have never seen anything like this."

"So, Agent Stevens, in your opinion, do you have what it takes to locate the AIA and Amell al-Gharsi before another attack occurs? If not, what steps do you need to take to accomplish this task?" Director Sprague jumped in to try and diffuse the tensions.

"Honestly, Director. I do. We need more time. We have one of their men in lock up. He is just now starting to talk. Give us some more time. See what we get out of him," Fred replied confidently.

"Agent Stevens, in your opinion, what are any possible roadblocks you foresee? And do you think the FBI can close out this investigation to the satisfaction of the American public?" Stone asked, continuing his line of questioning.

"Senator, the biggest roadblock I foresee is if and when this investigation moves overseas. Well, that's when politics gets involved, and border issues can slow us down. But yes, we *will* see this through no matter what."

A brief silence fell over the room. The members on the dais exchanged a look of satisfaction.

"Agents Stevens and Jones. That'll be all for now. Please wait outside." Senator Samms dismissed Fred and Tobias, and they departed the room and back out into the hallway.

"What do you think they are discussing in there?" Fred asked, now back in the safety of the hallway.

Tobias resumed pacing, clearly displeased with what had just transpired. "I'm not sure, but I think the entire hearing was to determine if we can handle this investigation," he said, not breaking stride.

"What do you mean?"

"I'm fairly certain they want to hand this over to the Department of Homeland Security. Possibly the CIA. They don't think we can do it. Dammit." He cursed, placing a hand on his clean-shaven chin. "No doubt, they are pondering their next move."

"They wouldn't, would they?"

"Come on." Tobias stopped for a brief second, giving his friend a side-eyed glance. "You know it's possible."

Fred sat thinking about the likelihood that he wouldn't get the chance to bring those responsible to justice for William and all the other agents who had lost their lives. Tobias continued to pace for what seemed like an eternity while the committee discussed its business.

If they were replaced, his next step would be retirement, as he had promised Sherry. He'd convinced her to let him postpone it to see the investigation through. But if they were going to take it from them, he no longer needed to stick around the Bureau. Nor would he want to. Now, the place reminded him of too much death.

The aide returned and motioned the two agents back into the room. Leading them back into the chamber and their seats. The two men affixed their blazers and ties and sat once again before the committee members as Senator Samms had reconvened the group.

"Agents, first and foremost, we want to thank you for being here today and for your brave actions that horrific day. Secondly, following your testimony, We're fully confident that you will find and bring the perpetrators of this horrendous attack to justice. We will support your efforts in any way we can."

Fred and Tobias looked at each other with shock at the turn of events.

"With that in mind, though," Samms said, pausing.

Here comes the caveat, Fred thought.

"Agent Stevens, you mentioned that your main concern was anything involving travel overseas, correct?"

"That is correct, Senator."

"In light of that concern, you will be assigned a liaison from the State Department. They should be able to help you navigate any of those potential entanglements. Do you think that will help?"

"Absolutely, Senator. Thank you." The committee's foresight took Fred aback.

"Thank us for finding these animals and stopping them before they cause any further damage to our nation," she responded. "Hearing is dismissed."

As they departed the chamber, Fred and Tobias were approached by Director Sprague.

"Gentleman, good job today," he said, shaking their hands.

"Thank you, sir," Tobias responded. The two agents were clearly thrilled with the outcome.

"I suspect the two of you have a plan to accomplish your mission. Correct?"

"We didn't want to say anything in the hearing, but we might have something to add."

"Well?" the director waited for them to divulge.

"The prisoner may have given us a way to infiltrate the group. It might just be possible to get an undercover agent in. From there, we might just find a way to locate Amell and take down the AIA."

"That's great," the Director enthused. "Put it together, send me the ops plan, and... Happy fishing, Gentleman. I have faith in you," he added, patting Tobias on the shoulder before turning to walk away.

That was all Fred and Tobias needed to hear. They now had the full support of not only the Director of the FBI but also the entire subcommittee. Now, they needed to make good on their promises.

"Celebratory drink?" Tobias asked as the two exited the Cannon House, about to climb into their waiting SUV.

"Gentlemen, if you have a moment, I would like to discuss some matters with you over lunch," came a voice over their shoulder. They turned to see Senator Stone approaching.

"Umm, Senator, I'm not sure we can discuss this matter outside of the committee hearing, can we?" Tobias asked, confused by the ambush.

"Sure we can," he responded dismissively.

Tobias looked at Fred, his eyes widening, his eyebrow raised, and he appeared unassured, asking what he thought. Fred nodded.

"Ok, Senator, where did you have in mind?"

"I have a standing reservation at the restaurant at the Acqua AI 2. It's not far from here. I'll take you."

"It's okay, sir, we can drive. We'll follow behind you," Fred interjected.

"Ok, suit yourselves then. I'll see you there."

****

The two agents hesitantly walked into the restaurant, following Senator Stone, who had been waiting for them outside. Both were still unsure if they should even be there. What could the senator possibly want to discuss with them?

The host immediately greeted them. The man knew Senator Stone reasonably well because they seemed to be on a first-name basis. The senator even asked about the man's family.

After some quick banter, the host led the group to a table at the back of the restaurant, away from other patrons.

"You guys like this place? Reminds me of home by the décor," the old man asked. "And they serve breakfast until 2 pm. "Which is great since it's the most important meal of the day," he added, laughing at his own joke.

"It's nice, but we do need to get back home. What did you want to talk about?" Tobias said, not trying to be rude. Still, he felt a little awkward about the situation.

"Let's eat first, and then we'll get to the brass tax and all," he said, smiling. The senator quickly ordered his food before the two men could object.

After the meal and sitting through the Senator's stories of big game hunts and his time in the service, Fred had heard enough. "Senator, We're a little short on time here, and you do want us to get back to work, don't you?" Fred interjected, cutting the man off mid-sentence as he'd done to him earlier in the day.

"Yes, I reckon I do, boys. As you now know, coming from my military background, it makes me sick to my stomach this attack. It directly attacked our way of life and everything this country stands for. I want to see these animals pay for this."

"I think we all do, senator," Tobias responded, with a sense of curiosity about where the conversation was headed.

"Great, we're on the same page, then. As a patriot and former military man, I know that sometimes things get messy in the field, if you know what I'm saying."

The phrasing of the statement gave Tobias pause. Before answering, he glanced over to Fred, who shrugged. Both men were clearly not on the same page as the senator. "Yes, I think so, sir. Sometimes, it doesn't always go according to plan, but we'll do everything we can to bring them to justice," Tobias replied.

"Well, you know there are many forms of justice, right?" Stone noticed the confusion linger on the agent's faces. "Let me break it down for you and get to the point straight away.

Sometimes, *I mean sometimes*, events and crimes are so heinous that there is no need for a trial. Especially if you know the accused committed the crime. The good American people do not need to relive this tragedy. Sometimes, a bullet to the head is all the justice needed. Catch my drift?"

Both agents simultaneously understood what he was asking them to do. "Sure thing, Senator. We will get the justice America demands," Tobias said, shaking his hand.

"Great, I knew you two were the right men for the job and great American patriots as well," he said, placing his napkin on the table. "And don't worry about the bill. Good luck, gentleman." The senator shook their hands again and walked out of the restaurant.

"Did that just happen?" asked Fred, watching the door close. "Did a U.S. Senator just tell us to execute al-Gharsi when we find him?"

"I believe he did," Tobias answered, just as shocked as Fred was. "I imagine he just said what every American thinks right now."

"We're not going to do that. Right? I mean, that's not justice. That's revenge." Fred immediately doubted he could bring himself to do it. From the look on Tobias's face, though, it seemed his friend was entertaining the thought.

"We gotta find them first," Tobias added, getting up. "Let's go." They exited the restaurant, finding their parked SUV. "Oh, and there's one more thing we have to discuss."

"What's that?" Fred asked, closing the door.

"This State Department attaché. I'll need you to play nice with them," Tobias carefully added, knowing full well that Fred didn't always work well with others outside of the Bureau.

"I can't promise anything," Fred answered, looking not too pleased with that turn of events. "It depends on how much he gets in the way," he added with a grin.

CHAPTER SIX

MCLEAN, VIRGINIA

Central Intelligence Officer Sophia Evans's phone vibrated across the nightstand. The light from the screen illuminated the small bedroom in the apartment, waking her from a deep sleep.

Her hand popped out from under a blanket like a submarine periscope, crawling spider-like across the glass top, searching and fumbling about.

Success.

Sophia's fingertips located their target and pulled the device closer, cracking open an eye and waiting for her iris to adjust to the bright light. A sequence of lines and blots formed across the screen.

Office.

"Uh-oh, this can't be good," she grumbled, sitting up.

Seated on the edge of her bed, she peered over her shoulder. Letting out a sigh of relief. Her girlfriend Carol hadn't moved a muscle and remained sound asleep. Relieved, Sophia put on her slippers and robe, sneaking out of the bedroom and into the living room before gently closing the door behind her and answering.

"Agent Evans, I need you to come in immediately. Your vacation has been canceled," her boss, Director James Owens, said.

"Yes, sir, I will be there in an hour," she responded, ending the call. Turning around, she caught a fleeting glimpse of her reflection in the mirror. A slender ray of moonlight had managed to infiltrate the gap between her living room curtains, enveloping her silhouette in an ethereal glow. The sight that met Sophia's eyes sent a shiver down her spine. Her long blonde hair appeared disheveled as if it had engaged in a grueling twelve-round bout with her pillow. Tangled and unkempt, it resembled a disarrayed mess. "Ugh, maybe it will take a little longer than an hour," she mused, assessing the disheveled state of her hair.

From the tone of Owens' voice, though, she could tell that whatever he called her in for would be important. She didn't even think to ask why. It wasn't really in her nature to question her boss anyway, and she wasn't about to start in the middle of the night despite her being on vacation. Her time off would just have to wait. Carol probably wouldn't be happy with it, but she'd understand.

Sophia quietly slipped back into the bedroom to wake Carol. "Honey, hey, wake up."

"What… What is it? Is everything ok?" Carol murmured, hardly lucid.

"I'm sorry, but I have to go," said Sophia, waiting for the backlash.

"But what about our trip?" asked Carol, sitting up and wiping the sleep from her eyes. "You can't leave now."

"I know. I'm sorry. It's a work emergency. " I'll call you later," Sophia said as she began collecting her clothes and headed to the bathroom, then turned back. "It probably won't take too long. Ok? Go back to sleep," she added, kissing her on the forehead before continuing and closing the bathroom door.

****

To her relief, Sophia arrived at Langley in just under an hour, barely beating her self-imposed deadline. One thing she couldn't stand was tardiness. A virtue instilled in her by her father.

The elevator chimed, and the doors slid open. Stepping out and into the vestibule, Sophia looked through the frosted glass door at the office, expecting to hear the buzzing noise of analysts working on whatever Director Owens had called her in for. Judging by his voice, it would be an all-hands-on-deck situation, though she heard nothing. She was even more stunned as she walked into the office, noticing it was eerily quiet. The office was empty.

She discovered rows of desks neatly aligned and computer monitors with screensavers dancing across their displays. No one had been in the room for some time. It was dark; the sensor lights hadn't detected movement yet. A single light emanated from an office at the rear—Director Owens'.

She made her way down an aisle between two banks of desks. The thrum of an electrical synapse firing just before the light above clicked on was the only thing she could hear as she walked.

I wonder what could be so dire, she thought as she went down the runway. The question was now burning her mind. Being woken up in the middle of the night like this and apparently being the only one he called, she really, really wanted to know what could have prompted such behavior.

As she approached Owens' office, the sound of his voice echoed through the door. The conversation seemed intense, punctuated by moments of raised voices. Catching fragments of his side of the dialogue, she discerned that Owens was far from pleased with the person on the other end of the line. However, it became evident that the caller held a significant position of authority, as Owens reluctantly acquiesced to something that clearly displeased him, judging by the forceful slam of the phone.

She decided to wait a few seconds before knocking to let him calm down, and she didn't want him to suspect she had eavesdropped. "Sir?" she said, knocking, poking her head through the doorway.

Director Owens looked up from his desk, over the brim of his square spectacles—worry lines etched into his gaunt facial structure. The life of a CIA operative is known to take its toll on people.

"Agent Evans," he said, managing a smile after his intensely heated debate. "Please have a seat," he added, motioning for her to take a seat.

"Good morning, sir," she addressed, sitting across from him.

"Good morning, Sophia. Sorry to bother you, but I have an assignment for you."

"Yes, sir. I assume this is something urgent?"

"Indeed it is. This comes straight from the DOD. I'm sending you to Milwaukee to aid the FBI in its investigation of the terrorist attack a few months back. You will be assigned to them indefinitely." He slid an envelope over to her.

"But, sir, I'm an analyst now. You know I'm no longer a field agent," she trailed off, not wanting to bring up the subject.

"I know, Sophia. That was tough on you," Owens interjected, not wanting to rehash it either. "You needed time after that, and I get that. However, this is technically not a field assignment. You won't be anywhere near the action. You're there to analyze and inform on anything they uncover. Just a support role."

"Why me?" she asked. She had no desire to return to field operations.

"Simple, you have the most knowledge of the Middle Eastern terrorist groups, you speak the language, and you're the best analyst here," he said with a grin. "Hell, one of the best I've seen in years. Not to mention, this is coming from the Department of Defense. We need to locate those responsible for the attack. They believe You're the best option at this point."

"Ok, sir," she said, relenting. "When do I leave?" As if she had a choice.

"Immediately," he answered.

Sophia joined him as he led her to the door. "There's a car outside to take you to the airport. You're to fly straight to Milwaukee. You're expected to be there by 10 a.m. Your contacts are Special Agent in Charge Tobias Stevens and the lead investigator, Agent Fred Jones."

"Am I correct in assuming you would like to be kept informed as often as possible?"

Owens nodded, pushing her out the door.

"Oh," she said, twisting, "I'll need-"

"You'll need all the reports related to the attack and investigation. I figured as much. I know you too well by now. I had all the reports sent over. I also added their personal files. Everything is in the envelope. You can read them on the plane. Also, you will go undercover as a State Department Official."

"Why, I thought we were supposed to be helping?"

"We're, but You're also there to monitor the FBI's handling of the situation. They were told to expect the State Departments' help, but the DOD wants us in on it too."

"Understood," Sophia responded. "Thank you for the trust, sir," she added.

"Just make sure we catch those monsters." He smiled as he watched Sophia board the elevator.

****

Arriving in Milwaukee just after 6:00 a.m., Sophia had a few hours to spare before she was expected at the FBI office. The best thing to do would be to check into the closest hotel she could find. Maybe catch a power nap and a bite to eat.

The flight over didn't take long, but it gave her ample opportunity to read the investigation reports, as well as both Tobias's and Fred's files. Feeling confident that she was up to speed after her quick nap, she headed for the FBI Office.

She pulled her Black Ford Edge to the FBI Office's main gate just before 9:30 a.m.

"Good morning," she said, addressing the guard. "I'm Sophia Evans from the U.S. Department of State. I believe I'm expected today." She flashed her badge to the guard.

The guard glanced at her badge before checking his log. "Agent Evans, my records indicate that you have a 10:00 a.m. appointment. You're a little early." The man's eyes drew suspiciously. The distrust was expected since the nation had just undergone a major terrorist attack.

"Well, you know what they say. If you're early, you're on time. If you're late, you might as well not show up," Sophia replied cheerfully.

The man smiled. "Ahh, military woman?" he said, letting his guard down.

"No, not me. My father was a career Army man, though. That was just one of his many sayings."

Still smiling, the guard continued, "Okay, Agent Evans, head straight for the parking garage over that way." He pointed to a four-story concrete and rebar structure to his right. The guard retreated to a small glass room and pushed a button. A loud beep followed as Sophia rolled up her window. The gate slid open to let her pass.

****

Fred and Tobias had engaged in a morning filled with heated discussions concerning Fred's task force composition. Tobias had compiled a list of office personnel whom he believed would be the most suitable candidates. Fred, however, was dissatisfied with the notion of having his choices dictated to him. His discontent primarily stemmed from the exclusion of both Ramirez and Franks, individuals he strongly believed should be part of the team.

Fred had been demanding their inclusion because he knew and trusted them beyond a shadow of a doubt. He had trained both of them just as he had with William and wanted them to be included. Before Tobias could refute Fred's argument, Tobias's admin knocked on the door, sliding through when Tobias called her in.

"Jill, good morning. What can I do for you?" He visibly tried to calm himself after the semi-heated exchange with Fred.

"Sir, the agent from the State Department is here."

Raising an eyebrow, he looked at Fred. "Wow, good. That was faster than we expected. It only took them three days. It's nice to see how fast our politicians work." The sarcasm was deep in the SAC's voice.

"Whatever," Snapped Fred, still simmering.

"Send him in."

She shook her head and quipped, "I will send *her* in."

Jill turned, opening the door the rest of the way, letting Sophia brush past.

Standing halfway, Tobias introduced himself. "Good morning, Agent-" Stopping, he realized no one had sent him a name.

"Agent Sophia Evans," she replied, stretching her hand to meet Tobias's and relinquishing her hold over the folders tucked under her arm as they fell to the floor.

Quickly collecting the folders, Sophia couldn't help but feel slightly embarrassed. Her face went beet red, accentuating her bleach-blonde hair as she flipped her ponytail back and stood up.

Fred couldn't hold back his scoff, rolling his eyes. He couldn't believe they had sent someone so green for such a critical investigation. His eyes caught Tobias's, who was not happy with Fred's reaction.

"Oh, shoot, I'm sorry. It's been a long night," she apologized, pushing her glasses back against the bridge of her nose as she stood. Her pale blue eyes glinted through the lenses as she shook Tobias' hand.

"Nice to meet you, Agent Evans. I'm Special Agent in Charge Tobias Stevens, and this is Agent Fred Jones, the lead investigator in this case. You will be working directly with him." He waved his hand at the seated Fred. "Please have a seat," he said, pointing towards the empty seat next to Fred. "First of all, thank you for coming. We can use all the assistance we can get."

"Is this your first case or something? You seem a little nervous," Fred interjected. Sophia registered that his tone suggested displeasure at her presence.

"Agent Jones! You *will* show Agent Evans the respect becoming of an FBI Agent immediately," Tobias decreed. Letting out the last ounce of frustration from their earlier conversation.

"No, it's fine, Agent Stevens," Sophia said, raising a finger and stopping Tobias before he could further scold Fred for his attitude. "For your reference, Agent Jones, no, this is not my first assignment. I just received it this morning and had to fly from Washington overnight." She looked the older man up and down. "Based on your present demeanor. You seem to have already assumed that I lack experience based on my appearance. Well, not that I need to prove anything to you, but I can assure you that I'm more than qualified for this. So, if you're done being presumptuous, can we please get started?" Sophia demurred.

Tobias laughed, amused by the woman's response. Fred put his hands up, drawing back. "Agent Evans, I couldn't have put it better. Fred, what do you have to say?"

Fred's face flushed red in embarrassment at the berating, mouth agape. He tried to apologize, but words failed him.

Sophia turned her head back to him. "There's no need to apologize, Agent Jones. I know you didn't mean to be a jerk," she said scathingly. "So, let's move on now, shall we?"

All Fred could do was nod. He had clearly been wrong.

"Well, now that's out of the way. Agent Evans, are you at least briefed on the investigation to this point?" Tobias asked.

"That I'm. I read most of the reports on the flight. The after-action reviews and memos are actually impeccable. The person who wrote those should be thanked. Very detail-oriented," she said, singing praises of their unidentified author.

"That was me," Fred informed, recovering from being put in his place.

"Outstanding reports, Agent," Sophia finished, giving the seasoned agent a nod of approval. "So, where are we today, then? The last report was two weeks ago."

"We're currently working on a plan to infiltrate the AIA," informed Fred, apologetic tone still lingering.

"Oh, how do you think we can manage that?"

"The one terrorist that we were able to take into custody has finally started talking," Tobias added.

"What makes you think that he's telling the truth?" Skepticism tinged her voice. "Why now, all of a sudden?

"So far, what he has given us has checked out." Sophia's expression suggested doubt. "Just out of curiosity, what is your area of expertise?" Fred asked.

"I was sent here because I speak Arabic fluently. I also know the AIA from my dealings in Saudi Arabia and other Middle Eastern countries. They're relatively new on the scene, having only popped up a couple of years ago. However, chatter mentioning the group had increased until it dropped completely off for a few months just before the attack." She returned her attention to Tobias, "So this plan, Agent Stevens, where are you with it?"

Tobias stood smiling. "You just so happened to pick the perfect day to show up, as it seems. We were actually about to discuss that. Why don't you accompany us?" Sophia and Tobias took a step towards the door.

"Um, before we do that, Tobias has to green-light the rest of my task force." Fred sensed an opportunity where he knew Tobias would feel obligated to give in.

"Alright," his friend and technically boss bellowed. "Fine, I give in. Take whoever you want."

A sly little grin crept across Fred's face. He'd finally got what he wanted.

Sophia looked bewildered, assuming she had accidentally

gotten in the middle of something.

"Good. With that settled…" Fred stood buttoning his jacket. "I'll go tell everyone who's on the team, and we'll meet in the conference room." Fred strode quickly out of the office, leaving Tobias and Sophia.

"I'm sorry, Agent Evans-"

"Please call me Sophia," she corrected.

"Ok, Sophia, again, I apologize. Sometimes, he forgets his manners. He's not normally this terse. It's… it's just he… we lost several agents that day." He led her from his office into and down a hallway.

"No, I understand. It was ten, correct?"

"Yeah." He looked off into the distance, remembering all of their names. "It's never easy losing some of your own. Let alone your partner."

"Oh, he lost his partner that day," she remarked, making a mental note of it and quickly searching her memory for the reports. Nothing she had read clicked. "Nothing in the reports mentioned that."

"It wasn't relative to the details of what happened," Tobias explained. "His name was William. Fred takes it personally. He feels he should've trained him better."

Hearing Tobias talk about the loss of Fred's partner brought her back to her own past. "I know all too well how that feels," she said with a frown. "Despite that, I will not sit here and take his shitty attitude the whole time. I'm here to help."

"I know I'll talk to him, but just give him some time; he'll come around," Tobias finished, opening the door to the conference room.

The glass doors of the conference room led to a rectangular room; the side walls were pretty barren, aside from a picture of the current president. The far wall was a little more impressive since it was decorated with a series of TVs. Above them were several clocks displaying the various times around the globe. In the center of the room was a sizeable oval-shaped glass table. An agent could be seen connecting wires to a standard-issue FBI laptop. He looked up, giving the pair a cursory glance before finishing the input of the last two cables.

"All done, sir," he said, walking by and taking his leave.

Fred entered with several agents trailing him, each taking a seat almost as if they had been assigned to them previously. Fred closed the blinds. Sophia took a seat next to Tobias. As he got to the last blind, another occupant entered. A man of Middle Eastern descent, he was finely dressed in a perfectly tailored suit. He had dark hair that was pulled back into a tight ponytail, complemented by a thick black beard.

"Agent Girgrah, nice of you to decide to grace us with your presence today," Fred said jokingly as the man took a seat.

Agent Girgrah looked around the table, directly at Sophia, and flashed a puzzled look at Tobias.

"Everyone, this is Agent Sophia Evans. She is our State Department attaché for the remainder of this case," Tobias informed the room.

Agent Girgrah stood, making his way toward Sophia. "It's nice to meet you, Agent Evans. You can call me Naseem." He welcomed her and shook her hand.

"Thank you. It's nice to meet you, Naseem. And," looking about the room, not knowing anyone else.

"Agents Franks, Ramirez, Johnson, Smith, Rodriguez, and White." Tobias pointed at each as he swept through the room.

"Alright, people, can we please dispense with the pleasantries and start planning this thing?" Fred quipped.

Fred and Tobias spent the next hour rehashing the details that the investigation had uncovered to this point. They discussed what their captive had divulged about the AIA. The most striking and terrorizing piece of information was about another terrorist cell that had already been activated and was possibly already planning the next attack. The prisoner had also given them a possible way to plant someone undercover.

"That brings us to the plan," Fred concluded. "We'll have to put someone inside."

"By someone, you mean me," Naseem interrupted, pointing to himself.

Fred nodded.

"Great, just making sure," he added, already rifling through all the horrible things that could happen to him if he's discovered.

"So we get Naseem to infiltrate the group at the bottom of the rung," Fred continued. "Work his way to the top or to someone with enough information to bring them down."

Sophia raised her hand.

"Yes, Agent Evans."

"Just a question: how do we get Naseem into the group right now? From my knowledge, if a group is about to commit a terrorist act, they don't normally bring in random people."

Fred was clearly annoyed by *her* disruption. "We know the name of one of their recruiters. So we're going to try to use him to get inside."

"But-"

"That's the plan, Agent Evans," Fred barked, shutting her down immediately. Fred was about to continue until Tobias spoke up.

"Wait, Fred, let's hear her out. It sounds like you have another idea, Sophia."

"Well, it's just that we know that doesn't work anymore. These groups have become a little more subtle than that. They no longer take 'believers' off the streets. Instead, from what I've seen, they recruit them in various ways."

"And how would someone in the State Department know that?" Fred asked. He could feel that something was off. He knew there was no way anyone from the State Department would have this much knowledge of the inner workings of terrorist groups.

"I read that in a report," she answered quickly.

Fred's eyes narrowed in suspicion, not buying her explanation at all.

"Agent Evans, can we speak privately outside?" By Fred's tone, it wasn't so much a question as a demand. He angrily pushed the door open and stepped outside. Sophia followed, head down.

"I'm not a dumb man, Agent Evans. Do you think I'm dumb?" Posing the question as a rhetorical one. Not even waiting for an answer. "So, if you truly want to be part of this team, I need to be able to trust you. And right now, I don't. So, I will ask a very blunt question, and I hope you can read this situation and understand that I want the truth, even if it goes against your programming and orders." Sophia gulped indiscreetly. "Who are you? Who do you actually work for?" Fred demanded.

"I told you I work for the State Department." She tried to defend herself and maintain her cover.

"Bullshit, I'm not buying that," Fred's voice rose.

"Fred," Tobias barked as he entered the hallway, his teeth clenched, baring them, and not wanting to shout too loudly. "Calm the hell down."

"No, she's lying to us," he shouted, jabbing his finger at Sophia.

"You know what. I'm not taking this from you anymore, Agent Jones. You're downright disrespectful," she retorted.

Fred was right; she could read the situation and tell that keeping the lie going would do more damage than good. Knowing her expertise and knowledge would help bring the attackers to justice. Her best course of action would be to confirm Fred's suspicion. After all, it wasn't as if she was on a life-or-death mission; keeping the cover intact was paramount to the mission and her success. On the contrary, a quick assessment of Fred suggested that maintaining her cover would only jeopardize the mission. She'd just have to break the news to her boss later. After all, these were fellow Americans looking for justice.

"You're right," she confessed.

Tobias jerked his head in her direction. "What?"

"Agent Jones is right. I'm not from the State Department," she said, shaking her head. "I knew I couldn't hide it from you for long after reading your file. Eventually, you would figure it out. You're smart," said Sophia revealingly.

"Wait, I'm still a little lost here," Tobias said, his eyes darting between the two as if he were watching a chess match.

"She's a spy. CIA, aren't you?" Fred accused, face red with anger, not attempting to keep his voice down.

"Keep your voice down," Sophia whispered, trying to calm him. "Yes, I work for the CIA."

"Why would they send a CIA agent to us?" Tobias questioned.

"I don't know exactly why," Sophia answered truthfully. "I received a call last night from my boss, instructing me to come here. I was told that I was coming undercover as a State Department official. That's all I know." Deciding right now wasn't the best time to tell them she was sent to monitor how they handled the terrorist group.

"So why lie to us?" Tobias was still slightly confused.

"I do not know why the ruse. I'm telling you-"

"If you say 'the truth,' I'm going to lose my shit," Fred snapped. "At this point, I wouldn't believe a word out of your mouth.

"Look, I wasn't happy about this from the beginning myself. But we're here now. Let's make the best of the situation. We do still have a terrorist cell to stop," Sophia said bluntly. "Quite frankly, I'm glad about this. I want everything out on the table. Hell, by just telling you this, I could get fired, which wouldn't help anyone. But I can help you stop the next coming attack. So, how about we keep all this between the three of us until we stop them?"

The two men pulled away, briefly discussing the proposal, before returning.

"Ok, agreed," Tobias declared. "We keep all this between us, at least for now. Can we all get back in there now?"

Fred and Sophia nodded. Sophia followed Tobias back into the conference room, taking their seats. Fred took another moment to soak in what had transpired.

"Agent Evans," Naseem continued, dismissing the interruption. "Do you know how I can infiltrate the group?" the impeccably dressed Arab man asked. "Without getting killed, preferably."

Fred re-entered, taking his seat. "Well." She paused, her eyes fixed on Fred, not wanting to overstep her bounds again.

"Go ahead, Agent Evans. If you've got a plan, I'm all ears," said a smirking Fred.

"Thank you, Agent Jones," Sophia continued, relieved. "Based on recent intelligence reports, the most effective way to gain acceptance into these groups is, surprisingly, through the internet."

"Through the internet, how do they do that?" Ramirez asked.

"Well, as you know, hundreds if not thousands of chat groups on the web and dark web spew out hate and anti-American sentiment. These groups troll the sites for anyone they feel can be indoctrinated into their cause."

"So that's how we get their attention?" Tobias asked.

"Correct. We start spewing anti-American garbage everywhere, and it will get noticed."

"How long would that take?"

"That's a good question, Agent Jones," she answered through clenched teeth, still seething at Fred. "Depends on what we say or can prove that we have done something big enough to catch their attention."

"Big enough, like?"

"I don't know yet. Maybe stage an attack of our own," Sophia pondered out loud. "We can put our heads together and think of something; I'm sure of it."

"Sophia, thank you for your valuable input. That's not a bad idea." Going along with the idea of possibly staging their terrorist attack. "I think we have a good solid plan here. All that is left to do now is to put it into action."

After the meeting, Fred approached Sophia in the hall, having calmed back to his usual self. "Good job today, Agent Evans, if that is your real name," Fred added with a slight tinge of sarcasm.

"That is my real name," she spat back. "Look," she added, calming. "I'm sorry for the deception. Again, that was not my idea. I wanted to be honest from the start."

"Whatever, I know how you CIA types operate. Just don't ever lie to me again. Or we'll have some issues."

"Never. Trust is essential, and this mission is too critical to mess up. I hope I can get yours back someday."

"You can start by helping me catch these assholes."

"We will; I will do anything it takes to catch them," Sophia said as Fred walked away.

He stopped turning his head over his shoulder. "What are you waiting for?" he asked. "These terrorists aren't going to find and kill themselves. Let's get to work."

CHAPTER SEVEN

Sophia sat in her car in the driveway outside Fred's house, making one more check of Naseem's chat room accounts. She hoped and prayed this would be the day they finally saw progress. They were four months into her suggested plan to infiltrate Amell Al-Gharsi's terrorist network, and no result yet.

The stress had begun to take its toll on her. She hadn't slept much lately, and dark bags had started to form under her eyes. Fred suggested she come over for dinner and take the weekend off. She didn't want to, but it'd been weeks since she last saw Carol. Things hadn't been going too well on that front for Sophia either.

Giving her phone a quick glance, she released a deep and foreboding sigh. There was still nothing outside of the usual rants and ramblings from Naseem. She shook her head, made one final check of herself in the mirror, and blew out another exasperated sigh. Uncomfortable with the newly formed bags and worry lines, she headed up the driveway.

Sophia was never one to play dress up for anything—a frequent criticism of her girlfriends. So, saying that she felt entirely awkward at this moment was an understatement. Pulling and tugging nervously at the too-tight black cocktail dress she was now wearing while juggling a wine bottle, she almost tripped but managed to save herself and the bottle. Standing at the door now, she gave another yank at the revealing dress, accentuating her figure in all the right places. She shimmied it into a more tolerable position and then pushed back her glasses up onto the bridge of her nose before knocking.

She took a brief look at her surroundings. A quick thought sprung into her mind, compelling her to leave. She could still get away, and no one would notice.

Too late. The door opened.

"Sophia, you're here. "Please come in," Sherry said, answering the door as she peered around, looking for someone else. "Where's Carol?"

"She couldn't make it, Mrs. Jones. She had to cancel the trip.

Some type of emergency meeting. She does send her regards, though."

"*Tsk,* that's a shame." Sherry's smile didn't subside at the news. "I still have you. I don't know what I would do if I had to go through another whole dinner with Fred and Tobias chattering about sports." The older woman moved aside to let her guest in.

"Don't worry, Mrs. Jones, we'll have our own conversations then," Sophia added with a smile. "Oh, this is for you guys," handing her the wine.

"Now, Sophia, how many times do I have to tell you? It's Sherry, not Mrs. Jones," she said as the two of them headed into the kitchen. "You're practically family at this point."

"I know, Mrs. Jo… Sherry, just a habit. It happens when you're raised in a military family." Sophia tried her best but couldn't help flashing a huge smile. The Jones' had been so welcoming to her.

After the rocky start between her and Fred, the two found out they had much in common. It seemed to be the only good thing about how long it was taking to get Naseem into the AIA.

"Anyway, come on, the boys are waiting." Sherry led Sophia through the front of the house, past the living room, into a hallway that eventually opened up into a dining room, which they passed through to enter the kitchen. Fred and Tobias huddled at the island counter, sipping away at their beers. Sherry turned to Sophia. "See, there they go, already gabbing it up about the Packers," she said, giving her guest an eye roll.

"I see that," Sophia said, smiling and nodding at Fred as he glanced over. "No worries, I'm here to rescue you from their testosterone." The inflection in her voice was loud enough for the two chattering men to hear the snarky comment, accompanied by a crooked smirk. Fred returned the smile, followed by a middle finger.

The pair's affinity for each other had shone through in unique ways as the two bonded. Fred initially saw Sophia as a threat. However, that feeling quickly disappeared once he got to know her. Now, the two were thick as thieves at work, developing an almost hive-like mind.

"Hey, Sof, what's up? No, Carol?"

"Sorry, my better half couldn't make it tonight. So you're stuck with just little ole' me," Sophia pouted, pretending to be offended.

"I wouldn't say better half, more entertaining half maybe," Fred replied, laughing at his own joke. Sophia returned it with a bird of her own.

"Fredrick, be nice," Sherry snapped. "She's still a guest in our house."

"Yeah, Fred, show some manners," Tobias added, hiding his smile behind a sip from his can.

"Anyways, let's eat. Dinner's ready," Sherry said, pulling the roast out of the oven.

"Mmmm, it smells great," Sophia remarked. "Beats takeout or room service."

"Honey, I told you we have a spare bedroom," Sherry said, placing the roast on the table. "You can stay here. Living out of that… that hotel can't be good for you."

Another broad grin from Sophia. "Thank you." She placed a hand on the other woman's hand. "I don't want to impose on you two. But thanks again."

It wasn't the first time that Sherry had offered their spare bedroom.

"Told you," Fred chimed in, sitting down.

Throughout dinner, the three agents did their best to avoid discussing the investigation. Sherry set up the get-together to get their minds off it after seeing the pressure and stress the months of little to no progress had put on them.

Tobias left soon after the dinner, but Sophia stayed behind at Fred's behest. He asked Sophia to follow him into his study, leaving Sherry in the kitchen, but as they moved to the other room, Fred turned to his wife. "Honey, leave everything," he said. "I'll be back in a bit to help clean up."

"Thank you, Sherry, for dinner. It was superb as always," Sophia followed up.

"Thank you, Sophia, and please give my regards to Carol."

"Will do."

Fred guided Sophia into his study, poured a glass of whiskey, and offered it to Sophia.

"No thanks, Fred; you know I don't drink," she said, placing her hands on her hips in annoyance.

"I know, but it's only proper to offer," he countered before taking a sip. "Anyways, I wanted you to stay back to discuss something." He took a seat in his chair, motioning for Sophia to sit as well. "I know this was your plan. And you know that I support it." Sophia nodded, confused. "But don't you think it's time to switch tactics? It's been four months, and we've made no progress in finding Amell."

She contemplated Fred's suggestion, thinking about how frustrated she had become at the lack of results to this point herself. She'd even thought about bringing it up to Fred after the weekend.

"Maybe," she said, relenting. "Let's wait until after Naseem gets back today. Then, we can gather everyone to sit down and devise another plan."

Fred smiled, pleased with how receptive Sophia was to abandoning the plan she'd worked so hard to put in place. "Well, I have some ideas. I think," he continued. "It might be possible to keep going with the current plan but tweak it a bit. Do something big," he added, placing his drink down and throwing his hands wide. "Something… something that might get Naseem noticed. Put him on the map of terrorists, so to speak."

"Good," Sophia said, being mindful of her facial expression. Trying not to give away her feelings, she was slightly offended by how quickly Fred had devised an alternative. She could tell he'd been thinking about this for some time. "Save it for next week. We can go over your idea with the rest of the team. Though, why ask me about this tonight?" she questioned.

"I wanted to give you a heads up and see if you were thinking along the same lines," he answered. "I want us," he said, motioning between himself and her. "To present a united front when bringing this to the team." He continued to explain. "We need to be on the same page."

"Fred, come on, you should know by now that I will back your play."

This was true despite her initial upset over the fact that he'd been thinking about a new plan. Admitting to herself that hers wasn't exactly working. Besides, she and Fred had developed that chemistry. She knew he was all about getting the job done, and he was smart. If he had another idea, it would be best to hear it out.

"I will always be on board for a better way. Just don't wait so long to bring it up." Fred gave a puzzled look. "Come on now, I know well enough by now that you didn't just come up with this tonight. You've been thinking about it." Fred nodded. "Next time, bring it up immediately. You know you're not going to offend me," she added with a teasing smile.

"Alright then, all settled," Fred said, standing. "Let me walk you out then."

The two made their way to the front door, Fred walking her all the way to her car and opening the door. As Sophia sat behind the wheel, Fred leaned in before closing the door.

"So, I don't mean to pry, but you know I care, so what did happen to Carol tonight? Are you still fighting?" Fred asked with genuine concern in his voice.

"No. I mean, a bit. More than we used to, certainly," Sophia admitted. "She doesn't understand why an IT consultant would need to be stationed for months on end helping set up a network." Sophia hadn't yet brought herself to tell Carol what it was she really did.

"Besides, this time, she canceled. Some big-shot attendee changed his travel plans, so she needed to help redo the scheduling.

"Ok," Fred said. "I can only imagine how hard it must be to lie to her about why you're staying here so long. I don't understand why you haven't told her that you work for the CIA. I know you can tell at least one person."

"I can, but… we're just not there yet," she said, shrugging.

"Ok," Fred conceded, not wishing to continue the line of questioning, seeing the look on his young friend's face. "Are you headed back to the hotel then?"

"I don't know, maybe. Might just go to a club and do

something like divulge state secrets." A wry smile crept across her face.

Fred laughed at the mere thought of Sophia going out to a club and doing anything remotely rule-breaking.

"Yeah, right, sure. Sophia Evans in a club. Ha-ha, I'd die if I saw that."

"Gotta show this dress off somewhere to justify the cost," she quipped, feigning to hike the slinky black piece up her thigh.

"Go on, get out of here," Fred cackled, closing her door as he walked away. He turned to the porch, watching Sophia back up and pull out into the road, still shaking his head as he pictured her in a club.

Driving away, Sophia had a thought, and it wasn't about going to a club; however, she also didn't intend to return to the hotel that had been her home for the last four months.

Instead, as always, she was thinking like the operative she was. She decided to go to the office and post on the message boards, hoping something would draw out a member of the AIA, as this could be her last chance.

****

She arrived at the office, fired up her computer, and then stopped; she had no idea where to start. Sitting, staring blankly at the screen, she pondered what type of incendiary post she could make that would draw attention.

The cursor continued flashing, taunting her. She knew she had to be careful about what and when she posted. Suppose someone was watching and monitoring Naseem's movements, trying to recruit him for the AIA; they would know that he should be getting off an airplane shortly after returning from Pakistan.

The team had been setting up fake extremist groups and placing Naseem as their handler. At this particular moment, he was returning from a trip after supplying one of these organizations with materials.

It was Fred's idea, believing that Naseem would need some credibility to make him a more attractive target for the AIA.

Signing into one of Naseem's accounts, Sophia began posting humblebrags about small things these groups get off on. Satisfied, she leaned back in the chair, anxiously waiting, staring at the text box. Hoping against hope that something would catch. Even after all these months. But sitting became too unbearable, so she started pacing to calm her nerves.

As the night ticked by slowly, Sophia sat once again, waiting for something to happen. Finally, succumbing to the sleep that had been hounding her for hours, Sophia's head hit the desk with a thud, her forehead thumping onto the space bar. The cursor lanced across the screen, leaving a trail of blank spaces in its wake.

Ding.

A message popped up. The speaker had been turned up so Sophia could hear it if she'd strayed too far from the terminal. The ping echoed in her head for several seconds before her unconscious brain could decipher what the noise was.

"I'm awake," she shouted, head shooting up. Her tired eyes were fixed on the screen before her. Her blurry vision focused on the text prompt. She rubbed her eyes, pinching herself to make sure it wasn't a dream.

It was a message from someone claiming to be Abdul Sanú.

Sophia's eyes widened, reading the name. It was one that she was very familiar with.

All the intelligence they had gathered about the AIA's operations had pointed to Abdul being Amell's number two, which their captive prisoner had confirmed. This guy was the one person on the planet who could tell them where Amell's base of operations was.

Sophia quickly rifled through her purse, looking for her cell phone. Finding it, she called Fred.

"Fred, wake up," Sophia could barely contain the excitement in her voice.

"Sophia, it's the middle of the night," Fred groggily responded.

"You need to get to the office now. We got a hit."

Fred, still a little drowsy, sprung straight up in bed. "What do you mean we got a hit?"

"What do you think?" Sophia blurted. "Someone claiming to be Abdul just replied to one of our posts."

"Abdul Sanú, the Abdul Sanú Amell's number two?"

"No, Abdul Sanú, prince of Persia," snapped Sophia. "Yes, Abdul Sanú." Fred could feel her eyes roll through the phone.

"Holy shit, I'll be there as soon as I can. Oh, and Sophia, good work."

"Thanks, now just get your ass here."

****

The elevator doors opened, and Fred entered the dark office. He could see one light on from Sophia's makeshift office at the very back of the room.

He could see through the window that Sophia had her head down, forehead resting against the desk. She was still wearing the same dress she had left his house in.

He knocked.

Sophia's head flung up. "Fred, you're here already," she said, wiping her mouth and ensuring no drool.

"Jeez, I thought you were going home."

"I… I decided not to. And good thing I didn't. If I had, we would still be nowhere."

"Ok, and where exactly are we now?" Fred asked, walking out of the office and heading to the break room. Sophia following.

"Closer than earlier tonight, that's for sure," she said, shrugging. "I haven't actually opened it yet," she added.

"Wait, you got me out of bed for something that could be nothing more than his porn site recommendations?" Fred fumbled around with the coffee machine, pouring in a cup of grinds. He wasn't entirely upset; he was just surprised that she hadn't read the message yet.

"No, the message came with a link to another site. I saw it and figured you would want to be here when I opened the link."

"Oh, ok, thanks. The sentiment is noted, but it could be nothing but a big fuck you."

The pot behind him spritzed. He sniffed the air, taking in the aroma of fresh coffee.

"I know, but I don't think that's the case here. That's not their M.O."

Fred poured a cup, then another one for Sophia.

"Ok, then let's go open it," he said, walking back to her office, still unconvinced.

Sophia spun her chair around, plopping back down on it. She clicked away at a few screens, getting back to the message board. Looking over her shoulder, Fred nodded.

"Okay, here we go." She clicked on the hyperlink in the text box. It connected her to another webpage plastered with the AIA symbol.

"Son of a bitch, they have their own website," she grumbled.

"Who cares? Everyone does," Fred sniped. "What does it say?" The entire page was written in Arabic.

"Give me a minute," said Sophia, scanning. "Ok, it says… just paraphrasing here, 'Soldier in the fight against the infidels, Allah wishes to accept you into his army. But you must prove yourself worthy of such an honor. You must complete a task that proves you're a true warrior of Allah. You will receive a message with your task. Once you have been proven worthy, you shall be enlisted into Allah's army.' That's it."

"Well, that's not exactly what we were looking for," Fred stated, disappointed. "But, at least it's an invitation."

"It is a start, Fred," said Sophia, rescanning the page to see if any hidden messages were embedded, trying to remain optimistic.

"It is," Fred agreed. "But the problem is we have no idea what this task will entail. What if they want Naseem to commit a terrorist act or, even worse, martyr himself?"

"I don't believe they are looking for a martyr; nothing in their past suggests that they would be."

"I know, but too much can go wrong here," Fred huffed, clasping his hands over his face as he thought about all the horrible things they might force Naseem to do.

"Ok, so we wait for the task. Run it by Tobias. If it's something we can do, we do it. Then we're in. Right?"

Fred shook his head in disbelief.

"You're right, as always. Let's wait it out and see what happens. Go from there."

****

Naseem's task was sent to them later that day via the same message board, which included another hyperlink. Agents Ramirez and Franks attempted to trace the origin of the messages but had no such luck.

The task itself proved to be reasonably simple. Naseem had to pick up an envelope from a P.O. Box and deliver it to a specified address without opening it or inquiring about its contents.

Tobias agreed to let the operation proceed, allowing Naseem to pick up and deliver the envelope without looking to see what it was. They set up surveillance on the building but didn't move in since this was a test to see if any recruits were law enforcement.

Sophia burst through Tobias' office two days later. "We got it," she blurted out.

Fred and Tobias looked at each other, confused. "Got what?"

"Abdul," Sophia crowed. "He responded. It was another link, but this page gave flight information and a boarding pass."

She could hardly contain her excitement, speaking as fast as she could.

"Slow down. Flight information to where?" Tobias asked.

"Orlando, Florida. They want Naseem in Orlando in two days to meet with Abdul."

Fred's face lit with a glow that Sophia had never seen before. He turned to Tobias, who had a smile stretching ear to ear. "We got'em."

"Sounds like it," his friend responded. "I want you and Sophia gone in the next few hours. Get Naseem up to speed. Fly down there, link up with the FBI office, and start creating a plan. I don't want Naseem going anywhere alone. I want eyes on him the entire time. We have no idea what they have planned," Tobias instructed.

"Got it, boss. Sophia? We've got work to do," Fred said, leading Sophia out of the office. "Go get the team ready; meet in the conference room in five minutes."

Heartland Strike

Sophia nodded. "Got it."

85

CHAPTER EIGHT

Naseem followed the flow of passengers departing his flight and heading into the terminal at Orlando International Airport, one of the largest airports in the country. He took a moment to orient himself, taken aback by the size.

He followed the crowd, allowing them to guide him to the baggage claim area. His mind raced on how and when the AIA would contact him. Moving through the crowded airport terminal, he tried to relax. He couldn't give the impression that he had formal espionage training. Sophia had warned him that it was possible they would be watching him every step of the way.

Standing at the baggage carousel, the hairs on the back of Naseem's neck prickled. A chill swept over his body as the open space around him began to disintegrate. Sensing that he was no longer alone, he turned slowly. Coming face to chest with a large Arab man easily standing all of six-eight.

The giant glowered intensely down at him. The tip of the man's long, dark beard, which covered a chiseled jawline, brushed against Naseem's forehead. The man's sun-beaten face sported a large scar running down its left side, cutting across his milky, glossy eye.

He stood there intimidatingly, wearing no expression at all. Naseem gulped, eyeing the brusque man up and down when his eyes fixated on another person standing behind the large mass. The second man was nowhere near as opposing; he was Naseem's height and build, but his face was every bit sun-weathered and beaten as his counterparts.

Not saying a word, the shorter of the two pointed to the sign the other was holding. Written across it was Naseem's name.

The man then pointed to Naseem. The agent nodded to confirm that they had the right person.

The smaller man spoke in Arabic, "Welcome, Brother Naseem. My name is Ashar, and this is Adeel," he said, pointing to his larger companion. "Please come with us. Abdul is waiting to see you."

"Nice to meet-" Adeel snatched Naseem's bag from the carousel and walked away. Ashar turned to follow.

"Ok, I guess I'm following you," Naseem murmured, throwing his hands up.

Heading for the terminal exit, Naseem scanned the area, searching for any signs of an FBI team following him. He saw none. No team had been trailing him. For his benefit, Sophia and Fred didn't discuss how they would be following him. Sophia felt it best he did not know so he couldn't inadvertently give them away.

Naseem voiced his concerns over the decision. However, Tobias decided to stick with Sophia's decision. For now, he would have to assume his backup was close by.

They exited the terminal to a waiting SUV. Asher opened the back door, motioning for Naseem to get in as Adeel loaded his bag. The trio departed.

Naseem took in the surroundings outside the blacked-out window quietly as he waited for his new friends to say a word or give him a clue about where they were taking him. Instead, the pair sat in complete silence, not even exchanging a glance at him.

After about forty minutes of silence, he was tired of waiting for them to speak. Naseem decided it was time to initiate a conversation and gather any information before meeting Abdul.

"Not much for talking?" Naseem asked.

Asher turned to face the agent in the backseat. "I prefer not to make friends with people who may not be around for long," Asher responded, staring straight into Naseem's eyes as the coldness of the words pierced through the agent.

"Hahaha." The man started laughing seconds later. "I joke, I joke. Adeel has been deaf since six, made so by an American bomb that exploded in our village. He doesn't like to talk since he can't hear himself. I, on the other hand, love to talk, but there is not much I can tell you. Abdul will explain everything in a minute. We're here." He pointed to an industrial building as Adeel turned down the side road where it was located.

He pulled the SUV into the parking lot of a small one-story factory building. They stopped at a grey metal roll-up gate along the side.

Following Asher's direction, Naseem stepped out of the SUV as the front door to the building opened. Out stepped a small, portly man with a long, jet-black beard, a white, decorative turban, and curly black hair peeking out from underneath.

He was not wearing the traditional Thoob. Instead, his dress style was much more Western—a pair of blue jeans and a white button-up shirt covered with a black windbreaker. The new arrival signed something to Adeel before he shuffled over to Naseem, who figured this was Abdul, judging by how Adeel and Asher regarded him.

"Assalamualaikum," the man leaned in and said, kissing Naseem on the right cheek, then repeating the gesture on the left.

"Waalaikum," responded Naseem.

"My friend, welcome to Allah's army. Come, come, let's go inside. You must be hungry, no? 'Cause I'm." Abdul threw his head back, tapping his belly and releasing a loud chuckle that caused his stomach to wobble.

He led Naseem into the small office building that adjoined the factory. Asher followed them and closed the door behind them.

"Wait, my bag!" Naseem cried out, only to return and find Asher blocking his path.

"Come, come, no worries, Adeel will take care of it," Naseem said.

At the same time, he couldn't help but wonder if he left anything inside that might give him away as a federal agent. No, he was more cautious than that.

Abdul continued to lead Naseem through the office, passing through one more door that led out into a larger room used as a loading bay. The ceiling vaulted up another ten feet. Pillars were strategically placed throughout the open floor plan, supporting the roof. Getting stuck in a large metal room with a group of terrorists wasn't a dream of Naseem's.

The agent's training kicked in autonomously as he began making mental notes of the factory's contents: Several Toyota pickup trucks, two larger cargo trucks, crates of supplies scattered throughout the room, two racks of firearms, and a wooden table.

Passing by the table, he caught a glimpse of the contents. Everything one needed to make a bomb—several, in fact, along with maps of the Orlando area. They had been planning a route to somewhere.

Not letting his eyes linger too long on the bomb material and maps, he continued to scan the area. Sofas, cots, and a refrigerator were in the far corner of the bay. It seemed they had been living at the facility for some time. Abdul started his spiel, giving Naseem a rundown of the facility, almost like an unofficial tour guide would do.

His chest seemed to swell with pride as he pointed out everything. Naseem had not paid attention to a word his host had said. He was more focused on familiarizing himself with the layout of the grounds.

Surveying the far end of the room, he carefully observed a suspicious transaction. The exchange struck him as incongruous within the setting. Two individuals had disembarked from a cargo truck that had recently arrived, clad in matching all-black military attire. Curiously, a patch on their shoulders caught his attention, though he couldn't identify its origin or meaning.

The two were clearly American, which only furthered Naseem's intrigue. One of Adbul's men handed them an envelope, followed by an exchange of words that looked pretty heated. After several seconds, the two men exited through the back door, leaving the truck behind suspiciously.

What had he just watched?

Abdul noticed Naseem had been distracted by the encounter, so he stopped the tour. "My friend, no need to worry about that over there. That is supplies from our provider."

Naseem quickly brought his attention back to Abdul's questioning gaze. "Sorry, just impressed with what you've built here." Through his years of undercover work, Naseem learned that flattery gets you everywhere, even off the hook for curious activity, or so he'd hoped in this case, as his heart thudded in his chest. Abdul's suspicious eyes gazed at or *through* him. Had he inadvertently given himself away? Did one moment of curiosity ruin the entire operation? He felt a droplet of sweat forming atop his forehead.

"Hahaha, it is pretty impressive," bellowed Abdul. His jovialness returned.

Naseem could feel the thud of his heart falling to the pit of his stomach as Abdul continued the tour. "We have big plans."

"That makes me happy. What do you have in store next?" Naseem questioned. "I mean, the Milwaukee attack was huge. How are you going to top that?"

Naseem figured that Abdul enjoyed hearing his own voice. He may be able to get him to divulge their plans.

"No, Milwaukee was a failure," scoffed Abdul. "We lost many brothers that day. No, it is easy to send a soldier of Allah in with a bomb to his chest to sacrifice for the cause. No, you will see that Amell doesn't believe in that nonsense. Soldiers fight to survive, not die."

"Well, that's a relief," Naseem quipped, shocked by the revelation that the AIA didn't believe in suicide bombers. This flew in the face of many Jihadist groups who believe suicide bombers are martyrs for the cause.

"Oh, did you come here to die, my friend?" Abdul stopped turning to face him. The question was phrased more sarcastically.

"No, not exactly. I came here to serve Allah's will, whatever it may be."

"Good, you will fit in very nicely." A smile returned to Adbul's face. "Now, come and sit with me. We have things to discuss before Amell arrives."

Naseem's eyes scrunched at the revelation, and he stopped in his tracks. The mastermind behind the Milwaukee bombing was apparently in the country and on his way. Whatever the group had planned would soon be happening. Trying to maintain his decorum, he asked, "Amell is coming here?"

It was a one-in-a-million chance. The team never fully believed that he would show up. Amell had only been seen once or twice, and no one knew his exact location. This would be huge if the team could catch him tonight.

"Yes, he is on his way." Abdul checked his watch. "Very shortly. This is why I want to eat now." Another tapping of his rotund belly.

"He wants to oversee the final preparations himself," Abdul said, his apprehensive gaze fixed on the floor—a sign of hurt.

Naseem picked up on the hesitation and crack in Abdul's voice. Possible dissension in their ranks? A possible window?

"So, does he normally do that?" Naseem asked.

"No, no, this is a first," the bulbous man sighed, sitting down.

"Does he… not trust you can achieve your mission?" He wanted to push Abdul but didn't want to overplay the situation.

"No, he trusts me, always has; it's just this mission is vital and will strike absolute fear in these infidel pigs."

Abdul's words signaled that he shouldn't push him anymore. The man may have an issue with the boss, but he seemed devoted to the cause.

The two men sat in brief silence as someone brought them food. Asher and Adeel, who had returned from wherever they had disappeared to, took their seats.

"Anyway," Adbul broke the silence, mouth full of bread, spittle flinging out. "I remember this one time…"

Abdul indulged in storytelling, further validating Naseem's suspicion that the man relished the sound of his own voice. Asher, visibly fatigued, let his head loll back in weariness, growing increasingly tired of Abdul's endless anecdotes. Even after thirty minutes, Naseem found himself growing tired of the repetitive tales about the days before America's interference in global affairs. He couldn't help but envy Adeel, who was fortunate enough to be spared from enduring the monotonous narratives. Nevertheless, Naseem couldn't afford to be consumed by his frustration. Somewhere in the recesses of his mind, he recognized the urgency of sending a message to his team, preferably outside, alerting them to Amell's impending arrival.

Behind him was an increase in chatter amongst 'Allah's Warriors,' followed by a spike in activity. Aside from Adbul, Asher, Adeel, and himself, everyone else in the warehouse began packing and loading equipment onto the trucks.

Whispers started floating around. Naseem wondered what was happening, but Abdul continued his story night until another man joined the group, sitting across from Naseem.

The new arrival's face hardened as he sat, affixing a steely gaze that sent piercing daggers through the agent. Shaking Naseem's confidence. He had seen a look like this only once before. A serial killer he had caught after the monster had murdered twenty people. The stare would strike fear in the most hardened of individuals.

Something was wrong.

"Abdul, not that I'm not enjoying your tales, but it was a long flight, and I came straight here. I need to use the restroom," Naseem informed. Thinking of something to get away from the new arrival. His presence set off every sense of danger in Naseem's body. Plus, he still needed to get the word out to Fred and Sophia.

"Ahh yes… yes, my brother, I'm sorry, the restroom is over there." He pointed to the back wall of the warehouse.

"Well then, please excuse me for a moment."

Abdul nodded as Naseem stepped away from the seating area towards the restroom. From the corner of his eye, Naseem could see the man with the thousand-yard death stare lean over and whisper something in Abdul's ear.

Yup, something was wrong.

Naseem's stomach was in knots, and his body shuddered with an uneasy feeling. He entered the restroom, closing and locking the door behind him. Next, he pulled up the left leg of his pants to find a small flip phone tucked away in an ankle holster.

He fumbled, trying to turn it on.

He didn't have long, so he quickly texted his team. Hopefully, waiting, team.

****

"I can't see anything," Sophia reported, staring through a pair of night vision binoculars. "There's not one window low enough to see anything." She resumed her pacing.

Unbeknownst to Naseem, Fred and Sophia had set up in a field behind the factory building, a few yards away. They had trailed

Naseem the entire way from the airport. Now that they had a location, they called the Orange County Sheriff's Office for assistance in closing down the area. They only had to wait for Naseem to signal them to move in.

"Sophia, calm down, just relax. He's going to be ok," Fred chirped, leaning back in the SUV. "Besides, your pacing is driving me bonkers. You and Tobias have the same issue. No patience."

"Hey, I resent that." She whirled to face him. "I have plenty of patience," she refuted, pretending to be affronted. "I waited for you to come around, did I not?" She flashed a smug smile, her eyebrow raised.

"Yeah, but that was only because I HAD to work with you," Fred fired back mockingly.

"Whatever, just admit it. You were wrong about me."

"I will do no such thing. I'm never wrong."

"Oh. What about the one time-" Fred held up a hand, stopping her mid-sentence, as he felt a vibration in his pocket. "What is it?" she asked as he pulled the phone out.

"It's Naseem. He sent a message," Fred replied, shooting up from his relaxed position. "Oh shit."

"What, what, come on, what does it say?" Sophia jumped up and down for a response, trying to snatch the phone.

"It says Amell is coming. The cover may be blown. Going back out, leaving the phone on." Fred read out loud, looking up at Sophia with eyes wider than she had ever seen before.

The phone rang, and Naseem's name popped up on the caller ID. Fred answered, looking up at Sophia. He appeared to be worried for the first time since they had met.

"What does that mean? Should we go in if his cover is blown?" She grabbed her M4 from the back, and she was about to rush the building.

"No, we don't move in," Fred barked, waving over the local S.W.A.T. unit. "Commander, just in case, get your teams ready to go." The squat, burly, brown-headed team leader nodded before rushing off to brief his team.

"Fred, if Naseem's cover is blown, they'll kill him," Sophia warned.

"And if his cover isn't blown and we move in now, we lose Amell, possibly for good. I can't risk that. Can you? We can end this here tonight."

Sophia scowled at him.

Knowing full well that he was risking the life of one of his own didn't make the decision any easier. But Fred knew he was making the right call.

Sophia's eyes remained fixed on him.

"Any sign of trouble, we move in. Ok?"

Sophia huffed but knew he was right. "Fine, I got it," she snapped.

Fred answered the call, hearing nothing but muffled noises and the sound of a toilet flushing.

****

Seeing that the message was received, Naseem attempted to calm his nerves. He took a few deep breaths and looked in the mirror.

"Keep calm; you don't know for sure if you've been made. Maybe it's just a delay in Amell's arrival or something," the agent said to himself, trying to ease his nervousness to no avail.

Dialing Fred's number, he slid the phone into his front pocket, hoping it would make the conversation easier for them to hear. Despite every effort to calm himself, he knew he was right. He had been made. The only question now would be, can he get out alive?

He flushed the toilet and washed his hands in case anyone outside had been monitoring him.

Naseem opened the door; the mood in the room had changed. The activity level had bumped up tenfold. Everyone hustled to load the cargo trucks. The weapons racks had been cleared, and the bomb maker had disappeared along with Asher and Adeel.

Abdul stood in the middle of the room, having an animated conversation.

Naseem took the chance to look about and figure out an escape route. He was practically in the middle of the factory. There were exit doors on either side of him, but he was too far away. If he attempted to run, he'd be shot. He could try to sneak out casually, but again, there were too many people. Someone would see him.

Abdul spotted him and waved him over.

Shit, too late now.

"Abdul, what's going on? Are we leaving? What about Amell? I was looking forward to meeting him," Naseem choked out, mouth running dry.

Abdul turned around and grabbed Naseem by the shoulders. "My friend, there's been a small development. I was hoping you could clear up a disagreement for us." There was a subtle stoniness in his words.

"Ok, I don't know if I can help, but I'll try," Naseem replied, trying to keep calm.

"For your sake, I hope you can. My friends Amir and Fahad tell me that you're FBI. I say no, you can't be. I recruit you. Personally, I tell them. Everything checks out for you. They say no, but a little birdie tells them otherwise. So, I say we ask you, then decide."

****

Fred held up his cell phone on speaker while Sophia also listened in. They could hear what appeared to be a conversation of sorts, but Naseem's jeans were muffling the voices.

Sophia drew back. "Did he just say FBI?" Fred gave her a look of uncertainty. They leaned closer, trying to hear. The voices grew louder. Then.

BANG!

CHAPTER NINE

The sound of the gunshot was unmistakable. Fred and Sophia exchanged horrified looks.

Had he waited too long to send in the backup? Was Sophia right? Fred knew now wasn't the time to play the what-if game. There would be plenty of opportunity for that later. He had to react.

"Move in, move in now!" Fred commanded, directing the assembled group of FBI agents and local Sheriff's deputies to advance toward the target building. Among them were esteemed members of the FBI's counter-terrorism unit, renowned for their expertise. Fred and Sophia had arrived in Orlando several hours ahead of Naseem, serving as the advance party team, collaborating closely with the local FBI and Sheriff's departments. Their role involved meticulous preparation, assembling a highly trained unit that was ready to confront any unforeseen challenges that might arise during the mission.

Everyone, including the counter-terrorism unit, scrambled into action, which led the charge.

Time was of the essence. Abdul would undoubtedly be on the move, knowing their position could be compromised. He was their only link to Amell at this point. He needed to be captured at all costs.

Fred snatched his M4 and followed the SWAT team, only to stop noticing Sophia hadn't moved a muscle since the crackle of the shot.

"Sophia, what are you doing? We need to move," he shouted, pulling her along. She wasn't budging. It was like something had cemented her feet to the ground.

Sophia stood helpless. A cascade of rushing emotions and nightmares ensnared the agent, freezing her in time. The muffled pop triggered an unwanted memory of her last assignment.

Her legs weakened, wobbling under the weight of the past, no longer able to hold her. She collapsed, falling to her knees. Disembodied voices of colleagues past screaming, encircling her, reigniting old nightmares.

"No, no, no," she rambled, covering her ears. "It wasn't my fault," she screamed into thin air.

Fred stood dumbfounded for a moment, unsure what to do. He tried once more to pull her to her feet. "Sophia!" He screamed in the young woman's face. His eyes caught hers, but there was nothing behind them. A thousand-yard stare. She wasn't looking at him but *through* him. "Sophia, come on, we got to go," he shouted again. The last of the strike team had filed out, heading to the warehouse. "Get your ass up and into the fight."

No response.

Somewhere subconsciously, Sophia could feel the pressure of Fred's hands upon her shoulders. She could see the man standing before her, screaming. She could see his lips moving, but his words were indistinguishable from the cries in her head. She wanted to respond, but no words formed. An overwhelming weight of dread had consumed her entire being.

"Oh, fuck it," Fred snapped. "Stay here then."

He had seen this before, the shock of past trauma flooding back. He couldn't help her, but he could help the assault team. He turned and took off after the team. Before disappearing around the edge of the building they'd been stationed behind, he glanced back at the kneeling Sophia. Still no movement.

****

Naseem flinched, clasping his hands over his ears, training a bewildered, almost offended look upon Abdul as the terrorist lowered the pistol to meet with his chest. A pencil-thin cloud of smoke wafted from the barrel as he brought to bear on the FBI man.

He gave Amir and Fahad a malevolent grin.

"What the fuck was that for?" Naseem shouted, ears still ringing.

"Well, my friend," Abdul's eyes narrowed in suspicion at Naseem. "It seems we shall have an answer to our disagreement soon."

"I told you I'm not FBI," the agent retorted, remaining

steadfast in his stance, somehow finding the fortitude to return Abdul's icy gaze. He needed to stall as long as possible.

The rotund terrorist laughed. "And so, we shall see. If you're not, then no one will come. *If* you are, then someone will be coming to rescue you. We'll kill you then," he snapped; the two men by his side whipped up AKs, pointing them directly at Naseem. Abdul's formerly cheerful demeanor washed away, replaced with a cold callousness.

Abdul was no fool; his plan would kill two birds with one stone. Flush out a rat and kill more Americans. He was right that shot would be bringing in the cavalry, or so Naseem hoped, not knowing the whereabouts of his partners. Suppose they'd followed proper protocol, though. They wouldn't have been too far from the target building. So, Fred and an FBI SWAT team would soon be barging through the doors.

Naseem's eyes darted around the room, looking for an escape route. He had to make the first move and do it soon.

Just then, a pallet of supplies crashed to the floor, drawing the trio's attention for a split second.

This was his chance.

Naseem launched himself at the closet of the three men holding him at gunpoint. Abdul, slow to react, took a hard right cross to the face. Bare knuckles crunched into his fat face, shattering his nose. The bulbous figure staggered from the blow. Naseem clawed, pulling him back and spinning him around while ripping the gun from his loosened grip, positioning the stunned terrorist between him and the other two, using their boss as a human shield.

The FBI agent jammed the gun into Abdul's temple before Amir and Fahad could react.

"Don't move, and I don't open your boss's head right here," Naseem warned, backing up. There was a flurry of movement as the remaining terrorists realized what was happening. They ran to encircle the agent.

Amir and Fahad shouted orders for them to stay back.

"You're coming with me, you fat bastard," Naseem hissed, dragging his hostage, inching closer to the exit.

"You're not getting out of here alive," Abdul fumed.

"We'll see."

More movement from his peripheral. Something flashed, creeping up to his right from behind a truck. It was a head poking out. Naseem whipped the gun around, squeezing the trigger. The man's head exploded in a spray of red mist. "I said no one fucking move," Naseem shouted. "Or tubby gets the next one."

More orders were shouted from Amir and Fahad.

The terrorists inched closer, closing in on Naseem and his hostage. He couldn't take them all, especially if they decided that Abdul was necessary collateral damage.

Naseem's heart raced, panic rising. Where was his backup?

Gunfire erupted from the parking lot.

****

The FBI counter-terrorism team emerged from the shadows, moving silently between buildings and descending on an open parking lot.

They had set their assembly area behind a row of buildings across the street from their target. This part of the city was primarily an industrial zone, so there were few people around. If any.

The streets were laid out in a grid lined with dull, unassuming one-story factories. The only thing separating them from their objective was a two-lane street and two parking lots.

The team stopped at the edge of the buildings, surveying the open expanse. No movement. The team leader gave the signal to move in. The first set of three men moved into the parking lot in a V formation, scanning their respective sectors of fire. All clear. The commander flashed a secondhand movement.

The remaining agents began to flood the parking lot, moving in precision without bunching up. The agents moved swiftly, advancing on their target.

The dark, quiet night evaporated as the prattle of a dozen AKs lit up the other side of the street in bursts of fire. The symphony of gunshots sent the advancing authorities scattering for cover.

Two agents who weren't fast enough were immediately struck dead by the barrage.

Upon Amir's warning, Abdul had sent several men to patrol the exterior in case Naseem had been lying. His move paid off as the two sides collided.

"Shit." The eruption of gunfire caused Fred to pause. Their element of surprise was clearly gone by the sound of it. Shaking off the disappointment, he continued. Bursting from a narrow passageway between two industrial buildings into a war zone.

"Contact, we have contact," a voice squawked over the radio—a parade of firework-like plumes erupting from both sides.

The once-quiet rural street had instantly become a terror-inducing kill box. The scene caught Fred off guard, but he managed to duck as a bullet zipped over his head. Spotting the man who took the shot, running between a car and a tree, he fired. The three-round burst killed the gunman.

Before anyone could return fire on his position, he dove behind a U-Haul truck as bullets pockmarked its side.

The battle raged on; both sides were caught in a stalemate. The terrorists had the better defensive position, but Fred had the numbers on his side.

****

The sounds of the full-on war rose loudly over the buildings, drifting down to the empty assembly area. Sophia, still on her knees, finally snapped out of her trance, unsure of where she was. "Wha… what," she stammered, remembering what had just happened.

"Oh god, Naseem," she said, anger swelling in the pit of her stomach. Yet another friend lost.

An overwhelming feeling of the need for revenge slapped her as she picked herself up. She clenched her jaw in rage and retrieved her rifle. It was time for her to get in the fight.

She jumped inside an SUV and threw it into gear, stamping on the gas pedal. The tires kicked up a spray of dirt as the vehicle sped forward.

With her death grip on the steering wheel, the SUV raced through the empty field. Sophia bounced inside, the chassis scraping against the dirt, hitting a dip, nearly losing control. Fighting to regain command of the two-ton vehicle, she angled it for the end of the row of buildings, readying to make the sharp turn.

The SUV swung around the buildings. Sophia hit the brake hard, drawing back in shock at the sight before her.

It took a minute to figure out that she had driven herself to a battleground. Muzzle flashes spat from both sides of the street.

"Damn, I did not think this through," confessed Sophia. "Oh, well. Here now." She stomped on the gas, sending the SUV rocketing forward into the fight.

Her arrival drew the attention of the terrorists as they saw the big black SUV speeding in their direction. Several broke off their engagement with the stalled-out agents, sending a fusillade in her direction. Bullets smacked into the chassis of the SUV. Sophia swerved as one shattered the passenger window, sending her ducking with a shriek. Unable to see where she was going, Sophia slammed the brakes, causing the car to fishtail.

A thump. The SUV was now riding on an island in the middle of the parking lot. She pushed harder on the brake, trying to bring the metal rocket to a stop. The brakes couldn't grip the wet grass, and another fusillade of bullets pelted the heavy vehicle.

Traction finally kicked in, slowing the vehicle just before it smacked into a light pole in the middle of the grassy island. It harmlessly tapped against the concrete stand. Running smack into the barrier would've taken her entirely out of the fight had she hit it full force.

She wasn't out of danger, though. The back window blew out in a spray of glass as rounds smacked against the back of the truck.

Flinging the door open, Sophia rolled out of the truck, crashing hard to the ground as pain seared in her shoulder. Still, she managed to scramble behind the front wheel well, taking in a complete picture of the chaos.

The strike team had spread across the parking lot and was now pinned between buildings. They took a glance around the other side. The terrorists were lined up and hunkered down behind any cover they could find, returning fire.

"Oh god, what did I get myself into?" she said, looking around for Fred.

There.

She spotted the lead FBI agent taking cover behind a truck to her left. Several rounds smacked into the side of the U-Haul. Tracing back their trajectory, she saw several of Abdul's men behind a tree. They had their sights set on Fred. She reached back into the SUV for her M4. Dropping onto her stomach, she had a clear line of sight of the two men from underneath the SUV. Lining up her shot. She fired.

A quick burst and one of them slumped over. Then, she quickly reset her sights on the other man. Sophia squeezed off another burst before he could decipher where the shots came from. The second burst dropped the other man, who slumped over his compatriot.

Getting to her feet, she rushed across the island, heading straight for Fred's location, not knowing there was a third terrorist nearby.

****

Fred peered around the U-Haul, seeing Sophia sprinting across the lot. From his vantage point, he could see the third shooter who had him pinned down a few seconds earlier. He now had his sights on another target, an easier one, running in the open.

Sophia.

"Sophia, get down!" he screamed. The urgency in his voice must have sparked an instant response in the running woman. She threw herself to the ground as a round exploded into the tree behind her. Fred rattled off a quick burst, sending the bearded man ducking back behind the tree he'd positioned himself against. He looked down at the sprawled-out woman, blonde hair covering her face. "Move your ass," he bellowed, *for Christ's sake*, shaking his head and sending another burst to give her cover fire.

Jumping to her feet, Sophia continued her sprint toward Fred's location, running full speed, as fast as her legs could carry her. Bullets flew all around; one thudded into the ground inches to her left. Another struck asphalt, and one whizzed by her ear, cracking like a whip. "Shiiiit! Fred, help!"

From his angle, he couldn't see where the gunfire was coming from. But, if he didn't do something quickly. Sophia wouldn't make it; they were zeroing in on her.

"Fuck." Swinging around the other side of the truck, Fred picked out the muzzle flashes of the gunman who was closing in on his target. "Gotcha." He whipped up his rifle and pressed the trigger. Bullets sprang from the barrel, hurtling at supersonic speed toward their destination. The man's body fell over as Sophia slid in behind the U-Haul.

"Thanks," she panted.

"Glad you decided to join us," Fred sarcastically stated, spraying another burst.

"Yeah," she said, head down.

Fred could see the embarrassment on her face. "You sort your shit out?"

"I'm good." She nodded.

"Good."

"Good," Sophia replied, this time accompanied by a smile. "Shall we put an end to this?"

****

The mini-war raging outside momentarily distracted Amir and Fahad. Naseem took advantage. He fired several rounds at them, sending them scrambling. Amir took one square in the forehead, blowing out the back of his skull.

The force from the shot drove him backward, crashing into Fahad and bowling him to the floor.

"Don't need you now," he said, kicking Abdul in the backside, spinning him around, and unloading several rounds into his bulbous stomach. The gun clicked empty. "Shit."

Tossing the gun to the floor, Naseem threw himself forward, diving for Amir's AK before Fahad could recover.

The agent scooped up the rifle, continuing his roll, stopping behind the safety of one of the few remaining crates before Fahad could open fire.

AK rounds showered the front side of the crate, raining splinters all around Naseem. There was no discernable pattern to the fire. Fahad was firing blind. He didn't know where his target was. He'd run his magazine empty in a second. Naseem knew this from his training. All he had to do was wait a moment for his opening. A bullet smashed into the container, narrowly missing Naseem's face.

"Shit," he exclaimed, snapping his head around, looking for the source of the new threat.

A large forehead and two beady eyes peered around from a pillar. "Fuck off," Naseem let loose his own AK.

The man slumped out from his cover as another shooter leapfrogged his dead compatriot. Naseem released another successful, deadly volley. The second body fell onto the first.

Fahad took advantage of Naseem's divided attention and slithered out of his position, having discovered where Naseem had taken refuge, and slowly moved in on his distracted opponent.

Having dispatched the two idiots who tried to flank him, the agent turned his attention back to Fahad.

Peering over the top of the crate, searching for the man, a series of bullets grazed off the top, nearly striking Naseem in the head. Fahad was practically on top of him.

Sensing an opportunity, Naseem laid down, spinning, pinning his feet on the crate. Lying on his back, he shoved off the wooden platform. The force sent him sliding out from behind his cover, catching his target completely off guard. He let loose a burst from the AK. The 7.62mm slugs ripped right through Fahad's body, spurts of blood spraying the pillar behind him with bright red spatter.

A roar erupted from another AK, rounds pocking the concrete floor lanced toward Naseem. The agent rolled from the new threat, clambering to a knee, spinning, and firing in their direction. The shooter stumbled back, cracking against the steel pillar, sliding down, leaving a trail of blood.

****

The gunfire on Abdul's side had slowed from a roar to a cat's meow. Either the strike team had taken out most of the opposition, or they were running out of ammo. Either way, it was time to finish the fight.

"Move!" Fred ordered, giving the signal to advance.

The strike team moved out, slowly advancing to their target building. Fred had the front doors in sight. A few claps of automatic fire here and there, and the strike team would finish off what was left of Abdul's men. Peeling from behind the U-Haul, Fred, and Sophia advanced toward the building.

Adeel emerged from inside, holding a large, tubular weapon. Asher sprang from behind, opening fire and driving the team back.

"RPG," Fred shouted, realizing what Adeel had hoisted onto his shoulder.

Wearing a sadistic smile, the terrorist fired the rocket-propelled grenade launcher. A bright flash of fire and a streak of smoke lanced across the street. Agents hurled themselves to the ground, the missile flying over their heads, crashing into the U-Haul truck, creating an explosive ball of fire.

The blast sent Sophia flying, landing a few yards away and hitting the ground hard with a thud and sprawled out as fire roiled behind her. Flames licked after her as she rolled away from them. One caught her left leg. Sophia screamed as the flame set her pants ablaze.

Fred, who had been in front of Sophia, leading the team to the building, had been far enough from the blast not to be affected by it. But upon hearing Sophia's cries for help as the flames danced up her pants leg, he sprinted back to her. The strike team, meanwhile, rushed forward, engaging the last remnants of Abdul's men.

Adeel and Asher broke into the night, using the blast as cover to escape while no one looked their way.

"Put it out, put it out," Sophia cried. The two frantically patted at the flames.

"Holy shit, are you ok?" Fred asked, putting the last licks out.

Both agents spotted Adeel and Asher slinking away from the factory, dodging in and out of cars. The strike team continued their advance on the primary target building, oblivious to their escape.

Sophia pulled up her pants leg. "Yeah, I think so. It doesn't look bad. Feels like a sunburn," she said, examining the burn site.

"You sure?" Fred asked.

Sophia nodded.

"Ok, stay here. The strike team will finish off the rest of the assholes and hopefully secure Abdul. If not," he said, turning to check on the two escapees. "Maybe those two can lead us to Amell in his place."

"Good idea. I'm coming with you." She stood, rolling down her pants leg.

"The hell you are. Stay here."

"No, I'm coming," Sophia objected. "See, I'm good," she insisted, putting pressure on her leg, walking fine.

He shook his head. "Defiant as ever," Fred complained. "Ok, let's go." There wasn't time to debate.

They started after Asher and Adeel.

****

Naseem scanned the area, realizing that he was alone. Everyone who had been inside was either dead or had run off.

"Well, I guess that's all of them," he quipped, dusting off his shoulders and congratulating himself. "Too bad no one was here to see this." Disappointment set on his face.

He headed for the exit, passing a cargo truck, and something fell inside. Naseem froze at the noise. Wanting to be sure no one was hiding inside, he turned to investigate. "Whoever's in there better come out," he called, sweeping the back tarp aside.

No one.

They may be trying to hide.

****

Adeel and Asher made it to the side of the building, thinking they had gotten clear. They broke into a light jog, fleeing the war zone while sirens blared in the distance.

Fred and Sophia closed in quietly, following the two men, trying not to be seen until the last second. Using the building for cover, their marks continued their escape, shuffling across the street in silent pursuit and taking refuge behind an abandoned car. They watched as the two terrorists trekked down the street. Asher slowed, retrieving a cell phone from his pocket, but why? They had no more men. Then it struck Fred.

"Sophia, wait, slow down," Fred whispered, pulling her back and ducking behind the car.

"Why? They're right there." She pulled her hand away from him. "They're getting away."

"No, maybe he's on the phone with Amell."

"You think he's still coming after all this?" She pointed behind them.

"Maybe," Fred answered, shrugging. "It's a chance I'm willing to take."

A black SUV tore around the street corner up ahead. Fred nudged Sophia as if to say, "I told you so." The two continued to advance slowly. The Range Rover came to a screeching stop near Adeel and Asher, nearly hitting both. The two agents continued to stay hidden, watching.

"Can you see who it is?" Sophia asked.

"No, it's too dark. Let's get closer."

Moving down the passenger side of the car, staying as low as possible, they crept in closer. Fred peeked over through the windows. The passenger and driver stepped out of the SUV, greeting the other two.

"Holy shit, it's him; go, go now, now!" Fred shouted, pushing Sophia to move. They sprung out from behind the car, guns drawn. "Freeze, get your hands up," Fred barked as they moved closer.

Asher spun, whipping up the AK. Before he could fire, Sophia's gun barked, striking the short Asher in the arm, forcing the wounded man to drop the AK. It skittered away.

"As he said, freeze," Sophia reiterated.

Asher, Adeel, Amell, and his driver, a thin man with wispy

black hair and a large patch of melted flesh on his left cheek, slowly raised their hands.

****

Naseem cautiously crested the cargo truck's tailgate, half expecting to find a cowering terrorist. Instead, he discovered a large blue tarp draped over a bulky object in the middle of the bed.

Naseem repositioned the AK to hold it in one hand, reaching out for the tarp.

"Gotcha," he crowed, throwing the plastic sheet aside. "Oh shit-"

****

A loud, thunderous explosion erupted from the factory, leveling half the building. The concussive force of the blast sent out a shock wave, blowing out all the car windows in the area. Fred, Sophia, Amell, Asher, Adeel, and the driver were also caught in the blast wave.

Fred was thrown several feet, crashing headfirst into the side of a tree. Sophia, faring slightly better, was flung to the ground several feet away. She hit the blacktop of a vacant parking lot hard.

Dazed and confused, with his ears ringing, Fred tried to stand but couldn't get to his feet.

"Sophia, where are you?" he called out, pawing around and looking for his gun. It took a few moments for his hand to clasp around the knowing steel, his vision slowly returning.

"I'm here," she answered, wheezing as she struggled to catch her breath. The combined forces of the blast and sudden hard stop against the ground knocked the wind from her.

"You ok?" Fred groaned.

"I'm fine. I just got the wind knocked out of me." The pair crawled to each other. "Jeez, your head," Sophia sibilated, seeing a gash streaking across Fred's forehead.

Blood trickled down the side of his head. "Ow," he yelped as he touched it. "I'm fine. Come on, let's get up. Maybe we got lucky, and the blast killed Amell and them."

The two helped each other to their feet, staggering, twirling, and inspecting the carnage. The shockwave exploded the windows of every vehicle and building in its radius. Glass crunched beneath their feet. Fred slumped against a car, using it to prop himself up as Sophia retrieved her firearm.

"Jesus Christ," Fred uttered disbelievingly.

Where a factory building once stood was now a thirty-foot ball of fire reaching to the heavens. Flames lapped over each other, clawing like animals for new sources of material to burn. Crackles and pops singing the praise of destruction inside, as unused ammo cans cooked off in the blaze. The heat reached dozens of yards away; Fred and Sophia shielded their eyes from the inferno.

"Oh my god, Fred, all those agents," Sophia gasped, covering her mouth with a hand. "We need to help them."

Grunts and moans reminded them they weren't alone. Fred spun, seeing Amell and his driver climbing back into their Range Rover. Asher and Adeel had been blown further away, but they, too, were recovering. Amell barked an order to the pair as he staggered into the passenger seat. The two, without question, turned and ran off into the night across an open, empty field.

"No, you don't!" Fred whipped up his gun, shouting, "Freeze!" Then, unloaded two shots that clanged off the hood of the Range Rover as it sped away in reverse back down the street. "Son of a bitch!" the agent spat angrily.

"You get those two," Sophia said, pointing to the escaping Range Rover as it reversed down the street. "I'll get them," Sophia exclaimed, pointing at Asher and Adeel, who were still shambling away.

Fred turned. "Are you-" Sophia had already begun her pursuit. "I guess so," he finished to himself. How was he going to continue his own pursuit? Looking around, he remembered. The truck that Sophia had driven in. Quickly sprinting back to the parking lot, he gave the raging fire a wide berth. Several of the raid team were recovering from the blast that had been further away when the bomb went off. He couldn't help them, but he could still get justice.

He spotted the SUV. Thankfully, it hadn't been caught in

either explosion. Reaching the open door, he peered inside. The keys were still in the ignition. Hopping in, he started the truck, throwing it into reverse, doing a full 180°. He whipped the front end around, speeding in the direction he'd just come from, catching a glimpse of Amell's SUV speeding away. He slammed the accelerator to the floor, speeding after him. From his peripheral, he could see Sophia running after the other two. Good luck, Sof, he thought as he raced after the man responsible for so much death and destruction. He was going to bring an end to it all tonight.

CHAPTER TEN

After glimpsing Sophia disappear into the adjacent field in hot chase of Adeel and Asher, Fred focused on his own pursuit. Applying more force to the gas pedal, crushing against the floorboard.

The Escalades V8 roared as additional air flowed into the manifold, giving the engine an instant surge of horsepower. The wheels struggled to grip the asphalt. The vehicle jutted forward, throwing his head back. The wane of the engine crescendoed, jolting to life with the sudden influx of combustion gases flowing through the system. The RPM meter flung into the red as the automatic transmission struggled to shift through the gears in time.

Fred's eyes stayed on the road, focused ahead. He could still make out the headlights of Amell's Range Rover in full retreat, which had been unable to make a U-turn on the narrow road, slowing their escape.

The Ranger Rover suddenly made a hard 90° turn, reorienting its front end and heading north down a new street, speeding off. Closing the distance, Fred saw the turn ahead, knowing he couldn't make the tight turn at full speed. Could he drift an SUV? Now was the time to find out.

Reaching the T-section in the road, he slammed both feet onto the brake and jerked the steering wheel hard to the left with both hands, causing the tires to squeal through the turn. The Escalade banked heavily, the driver's side tires lifting, tipping the SUV.

"Come on," Fred prayed, holding the turn. The truck slammed back onto all fours. Fred fought the wheel to regain control of the fishtailing vehicle, straightening it out, and narrowly missed a center divider and its stop sign. "Fuck," he spat, looking in the rearview mirror not only at the past obstacle but the burning fireball. He was also worried about leaving Sophia behind. However, Sophia could take care of herself. Besides, he had a problem of his own, and it was fast approaching.

The two speeding vehicles were headed straight for the bright lights and bustling traffic of a major intersection. The last thing he wanted to do was take the chase into a heavily populated area, but

111

he didn't have a choice. There wasn't enough time to catch them before they reached it. Tensing, Fred prepared for the inevitable. A high-stakes car chase.

****

"What the hell," Sophia panted, climbing a small hill. Despite their possible injuries from the explosion, the two suspects she was chasing maintained their lead on her. They were much faster than previously thought.

She ran as hard as she could, legs pumping, arms swinging, sprinting down the backside of the hill onto another street. Every step she took burned more and more, her pant leg scraping against the burns. Still, she pushed through the pain.

Steadily gaining on her prey, the thought rushed through her mind, "When I catch them, how will I subdue them?" She shook off the thought. First, she had to catch them.

Asher appeared to be fatiguing, thankfully. His knee gave out several times, but he luckily recovered before stumbling. If anything, she could definitely outlast the two men.

Asher's luck finally ran out, tripping over a curb and stumbling into a full-gainer, head over heels—a perfect opportunity for her to take a shot. Sophia stopped, pulling up her M4, and squeezed several rounds out of the chamber.

Before they could strike their target, his partner, the massive mountain of a man, had snatched Asher off the ground like a parent reclaiming their child. The slugs plowed helplessly into the concrete.

"Shit!" she cursed, readjusting and firing again.

Dry, empty magazine.

Adeel flashed a sardonic smile she could make out from down the street. Slinging the rifle aside, she drew her Glock. "Smile at this fucker," she hissed angrily, popping off several rounds.

The first struck Asher in the side. He collapsed, only to be supported by his friend. Adeel took the second round to the arm for his troubles, which didn't seem to faze him.

He continued lumbering forward, scooping up his brother,

throwing him over his shoulder, and ducking around the corner at the end of the street.

"Oh, come on," Sophia moaned, throwing her arms up in disbelief, continuing her pursuit.

****

Amell's Range Rover barreled through a red light, blasting into the intersection without slowing down, and turned left. A symphony of car horns blared into the night as their drivers smashed their brakes, causing multiple rear-end collisions. With no alternative but to follow, Fred gritted his teeth and tightened his grip on the steering wheel.

"Here goes nothing." He plowed into the intersection.

An unsuspecting motorist who had barely escaped T-boning the Ranger Rover swerved again as Fred's SUV flung through the intersection. The two chassis' came within inches of meeting. The two vehicles were so close Fred could see the terror in the woman's eyes as she lost control of the wheel. The BMW X5 bounded onto the sidewalk, slamming into a bus stop.

Glass and aluminum exploded into the air, raining back down all around the woman's crinkled SUV. "Sorry," Fred mouthed, knowing she couldn't hear him.

Peering into his rearview mirror, Fred took one quick, doleful look back at the intersection and the destruction they had wrought. A jumbled mass of cars crinkled and tangled together in a heap of devastation. It looked like a demolition derby, like the ones his father had brought him to as a youth. The vehicles' drivers were in the middle of the intersection, some with hands in the air, others had them on their hips, wearing bewildered looks, unsure of what had happened.

To Fred's relief, the woman he had just sent careening into the bus stop was one of them. She appeared to be ok.

****

Once the two men had rounded the corner, Sophia had briefly

lost sight of her aim. Now, rounding the bend herself, she easily picked up their trail. It wasn't hard; all she needed to do was follow the line of blood dotting the sidewalk. She'd definitely hit both her targets as two separate lines of blood were discernible, creating a trail. Following the droplets, they led her from the concrete sidewalk to a fence that contained a parking lot on the other side.

Hopping over the chain-link fence, she crossed the empty lot, letting the trail lead her now as the two men had seemingly vanished in the night. A building began to take shape in the darkness. As she drew closer, each new splatter grew larger than the one before. Indicating the pair was slowing down, and judging by the amount of blood, one had been badly wounded.

Asher, most likely, as she'd struck him in the side. Maybe the bullet had pierced a kidney or the liver. Whatever organ she'd hit, the man wouldn't be long for the world without serious medical attention, possibly tipping the scales in her favor as well. Once she did catch them, the only one that would pose a major threat was Adeel.

Upon approaching the building, Sophia saw that the front door had been smashed open, leaving shards of glass scattered across the ground. She found where the two had gone. If you can't run, hide, right? She thought.

Pausing at the shattered doorway, Sophia reached into her pocket, only to find that her phone was not there. She'd left it in the car. No way to call for backup. Looking around, seeing nothing but night, was she really about to enter a dark, confined space, pursuing two terrorists with no backup?

Seeing no other way, she had no option. Plus, she wasn't about to let them escape. "Guess I'm going in." Admitting it wasn't the best plan, but it was the only option. Reaching into her jacket pocket, she pulled out a small flashlight attached to her keychain. With a deep sigh, she flipped it on and entered the dark building, not knowing what she'd encounter inside.

Finding herself in a dimly lit hallway, she crept forward. The parking lot lights faded as she descended in, darkness closing in all around. She was left with nothing but the beam from her light and the illuminated exit signs.

Sofia gulped; now would be a horrible time for a zombie to creep out. Too many horror movies with Carol, she thought, shaking her head. She stopped briefly to let her eyes adjust and continued down the hall, making every effort not to make a sound.

One foot over the other.

The cold air from a nearby A/C vent hit the back of her sweat-filled neck, sending a shiver down her spine.

It had been years since her training on "The Farm," the CIA's training camp. She was trying to recall how to sweep a building, and it all came rushing back as if it were yesterday.

She approached the first open door. I must be in the office section, she thought. She shone her light down the rest of the hall, seeing several more entries.

Sophia drew a deep breath, her heart a low simmering thud in her chest. She had moved to the edge of the wall, just before the cracked door, and peeked inside. No immediate danger. Still, the simmer rose to a full boil, heart popping like spaghetti sauce. Knowing what was about or could happen. Sweat beaded down her face; her legs were heavy, and her mouth was dry from the run.

Readying herself.

She threw open the door, rushing inside the dark room, gun drawn, flashlight sweeping side to side. No movement: no zombie, boogeyman, or terrorist came jumping at her.

Relief washed over her. An odd thought occurred to her as she scanned the room. Her decision to wear contacts instead of glasses this morning paid off. Had she worn her spectacles, they would've certainly fogged up in this instance. An odd time to have this thought, but adrenaline can do strange things. Ignoring the random thought, she continued searching the room. Pausing for a moment, she spotted a landline on the wall. She removed the headset, hearing a dial tone. She quickly dialed 911 and dropped the phone, letting it hang off the hook.

Sophia finished sweeping the space and moved back to the entrance. Another deep sigh: no one was in the room. An empty office.

"Ok, Sof, one room down, X more to go. I can do this." She calmed herself, sliding back into the hallway and moving to the next office.

****

Amell barreled through another intersection, this time with considerably less resistance than the previous, having hit the green light.

Fred still followed in pursuit. Suddenly, he heard a squelch from the dashboard. The law enforcement vehicle had a radio. A disembodied voice spoke.

"All emergency responders report to 915 Lake Street. We have a triple 9. Multiple officers and FBI agents down," said the police dispatcher.

Fred ripped the receiver from the mount. "This is FBI Agent Fred Jones. I'm in pursuit of the suspects. Need backup. I repeat, in pursuit of the suspects, need backup."

"Agent Jones, what is your 20?" the female 911 dispatcher responded in the calmest radio voice he'd ever heard.

"I don't fucking know. I'm not a local. Wait, hold on." Seeing another intersection fast approaching, the two SUVs tore through it. Fred caught a look at the street sign. "Oh-oh, I'm headed westbound on Irlo Bronson Highway in pursuit of a black Range Rover. Two occupants, presumably armed and dangerous," he reported.

Fred tossed the receiver to the floor upon hearing the wailing of horns. The Ranger Rover had blown through another intersection, clipping the backend of a VW, spinning it around, and coming to rest in the middle of the six-lane square, directly in Fred's path.

"Oh fuck!" Fred swerved, swinging the car left into another lane, then right, circling the stalled VW. Fred peeked back at the VW to see it get rammed, ironically by a super-jacked Dodge Ram, which crushed the small car. "Shiiiit." Fred's eyes bulged as he turned his head. There was another obstacle bearing down on him. This time, a yellow cab.

The driver must have been busy texting since he didn't see the near-collisions as he entered the cluttered square from the oncoming side.

Damnnnnn! Fred jerked the wheel hard left again, missing the front end of the cab. The rapid swerving sent the Escalade's rear fishtailing.

Fighting with all his strength, Fred straightened it back out, making it through the deadly obstacle course. "Phew, that was close-"

A bullet pinged off the hood of the truck. "Shit." More rounds pocked the front end of the SUV. Fred swerved the truck, trying to stay out of the path of the bullets.

Ahead, he saw Amell hanging out the passenger's window, trying to line up another shot. The terrorist leader fired again; this time, the bullet smashed into the passenger side of the windshield. Fred watched as the spider cracks slowly spread, obstructing his view.

****

Sophia continued down the dark hallway, creeping along the linoleum tile as quietly as she could. She reached the next office door. It was closed. Flicking the flashlight off, she reached for the doorknob and turned it slowly. She could hear the bolt sliding in the deafening quietness. The door popped open.

With the same familiar routine as before, she inhaled deeply, calming herself as she stepped inside. She swiftly scanned the room from side to side, experiencing a sense of partial relief as she discovered it was empty. The office layout mirrored the previous one, facilitating a quicker and more efficient clearing process.

Satisfied that no threats lingered here, Sophia lowered her guard for a brief moment.

A *wumpth* echoed in the silent building. It'd come from the hallway. The noise startled Sophia: she spun around, drawing her Glock 22. Her left hand flung wildly, connecting with a coffee cup on the edge of the desk. Her eyes widened as she felt her hand bang against the ceramic surface, catching the object that had fallen from her peripheral vision, instinctively sticking her foot out with a cat-like reflex. The cup connected with the tip of her shoe before rolling off harmlessly onto the tiled floor, rocking to a stop. Her shoe braced the impact, and the cup hardly made a sound.

One crisis averted. Sophia turned her attention back to the noise. It sounded like someone had closed or opened a door in the hallway. She glided back to the doorway and peeked around the corner down the hall.

No one was there, nothing but darkness.

She surveyed the area and spotted another trail of blood droplets. She was on the right track; they were still inside the building.

****

Amell was still hanging out the side window as the two SUVs rocketed down the streets of Orlando. There was a short-lived lull in the gunfire as he and the driver exchanged weapons before the firing recommenced.

The terrorist leader sent another barrage at Fred's Escalade. Bullets pinged off the front end, and the windshield cracks stretched its entire length, almost blocking his view. Fred swerved the SUV to the other side, escaping the path of the oncoming bullets.

Though he had overcorrected, veering the Escalade into oncoming traffic. A speeding car barreled toward him, its horn blaring.

"Shit." Fred cut the steering wheel back to the right and straight into the path of Amell's gunfire. Another round struck the windshield as Fred dropped back. "Oh fuck it." Fred drew his weapon, a Glock 19, firing several shots into the windshield, shattering what was left of it. The wind came rushing into the cab of the truck.

Ahead, Amell was pulling away, his driver expertly navigating the densely populated street, swaying in and out of the lanes. Fred punched the accelerator again, and the engine roared to a loud, lion-like sound—a burst of speed.

The two speeding vehicles were screaming down the road, Amell still firing. Bullets whipped past into the night. Others were scything off the chassis of the Escalade. The racing cars were fast approaching a sea of red lights. The traffic light had switched to red. All the motorists ahead had begun to brake and come to a lawful stop, unaware of the deadly chase behind them.

The Range Rover obstructed Fred's view of the wall of stopped cars. However, a hand appeared from the cab, gripping Amell's thawb and pulling him back inside. He suspected something was amiss. This was confirmed only when the lead SUV veered to its left onto the sidewalk, smashing through a speed limit sign that it had exceeded. Repeatedly sounding their horn, they scattered the few pedestrians and sent them reeling for their lives.

Seeing the traffic jam and not wanting to follow the same route, Fred swerved into the oncoming lane of traffic, nearly missing the last row of stopped vehicles. It was now his turn to pound the horn. Fred screamed, waving his arm out the window like a lunatic. "Get out of the way! Get out of the way, dammit!" Like they could hear him.

Cars bobbed and weaved out of his path as he sped along. Their lights swiped by so quickly that they all blended into a solid, illuminated wall.

Clearing the intersection and the swath of stopped cars to his right, he spotted Amell's Range Rover, briefly locking eyes with the man behind the wheel.

Fred recognized the driver immediately from a photo. It was Hasan Althani, Amell's enforcer and personal bodyguard. A true believer, this man would do anything to keep Amell safe and destroy America.

****

Sophia continued to follow the blood trail to the end of the hall. It hooked left down another corridor. At the end was another wooden door with a sign on the front that read, "Now Entering the Workspace. Use Caution." She was positive this was the one she heard close.

As she got closer, the blood drops grew larger, culminating in a pool at the base of the door. They'd definitely come this way.

Opening the door slowly, Sophia walked into the new room. Unlike the previous section, a bit of light came in from the back. Ahead, she could see rows upon rows of sewing tables, topped with heavy machines, lined up in neat, orderly columns of three, stretching from one wall to the other.

A light shone through a porthole in the door at the back of the workspace. A sign on the door read, "Dye Room." There was no way they were dumb enough to be hiding in the most brightly lit room. Right?

Sophia raised her Glock as she tiptoed toward the Dye Room.

****

Hasan flashed Fred a snarled grin, then jerked the Ranger Rover hard to the left, swerving straight into Fred and crashing into the side of the Escalade. The ear-splitting grind of the Chassis pierced through the shattered passenger window.

The crunching of the metal and fiberglass was distinct as the two speeding vehicles rubbed against each other, each jockeying for dominance. Fred pawed at the steering wheel, fighting to keep the SUV straight.

Glancing over, the two men locked eyes in a staring contest as the two vehicles scythed against each other. There was nothing behind Hasan's eyes but pure hatred. Fred knew the man would not be taken lightly, nor would he be taken alive.

In the flash of a second, Hasan yanked the steering wheel, separating the two SUVs. As the two metal demons peeled apart, the side mirrors were ripped from their mounts. Fred watched as they bounded down the road from the rearview mirror, hoping they didn't hit anyone or smack into a car.

They did neither, but something was about to hit him. Hasan was preparing for another strike. The terrorist swerved at him.

Fred stamped on the brakes, and a cloud of smoke from the burning rubber pads erupted from under the wheel wells. Fred slung forward, managing to brace himself just in time before crashing headfirst into the wheel. The maneuver worked. Hasan's

Range Rover narrowly missed ramming him.

Two cop cars careened around the corner several yards ahead, blocking the street and racing toward the two SUVs. Fred's backup had finally arrived, to his relief. If this chase continued any longer, a lot of people were going to get hurt.

Clearly, Hasan had also seen the reinforcements. They needed another way out before they could try and box him in. He turned the Range Rover down another road; this one was a little less populated. Fred saw his chance to end the chase. With no concern for endangering civilians and with backup on the way, he executed a pit maneuver. Spin out the Range Rover. He'd done it a dozen times in driver training, though he couldn't recall ever having to use it in the field. First time for everything. He stamped the accelerator again, closing in to make a move.

****

Sophia reentered the printing room, having searched the dye room to no avail. There was no one inside. Puzzled, passing several of the large industrial printing machines. She was sure that she had checked the entire facility. Aside from the blood trails, there had been no sign of her escapees.

Had they somehow doubled back behind her and got out?

No, they were still inside, and she was sure of it. Then, as she was about to recheck the offices, something caught her eye.

A flash. It was quick, but she'd seen something move.

A dark shadow-like blob was moving in the darkened corners of the room. Whipping up her gun, she spun to investigate. More thoughts of ghosts or malevolent demons put her senses on high alert. *Definitely no more horror movies for a while*, she thought.

Step by step, her muscles clenched tighter as she moved toward one of the printing machines. She flicked her weapon off the safe, slowing her breathing. The hairs on the back of her neck stood up as she spotted an irregular shape on the ground. Squinting, she strained her eyes to make it out. It jerked.

Sophia flinched, too, her fears spiking. Whatever the object was, it was alive. Another flinch, her heart along with it. What could it be, inching closer?

A foot?

Sophia gulped, ready to pounce. She sprung forward around the printing machine, weapon pointed. Slightly to her relief, it was Asher, lying helpless on the floor, hands clutching his side, and not an imagined beast. Nope, just a very real one, and one that had already killed many people tonight.

The wounded man glanced up at her, helpless, fearful. "Where's your buddy?" she asked, gun still trained at the terrorist. He may be wounded, but his friend was still missing and nowhere to be found. She was not about to let her guard down. "Tell me," she snapped, looking around but keeping one eye on the downed man.

He managed to crack a half smile. "Th… ther… there." He pointed behind her.

Another shadow sprang from the darkness, screaming, "Ahhhhhh!"

It was Adeel charging full speed at Sophia. Too slow to react, she took a devastating shoulder check, sending her flying backward and knocking the gun from her hands.

Pain seized her body, hitting the hard concrete floor as she slid. Aching and slightly out of breath, Sophia struggled to stand up. Darkness enveloped her. Adeel leered over her, grunting like an enraged bull, his face snarled in anger.

He reached down, scooping her off the ground with ease. Feet dangling in the air, his colossal hands wrapped around her throat, shaking her. Sophia could only stare into the bottomless pits of his cold, coal-colored eyes.

This was going to be the end of her.

****

Fred's Escalade was in full throttle as it barreled down on Amell's Range Rover, the two speeding bullets racing down the empty street. Then, swerving to his left, Fred drew the front end closer to Hasan's rear fender on the driver's side.

As the agent pulled out from behind the SUV, Hasan instantly knew what Fred was about to attempt. Snatching the gun from Amell, he blindly fired two rounds out the window.

"Shit," Fred gasped, ducking down, punching the brake, and dropping back.

Attempt one failed.

Running out of the empty street and now angrier than ever, Fred steeled his jaw, knuckles turning white as he gripped the wheel harder. He moved back into position for another attempt, but this time on Amell's side.

****

Adeel's colossal hands squeezed around Sophia's neck, dangling her in the air as he shook her back and forth. She needed to break free from the vice-like grip of the behemoth. She was struggling to breathe, feeling her windpipe shrink.

The only thing she could do was dig her fingernails into his forearms. Adeel's face changed from anger to pain as she ran her fingers down his arms, splitting skin. The giant let out a wail, effortlessly heaving the woman ten feet into the air.

Sophia's spine bowed, crackling as she crashed into a wall, breaking through the drywall. Every ounce of air in her lungs was expelled as she slithered down the cracked wall. Sophia crawled across the ground, gasping for air, looking for an escape route. Looking behind, Adeel had recovered and lurched forward to end his prey.

****

The Escalade's V8 engine roared, air whipping through the windshield-less cab. Fred pulled back out from behind, drawing alongside the rear quarter panel of the Range Rover. Swaying out to the right, Fred braced for impact, yanking the wheel hard to the left and sending the Escalade smashing into the rear of the Rover.

The Range Rover slewed, its tail end sliding out, turning ninety degrees, and drawing it perpendicular to Fred's SUV. All three men were now staring at each other in disbelief. Fred could practically reach out and grab Amell.

The Escalade was pushing the Range Rover forward, tires skidding at an awkward angle that couldn't hold. Then, in an instant, the Ranger Rover was gone. It flipped side over side, flying through the air over the Escalade. The Rover crashed back to the ground in an explosion of car pieces. With the pressure from the SUV gone, Fred lost control of the Escalade, plowing into a steel metal pole.

****

Sophia lumbered to her feet, every part of her body ablaze with pain, nerve endings wanting no more, gasping for air. Adeel roared, cocking back his right arm and balling his hand into a fist. He swung with a sadistic smile on his face. Sophia ducked just in time, and his fist smashed through the wall. Had she not moved, the blow would've likely concaved her face.

The young woman tried to roll away, but her attacker's large wingspan snatched her back with his left arm, throwing her back into the wall.

Adeel clamped his large hand around her throat, pinning Sophia up against the wall, feet in the air again. He squeezed harder and harder, slamming her against the wall repeatedly.

His fingers compressed tightly around her throat like a python would, squeezing the life from her body. Sophia could feel a blood vessel in her eye pop. Her eyes bulged as he pressed harder. Dark spots danced as her vision became blotchy.

The room started going black.

****

The approaching sirens shook Fred awake. His head rested against the steering column's airbag. The world around him slowly came back into focus as he reached up to his forehead, pulling back a blood-soaked hand.

A metallic taste stung his mouth, and he spat a gob of blood. Sirens in the distance grew closer and closer with every second.

He remembered where he was and what had just happened.

He needed to get to Amell.

Opening the car door and unfastening his seat belt, he rolled out and plopped to the ground. Feeling nothing broken, heart-pounding, still hazy, he searched for his gun. He stopped when he heard glass shattering from the Range Rover. Seeing the two men emerge from the crumpled-up car. Hasan was helping to support Amell.

Having just taken a second blow to the head in less than an hour, Fred was now fighting to stay lucid. The world was swirling around him, head pounding.

****

Sophia was losing consciousness as her life was choked out of her. The stories of your life flashing before your eyes in the moments before death were true. Images of her past came between intermittent flashes of Adeel's cold-hearted, ruthless face.

Her legs flailed in the air, gasping for breath, tears trickling from her eyes as the images of her life played out like a movie. She locked onto an image, like pausing a movie. It was of her at a dinner with her new family, Fred, Sherry, Carol, and Tobias. Something she'd never get to experience again.

Sophia's head lolled to the side, taking her final breath.

No. She wasn't going out this.

Summoning her last ounce of strength, she reached to the right, desperately clawing at the wall for a picture frame she had spotted earlier. Her hand gripped the frame; she tore it from the wall, swinging it as hard as possible. The frame shattered into splinters of wood and glass, striking the side of Adeel's head.

The blow hardly fazed the man; he laughed at the useless last-ditch effort to save her life. The sadistic smile he flashed back was met with a cold gaze in his eyes, easily the most terrifying thing she had ever seen, and it would be the last thing she ever saw.

His pause at that moment gave Sophia one last window of opportunity, still holding a fragment of the frame in her hand. She had the perfect place for it to go.

Her right hand fully extended, and she drove the spike straight into Adeel's left eye socket. He howled in pain, dropping to his knees, releasing his grip on Sophia. She crumbled to the floor.

****

Fred's vision blurred the world, transforming it into a series of images and snapshots around him. One moment, the approaching men were twenty feet away; the next, they were ten. Then, they were practically on top of him.

He tried to stand, only to fall back to the ground, his legs unable to support him. The unmistakable feeling of a cold gun barrel pressed against his bloody forehead. He reached up with his left hand, trying to grab the gun pointing at his face. Hasan kicked it away.

****

Sophia gasped, taking in as much air as she could as her hand rubbed her bruised throat. Adeel was still wailing in pain on the floor, rolling about, and hand reaching for the protruding object, effectively out of the fight for now, though. However, there was still one possible threat left. Asher.

Sophia scrambled in the dark, running her hand across the cold concrete slabs of the floor, looking for her gun.

A terrifying click sounded in her ear. It was the hammer of a gun cocking back. Sophia looked up to find Asher propped up against a printing machine, hand still clutching the abdominal wound, pointing the barrel of her own gun in her face.

****

Amell stood in front of Fred, examining his opponent, the man who had chased him through the streets of Orlando, halting his second attack.

"Now you die, infidel." He squeezed the trigger.

Chink.

The gun was empty.

"Noooo," he shouted, kicking Fred square in the jaw.

Searing pain shot down Fred's spine as his head snapped back, falling stomach-first on the pavement. Several police cars slid around the corner, sirens blasting, announcing their presence.

"We've got to go," Hasan said, pulling on Amell's arm.

The last thing Fred saw before finally succumbing to his injuries was the most wanted man on the planet ran off into the darkness as he was encircled by police cars.

****

With no more fight, Sophia closed her eyes as Asher squeezed the trigger.

BOOM!

The deafening echo of the gun going off reverberated through the room. Sophia flinched at the sound. As the echo subsided, she was still breathing. She slowly opened her eyes to see Asher's body in front of her. Half the top of his head was missing, and his body twitched on the floor.

"Ms., Ms.... get... get your hand up."

A voice shouted, emerging from the darkness, the flashlight blinding her. Behind the light, a fresh-faced, blonde-headed man in a police uniform came rushing at her, kicking the gun across the floor.

"I... I... I said, get your hands up."

His gun was drawn on her, hand trembling, voice cracking. Clearly, this was the first time he had ever shot someone.

Sophia raised her hands, trying to speak, but no words came out. Unable to talk, she pointed to the back of her jacket. Across the back, the huge, bold, yellow letters read 'FBI.'

The officer realized who she was and grabbed his radio.

"Dispatch, I have the other FBI agent and both suspects. One KIA'd." Peering over, he saw Adeel writhing in pain, hand clutched around his eye.

"The other...um, the other is seriously messed up but alive."

The officer helped Sophia to her feet as other officers poured in. "Come on, Agent Evans, let's get you to a hospital."

CHAPTER ELEVEN

The pilot activated the seatbelt sign in the cabin of the G5 private jet, initiating his approach to the runway. The only other passenger on the plane was a flight stewardess who approached Sophia. Tapping her on the shoulder, Sophia jolted up, panicked from a deep sleep; her right hand reached for an invisible sidearm. The young lady leaped back in fright, nearly stumbling over her feet.

Still frightened by Sophia's autonomic response, the stewardess gathered herself, one hand clutched over her heart. The other outstretched, showing she meant no harm.

"Agent Evans," she said timidly. "It's ok. We're about to land."

Looking around the plane's cabin, Sophia eased back into her seat. There was no danger.

"I… I'm sorry," she apologized in a low, hoarse voice, her body aching and tiredness still gripping her, even though she'd slept the entire flight.

The stewardess nodded, accepting the apology, and shuttled off, disappearing behind a curtain.

Sophia hadn't entirely recovered from her battle with Adeel five days ago. Her body still sported the signs, bruises running down her back from the wall, along with other cuts and scrapes. She had a deep hand-shaped bruise around her neck, the finger lines still popping out.

The longest-lasting effect from the fight was on her damaged vocal cords, which altered her voice. She spoke with a lower, raspier inflection now. The doctors were unsure whether they would ever fully recover. She would have to get used to the possibility that her voice would be forever changed.

The worst thing for her was that she had to relive the altercation repeatedly whenever she saw the bruises in the mirror. The sick, malevolent look on Adeel's face still haunted her each time she closed her eyes. It was the closest she'd ever come to death and an experience she'd rather not want to repeat. But she wasn't the only owner of a near-death experience.

Not only had one of Amell's henchmen nearly killed her, but Amell himself had nearly killed Fred. Had the cops not closed in as quickly as they did, Fred would be dead, a thought she couldn't stomach. The older FBI agent had become a surrogate father to her over their time together. Not seeing his salty hair and broad smile, gazing around the cabin, made Sophia lament that she had to leave him back in Orlando.

She had suffered numerous injuries herself, but Fred made off worse. Having taken multiple blows to the head, Fred had fallen into a coma, and the doctors weren't sure if he'd recover from it. She wiped a tear from the corner of her eye, just thinking about what Sherry must be going through. She wanted to be there by her side, but her desire for justice and revenge had taken precedence over that.

So, when Director Owens tried to remove her from the investigation, she did the one thing she never thought possible. Defy orders. Breaking the sacred chain of command by going through Tobias, requesting his intervention. He had flown out to Florida upon hearing the fate of the mission. Together, they used the information gathered from Adeel's interrogation, which was time-sensitive, to have her reinstated on the case. They pushed the DOD using her expertise and knowledge of the case and the AIA to convince them that Sophia was the best person to bring the terrorist group down before another attack.

The power move paid off.

The information gathered by the CIA and NSA indicated that Amell had somehow managed to escape the United States and return home. Adeel also provided a critical piece of information. After the Orlando bombing, Abdul, Asher, and he were to meet with an arms dealer in Yemen to purchase more weapons and explosives for future attacks.

The arms dealer was Tarik Salem, the world's most wanted arms trafficker in the Middle East.

Sophia easily obtained approval for the mission. All she had to do was put together that intelligence along with the promise of finding and capturing Amell.

As the plane landed, Sophia gathered her equipment. First, she had to meet with a CIA asset in Saudi Arabia, and they would take her to a safe house, where she would meet up with a U.S. Navy SEAL team. From there, they would plan the sting operation for the sale. As Adeel had made it clear that Amell would still need the weapons from Tarik, he would most assuredly send someone else to get them.

Sophia stepped out of the plane's cabin, immediately taken aback by the rush of heat flooding her body. It was warmer than expected for this time of year. The air here was in stark contrast to that of Orlando. There was no humidity, just dry, hot air being blown in by the winds.

The sun had already begun its slow fading descent into the western horizon, marking late afternoon. It still didn't bring any respite from the baking orange ball overhead.

Shifting from the dull luminescent lights of the plane's interior to the oppressively assaulting glow of the sun, Sophia scrambled to throw on her Oakley sunglasses before being permanently blinded.

She peered over the landscape, a flat desert stretching for miles beyond the small hangers to her left and right. Waves of heat danced off in the horizon over the paved runway.

"Awesome, maybe it's a good thing Fred's not here. Or I'd be listening to him griping about the heat already," she remarked to herself as she descended the flight of stairs.

There was no one in sight.

Sophia had expected someone to come to receive her. If not the asset, then at least someone connected to them would be waiting for her. Aside from the flight crew and stewardess retrieving her bag, no one else was around.

The CIA-chartered flight had been granted permission to land on a private runway, away from the main terminals of Jazan Airport.

Could the asset have received incorrect information? She thought. The stewardess hesitantly approached Sophia to hand over her luggage.

"Ma'am, is something wrong?" the stewardess asked.

"Yeah, there is no one here to meet me," she answered, indicating the empty tarmac. "What am I supposed to do, walk from here?" she complained to the still-frightened woman who could only manage a shrug for an answer.

Just then, a black Jeep Grand Cherokee ripped around the hanger at the end, speeding down the runway.

"I think your ride's here," the stewardess pointed out, handing Sophia her bag.

The agent turned to see the approaching car, then shot the stewardess an apologetic smirk. "Sorry again. I'm usually not this irritable."

"It's ok, ma'am. I know these international flights could be a drag," the young blonde remarked.

"If you only knew what I've been through over the last week." Subconsciously arching her back, feeling each bruise. Every part of her body was still sore from the fight.

The stewardess smiled back, running her hand across Sophia's shoulder before walking away. Sophia hid her painful grimace as the woman unknowingly brushed one of her many bruises.

The Grand Cherokee screeched to a halt a few feet in front of Sophia. The driver sprang from the vehicle hurriedly, rushing to grab her bag while apologizing profusely in Arabic. She couldn't quite nail down which dialect, though. It sounded mostly like Najdi Arabic, but she was not a hundred percent certain.

But since most people who spoke Arabic were familiar with MSA, Modern Standard Arabic, she answered back using the most known dialect.

"It's quite all right, sir. I'm just in a hurry to meet someone," she stated, handing the man her bag.

The passenger door opened, and another man stepped out, shouting to the driver. Sophia recognized the voice. She looked up, and standing before her was a man of medium build and height. He had curly black hair and a medium-length beard, wore blue jeans with a light blue button-up shirt, and sported dark aviator glasses.

"Oh, my goodness, is that Yousef Ali?" she exclaimed, walking up to hug the man. He stuck out his hand for a shake instead.

"You never know who's watching," he said, looking around.

"Oh… oh, forgot. Yes, Sorry. How have you been? I had no idea I was meeting you," she said, shaking his hand.

"I have been good," he answered with a smile. "It's great to see you again." It's been…"

"Three years," Sophia said, knowing exactly how long it'd been. Their last engagement corresponded with her last time in the field. An operation she'd never forget.

He snapped his fingers. "That's right, three years. Man, time flies. They said I was meeting someone from Langley, but I never, in a million years, expected you."

"I never expected to be in the field again. So…" Her thoughts trailed off to that last assignment, briefly reliving the moments again, just as she had done earlier with Adeel's attack. Her eyes wandered, looking away to the ground as Yousef spoke.

"Yeah, not since…" Yousef picked up on Sophia's body language and immediately stopped. "Um… So, shall we go? It's a bit of a drive to the safe house."

Changing topics, he ushered her to the Jeep.

"We shall."

The surprise reunion with Yousef was a welcomed distraction for Sophia. The two had gone through The Farm together. The CIA training ground for new recruits. The two battled each other for top honors, where Sophia would eventually beat him out in just about every trial. Almost setting new records for the highest scores in the process.

After graduating, the pair had been assigned several missions together before she left to become an analyst. She had always been fond of him, thanks to their friendly rivalry, and considered Yousef a good friend. He was also a great agent.

"I'm glad you're with me on this one," Sophia said from the back seat as the car set off to the safe house.

"Me too. But hey, I have to ask. What's up with the voice? When did you start smoking so much?" Yousef joked.

"Hahaha, very funny," she said, reaching up and punching him in the arm. "No, it's a gift from one of the terrorists I was chasing.

See, it even came along with a nice necklace." Sophia pulled down the collar of her shirt to reveal the bruises around her neck.

"Damn, I'd hate to see the other guy."

"If you did, he'd only be able to see you with one eye," Sophia retorted.

"Ahhh, good old Sophia, won't take shit from NO man. By the way, speaking of no men, how are you and Carol?" Yousef asked.

Despite growing up Muslim his entire life, he didn't care much that Sophia was into women. He never treated her differently based on how she lived her life. That was her decision, and what should that matter to him?

"Um, to be honest, not sure at this moment. Things have been a little rough lately." This was the first time she even thought of Carol in a few days. "Working on this and being away for so long has not done us any wonders," she added.

"Yeah, well, I suppose it's, unfortunately, part of the package, I guess," he said, referring to the job.

"Sure is."

Sophia sank into her seat, thinking about how she would explain everything to Carol when she got home.

"So it took something this big, a terrorist act, to pull you from behind the desk and back to where you belong. In the field." Sophia shot Yousef a glare from behind her sunglasses that seemed to burn straight through them and into the Arab. "I always told you, even after Belgrade. You belong in the field. You're too good of an officer." He turned to look directly at Sophia, making his point.

"You might be right, but we'll see." She knew he was right deep down.

She turned to stare out the window as the buildings whisked by. The concrete columns of buildings eventually turned into a vast open canvas of blanket desert.

"I take it then, you've been read in on the mission?" she asked.

"Hard not to be. Terrorists attack our homeland. Everyone in the intelligence community followed the hunt as closely as possible."

"Good, then I don't have to catch you up."

"Nope."

"That's a load off me. Knowing how slow you are," she said, giving him another playful bump on the arm.

"Hey, I wasn't slow. I just didn't want you to feel bad when I smoked you in every class."

"Wow, you need to have your memory checked. As I recall, I finished at the top of the class."

"Well, I've learned a few new things since The Farm."

"I'm sure you have, Yousef. "I'm sure you have," she said, smiling and giving him a thumbs-up gesture as if to confirm his own belief.

"Shut up," Yousef snapped, playfully pouting. "Good, we're almost there," Yousef said, shifting in his seat and retrieving his wallet.

The driver slowed, pulling up to a checkpoint. "Shit, I forgot, put this on really quick," Yousef said, tossing a plain black Hijab in the back for her.

Sophia quickly wrapped the Hijab over her head just before Yousef rolled down his window. After a brief conversation and exchange of a few Riyals, the guard waved them through without inspecting the vehicle.

"What was that about? And where are we almost?" Sophia asked as the car cleared the barricade.

"That, oh, that was nothing. Just a random stop. Some groups have been filtering in from Yemen to escape the violence there," Yousef answered. "And we're almost to the safe house."

"Great, the sooner we get this done. The sooner I can get back."

"In a rush to make things right with Carol, I see," said Yousef, grinning from ear to ear.

"Yes, but I also left my partner in Orlando. He's been in a coma since the attack we stopped."

Yousef's head snapped to the back seat. "Oh, wow, it's like that for you now," he continued, chiding her.

"Eww, no. I don't cheat. You know me better than that. My FBI partner, Fred," she clarified, seeing the perverted look on Yousef's face. "He was injured in a car chase, and I want to get back to him. With some good news, hopefully."

"Oh, ok." Yousef's face fell flat as the image he'd cooked up evaporated. "Well, then, when we arrive at the safe house, we'll introduce you to your SEAL team, if they have arrived yet, and go from there."

"How long?"

"Another twenty minutes, give or take. It'll give us some time to catch up. I've read the briefs. Detailed as always with you. But I want specific details. Like, how is it working with the FBI?"

"Well," Sophia huffed jokingly. "Let me tell you…"

Thirty minutes later, the delay occurred when they were stopped at another random checkpoint, which took a little bit longer to clear. The Cherokee pulled up to a nondescript-looking compound with a high concrete wall topped with razor wire. They pulled up to the front, with the driver stopping a few feet from a gate.

Yousef stepped out of the Jeep and punched a code into a keypad, opening the gate before climbing back in and motioning for the driver to continue. The gate automatically closed behind them as they entered.

Sophia took in the compound, surrounded by high walls on three sides, topped with new-looking razor wire, and the fourth side was the gate they had just entered through. She was confused by the living arrangement. "I thought you were supposed to blend in," she said.

"Oh no, this is a high-class assignment," Yousef said, fixing an imaginary bow tie. I'm supposed to be an expert on antiquities for an excavation site nearby. So, this is where we house everything found."

"Hahaha, okay, that's the funniest thing I've heard in a while. Antiquities expert, you?" Sophia laughed, chastising her friend.

"Hey, like I said. I've learned a few things," Yousef fired back in mock offense.

The Jeep bounded up a flagstone driveway, coming to a stop in front of a three-story building. The three occupants exited the vehicle; the driver ran around to the back, retrieving Sophia's bag. Before running off, he set it beside her and left the walled compound through a side door.

"Where's he going?" Sophia asked, pointing towards the running man.

"Home. Some of the diggers working the site live just outside the wall. Waleed's a good man; we can trust him," Yousef added, seeing the uncertain look on Sophia's face. "The agency pulled some strings to get him out of Afghanistan, so he helps us out."

"Good to know," she remarked, warily watching him disappear through the door.

Dismissing her suspicions of Waleed, she followed Yousef up the path to the front of the house. It looked completely out of place from the outside, made of concrete, with glass windows. Power lines ran to the house, which was connected to a generator building located in the far corner of the compound.

Yousef was living it up out in the desert.

The compound was surrounded by a makeshift town of mud-brick dwellings constructed by workers from the newly excavated archaeological dig site. It just so happened that a historical site may have been uncovered not far from the border of Yemen, on the outskirts of Jazan. The CIA had managed to put Yousef in charge of it. His assignment was to monitor the tension in the region as hordes of refugees had been fleeing the battle-torn cities of Yemen. As she saw the ultra-modern office building, she could not hide the amazement on her face.

"Oh, you haven't seen anything yet, my friend," Yousef said, pumping his eyebrows as he approached the door. "The outside is just the tip of the iceberg here."

"I'm just wondering why you get to live here and everyone else outside gets to live in mud huts," Sophia said half-jokingly.

"Well, you can thank our government for that one. But come inside. We'll see if the SEAL team has arrived yet."

Yousef opened a small box on the side of the front door, placing his index finger on it. A fingerprint reader lit up with a green glow, scanning his digit, authorizing its user, and displaying a digital keypad. Punching in the password, Yousef was prompted to give a voice recognition code. Afterward, a mechanism on the other side clicked, and then the door opened.

As they walked into the building, Sophia realized how right Yousef had been. She had not seen anything until she saw what was on the inside.

On the first floor in the center were several already excavated artifacts wrapped up, ready for transport, with clean rooms to the right and offices to the left. Several workers were packing up and getting ready to leave for the day.

"I thought this was just a safe house," Sophia asked, her forehead wrinkled in confusion as she looked at Yousef.

"It is. We have the second and third floors. We had to agree to let the Saudis use the building to analyze the artifacts. But everything else is ours. Come, the elevator is in the back." The pair entered the elevator.

"Living quarters are located on the third floor, adjacent to the offices on the second floor. I'll take you to your room. Then meet me on the second floor in about… ten minutes," he said, looking at his watch. "If the team is here, I'll gather them, and we can start."

****

Setting her bag in the corner of the small, eight-by-eight room, Sophia sat on the bed for a moment, taking in her surroundings.

It had occurred to her that, over the last week, she had barely had any time to herself. Face-planting in her hands, she was still tired despite having slept nearly the entire flight.

Now was not the time for rest, though. Retrieving a pill bottle from her bag, she slid two painkillers into her hand and gulped them down with a swig of water. It was time to meet the team, hopefully.

Sophia exited the stairwell on the second floor. Again, amazed by the level of setup. Most safe houses were just rundown hideouts with U.S. governmental upgrades. This one, though, had several offices along the south wall of the floor. The main floor was completely open, sans a few cubicles.

Seeing Yousef further down the hallway, she went to meet him. Having to do a double take as she walked past a gated room.

Apparently, it was an armory, as evidenced by its contents. Inside were enough weapons to outfit a small army. She noticed the look on his face as she drew nearer. Yousef was standing outside of what appeared to be a small conference room. He was wearing a concerned look, his face wrinkled.

"What is it? Are they not here yet?" she asked.

"No, they're here," he said, shaking his head.

"Ok, then what is it? I know that look." Sophia had seen Yousef's worried expression before, and here he stood, wearing it again.

"Nothing, they're just… a little amped up, is all. And I know how you are. Try to remember that not everyone shares your same love of detail. Let's just walk them through quickly," he said, trying not to offend Sophia about her anal-retentiveness.

"Whatever, I'm not that bad," she griped. Rolling her eyes, she shoved him out of the way and entered the room.

The eight occupants instantly ceased their activities, snapping to attention as Sophia entered. A faint whistle lingered from the back of the room.

"Man, she's hot," someone said under their breath.

"So that's our new handler. I want to handle that," another said, drawing a chuckle from the man standing next to him.

"Tex, knock it off. Show some respect for once," came an order from the left side of the room.

Sophia's eyes fixated on the man who had given the order. A lean, athletic-looking man with a strong square jaw hidden behind a thick beard and dark, intense eyes. He had the presence of someone in command. He gave a quick salute. "Ma'am, sorry about that," he said.

"I take it you're the team leader," Sophia questioned, reaching out to shake his hand. "Please don't call me ma'am either. And I'm not in the military, so you don't have to salute."

"Understood. And yes, I'm indeed the leader of these misfits. Chief Petty Officer Marshall Wallace. And you are?"

"Agent Sophia Evans, I will be your CIA handler for this mission."

A groan emerged from the room when they heard the letters

"CIA."

"Great, another CIA mission. Don't you guys have special teams for shit like this?"

Sophia faced the man who said it. "What is that supposed to mean, sailor?" She'd worked with Special Forces teams in the past. To the best of her recollection, none of them were too thrilled about it either. Too much secrecy, she figured.

"Nothing, that over there is Ryan Sands, my number two," Wallace added, cutting off the stout, curly-haired soldier before he could answer.

"First off," she said, disregarding the comment, wanting to make sure they got off on the right foot. "I want to tell all of you," she addressed the room. "Thank you for the extraordinary work you do. And I know your team was on its way home before being recalled for this mission. For that, I'm truly sorry. But it's for a very good reason, as we'll cover here. Also, just call me Sophia, ok? Chief Wallace, can you please introduce me to the rest of the team?"

"That over there, the rude whistler is Bobby Jenkins. We call him Tex, though."

"Sniper extraordinaire, smart-ass aficionado," the man in the corner, wearing a cowboy hat and a toothpick sticking out of one side of his mouth, proclaimed. He spoke in a sharp Texan accent.

"Holy shit, guys, Tex just said two large words," blurted out another team member.

"That is Marcus Tyus over there," he said, pointing to an African American gentleman. He smiled, exposing a gap between his two front teeth. "The others are," he said, moving left to right across the room, pointing. "Victor Gutierrez, also known as 'Gut,'" he said. Gut was a medium-height, well-built man with close-cropped black hair. "Ahmed Alwani." An Arab with a scar down one side of his face. "Damon Johns." A burly-looking man with a softer demeanor than his looks would suggest. "And finally, Michael Walsh." He had thick-framed glasses that hid his green eyes and a gaunt-looking face that didn't match his square body.

"Good, nice to meet you all. Now that the introductions and interruptions are over," she said, staring at Tex. The man sheepishly nodded. "Can we get started?" Sophia moved to the center of the room, looking back at Yousef. "Is everything ready?" she asked.

"It's all here, everything you wanted and needed." He waved a hand at the setup.

The room had been laid out like a school classroom, with three rows of long tables and several seats. At the head, a large whiteboard stretched the length of the wall. On the front table were a computer and projector, casting a blank white screen onto the board. Yousef, who had followed Sophia, grabbed a clicker from the wall and pressed a button.

The clear glass became a sheet of solid white, blocking the view into the room from outside.

"Yes, please get started," Wallace said, waving his hand and giving his team a dark stare, suggesting that everyone keep their mouths shut.

Sophia removed a small flash drive from her pocket and inserted it into the laptop's USB port. "Ok, then, a quick rundown of why you're here and not on your way home," Sophia said, clicking several keys on the computer. An image of a tan-skinned man with a crooked nose, long black hair, and a thick, stubbly beard popped on the screen. "We're here to surveil and potentially capture this man." She pointed to the image. "This is Tarik Salem; he may have intelligence that will lead us to Amell al-Gharsi. The man who orchestrated the attack in Milwaukee and the failed attempt in Orlando also."

Tex's hand shot up into the air. "Um…"

"Yes, Tex, am I moving too fast for you already?"

The room erupted with laughter.

"No, ma'am, I'm used to the speed, but how do we know where Tarik is going to be?"

"Shockingly good question. One of the men we captured in Orlando provided us with the time and place they were supposed to meet him."

"Then how do we know the meet is still on if the men he was supposed to meet have been captured?"

"Tex, shut up, let her continue," Wallace ordered. "Or you'll be doing laps all night."

"No, that's all right, Commander. It is a good question. And to answer you, Tex, Amell needs what Tarik is selling him to continue his crusade against the West. We do not believe he has any other options. So, we stake out the meeting place and hope it's still a go."

"What's the plan then?"

"That we'll go over tomorrow," Sophia said. "This is just a brief catch-up."

"Ok, that's all I needed." The Texan tipped his hat.

"Great, now that he has all he needs," Sophia said, singling out Tex. "I would like for Chief Wallace to stay behind. The rest of you are dismissed."

The sailors filtered out of the room one by one. "I didn't mean any disrespect," Tex said, passing by. Sophia nodded before approaching Wallace, waiting for the men to leave.

"I trust your men can do the job?" Sophia mused, with very little doubt, that this team could do the job by their demeanor during the briefing.

"They can do the job." There was no waiver in the Commander's voice.

"Good. I cannot express enough how important this op is."

"No need to. We know what's on the table here. Don't let the joking fool you. My men are highly trained, and we have never failed to execute a mission." Wallace's confidence buoyed that of her own.

"Get some rest, then." Sophia turned, opening the door to the conference room, and stood in the doorway. "We have a big day ahead of us tomorrow. We've got an arms dealer to catch."

CHAPTER TWELVE

The next morning, Sophia, Yousef, and the SEAL team had an early start to the day, waking up around 4 a.m. to go over the plan. Once they had gone over it, they proceeded to recap it in great detail five more times per Wallace's request. He wanted to ensure his team was prepared for anything; everyone understood their assignments and was aware of all contingencies in case something went wrong. After all, they were about to embark on a mission to capture a wanted arms dealer in the middle of a Saudi Arabian city, in the middle of its busiest market, in broad daylight.

What could go wrong?

The team loaded up and set out; once Wallace had been satisfied, they were ready. The drive to the meeting location led the group through the city of Jazan. The sun was out in full, reaching its apex in the sweltering mid-afternoon sky. The oppressive desert heat clawed at Sophia despite the van's A/C pumping to its max. Beads of sweat covered her forehead. She casually used the excess linen from her hijab to wipe them away whenever she got the chance.

As they crossed over from the barren desert outskirts into the city, Yousef became an impromptu tour guide, pointing out all the small, fascinating details of the town that he had learned. Sophia, though, was only half-heartedly listening to the history lesson.

Her mind was elsewhere as it had been each time it wasn't focused on something. The moment she had a chance to let her thoughts linger, they returned to the same thing. The events of the Orlando incident. They replayed on an endless loop in these quiet moments. What could she have done differently to save her friend Naseem that night? What different decisions could have been made that would have kept Fred out of his coma?

Then she'd hear Fred's voice in the back of her head saying not to go there. *Rehashing is counterproductive. What's done is done. Keep focused on the mission,* he would say.

Amell was the goal. The losses would be meaningless if they let him slip through their fingers again.

****

As they crossed the last checkpoint into the city, the simple mud-brick structures of the desert-dwelling locals vanished. Instead, the aesthetics of their surroundings slowly became more recognizable as the backdrop began to take on the feel of a modern American city.

"Naqil," Yousef spat in Arabic, waving his arm out the window of their Range Rover and urging the traffic to move. "It seems every day the city gets more and more crowded," he added.

"By the looks of it, more modern, too." Sophia pointed ahead. The steel skeleton of another skyscraper loomed in the distance.

Even the streets gave off the vibe of an American lifestyle. Horns blared through the congestion. Children ran through the streets as adults milled about the city, moving from one place to another.

Twenty minutes in and a few Arabic curse words later, Yousef pulled off to the side of the road. "We're here," he said, signaling ahead. "We should walk the rest of the way in."

Disembarking the Range Rover felt like stepping into a furnace as the sun blared down on Sophia. She quickly put on a pair of sunglasses and followed Yousef's lead. He knew precisely where the café was and the best place to get a good vantage point of the entrance.

They walked down the streets, passing the rows of stalls. Sophia was amazed by the variety of items being sold. There were perfume stalls, jewelry makers, carpet sellers, and electronic shops, all practically on top of each other in the crowded market. Most were selling outdated equipment by American standards but still fetched top dollar here.

They reached a sandwich shop across the street from their target building. The pair took a table on the patio, with a perfect vantage point and sightline to the front entrance of the restaurant, which sat at the corner of two intersecting streets across from them.

The entire corner felt like a busy city neighborhood in New York or Chicago. Sophia could see the shop vendors screaming and haggling over prices with their patrons. More horns blared at pedestrians who used the road as a makeshift sidewalk, blocking the streets so no cars could pass. It was so loud that all conversations resembled a screaming match between two people. She wondered if they would be able to hear each other over the comms.

Yousef resumed his history lesson of the city as they sat, unaware that Sophia had stopped listening long ago. Although she managed to throw in a few ahhh's and umm's to keep him going.

A wave of distinctively different aromas wafted down the street, all competing for Sophia's attention. The smells of freshly cut flowers and spices, such as cinnamon, ginger, and mint, overpowered her senses. Then came a truly pungent scent. Her nose twitched and crinkled as it crept up her nasal passages.

"You get used to it," Yousef said, seeing her face contort at the acrid smell.

"Get used to what?"

"The fish smell." Yousef waved his hand across the market.

"Where is it coming from? It's... so overwhelming, I mean, jeez." Pinching her nose shut with her forefinger and thumb, she held back a gag.

Yousef laughed at the sight. "I forgot you don't like seafood. One of the vendors here sells fresh fish. He goes out every morning, catches a bunch, and brings it here to sell."

"Well, that's all good, but it's noon now, and it smells like it's going bad."

"Well, hopefully, for your sake, this won't take that long, then," he said, not even trying to hold in his amusement at her despair. "Take a whiff of your coffee," Yousef added as the waitress set it down, glaring at the young American. "The Arabian beans are fresh and extremely strong. It should dull the smells."

Sophia inhaled the aroma of the coffee, a smile of relief stretching across her face as Yousef continued. "You know that the Jazan market is one of the oldest in the region. It has been around for over a hundred years."

"Are you really going to continue the history lesson, Professor Yousef?" Wallace questioned, his voice cutting into the comms units in their ears. "We've been listening to the lecture for an hour now."

"Yeah, kind of wishing you left me behind back at the safe house like Johns and Walsh," Tex jested, but in a way making it clear he wasn't joking.

Sophia grinned, watching her friend frown at the interruption, and added a laugh of her own. "Chief, is your team in place and set to go?"

"Yes, ma'am, we're all here."

Sophia casually glanced around the square, not seeing any of Wallace's team, which was a good thing in her book. If she couldn't see them, looking for them. Then, it was doubtful the team could be made by any of Amell or Tarik's men.

"You sure?" Yousef asked, shaking off his anger at being interrupted.

"My team knows what we're doing," Wallace replied pridefully. "Ryan and I are across from you in the market. Don't look," he snapped. "Gut and Tyus are at the ends of the streets. Ahmed is inside the restaurant, and-"

"And I'm across the street on the roof watching your ass-"

"Tex!"

"Your six," the big Texan finished in his Southern drawl. "Jeez, boss, what did you think I was going to say?"

"It's quite all right, Wallace. Let the *boy* be himself," Sophia strongly emphasized the word boy for the whole team to hear. The slight underhanded remark drew a chorus of oohs from the rest of the unit.

"Ouch, Sophia, ouch. You'll come around to my charms. Just wait."

"Team heads up. I think something is happening here," Tyus cut in, stopping the banter.

"What do you see, Ty?" Wallace asked.

"Black Explorer is approaching, and it doesn't look like they're here for a Sunday shopping trip. Got some real unfriendly-looking passengers."

"Ok, team. Game faces on. It sounds like the Intel was right. Sophia, do you have any idea what Amell's guy looks like?"

"No idea. It was supposed to be Abdul Sanù, his number two. However, given that he's currently deceased, I'm not entirely sure who is taking his place. They could already be inside."

"Ok, Ahmed, be vigilant."

"Yes, sir."

The Explorer pulled up to the restaurant, nearly bowling an older couple over as it jolted to a stop. A thick-necked Arab in a black suit jumped out of the passenger's side. The older gentleman, upset at almost being run down, moved to confront the new arrival, but a sneer from the suited man drove him and his wife away like they'd seen a demon.

The looks of recognition on the fleeing couple's faces told Sophia that whoever they were, the locals knew not to mess with them. Satisfied at driving the couple away, the suited man surveyed the market before opening the back door.

From the back of the SUV outstepped a man wearing a long black thobe with embroidered gold trim around the neck and sleeve cuffs. On top of his head, he wore a matching keffiyeh with a gold circlet. The keffiyeh ran longer than usual down his back and covered the right half of his face.

The man slowly turned, facing out to the street. He was barking an order to his driver. Sophia squinted through the desert heat, trying to get a good look at him. A gust of wind blew the keffiyeh aside at the right moment. Exposing beyond the covering, a mottled melding of melted flesh, kissed by fire.

He grabbed a cane from the back seat before the driver drove off, covering his face back up as he entered the restaurant.

"And GQ's ugliest terrorist alive award goes to Mr. Arm's dealer. Why am I the one who gets to stare at him through the scope? He looks like old dog meat," Tex complained.

"That's definitely Tarik," said Sophia. "He got those scars and limp from us about four years ago," she continued. "We thought we killed him in a drone strike, but he somehow survived, badly burned on 20% of his body, and his right leg crushed in the rubble. We were wrong, clearly, as he popped up a year later, rerunning his guns," Sophia explained.

"Keeps the saying true, though. Cockroaches always survive,"

Ryan joked.

"Hey, boss, I can end this right now. Put one in this dude's head. No guns, no attack, no war for Amell, right? Give me the word, and we can all go home right now," Tex added.

"Stow that trigger finger of yours, sailor."

"That's not how this works, Tex," groaned Sophia, clearly annoyed by his simplistic thinking. "See, that's why we would never work; you're too simple," she chided.

"Damn, Tex, she's got you twice now," Ryan instigated.

"She can come and get me anytime," Tex professed, his smile piercing through the radio.

"Ahmed, Tango One is headed your way. You're up," Wallace interrupted. "And Tex, you've got no chance. Sophia can count to ten without using her fingers. You're not her type."

"And just how would you know my type?" Sophia objected in mock.

"I see Tango one. He's approaching the hostess stand. It appears that they know him pretty well. He's being shipped to the front," Ahmed narrated, recounting Tarik's movements. "Looks like this may be a favorite hangout of his."

Indeed, the restaurant's employees knew Tarik very well. Even the manager, an older gentleman with greying hair and a salt-and-pepper beard, ran forward to greet the arms dealer. However, his reverence was more a result of fear than genuine respect.

The two briefly exchanged words. Then, the manager led Tarik and his bodyguard to the back of the restaurant, passing Ahmed, who was seated at a table in the far corner of the room, as per his request. The location gave him a perfect vantage point of the whole restaurant.

Someone was already seated at the table, and he irritably looked at his watch as the two men approached. The sailor still had a good line of sight to the meeting spot.

Ahmed watched silently as Tarik's bodyguard asked the seated individual to stand. The man said nothing, staring at Tarik without breaking eye contact and ignoring the bodyguard. The staring contest between the two men flooded the café with tension. Finally, Tarik took a seat across from the terrorist. His over-watcher did the same. Though under his suit, Ahmed could clearly see a bulge.

A gun.

"Guys, something's happening," Ahmed reported, referring to the stare-down. "The bodyguard is also armed."

"What's going on?" Sophia asked. The tension and anticipation in her voice were palpable through the radio.

"I think the person Tarik is meeting with is already here. He's been inside the entire time and doesn't look happy. Should I move in?"

"NO!" Shouted Sophia, her voice distorted through the feedback, causing the team to flinch from the static. "Let it play out. It had to have gotten out that the attempt in Orlando failed. Tarik is probably hesitant to do business right now. So, stay put unless you can get closer to hear anything."

"Boss?" Ahmed asked, hesitating about following Sophia's order, looking for a second opinion.

"You heard the lady. Do what she says. This is her op, guys," Wallace reiterated, providing the CIA agent with full support.

"Can you get closer?" Sophia asked.

"I think," he said. "Let me try something." The soldier spotted a sign for restrooms near the table where Tarik and the unknown terrorist were sitting.

Ahmed slowly rose from his table, leaving several Riyals for the waitress. He moved casually towards the meeting, veering toward the hallway that led to the restrooms. He stopped before entering, though, hanging just around the corner for a moment. Then he reentered the dining room area, sitting at a table a little closer now, hoping the bodyguard wouldn't suspect anything.

He didn't. All three intently focused on the meeting, which hadn't even started yet. Neither party had spoken a word. Instead, they sized each other up silently. Sophia was right; the arms dealer seemed to be hesitant.

Then, a large envelope was slid across the table. Tarik's bodyguard opened it to expose a stack of American hundred-dollar bills. Tarik nodded and eased back in his seat as the suited man hurried the cash from sight. The offering looked to have erased the brewing tension, at least temporarily.

"Ahmed, do you have anything?" Sophia barked at the soldier again impatiently.

"Hold on," responded Ahmed. He listened intently, but the restaurant chatters only allowed him to make out a few words. "I think the man he's meeting with is named Hasan."

Sophia's face fell flat, balling her fist up, recognizing the name—the same Hasan who'd put Fred in a coma. "Oh, crap," she muttered.

"Wait, who's that?" Wallace demanded, sensing the CIA agent's recognition of the name. "He was not in the briefing."

"I didn't think he'd be here," she rasped, trying to suppress her anger. "Hasan Althani, Amell's enforcer and dirty worker. It might mean Amell and Tarik's relationship has soured if he's involved now."

"Wait, wouldn't that help us turn him then?" Tex asked a legitimate question. "I mean, enemy of the enemy, right?"

"He was not sent here to kill Tarik," Sophia added, surprised at Tex's question.

"Anyway, team, this doesn't change the mission. Stay on point. We need to bag Tarik."

"No," Sophia objected. "Hasan is now the primary target."

"We can't change the op mid-stream," Wallace protested. "That's what gets people killed."

"It's not that big of a deviation," Sophia countered. "We're still bagging one man. It's just a different one. Besides, wouldn't Hasan be the easier target? You don't have to deal with the bodyguard."

"Um, maybe not," Ahmed interrupted. The conversation between Tarik and Hasan just wrapped up. A deal had been struck between the two parties. "Looks like Hasan's got company," Ahmed added as two other men approached the table.

"We still stay on, Hasan," Sophia ordered.

"Wait, hold on. There seems to be a last-minute change," Ahmed reported.

"What type of change?" Wallace asked.

"Tarik's guard is going with Hasan. It sounds like he wants

assurances that Amell's operation is still safe. Sophia was right. Word got out that Amell let in a mole." Ahmed watched as the two sides headed for the front door.

"Well, that puts three men with Hasan. Do you still want us to go after him and let Tarik go? Tarik's the easier target now," Wallace inquired. Sophia didn't answer. "Agent, who will it be?" Still, no answer, and Sophia was trying to reconcile her emotions.

"I think this gives us an opportunity here, boss," Ryan cut in with an idea in Sophia's hesitation.

"I'm all ears. Let's hear it."

"Ok, we can follow both of them. We're assuming that Tarik will turn on Amell. If he doesn't, we're screwed. If we follow Hasan, he'll lead us straight to Amell. So, we split the team and follow both of them."

"Great idea. Sophia, what do you think?"

No response came from the CIA agent. The second Ryan mentioned splitting the team up, her eyes glazed over, heart plummeted into the seat cushion. She started to sweat, her hands trembling. The busy, noisy street became silent. Echoed screams, followed by gunshots, played through her ears. The young agent's eyes darted around the café patio.

Across the street, Wallace could see her reaction. "Sophia, what's the order? What do you want us to do?"

Still no response. Yousef tried to snap her out of her trance. "Sof, they need a response. Give them your order," he said, snapping his fingers in front of her face.

"I… I… I…" Sophia couldn't speak; her throat ran dry.

Not waiting for Sophia to snap out of it, Wallace gave the order instead, taking over command. "Fuck it. We're going with Ryan's plan. Split up. Ryan, Tyus, and Ahmed follow Hasan. Gut, Tex, you're on me; we're going after Tarik. Yousef, grab Sophia, and meet us at your Rover."

The small unit split into two teams, each scrambling to their respective vehicles. Yousef grabbed Sophia's arm, yanking her out of the chair and dragging her down the street as they headed towards their Range Rover.

Sophia finally came, too, while they were en route.

"What… what happened?" Sophia asked, confused as to why and where they were headed.

"What the fuck was that, Sof? I know you process shit differently, worrying about everything that could go wrong, but you totally froze."

"I… I don't know what that was." She lied, knowing full well exactly what had happened and why. The mere mention of splitting the team up took her back to Belgrade.

Yousef could tell she had lied to his face, and he knew what was wrong, as evidenced by the look in her eyes. "Don't tell me that was all about Belgrade again?" he asked. "Jeez, I thought you were over that. I thought that's why you came back to the field."

Getting closer to the Range Rover, Sophia looked Yousef square in his eyes. The look was unmistakable, her eyes pleading with her friend not to say anything. "Please don't-"

"I won't," Yousef said reassuringly.

The two pushed their way through the crowd to the truck. Wallace was waiting for them by the passenger side door. He waved to get their attention. As they got closer to the car, Sophia could see the anger in Wallace's eyes.

Sensing his extreme displeasure with her, she didn't look directly at him; instead, she jumped into the back seat. Gutierrez hit the gas when she closed the door, pursuing Tarik.

Wallace immediately snapped his head back once inside the truck and stared at Sophia with a burning gaze. "What the fuck was that?" he demanded.

Sophia could feel her stomach sink to the floorboard of the SUV, her face flared beet red, all the more noticeable by her typically light complexion.

"I… I… was just-" She stopped herself before lying to Wallace and making up an excuse. "It will not happen again. I'm sorry."

Wallace was surprised by the response and the fact that she owned up to the hesitation. "Good, it better not. Any, and I mean any, hesitation in the field can cost my men and me our lives." His anger was seething out of him at this point.

"Copy that. As I said, it will not happen again," she replied, still flushed with embarrassment and frustration at having frozen again, just as she had in Orlando.

Sophia stared a hole through the bottom of the vehicle, not saying a word as Gutierrez navigated the street following Tarik.

Tex leaned over to her. "Don't worry about that. He wants to make sure everyone makes it home in one piece; that's all," he said with a grin. "Chin up; you'll be quicker on the draw next time." He flashed her a quick wink.

"Thanks, Tex." His words lifted her spirits. Especially coming from Tex, with no sarcasm or sexual undertone, really shocked her. But that was what she needed to hear.

"Gut, don't get too close. Hang back a bit," Wallace barked, having turned his attention to trailing Tarik.

The team followed closely behind Tarik's Land Cruiser, maintaining their distance and trailing them through the city. The original plan that had been put in place was to follow the arms dealer back to his hideout before snatching him up. That way, they would also be able to alert the Saudis to his cache of weapons, killing two birds with one stone. They could take the arms dealer and his guns off the board simultaneously.

Tarik led them out of the city to a small village located halfway between Jazan and the Yemeni border. There were a few houses lined up just off the main road. Tarik's Land Cruiser turned off onto a small dirt trail leading away from the main village to a home in the distance.

"Where is he going?" Gutierrez wondered out loud.

"I don't know, but keep going, don't follow," Wallace ordered. Gutierrez kept straight on the road, not turning off to follow Tarik. Wallace turned to Sophia. "Where is he going?"

"I have no idea. Nothing we have tells us where his stash is. And there has never been a mention of this village in his file. So, your guess is as good as mine." Sophia shrugged.

"Yousef, what is out there?"

"How do I know?"

"Well, you gave such a good history lesson earlier today," Wallace chided. "All that shit's gotta be good for something."

"That doesn't mean I know every inch of the country," Yousef fired back sarcastically, shaking his head.

A few miles later, the team pulled off the road into a gas station to regroup. Yousef contacted the safe house and requested satellite images of the area so that they could plan their next move.

****

Several hours later, the team closed in on the house as night settled in. The satellite images Yousef had pulled up on his laptop showed nothing unusual in the area. It appeared to be a small farm. The inference indicated that four people were present at the house. Two inside, one in the car and another walking around the house.

"Tex, are you in position?" Wallace radioed.

"Yes, sir, eyes on the driver in the car." Tex had situated himself on the tallest hill he could find, several hundred yards away. He had his sights set on the driver in Tarik's Land Cruiser.

"Sophia, any sign of the roving guard?"

"Not yet; he walked around to the back two minutes ago. That gives you about two minutes until he comes back around." Having watched the house for several hours, they had timed the routes of the guards.

"Ok, Gut and I are moving in. Tex, when I give the word, take out the driver." Wallace and Gutierrez darted across the desert landscape, hunched over, stealthily closing in fast on the Land Cruiser. "Now."

The guard was leaning out the door, smoking a cigarette. Tex fired one shot from his silenced M40A5 sniper rifle. The .308mm round shattered the passenger window, striking the guard in the head.

He slumped over and fell out of the car. "Ha-ha, poor bastard never saw that coming," Tex muttered. "Driver down."

Gutierrez and Wallace ran past the now-deceased guard to the house's front door. Gutierrez slid a lock-picking kit out of his pocket and attempted to pick the lock.

"Guys, the other guard is about to come back around. You have less than a minute." Sophia warned, keeping a close eye on her watch to time the route.

"We're in," Gutierrez whispered, opening the door. The two soldiers quietly entered the house, closing the door behind them.

"Tex, if you get a shot at the rover, take him out."

"Roger that, boss. I'm happy to oblige," Tex responded with a smile, swinging the sniper rifle around to where the man should appear shortly.

Inside the two-story wood-frame home, all was quiet. There were no lights on. The pair slipped on night-vision goggles. The dark interior instantly lit up a bright shade of green. They found themselves inside a living room, and the goggles made it easy to pick out the furniture.

A couch lined the center of the room, and an older boxy TV was on top of a coffee table. A La-Z-Boy recliner sat in the corner, facing a bookshelf sparsely decorated with books.

Wallace tapped Gutierrez on the shoulder, pointing ahead to a hallway. The two advanced, tiptoeing to the first room on the left side. The junior team member moved, ducking inside with another brief hand movement from his chief, sweeping his M4 around the new space. Wallace followed closely behind.

Kitchen.

It was empty. They filed back into the hallway, checking the other two rooms before moving upstairs. All they found was the bathroom and a laundry room that also served as storage space. They continued clearing the house.

****

Tex stared through his night-vision scope, waiting, knowing that his target should appear at any moment.

A flash went off as the man in desert fatigues emerged from behind the house. He passed under a wall light obscuring Tex's view as the bright light temporarily flared in the scope.

"Damn it," he cursed, waiting for the unsuspecting soldier to reappear.

There he was, striding down the front steps, approaching the parked Land Cruiser, which was currently serving as a makeshift casket for his comrade.

"Just a little closer, buddy, just a little closer." *Pfft,* another shot. The second guard's body fell to the ground. "Guard's all taken care of," he radioed.

"Good shooting, Tex," Sophia congratulated the sniper, returning the kind words he had said to her earlier in the day.

"Thanks."

****

Wallace and Gutierrez reached the top of the second floor. It was nothing but a narrow hall with four doors. Two doors were set into each side. A cast of yellow slipped from underneath the door at the end to their right. Gutierrez signaled to Wallace.

They advanced on the bedroom door. Wallace positioned himself against one side of the doorway, with Gutierrez on the other side.

Wallace held up three fingers, slowly putting one down at a time—a silent countdown.

Gutierrez kicked in the door as soon as the last finger went down. It flung open, breaking from its hinges in a shower of splinters. The soldier barged through M4 at the ready, followed by Wallace.

Startled by the interruption, Tarik turned to see the two-armed intruders approaching him. He pushed away from the man, who was bent over in front of him and reached for a pistol on the nightstand.

Stunned by what they had seen, Wallace and Gutierrez drew first. Wallace fired two shots. One round hit Tarik in the hand, sending the pistol flying, and the second round went through the leg. Gutierrez moved on the naked male companion thrown to the floor, placing his boot on his head and sandwiching him onto the floor.

"Wallace, Gut, is everything alright in there?" Sophia barked over the radio, worried by the long silence that had fallen inside the house.

"Sophia, Yousef, bring up the truck quickly and get the med kit; Tarik's been hit," Wallace ordered, Tarik's screams echoing in the background.

Yousef slammed the brakes as the truck came to a screeching halt at the base of the steps, kicking up a cloud of dust. Sophia hopped out with the med kit, racing up the stairs to the bedroom.

Several moments later, the team emerged from the house, with Sophia and Wallace supporting Tarik, battlefield dressings covering the holes Wallace had put into their captive.

He tried to squirm from their hold, but Wallace clocked the injured man in the back of the head.

He slumped in their arms.

Gutierrez followed behind with his companion.

"Tex, Gut, take the Land Cruiser and bring him." He pointed to Tarik's lover, loading the now unconscious Tarik into the back of the Range Rover.

"Great, we get the blood vehicle," Tex wailed, throwing his hands up in protest, opening the driver's side door, and sweeping the blood-soaked shattered glass from the seat.

"Yousef, you're driving. Get us back to the safe house immediately. We're going to have some questions for this piece of shit when he wakes up," Wallace said, climbing into the back seat with the prisoner.

Sophia slammed the door shut before getting into the passenger seat. Yousef punched the accelerator, speeding off into the night.

CHAPTER THIRTEEN

The two SUVs raced down the dark desert road at full speed toward the safe house—the only vehicles on the lonely highway belonged to the SEAL team.

Yet, Yousef continued to check the rearview mirror nervously and routinely every few miles. He expected Tarik's men to magically appear despite having killed his guards at the farmhouse.

Tarik had no time to call for help when Wallace snatched him and his companion out of bed, and Yousef knew this. Still, out of an abundance of caution, he continued to check. Each time he did, he saw nothing but the bobbing headlights of the Land Cruiser behind him, which relaxed him until the next check.

"We're getting closer; you should call the safe house now," Yousef alerted Sophia as the Ranger Rover sped past a road marker. The Arab tilted his head to read the numbers.

Sophia already had her phone to her ear. "On it," she said huffily. Irritation was evident on her face. "Yes, I just gave you the authorization code. We're coming in with passengers and need a medical team on standby." Sophia gave Yousef an exasperated eye roll. "Yes, a med team, jeez."

The Range Rover smashed into a pothole, sending its occupants headlong into the roof. None had thought about buckling up in the scramble to get the injured Tarik to the vehicle for extraction.

The unconscious arm dealer's neck bent upon impact, jarring him awake. "Ow," he screamed, clutching his injured leg with his hand and cursing in Arabic.

"Jackass is awake," Wallace muttered, waving his gun in Tarik's face. "Don't do anything stupid," he advised the injured man, though he was clearly in no shape to be doing anything. The order drew another obscenity-laced tirade from Tarik. He may have been too injured to do anything physically, but his mouth still worked. It was doing so in overdrive, hurling obscenities at the team, recognizing they were American.

"I don't understand, asshole. Speak English."

"Fuck you. You American infidel," came Tarik's retort, this time in English.

"Well, at least he speaks English. That should make the interrogation easier." Wallace fixed a malevolent grin on the irate man. "Unless he resists." Throwing up air quotes with another smile.

"Wallace, will you please shut him up? I can't hear," Sophia huffed, getting back on the phone. Her frustration was primarily directed at the person on the other end of the line.

"Gladly. Night, nighttime again," the sailor said with a smirk, eyes darting towards his handgun before pistol-whipping the arms dealer again, knocking him out cold. "Is that better?"

"Yes, thank God. No medical team, such as a doctor? Doesn't anyone at the safe house speak English?" she yelled, annoyed, turning to Yousef.

The Arab shrugged. "Maybe bad reception."

Jabbing an angry finger at the end button on her phone. "Maybe, just get us there," she snapped.

"Yes, ma'am," Yousef responded sarcastically. The corners of his mouth twisted up.

"What's that look for?" Sophia asked, puzzled by her co-worker's expression.

The agent thumbed at their unconscious passenger. "You just captured Tarik Salem," he said.

"We," Wallace corrected from the back. "We just captured Tarik Salem."

"Yes, yes, ok. We," Yousef reiterated the need to change the pronoun to include the SEAL team. "Do you know how big of a win this is for the agency? Shit, for you?"

Sophia looked out the windshield into the darkness, contemplating the implications of this success. The lights of the safe house's compound walls came into view, allowing her to take in the momentous moment.

Tarik Salem's name had become synonymous with terrorism for the better of two decades. Like every international agency and even Saudi Arabia's secret police force, the Mabahith listed him as one of their most wanted.

Yet, here she was, a CIA analyst plucked from her isolated cubicle, assigned to a task force she didn't want to be a part of. Then, flown halfway around the world to link up with a SEAL team. And now, she, no… they, had caught the man no one could.

Wow, we did it. We just scored a big win against terrorism worldwide, she thought.

"I'm not concerned with winning right now," Sophia said, retreating from her thoughts. Her eyes focus on the rearview mirror, locking onto the unconscious man. Now wasn't the time to be celebrating. The mission was only half over. Her thoughts turned to how she would take down the arms dealer extraordinaire. "Besides, catching him is only half the battle. Now we have to get actionable Intel, like where Amell is hiding," she added, dampening Yousef's mood.

Sophia knew they needed to turn Tarik and do so fast before Amell caught word of his capture and disappeared into the wind.

"Yeah, but we have a pretty big bargaining chip behind us," Wallace said, pointing to Gutierrez and Tex's trailing Land Cruiser.

In their raid, the two commandos had managed to secure a second detainee that Wallace was referring to—the unknown bedroom compatriot of the terrorist. It was unmistakably clear what the two were doing in the bedroom together. Engaging in a sexual encounter when the soldiers barged in uninvited.

An act that was against the beliefs of the Arab world. As well as illegal in Saudi Arabia.

Most Middle Eastern countries, for that matter, still had laws making homosexuality illegal, and it was generally frowned upon amongst hardcore Jihadists as well.

Sophia glanced in her side mirror at the speeding headlights of the SUV behind them. Her mind had already started turning over how she would use this new golden nugget of information to her advantage during the interrogation.

Men like Tarik ruled by fear. His strong reputation and penchant for violence only enhanced that feeling in his rivals and subordinates. All she would have to do was release him and spread the word amongst the people. A smear campaign of sorts.

Something that the CIA excelled at, having had decades to perfect the tactic.

Eventually, if it got repeated enough, someone would believe it. Then, when Tarik least expected it, he'd have a knife to his throat, a gun to his head, or a noose around his neck. Either way, Tarik Salem would be dead.

That gave Sophia the proverbial ace up her sleeve.

****

The safe house's concrete walls and steel gate came into view five minutes later, just as Tarik woke again.

"We're here," Sophia announced, letting out a sigh of relief.

Yousef sped through the open gate, soon followed by Gutierrez, as they raced around the back of the building where a team of CIA operatives and a doctor awaited them.

The two-vehicle convoy came to a screeching halt. Wallace jumped out the back, waving for the medical team to assist. "Got one wounded here," he said, moving aside, allowing the team of white coats to pull the arms dealer out, dropping him into a wheelchair, and rushing him inside.

"I thought you said he was only shot," one of the doctors asked, signaling to his face, inquiring about the broken nose.

"He got rowdy," Wallace quipped.

The doctor nodded, then followed his patient inside.

"Boss, what do you want to do with this guy?" Tex asked, pulling the younger Arab out of the Land Cruiser. The captive Arab pulled away from the bulky Texan to run. The soldier swept out his leg, catching the barefooted man and tripping him.

Tex instantly dropped his knee into the back of the man's neck.

"Where the fuck do you think you're going? You've got nowhere to run, Jack."

"See, you made a new friend here," Wallace joked, walking up as Tex hauled the half-naked prisoner to his feet.

"Yeah, this here is Rasheed." Tex pulled him tighter as he tried to wiggle away again. "He likes long walks on the beach, knitting in the winter, and is your regular fucking chatterbox. Wouldn't shut the fuck up the whole way. He at least speaks English."

"Hmm, you don't say." Wallace stared intently into the young man's eyes, squinting as he leaned forward, their faces just out of reach so Rasheed couldn't head-butt him. The silence was palpable as the two men eyed each other. Rasheed snarled, breathing heavily, looking about, ready to pounce. Wallace stayed the course, staring him down. Seconds passed, and then Rasheed broke eye contact, looking down. Submitting. "That's what I thought." Wallace stood upright again. "And what does chatterbox have to say now?"

"I did nothing wrong. I love America. This is okay in America, no?" The Arab was clearly nervous about being caught in the act of being with another man as his anger dissipated.

"Sure, what you two were doing is okay," Wallace said, glancing between his fellow soldiers and shrugging. "We're not here for that. We're here for the son of a bitch you were doing it with," he said, jabbing his finger into the scared man's forehead.

"Rasheed may love America, but that man… he hates us. And he tries to kill American sailors like me and my friends here. So, for you, that's a problem because I don't believe you, but we'll find out how much he loves you."

Turning to Yousef, he asked, "You got holding cells here, I assume?"

"Not really, but I'm sure we can cook something up. Agent Hanks here will escort you. Agent?"

"Yes, sir." A plain-clothed, unassuming man jogged over.

"Take Chief Wallace's men and find a place to secure the prisoner," the lead CIA agent ordered.

"Absolutely. Come with me," he said, leading the sailors away.

"Where've you guys been?" Tex chortled, passing Johns and Walsh as they made their way in. "You missed all the fun," he said, patting the pair on the shoulder as he walked past.

Sophia stayed out of the scuffle and watched the team from a distance. After Gutierrez and Tex departed with Rasheed, she strode past Yousef and Wallace, head down. "I'm going to prepare for the interrogation for when Tarik wakes up," she said quietly.

Sophia and Wallace hadn't had a real conversation since the events earlier in the day when the meeting had gone sideways, and she'd frozen up.

Despite Tex's best efforts to comfort her, there was still a hint of embarrassment about her. She wondered how much confidence the Commander would have in her moving forward.

"Sure thing, Sophia," Yousef answered as she continued past them. The Arab went to follow when Wallace reached out, yanking him back.

"You and I should have a conversation." From his tone, Yousef could tell this was not a request but more of a demand. "Come here."

The soldier forcefully dragged the CIA agent by the arm down the hall, pulling him into an office room and ensuring no one was following them.

Yousef pulled away, rubbing his arm with a bewildered look.

Wallace closed the door, locking it behind him, and then took a few deep breaths to collect his thoughts.

"Look, I don't know what this is about, but it can wait," the agent said testily, moving towards the door.

The soldier snapped around, blocking it.

"Get out of my way, Commander," Yousef barked, still rubbing his arm. A bruise had already set in. He tried to shuffle past, but Wallace moved again, putting himself between Yousef and the door. "I need to ensure my people are setting up the interrogation room."

The two men were toe to toe.

However, there was no way Yousef could take on a highly skilled warrior like the SEAL team leader, and they both knew it.

"No! This can't wait. You know exactly what this is about."

Yousef rolled his eyes, backing off. Wallace was right. He did know why he was being cornered. "Ok, go ahead," the agent relented.

"I've gathered from the way you two speak that you've known each other for a long time. Am I right?"

"Yes, Sophia and I go way back to our days at The Farm."

"Ok, so what the fuck happened out there today?" Wallace

shouted. "Did she freeze up? Is she even a fucking field operative, or are we running about putting our lives in the hands of a desk jockey? That's the impression I was given today. My sailors' lives are in my hands, and I will not trust them to someone who has no fucking clue what to do. Every second matters out there," he shouted, pointing in a general direction. "In the field, a moment, a fraction of a second of indecision, can mean the difference between life and death. So what is her deal? Because I will not send my team back out there if I can't trust her to do her job."

Yousef raised his hands, backing away from the enraged sailor who was steadily encroaching on his personal space during his tirade. He was caught between loyalty to his long-time friend and the mission. He took a deep breath, knowing that the SEAL team leader was correct. They had gotten lucky earlier, but next time, they may not.

"You're right," Yousef admitted. "She froze out there. Technically, she is no longer a field operative. The admission drew a questioning glare. "She's been out of the game for the last three years, working at Langley as an analyst."

The sailor turned, throwing his hands up. "Great, I'm working for a desk jockey who's in over her head. So, why is she in charge, then?"

"She had been following this group since they attacked Milwaukee, along with an FBI partner, who was injured in Orlando chasing this Amell. She knows more about them than anyone else and is probably the only person who can do this."

"Not from what I fucking saw today. She's going to get us all killed, freezing up like that. I can't trust her out there."

Again caught between loyalty and mission, Yousef carefully picked out his next few words. "Look, she knows more than most what a bad decision in the field can mean. She knows she screwed up, and it won't happen again."

The sailor sensed there was more to the story by how the agent parsed his words. Having worked with other spooks before, Wallace knew how they sometimes withheld vital information. "If you know more than what you're telling. I need to hear it. Now." He started advancing on the Arab, his words seeping with a veiled threat. "What do you mean by she knows more than most?"

"I… I just mean the woman beats herself up more than anyone else could."

"No, go back to the part about her knowing what a bad decision could mean."

Yousef paused, thinking for a second if he should continue. "Look, it's not my place to say. You should really talk to her."

"Come on," Wallace spat angrily. "Man, you guys really don't like giving straight answers, do you? All lies. That's all you guys ever do."

Yousef tensed, straightening his back. "Hey, just because we're spies doesn't mean we always lie." The insinuation affronted him.

Wallace gave him a sly look with one eyebrow raised.

"Look, man, all I need to know is, can she be counted on when the time comes? Why was she on desk duty?"

"Ok, fine," said Yousef hesitantly, finally giving in. "Sophia is, was, and probably always will be the best instinctual field operative I have ever worked with. At the top of our class, brilliant, and never failed at anything in life. If she puts her mind to anything, consider it done. She shattered records at the farm like they were nothing. A complete natural for this job-"

"So, what happened? Because that is not who I saw."

Yousef decided that Wallace needed to hear everything, so he continued. "Three years ago, we were running an operation together in Belgrade. We were tasked with surveilling Sergey Koslov."

"Sergey Koslov, the arms dealer?" Wallace's head cricked, recognizing the name. The name had crept up during a few mission briefs over the years. He was a well-known bad guy.

"The very same one," Yousef confirmed. "We got a great tip about where to find him from some of his past associates who had been captured. We looked into it, and low and behold, we found him where they said. We then contacted Interpol and established a joint operation. We surveilled him for two weeks, just waiting for him to slip up and make an incriminating move. You know, anything that Interpol could sweep in and pick him up on and send him away for life. One less arms dealer in the world, right?"

"Well, did he?"

"No. In fact, that asshole either figured out or was tipped off that we were on to him. So he sets up a bogus arms deal, knowing we were watching. We go to the meet and get all the photos and evidence that Interpol needs to make an arrest. Sergey and the fake buyer go to leave. We figure that if we continue to tail them, we can pick up Sergey and the buyer in one night. They go in separate directions, obviously."

Wallace took a seat, listening as Yousef continued to speak.

"Sergey goes one direction, the buyer the other way. So Sophia makes the call to split up the surveillance team, right? Sophia and I follow the truck, the buyer. We want to get a good ID on him. The Interpol agents with us follow Sergey to make the arrest. We go ahead and, with a local unit, stop the truck. When we search for it, it's empty."

The agent continued taking a seat of his own. "Somehow, they switched the trucks. At this point, we know that we've been had. Sergey, meanwhile, leads the Interpol team into an ambush. We tried to radio them to warn them, but we were too late. All we could hear on the radio were the gunshots and the agents screaming for assistance. By the time we arrived, they were all dead, and Sergey had vanished. No one has seen him since. So yeah, she knows bad decisions. And I would assume that when the suggestion to split the team was made today, it... it may have triggered her." Yousef concluded.

Wallace sat stunned, listening to the story and unsure of what to say. "Shit, man, that's bad," he remarked. There wasn't much else he could say to that. "That wasn't her fault, though."

"I've told her that, and her superiors told her that. Interpol's investigators told her the same thing. She doesn't see it that way. Her op, her responsibility. So, ever since then, she hasn't really been the same. After the investigation was settled, she attempted to return to operations again. But for whatever reason, she's incapable of making on-the-spot decisions. Or folds when something doesn't go according to plan. I guess. There's probably more to it, but I got transferred here shortly after, and we really haven't spoken that much since. They wound up transferring her to an analyst role, perhaps hoping she'd overcome whatever demons were in her head instead of completely ending a promising career. I thought she had overcome them when I saw her back doing field ops."

"I see… I see," Wallace said, stroking the hairs of his beard. "Ok, well, that's good to know. I can work with this, buddy, thanks." The sailor got up, patting Yousef on the shoulder, and opened the door. "I think I know exactly how to help her," he thought out loud. "First, I have got to find out what happened with Ryan's team."

Yousef was taken aback by the sudden change in demeanor and confidence that he could help Sophia. It took a moment for it to dawn on him. Sophia would know who told her secrets. "No. Wait, you can't-"

Yousef ran after him, trying to catch the soldier before he confronted her. But he was out the door in a flash. Yousef didn't want to hurt Sophia's feelings or have her trust in him eroded by divulging her personal information.

But it was already too late. He spotted Sophia coming down a flight of steps ahead of him.

The Arab cringed as Sophia and Wallace passed each other, waiting for the blowup. To his surprise, Wallace didn't say a word; the two nodded in silence at each other as they passed.

"Hey, there you are," Sophia said. "What were you two talking about?"

Relief washed over the agent. "Wha… what?" Yousef asked, watching Wallace disappear into another room.

"Never mind, I don't care. I wanted to check on Tarik's status. Where did they take him?"

Yousef continued to stare past Sophia.

"Yousef, where is Tarik?" she asked again, waving a hand in front of his eyes.

"Um… um, come this way." Yousef snapped out of his fear and led Sophia to a makeshift medical room.

The doctor, a tall, slender Arab, had just finished with Tarik. He was speaking with the two agents posted on guard.

"Doctor, how is he doing? When can I question him?" Sophia asked, walking upon the trio.

The doctor turned, mildly annoyed by the American's hastiness. "He's fine and in stable condition," he said.

"Both shots were through and through. So, all we did was stitch up. Give him about an hour, and he'll be ready. Just take it easy on him, though. I don't want to have to re-stitch the patient," the doctor said accusatorily before departing.

"Well, shit," Sophia said, peering through the door at the arm's dealer on a stretcher. "Come get me in two hours. We'll start the interrogation then, I guess." She looked at Yousef, not allowing him an opportunity to answer before walking off.

"I need some rest," she called down the hall.

****

Several grueling hours later, Sophia and Yousef emerged from the hastily converted interrogation room, dark circles under their eyes. Sophia's hand clasped over her mouth, unable to fight back the yawn she'd been holding for the last thirty minutes.

Night had long given way to daylight as the two entered a small break room. Yousef fumbled with a coffee machine. They both took seats, waiting with bated breath for the machine to finish dispensing. They were both weary and beleaguered from their hours-long interrogating of a very uncooperative subject. Tarik had put up a formidable defense. Yet they were still quite satisfied with the outcome of the conversation with Tarik.

The sleep-deprived agent caught sight of Wallace talking to Ryan in the corner. With a hand on Yousef's shoulder, the two nodded congratulatory at each other as Sophia veered off, making her way to the two SEALs.

She wasn't in the mood for any more talking. Her throat hadn't fully recovered from the beating it had suffered at the hands of Adeel, and now she was parched. However, she did want a progress report on Ryan's mission, which was tailing Hasan after they'd split.

"Ryan, you're back," she said, interrupting his conversation with Wallace. "What happened with Hassan?" Sophia was still unable to make eye contact with Wallace. She would look away every time he looked at her.

Sophia had always been tough on herself, routinely obsessing over the most minor errors. She was a relentless perfectionist. This helped her gain top honors in school and pushed her through The Farm and everything else she put her mind to, something that her father had instilled in her from an early age before he had been killed in action two weeks shy of her thirteenth birthday.

"Accountability," as he would say, "was the measure of a decent human being." Always hold yourself accountable for your actions—a lesson she had really taken to heart over the years since.

Ryan turned to face her; his expression said it all.

"Not good. I'm afraid. Not good at all." He still said it out loud, though.

"You didn't kill him?" Ryan shook his head. "Did you get made? Do they know we're on to them? Ryan shrugged in the negative. "Then why not so good?"

"We lost him," he said glumly. "But I don't think he spotted us. So we should be good on that front."

"I'm confused. You don't believe you were made, so how did you lose him?" Sophia was puzzled how a highly trained SEAL could lose someone in the open desert.

"Simple. They crossed the border into Yemen. I didn't think our mission parameters allowed us to make an incursion into a hostile country with only three men." He checked with Wallace to confirm what he already knew. His superior shook his head.

"Oh, that makes a lot of sense then."

Wallace and Ryan looked at each other, just as confused as Sophia a second earlier.

"Tarik just told us that is where Amell's base of operations is located," she added, feeling the need to explain. "Well, more specifically, an Island off the coast. Perim Island in the Gulf of Aden is where they are."

"Cool, at least we have something to go off," Ryan quipped, happy that the team had managed to get something actionable.

"Ryan, go get something to eat and rest up. I have a feeling we'll be on the move soon," Wallace emphasized with a crick of his head, hinting for him to get out of there.

"Yes, sir," the sailor blurted before shuffling off.

"I should probably try to do the same." Sophia gave an exaggerated yawn, stretching. "Lots to brief Langly and the DOD on later."

She tried to slip away, the awkwardness palpable between the two.

"Did Tarik give up anything else?" Wallace asked curiously. "You guys were in there quite a while."

Sophia stopped to ponder the question, her tiredness delaying the electrical synapse that affected her comprehension.

"I mean, anything my team needs to know?"

According to CIA policy, any and all information that Tarik divulged during the interrogation was highly classified and strictly need-to-know. And Wallace wasn't need-to-know. Something Sophia knew all too well. What the terrorist gave away, willingly, very willingly, wasn't of operational concern to him or his men.

Sophia thought for a second, eventually deciding to violate the policy, either due to exhaustion or a desire to extend an olive branch; she wasn't sure. Pulling the SEAL team leader into a room, she said, "He gave up some interesting information that I have not quite figured out yet."

Curious, the sailor pushed. "Like what?"

"It took a bit to break the man. I assume it was more about making a show of how tough he was than protecting Amell. Because when he did start talking, it was like he wouldn't shut up," she laughed, thinking about the exchange.

But she saw the surprised look on Wallace's face. "I know." She shrugged. "It felt extremely odd."

"Do you think he was lying then?"

"I thought so at first, but then I could see why he rolled over so easily with what he was saying and how he was saying it. I mean, after all, Amell was the reason he got caught after two decades. So, that might have been a bitter pill to swallow. So maybe he started talking out of spite or as a form of revenge."

"So why did he roll over then?"

"He told us that Amell had betrayed the cause, going against the very belief of the jihad, and how he'd become just like the infidels he was fighting against."

"Okay, that's nondescript, but at least we know where to strike next."

"Speaking of, I have to get some rest. I have a call with the DOD in a few hours to brief them on our mission." She headed for the door before Wallace grabbed her arm.

"Look, I want to apologize for yesterday," the sailor said. I shouldn't have yelled at you in front of everyone. That was wrong."

"No… No, you have nothing to apologize for. You were right; I froze out there. And as I said, it will NEVER happen again." Sophia made it very emphatic that she meant it.

"Well, that's good to know. I still wanted to apologize, though. We all have things in our past that are hard to shake."

"What does that mean?" Sophia's voice flared into a high-pitched, offended tone, her eyebrows furrowed. It sounded like he knew something about her.

"Look, don't be mad," he warned, trying to defuse the situation. "But I talked to Yousef. I needed to know if I could trust you in the field."

Sophia's eyes widened, and a warm spike shot up her spine; her nose and lips arched to one side, quivering. Her blood boiled as she stood seething.

"He kind of told me what happened in Belgrade."

"HE DID WHAT!" she screamed, slamming her foot as she stormed towards the door. "I'm going to kill him."

Wallace jumped in front of her, holding her back by the arms. She ripped away.

"Wait… wait," he pleaded. "Just breathe. Don't be mad at him, be mad at me, I asked him. Hell, I practically forced him to tell me. I needed to know that I could trust you to make the right call out there with our lives."

Sophia huffily paced back and forth, trying to calm herself. "And, well, can you trust me then?" She spat. "And speaking of trust," she said, whirling on the sailor. "You should have come to me and asked, not gone behind my back and asked my friend."

"You're right. I should have, but would you have told me the truth?"

The question made Sophia pause. Wallace had a good point—not sure if she would have told him or not. "Well, you still should have come to me," she snapped, regaining her composure after realizing she wouldn't have said anything about Belgrade had he.

"Like I said, though. We all have things in our past that haunt us. You're not the first to make a bad call in the field, and you won't be the last," he said, managing a slight smile. He'd made a few in his past. "No one's perfect. But you can't let one decision define your career. At some point, you have to move past it."

"How do you get past the fact that it costs people their lives? They were my responsibility, and I let them down." Sophia sat, trying to hold back the tears.

"The same way you do from all mistakes. You learn from it. Also, they knew what they signed up for. Shit, we all do. I could tell you the names of every sailor I have lost under my command." Wallace sat next to Sophia on the couch, feeling a little more at ease as he put his hand on her shoulder.

"You can?"

"Of course. Any commander worth his salt could do that. We learn from those mistakes and try never to repeat them. The one thing you have to remember is that nothing ever goes according to plan out here. When something goes wrong, I just think S.H.O.T."

Sophia chuckled, wiping away a tear. "Well, I guess I'm screwed then. I don't drink."

"Not take a shot. It's an acronym I use. It stands for 'Shit Happens Out There.'"

"Oh… ok, that makes more sense," she responded sarcastically.

"You can't control everything, and shit happens. Take it in, learn from it, and move on." The sailor stood. "We get up and get back on that horse. Our country still needs people like us. So we keep going."

"Thanks, Wallace. That is… well, surprisingly insightful for a sailor," she added with a grin.

"I'm going to let that insult go," Wallace said, returning her grin. "You know, SEALs aren't just killing machines. We can be thinkers, too."

She let out a deep sigh. "I know. I didn't mean it that way."

"I know. So we good?" He patted her on the shoulder.

"Yeah, we're good." She stood. "As long as you think you can trust me."

"Then," he said, making a show of thinking hard, rubbing his temples. "I guess we're all good."

The two exchanged a moment of camaraderie. "Then get some rest and get your team ready," Sophia said. "I have a feeling we'll be going to Perim Island very shortly. We still have a terrorist to catch."

CHAPTER FOURTEEN

The night was still, except for the low hum of the outboard motors powering two slate-gray Zodiac Hurricane boats as they traversed the Gulf of Aden.

The water had been abnormally choppy as the boats bounced, hitting the small waves and spraying saltwater into Sophia's face. Being bobbed up and down in a small craft would have made her queasy on any other occasion. However, that was not the case this evening, out in the ocean, far away from any city's barrage of artificial lights.

The stars danced high above in all their opulent radiance, casting an illuminating glow. They felt so close that she could pluck one and put it in her back pocket to keep it if she reached up. For the first time in a while, thoughts of Carol sprang up.

One of their first dates was to the Phoebe Waterman Haas Observatory to watch the stars. Thinking about that night made her smile as she picked out her favorite constellation, Cassiopeia. They had spent the rest of the evening debating the merits of naming a constellation after a defeated dragon rather than the warrior Athena, who had killed it.

Alas, the memory was jarred out of her mind by another splash of salty water. It had been nearly two weeks since they last spoke. Two whole weeks and not once until now had she thought of her. That couldn't be a good thing, and that thought wiped the smile away just as fast as it had come.

Now is not the time for this. We have a mission to accomplish. Sophia reminded herself.

The *mission*. The thought of it snapped the rest of her feelings away. This wasn't going to be an easy one.

Less than four hours ago, she had stood at the head of a room, briefing the eight-man SEAL team and Yousef on what that mission would entail—the capture of one Amell al-Gharsi. After learning that Amell's main base of operations was on the volcanic island of Perim, off the coast of Yemen, from Tarik, there was a scramble to gather as much Intelligence as possible. In just a few short hours, they were given a treasure trove of information to help plan their operation.

Wallace was showing the commandos several satellite photos of the area. He also drew up the incursion plan, picking a small cove on the island's southern side, hidden between the surrounding mountains. They made sure that everyone had input on how to proceed with the mission.

She sat back in awe, watching them plan out everything to the letter. From the incursion point to how long it would take to reach the compound, the best way to snatch and grab and then make their retreat. It was like a professionally choreographed dance.

Their biggest concern was the opposition forces. According to intelligence reports, the island housed around 150 to 200 men. All terrorists, eager to kill Americans.

Why the Department of Defense ordered the team to go in upon learning how outnumbered the small squad was baffled her. She had requested Saudi assistance, but Washington vehemently denied it. She guessed that they wanted this strictly to be a black ops mission. So it was just her ten-person team against two hundred. Or, as Tex put it, the AIA's worst nightmare.

"Tex cut the engine," Wallace whispered.

Sophia was rudely brought to the present. She shook her head and squinted, staring into the darkness, wondering why they were stopping.

Wallace handed her a pair of night-vision binoculars. The world lit up in a green tint as she pressed them to her eyes. In the distance, she could make out a small C-cut bay, mountains rising around it on the other three sides—their landing zone.

"We'll paddle in from here."

"Sure thing, boss. Time to row, row, row our boat, mightily down the stream to merrily, merrily, merrily, kill some terrorists," the Texan sang off-tune before cutting the engine. Wallace signaled for the second Zodiac to follow suit.

"I thought all Texans knew how to sing," Wallace quipped, handing Tex and Gutierrez an oar.

"Hope you at least paddle better," Johns smirked.

"Hey, I'm a great singer," the Texan shot back, snatching the oar. "You should've seen my American Idol audition."

"Yeah, Simon probably said you sing like two horses fucking in a wood chipper," Gutierrez joked. Wallace and Johns shared in the laugh. Tex glowered at them as he began to paddle.

Sophia could only shake her head. This was the team she had to lead into battle to capture Amell.

A rogue wave hit the boat, shuffling the occupants, the coarse fabric of her bulletproof vest chaffed against her neck. She pulled the vest down, hoping it would allow her to breathe more easily.

The island came into view through the darkness. She was suddenly hit with a dark sense of foreboding. She'd felt it when the General ordered the mission, but she tried her best to push the dread and anxiety aside. These were good men, experts, and sailors who knew what they were doing. She had to trust them and herself.

As the island approached, the demons of old inundated her. She was in charge again, leading a strike team into danger. Sophia's heart started to race. The pounding grew stronger with each stroke of the paddle.

Ten minutes later, they were on the island. Wallace jumped from the boat, dragging it to the shore. Tex, Gutierrez, and Johns leaped out, moving to secure the beach as the second craft came ashore, its occupants joining them.

Wallace reached back after securing the boat, helping Sophia down. Not moving, she stared blankly at the Petty Officer, knowing what she was about to lead them into. Her dad's voice in her head said, *Come on, girl, soldier up. America needs you.*

"Sophia?" Wallace whispered, snapping her back. She took his hand as they disembarked the boat. "Hey, we've got this," he added, seeing the paleness of her complexion in the starlight. He winked, then broke off to join his team.

Yousef approached, ducking between the boats. "Hey, come on. Let's go bag us another terrorist," he said as the two CIA agents joined their elite SEAL team squad.

Wallace surveyed the ground ahead, picking out the lowest mountain peak they'd spotted from the satellite photos. Amell's base camp and training grounds lay on the other side of the ridge. The team would have to make a quick ascent to reach it in time to take advantage of the cover of darkness. Turning over his wrist, checking his watch. The others followed suit. Synchronizing their watches.

"Alright, guys," Wallace said.

"Ahem," Sophia pretended to clear her throat, glaring at the Chief.

"Alright, TEAM. We have 3 hours before sunrise, and I would like to be on our way home with our target by then. So, let's get a move on it."

With a wave of his arm, the squadron moved off the small beach.

****

The island was shaped like a crab, with Amell's training camp situated in a bay between what would be the claws on the other side of the eastern mountain range, which protected their landing zone. Despite the obstacle and the fact that neither of the CIA agents had any real climbing experience, they made a great time reaching the base camp in just under two hours.

The team navigated south, descending from the peak, as the bay was protected to the North by the Aden Sea, with mountain ranges protecting its eastern and western flanks. The only other option was coming in from the hilly south side.

The team nestled in at the bottom of one hill while Wallace and Ryan low-crawled to the crest of the dirt hill. The view overlooked the entire camp, providing a perfect vantage point.

Looking down into the depression, they could see nearly the entire layout of the ground. The island had been used as a coal refueling point for ships in the early 1900s, but most of the buildings were in a state of near disrepair.

Instead, the AIA members had resorted to making houses from a mud-brick mixture. Some lived out of tents; others used the more intact houses as dwellings. In the center was a large open field. To the east end, it appeared they had set up a firing range against the mountain. The layout had no actual discernable pattern to it. The soldiers built their houses wherever they could—everything matched the satellite photos.

Wallace drew an overlay photo from his rucksack before sliding back down the hill, rejoining the team.

The camp had a few newer-looking structures. Two metal-framed buildings lay on the outer perimeter of the base. Towards the middle section, a new concrete housing structure was built. Most houses had no signs of electricity except for the main house. Everything else looked as if it were lit by candlelight.

"Boss, I think those are the ammo and weapons depots," Ryan said, pointing out the metal-framed buildings in the picture.

"I think you're right."

"And I take it that larger fucking house is where asshole lays his head at night," Tex questioned, indicating the concrete building in the center of the camp.

"I don't see any guard towers, posts, or anything other than a few roving guards around the perimeter," Ahmed reported, crouch walking back, Walsh behind him. Wallace had sent both sailors ahead to check the perimeter defenses.

"Yeah, I don't think they were planning on anyone crashing in on them." Yousef took the time to throw in a rare sarcastic remark.

"Well, easier for us then. Everyone, listen up, Rye, Tyus, Ahmed, Gut, Johns, you're on me. Tex, you stay up here, call the shots. Walsh, you spot him."

"Damn, it sucks being such a good sniper. I never get to have any up-close fun," Tex complained.

"Well, you have nothing to say about that when counting up your kills. Do you?" Ryan poked at Tex's affinity for keeping track of his kills over the radio.

"Good point, asshole. I wouldn't have so many if you learned to shoot straight, though."

"Shut up, you two," Wallace interjected, regaining control of his team.

"Ahem, so what do Yousef and I do then?" Sophia asked, although she already knew the answer.

"Keep Tex company," Wallace said, smiling, knowing that

was the last thing Sophia wanted to hear. His laugh lines deepened as he saw the young agent's eyes rolling to the back of her head.

"What if something goes wrong down there?" Sophia still had that nagging feeling in the pit of her stomach.

"Well… then come down to the perimeter with Gut and help lay down cover fire for our escape." Was Wallace's nonchalant response. "Ok, everyone got the plan?" He paused, waiting for the team to nod their heads. "Great, we have an hour before sunrise. Let's get in and out quick and be done."

In those words, the infiltrating team made their way up and back down the other side of the hill, leaving the others at the top. Sophia watched nervously as the group crossed a quarter of a mile of flat open ground before reaching the camp's perimeter.

She could see their movement through her night-vision goggles as they surgically moved in tandem through the empty void with nothing to disguise their approach but the darkness. Which only grew as the moon descended behind the mountain peak on the horizon.

"Relax, girl. They got this. We do this all the time." Tex could feel the tension emanating from Sophia as he lay next to her, looking on.

"What? I'm calm," Sophia snapped back, not believing it herself.

"Ha-ha, calm my ass. You're barely breathing. Take a breath, hold it, and watch the fun," Tex drawled, sliding out a toothpick from a plastic container and popping it into his mouth. "Look, if you want something to do, help me."

"Help you do what? And so help me god, one sexual comment and…"

"I would never. Yeah, I would." He took a second to think about it. "But sniping is actually a two-person job. Be my spotter." Sophia looked past the burly bearded Texan, seeing the offended expression on Walsh's face. "What? He can go and cover our six. Take Yousef with you," Tex suggested, to the chagrin of both men.

"You're a real piece of work, man," Walsh groaned, handing over the scope, smacking Tex on the back of the head before sliding down to watch their rear.

"You see a target call out the location and distance to me, but get on the other side." Sophia had taken up a position on the right of Tex. The ejector port side of his MK13 sniper rifle.

Sophia made her way around Tex, first sliding back a few feet before low-crawling back up on the other side. Yousef inched closer, leaning into Tex's ear. "Hey, Hoss. You know she plays for our team, right?"

"What?" Tex blurted, not wholly understanding what Yousef was referring to.

"She likes women," Yousef said bluntly, loud enough for Sophia to hear.

"What, no shit?" Tex exclaimed, looking at Sophia as she returned to his left side. "You're a lesbian?" Obviously, he still didn't entirely believe it. "Holy fuck, you are," he said, reading the answer in her eyes. "Damn, we do have something in common after all," Tex gasped, shocked by the revelation. "I think I just found my new best friend and wing-woman."

Sophia sighed in disbelief at Tex's response. "Why am I not shocked by that? But… I guess I could be your wingwoman," she said hesitantly, not entirely sure what she was getting into. "But I'm *not* wearing a cowboy hat or doing any line dancing," she said emphatically.

Tex's mouth creased, barely able to contain his laughter long enough to say what he'd cooked up. "How about ass-less chaps?" His toothpick slid out of his mouth, catching it just in time. Sophia huffed in disgust.

Wallace triggered his throat mic, drawing their attention back to the mission. "Switching to open comms, Alpha one in position Alpha four; how are we looking?"

Tex and Sophia looked through their night vision. "All clear, boss." Tex gave the team the green light to move in.

"WAIT. Tex, two o'clock on the roof," Sophia shrieked.

"Shit," Tex quickly shifted positions, catching a guard coming around the edge of a building and zipping up his pants. He fired one shot, and the man fell. "Phew, good call. Alpha one, you're all clear tango down." The sailor gave Sophia a wide-eyed look. The Texan was unsure how he could've missed the patrol guard.

"Are *you sure* this time?" Wallace grumbled through the mic, dripping with anger.

Had that soldier spotted the team before they even entered the training camp, the mission would have been over in a flash. Outnumbered twenty to one, they couldn't afford the slightest mistake.

Tex pressed the scope to his eye once more, conducting a sweep of the area. Still no movement aside from the dancing licks of flames from a barrel fire. He glanced over at Sophia, who had also finished a sweep of the shantytown. She nodded in the affirmative. "Yeah, we're sure. Proceed."

Given the all-clear again. The incursion unit pressed forward, moving towards the center house. Midway, the team abruptly paused at a crossroads. Sophia looked on, bewildered.

"Wallace, why did you stop? The house is just a hundred yards ahead."

She watched as they changed course, cutting right instead of continuing straight.

"Wallace, where are you going?" she growled. "Get back on mission." The sinking pit in her stomach returned. Was the mission already going off the rails? "Tex, where is he going?" she whispered.

The sniper quickly surveyed the map of the camp. "I think they're headed for the ammo depots," he answered. However, he seemed unsure of his answer.

"Wallace, where are you going? You need to get to the house. That's an order," Sophia commanded. With each passing second of non-answer, her blood boiled. Wallace was disobeying a direct order.

"Don't worry," the commando replied, annoyance embedded in his tone. "I've got an idea, and we've got the time." He checked his watch; they still had thirty minutes before sunrise.

"For what?"

"I want to take a peek inside their ammo depot. See what they have. We've got some explosives with us. We can cripple their supplies," Wallace explained. "And possibly provide a distraction to cover our exfil."

Sophia grumbled; this wasn't part of the plan. But after taking a second to think about it, she knew that Wallace was right. Just because they took Amell off the board didn't mean someone else wouldn't take his place. They had already taken out their weapons supplier, and now they could take out whatever weapons they already had—effectively crippling the entire AIA once and for all.

"Ok, but make it quick and get back on mission," hissed the CIA agent. "We're running out of darkness," she added.

"Yes, Mom," Wallace responded, drawing a little chuckle from Tex.

Sophia glared at him. "Oh, shut up, Chuckles," she spat, returning to her goggles and watching the sailors surgically make their way through the terrorist's village.

Wallace's team continued to the ammo storage depot. Reaching the front door, Wallace ordered Johns to pick up the lock. Then, with Sophia watching from the hill, the team entered the building, and they were gone from her sight.

****

Inside, they fanned out across the floor, securing the area for any hostiles. Seeing no one in sight, they began inspecting the equipment crates sprawled out across the storage room.

"Boss, come here, look at this." Ryan waved Wallace over as he shone his flashlight down into a crate.

"Shit, that's enough C4 to level a city block," Tyus added, checking a crate of his own.

"What the fuck?" Wallace questioned, pulling an M4 rifle from the crate Ryan had pointed out. "This is American. How in the actual fuck do they have American guns?"

"Got some over here, Chief." Wallace whirled around to see Ahmed holding up a claymore mine. "And they got some .50-caliber sniper rifles, too." He thumbed to a crate behind him.

"Boss, this is enough munitions to equip a sizable army." Where the fuck did they get all this stuff?" Tyus looked around the room, mouth agape at the mass amount of weapons and ammo stored there.

"Good question, Tyus," Wallace responded, lowering his flashlight to the side of the crate, coming across a company logo.

He had seen the symbol before but couldn't quite place it. However, it was definitely familiar.

"Guys, we're on a clock here. Let's just plant the explosives and get moving. Especially before our handler loses her shit," Gutierrez reminded the team.

The others exchanged looks with Wallace. "You heard 'em. Plant 'em, and let's get moving."

****

Sophia nervously wiggled her feet, watching the storage building, waiting for any sign of the commandos. As time slowed to a crawl, she grew increasingly impatient with every passing minute. That horrible feeling that something bad was about to happen punched into her gut. Each blow grew harder until it felt like a battering ram churning her insides.

"Something is wrong. Maybe there was a guard inside, and they got discovered. I'm going down there." She tried to stand but got yanked back down, face-planting into the dirt.

"No, you're staying put," Tex snapped at her for the first time. His usually cheerful manner was gone, replaced with a more pointed and direct tone. "If something went wrong, we would have heard about it by now. Either gunfire or over the radio. So keep your ass here with me."

Spitting sand crystals, Sophia picked her face out of the dirt in a state of shock and couldn't believe what had just happened. Had he really just done that? Choosing to ignore her anger for the sake of the mission, she figured he wouldn't have done something that drastic for no reason. "Well, they are in a metal box, right?" she commented, choosing to move on from what had just happened. "What if the radios don't work in there?"

"We would've still heard gunfire, or they would have sent a signal or something." Sophia did bring up a good point about not having a radio signal, but Tex felt it would be best not to play into her fears. So, instead, he reassured her that everything would be fine.

Several silent but nerve-racking minutes passed with no word or signal from Wallace's team. Suddenly, the sailors burst from the front door of the building. Wallace flashed a thumbs up in their direction. "We're all clear here. Sorry, we lost communication inside. Explosives are set. Resuming course to the target building."

Sophia, relieved to see the team, let out a huge sigh. "Good, stay on track this time. You need to move." She checked her watch. They had fifteen minutes before sunrise. They were cutting it extremely close.

"Roger that, moving."

Using the buildings for cover, the team moved stealthily through the camp. Most of the AIA forces were fast asleep in their bunks, blissfully unaware that a SEAL team had located their base of operations and was moving closer to capture their leader.

"Alpha one, stop. Two tangoes to your left, approaching in between the buildings. " I don't have a shot," Tex warned, seeing the two perimeter guards flash through his scope for a second before they walked out of sight behind the building.

Sophia's heart stopped, and she clenched her teeth, fearing what could happen.

Wallace threw up a closed fist, signaling the team to stop moving. They stopped completely in single file and pressed up against the house they were passing, waiting quietly for the two guards to cross their path. One wrong move would compromise the entire operation, and they would most certainly not make it out alive.

He could hear the two men talking, and the smell of a cigarette had perforated the area. Wallace shot Ahmed, who was standing behind him, a look. That was all the SEAL needed to know. He slid out a K-bar knife, gleefully unsheathing it. Wallace produced one of his own. The two sailors readied themselves to pounce.

The two men came into full view of Wallace, who was still pressed up against the wall. Continuing their conversation, they walked right past the team, not knowing their death warrant had just been signed.

The two sailors pounced from the wall, K-bars in hand. Wallace was on top of his man in two steps, his left hand clasped around the guard's mouth. He drove his K-bar through the back of his neck. The knife pierced straight through, puncturing the terrorist's trachea.

The guard tried to scream, but all that came out was a gurgle as his body shivered one final time, the blade severing his spinal cord at the neck. Warmblood oozed over Wallace's hand as he eased the dead man's body to the ground, pulling his knife out and wiping it on his pants.

Sheathing his knife, he glanced at Ahmed, who had just done the same. The two synchronized their strike perfectly. Ryan and Gutierrez swept in, dragging the bodies out of sight.

"Tango's down, moving," Wallace reported.

Sophia could finally breathe again.

Another obstacle was thwarted by the quick reactions of the highly trained SEAL team. They continued to inch closer to the target house.

Sophia could finally feel more at ease with the operation and that her gut feeling was wrong. But simultaneously, she didn't want to tempt the fates. The team had still not captured Amell, and on top of that, they still had to get out with him.

"Alpha four, Alpha team has reached the target house. About to enter," Wallace radioed as they reached the front door.

"Remember, alive if possible. If not, kill and confirm," Sophia reminded the team of their orders one last time.

"Roger that." Wallace and the team slipped out of view once more.

****

The house was a single-story building; the interior lacked all the usual comforts of a traditional home. Instead, the living room had two rows of six cots on either side of it. Three guards were still fast asleep in their beds—one snoring like a freight train, something the others must have grown accustomed to, as the occasional loud snort did not seem to affect them.

These were likely Amell's private guards. Soft Arabic music played on the radio in the kitchen. One half-awake guard sat playing a card game by himself. His head nodded, slipping off his hand every few seconds, jolting him awake briefly before his eyelids closed again. The entire house smelled of hookah smoke, which undoubtedly masked the musk of a dozen men living in a small room who had not showered for days.

Quietly, the SEALs moved in, creeping around the edges, keeping out of the low light of the lanterns placed around the living quarters. They lurked in the shadows like a pack of hyenas waiting to strike their prey.

Ryan, Ahmed, and Johns took up positions over the sleeping men. Gutierrez inched closer to the unsuspecting, drowsy card player. Tyus stayed back, watching the front door. Wallace held up three fingers to count down like a band conductor.

Three... two... one.

On one, the sailors struck in a coordinated attack with their K-bars. Ahmed, Ryan, and Johns drove their blades into the ears of the sleeping men. Blood oozed out, dripping on the dirt-covered concrete floor and pooling around the dead bodies.

Gutierrez ran his knife across the cardman's neck, spraying bright red blood across the kitchen, spattering on the front of a lantern, casting a dim red tint over the room. It was the last time the man's eyes would close.

The sailors stacked back up on Wallace. "Tyus, stay here. Watch the door," Wallace ordered. The medic flashed a thumbs up. "The rest on me."

Ryan, Ahmed, Johns, and Gutierrez followed their leader down the tight hallway to the bedrooms. Passing a door on his left and one on his right. Ryan and Ahmed broke off to clear each room before converging on Wallace and Gutierrez, who were waiting outside the master bedroom.

Ryan brought up the rear, squeezing Ahmed's shoulder. Feeling the pressure, Ahmed knew his companion was in position. The Arab squeezed Gutierrez's shoulder, who repeated the signal on the Chief's right shoulder. The team was ready.

Wallace slowly tried the doorknob, turning it ever so slightly until it reached a stopping point. The door was locked. "We're breaching," the leader whispered, taking two steps back.

CHAPTER FIFTEEN

Everyone braced for the moment. The entire operation depended on their ability to snatch Amell without raising any alarm. If he was alone behind the door, and Wallace was quick enough, they could corral the terrorist leader quickly and still have a chance of escaping alive with their prized target.

However, if the slime ball slept with guards watching over him or any female companion who might scream upon sight of a bunch of strange men in military gear, it could get ugly expeditiously.

Wallace drew his leg back. The team collectively drew deep breaths, readying for whatever came next.

The Chief launched forward, driving his leg into the wooden door and delivering a hefty kick. It splintered from the door frame in a loud crack, flying open. Wood chips flew in every direction.

Wallace burst into the room, rifle darting side to side, looking for targets other than the one in the bed. The others followed closely behind.

A startled Amell shot up, eyes wide with a mix of terror and surprise. The terrorist's leader lunged for his AK. Wallace, snapping into action, sprang forward.

His face lit on fire before Amell's hand could clasp around its barrel. A burning swath of pain radiated from his cheek across his face like ripples through a lake. Warm, oozing blood gushed from his freshly broken nose. Wallace had delivered a savage blow with the butt of his M4A1 carbine, striking him across the face. He was about to scream out in pain, but Ryan's hand clamped across his mouth.

Ryan shrieked, ripping his hand away. "Shit, the fucker bit me." He snatched a nearby pillow and pushed it against Amell's face with one hand. "Can you believe this fucker?" he spat, checking the bite wound. Two semicircular teeth marks were imprinted on the side of his palm.

"I think you're gonna need a tetanus or rabies shot, bro," Gut joked.

"Just secure the prisoner," Wallace snapped.

Amell thrashed around the bed as his attackers converged on

him. Restraining his movements, Ahmed removed the zip ties from his back pocket and tied Amell's hands and feet. Removing the pillow, Wallace jammed a gag into his mouth. He then slapped Amell across the face several times to get his attention.

"Listen here, shit bag," Wallace said, jamming his finger in the terrorist's face. "We're taking you to face justice one way or another. You copy that?" Wallace stared unwaveringly into Amell's eyes, showing he meant every word he said.

Amell intensely stared back. His eyes were black as coal, and his irises lit with intense fury, anger, and rage. Wallace knew he wasn't going to go easy, though.

The tense staring match was interrupted by Tyus's voice on the radio. "Boss, we've got movement. We need to go."

"Shit. On the move. Get him up." Wallace signaled for Ryan and Ahmed to pick up Amell. They headed back to the living room.

As they exited the hallway into the living room, the front door opened, and a man stumbled into the threshold. His eyes, looking down intently, focused on where he was, planting one foot in front of the next. Not registering, a band of Americans was in the house, their leader slung over one of their shoulders.

Everyone paused. Stuck in a state of stasis. The man slowly raised his head, sensing something was amiss. He locked eyes with Wallace. The two men gazed at each other briefly as recognition stretched across the man's face before he could react. Tyus had been hunkered down on the other side of the door, waiting for the man to take another step. When he did, trying to unsling his rifle, the commando leaped out, driving his knife under the guard's chin and jabbing back out the top of his head. His body fell forward, lifeless, only to reveal a second guard standing behind him.

He, too, looked as if he suffered from the same affliction as his now-deceased buddy—a night of smoking opium. The man's clothes reeked of the drug. It was practically wafting off of him in a cloud, like Linus from The Peanuts.

He stumbled forward, seemingly unaware that his friend's corpse was only a few feet ahead of him and that he'd soon be joining him.

189

Wallace let three rounds lose from a silenced M4A1, striking center mass and blowing a hole through his back. The force from the bullets staggered the terrorists. He fell backward and out of the house.

Tyus sprang from the house to retrieve the second body, pulling him back into the dwelling, spinning to see the dead man's AK still lying in the dirt.

"Shit, his gun," Tyus went to retrieve the rifle.

****

Tex watched the body of a terrorist stumble backward, collapsing to the ground through his scope. "Well, that's one dead one-hundred-ninety-nine more to go," he chided, chuckling at Sophia's nausea.

"Is there a certain body count for you guys where you just become desensitized to all the death?" she asked, genuinely wondering. She hadn't killed many people. In fact, she had only dropped three bodies in all her years of service, but she would occasionally see their faces in her sleep. She knew their names and almost everything else about their lives, which she had prematurely shortened.

Tex thought about the question for a second. There probably was one, but he didn't remember when the emotion of killing subsided. To him, this was his job. Sure, the first few were hard. He even threw up after his first kill. But now, it had almost scarily become second nature for him.

"Hey, I look at it this way. It's either them or me. And it sure as hell isn't going to be me." He surmised, between chews on his toothpick.

Sophia regarded him for a moment, unsure whether to feel sad for him or happy he didn't have to suffer the same feelings she did.

"Hold up," he said, turning their attention back to the house and seeing Tyus drag back the dead man. "The gun, you fucking idiot," he rasped as his teammate could hear him. Something else caught his eye, too, though. Two soldiers were approaching when he saw Tyus re-enter the street. "Get back," he yelped into the radio.

****

The urgency in the sniper's voice put Tyus's senses on high alert. He checked his surroundings and saw the two perimeter guards pass at the end of the small block. He dove back into the house, kicking the door closed behind him. Johns helped him to his feet. "Can't go that way," he snapped to the team inside.

"Good job looking out for us, man," he thanked Tex.

"Ok, back to the bedroom out the window," Wallace ordered the team.

"Alpha One, everything ok in there?" Sophia and Tex stared intensively as the two soldiers continued their roving pattern. Apparently, they had not seen Tyus.

"We're good. We have bingo, looking for an alternative route back," Wallace answered, racing to the back of the house. "The main entrance is cut off by a guard patrol. Is the other side clear?"

"Fuck," Tex spat, shifting positions, unable to get a clear view. They were on the wrong side of the compound to see the backside of the house from their vantage point. "Fuck, can't tell from here, sorry, chief," Tex responded.

Back in Amell's room, Johns slammed the door shut behind them. He and Gut slid a dresser in front of the door. "What do we do, Chief?" Ryan asked.

Wallace surveyed their surroundings, thinking. He couldn't see any other alternative route. "Ok, we go out the back," he ordered.

He remembered the camp layout from the aerial photos. The house was situated against a dune, creating an alley between the sand and the home. The team would have to traverse the alley and use the buildings as cover to return to their insertion point.

Johns took point smashing out the back window with the butt of his rifle, hoping to clear the small pathway. "Clear," he called back to the others.

Wallace and Gutierrez exited next, securing the rear of the

alley. Ahmed, fourth up, began to climb through the window. He was halfway out when Amell sensed an opportunity. As none of the soldiers had kept an eye on him, he decided to strike.

He kicked Ahmed out the window, then spun around, delivering a head-butt to Ryan, who was trying to re-secure him. Knocking the soldier back, he created enough room for himself to make a break for the door. He broke before Tyus could react. But Ryan caught himself before falling, managing to jab out his foot in time to catch Amell mid-stride.

The terrorist fell forward with his hands bound. He couldn't brace himself. He smacked headfirst against the concrete floor. The only thing breaking his fall was the thick, no doubt overpriced, stolen rug.

Hearing the commotion from outside, Wallace poked his head back through the window. "Rye, you guys ok?" he asked as Gutierrez picked up Ahmed, dusting him off.

Rubbing his forehead, Ryan said, "First, the son of a bitch bites me; now he head butts me. Is he a warrior or a fucking five-year-old?" He tried to calm himself, pacing back and forth around the room.

"Just check on him." Wallace noticed that Amell was still lying face-first on the ground.

Ryan stood over Amell and kicked him. He didn't move. So the sailor bent over to check for a sign of life, praying that he had died from a brain aneurysm from the blow.

"Son of a bitch," he complained, unfortunately finding a pulse much to his displeasure. "Bastard's out cold," he reported.

"Good, that'll make him easier to move. Get him out here. Alpha four, this is Alpha one. We had a bit of a delay, but we're on the move now."

"What about the package?" Asked Sophia.

A thud like a sack of potatoes hitting the floor caused Wallace to glance over his shoulder. Amell's unconscious body was lying face down in the dirt. Ryan leaned out the window and shrugged. "Package is currently unconscious," he reported.

"What the fuck?" Sofia barked.

"Sorry, he slipped." Ryan feigned an apology.

Wallace lifted the terrorist leader over his shoulder, then moved out. Using the structures for cover, they bounded from building to building in two-person teams. Ryan and Gutierrez cleared the gaps first, followed by Wallace carrying Amell, with Johns providing security, and then Ahmed and Tyus brought up their six.

Sophia watched from the ridge line as they moved in and out of sight between the buildings. With each gap they cleared, the sinking feeling of dread dissipated, giving way to an anticipation of joy.

They were about to accomplish an out-of-this-world feat of Special Operations brilliance–sneaking in and out of a terrorist camp and extracting their leader without being seen.

She allowed a second of happiness to overcome her stoic face, letting loose a slight smirk as she nudged Tex's shoulder. Together, they watched the team leapfrog buildings.

****

Down in the compound, the team reached the second last set of buildings before the final quarter-mile stretch of empty ground. After that, the ridge, and on the other side, they'd be practically home free.

Ryan and Gutierrez went first, crossing to the last set of protective buildings. They stopped, finding suitable ground to turn and lay down cover fire for the next pair. Spinning and kneeling, they surveyed the area for movement. Seeing none, they motioned for the next two. Wallace and Johns were up next. Wallace readied Amell onto his shoulder again, preparing for the twenty-yard dash. Seeing the all-clear signaling, they moved out, breaking into a light jog into the open expanse.

Amell stirred awake, realizing he was being spirited away in the middle of darkness. He wasn't going to make it easy on his capturers, though. He began thrashing like a fish out of water, trying to wiggle free.

Wallace, mid-stride, wholly unprepared for the sudden flurry of motion, lost his grip on his passenger, causing him to drop to the ground.

"Shit." The sailor stopped and tried to resecure Amell, who was now fast crawling in the dirt, trying to escape.

Wallace grabbed him, rolling him over, but the Arab lashed out with his bound fists. Wallace just managed to dodge the blow, delivering one of his own, knocking him out again.

Sophia watched through the night vision, eyes wide as saucers, as Wallace struggled with Amell. Once he had secured the target again, she let out a sigh of relief.

"Phew, dodged that one," she exclaimed, wiping fake sweat from her brow.

No sooner than she muttered the words, a bright muzzle flash lit the corner of a rooftop. It was followed by the crack of displaced air, which cut through the silence. All Sophia could do was look down in horror as her worst fear was becoming realized.

The dirt around Wallace erupted into several dozen geysers, cascading earth all around as bullets hammered the ground. The SEAL leader threw his body over the unconscious Amell. After what it took to capture the terrorist, he was going to take him out alive, even if it meant sacrificing himself to do it.

Johns pivoted at the whip-cracking sound of hot lead rocketing past his head. "Alpha one taking fire," he shouted, unleashing a barrage toward the muzzle flashes.

"Goddammit," Tex spat.

"Move," he pushed Sophia aside. He shifted positions, peering down his scope. Centering the crosshairs on the gunman's forehead. "Fuck you!" The sniper squeezed the trigger of his MK13 rifle. A millisecond later, the shooter's head was reduced to a spray of pink mist. "Shooter down, shooter down."

It was already too late; their presence was no longer a secret. Shouts and yells rose from all over the camp. Two men sprinted out of the building to Johns' left, AKs drawn, searching for enemies.

"Alpha eight, tangos on your left," Ryan warned. Johns dropped to the ground, opening a clear shot for Ryan. Who fired his M4A1, spitting out two three-round bursts. Both gunners fell face-first.

"Move, move, move," Wallace ordered, scooping Amell up and hoisting him over his shoulder again, making a mad dash for the safety of the building cover, where Ryan and Gutierrez were laying down cover fire. "Tex, Walsh, provide cover."

****

Walsh sprinted to the top of the ridge, and Yousef followed behind. "Cover the left; I've got the right," Tex barked, aiming for another terrorist racing to the edge of the building where his buddy had been standing. Another shot eliminated the threat before he could fire.

Sophia covered her ears.

From their elevated vantage point, Walsh surveyed the battlefield. The once-quiet, sleepy shantytown now buzzed like a beehive. Men were pouring out of every nook and cranny, scrambling about in a chaotic jumble, half asleep and half unsure of where to go. It was clear these weren't terrorists of the highly-trained ilk.

"Chief, you've gotta get out of there." Tex lined up another target.

"No shit," Wallace barked back, recovering the unconscious Amell. Slinging him back over his shoulder, he continued. "Ahmed, Tyus, get a move on it." They reached the next set of buildings safely. Johns scrambled around the corner seconds later, ducking as rounds blasted away at the façade of the building, causing Ryan to jerk back before losing the side of his face.

The two remaining sailors sprang from their cover, sprinting into the gap separating the last two rows of houses. Before they could reach the other side, they were spotted by three men who had just exited one of the mud-brick dwellings, launching a fusillade at the SEALS. 7.62mm rounds pounded the ground, chasing after the duo, zeroing in on their targets.

Ryan and Gutierrez opened a series of blasts, covering their buddies as they ran, killing all three enemies. "Let's go!" The two waved them on.

****

A clatter of gunfire erupted from an adjacent rooftop. Walsh spotted the threat and aimed. The man's head exploded. His headless body lurched forward, tumbling over the low wall. "Four." He held up four fingers at Tex, announcing his kill count.

****

The two SEALS reached the last building, breathing heavily and reconnecting with the rest of the team and their passenger. However, unfortunately for them, they were still not out of danger yet. There was one last hurdle to overcome. A stretch of 300 yards of flat, open ground before the ridge with no cover. And they would be pursued by an entire camp of angry terrorists.

Each man looked at the other as if they were silently saying their final goodbyes, hearing the roar and battle cries of their enemies as they approached. "Remember, men, the only easy day was yesterday." The commander drew a crooked smirk. It was the Navy SEAL motto and a call to arms.

"Hooyah," the unit responded in unison.

They broke off into a dead sprint. Wallace led the way, with Amell still slung over his shoulder. After twenty yards, Ryan and the others spun, dropping to a knee in a straight line, spaced out several yards, building a wall of cover fire.

Tex and Walsh were picking off targets from the hill three football fields away. The unit laid down cover fire in a tactical withdrawal, allowing their leader to make his mad dash to safety.

Sprinting towards the ridge, Wallace could hear the whistle and crack of bullets zinging by his head. The AIA wasn't about to allow their leader to be whisked away so easily. Racing forward, his legs began to wear, trudging along the denser dirt track, tiring from the extra weight on his shoulders, but he was trained for this.

He flashed back to BUD/S training, lifting and holding a boat over his head for hours as the waves of the Pacific Ocean pounded against his exhausted body. If he could make it through the SEALS' intense training program, he would undoubtedly make it through this.

****

AIA forces continued descending on the defensive line and the rest of Wallace's squad. The SEALS plucked out the closest and most pressing threats, trying to suppress their advance as a hailstorm of lead rained upon them.

"We need to move," Ryan yelled, firing several bursts into the crowd of encroaching AIA, which felled two and scattered the rest. "Tactical withdraw, men," he ordered.

Meanwhile, the terrorists, using their inaccurate AKs, tried in vain to strike any of the SEALs. However, it would only be a matter of time before one lucky jihadist found pay dirt.

"Go," Gutierrez shouted back.

"Moving." Ryan fired another volley, then jumped to his feet, dashing back several yards behind the firing line. Find a suitable position, spin, drop to a knee, draw his weapon again, and fire several more rounds.

"Set," he screamed.

Tyus followed suit. Then Ahmed, followed by Gutierrez, and finally Johns. They moved back in with almost perfect surgical precision. First, one sailor tactically withdrew several yards while the others provided cover fire. Then, the next would be on the move.

The team was making headway back to the ridgeline. Tex and Walsh still provided overwatch support. The SEAL team followed this maneuver to the T. All the while, Wallace was absconding with their prize.

****

"Sophia, Yousef, get down there and help cover them," Tex ordered between shots. "Ten, eleven," he continued, counting his kills.

Without hesitation, Sophia and Yousef slid down the hill, moving a few yards into the open clearing and spreading out so they wouldn't accidentally shoot one of their own.

Sophia watched Wallace draw closer, waving him on between semi-automatic bursts, urging him to run faster. AK rounds sizzled past, burrowing into the mound of earth behind her. One round struck mere centimeters from the running SEAL. She felt a gasp escape her throat, her heart leaping up to take its place. To her astonishment, he was going to make it, which meant they still had a chance to escape with Amell.

****

Wallace rushed past Sophia a few seconds later, trying to get up the hill. His feet slipped, the loose dirt robbing him of his traction.

"I'm going to go get him," Tex shouted across to Walsh, laying down his rifle. He reached out to grab Wallace's hand while still holding Amell. The burly Texan helped pull his leader up the last few feet of the hill. The three rolled down the backside, tumbling over each other.

Laying still for a few seconds, catching his breath, Wallace sat up, hearing the continuous clatter of automatic machine gunfire. "Tex, how about you prep a gift for our friends?" the leader wheezed, getting to his feet and dusting himself off. "Oh, and watch, asshole." He pointed to the still-unconscious terrorist leader.

"Gotcha, boss," Tex ran over to their pile of packs lying on the ground, rummaging for a particular one. A smile creased across his face. "Oh yeah."

****

"Come on," Sophia urged as Ryan was the first of the team to reach her, spinning and now laying down fire for the others.

"Yousef, Sophia, get your asses up the hill," Wallace called down, taking up Tex's rifle. "Ry, I think it's time for fireworks."

Sophia turned and started up the hill, slipping back several inches before recovering and trying to scale up again. But the dirt beneath her kept giving away. Wallace abandoned the sniper rifle, reaching out to help pull her to safety, and stretched to take her hand.

The mound exploded inches above her fingers; she shrieked as a round burrowed into the hill. Wallace snatched his hand back. Sophia slid helplessly back a few inches, covering her face, feet digging to stop her descent.

Someone had her nearly zeroed in. "Walsh," Wallace snapped, drawing the sniper's attention.

The sailor pivoted, tracing the trajectory back. Through the lens of his enhanced vision, the attacker had just finished reloading. They fired simultaneously. Walsh was a microsecond faster, blowing a gory hole through his chest.

But the AIA soldier had also struck his prey.

****

An intense searing pain engulfed Sophia's right upper arm as her skin ripped apart and dirt particles showered her face.

The bullet nearly missed the bulk of her arm, just grazing her. But having never been shot before, the pain was still immense.

"Fuck. I'm coming. Ryan, keep covering us," Wallace bellowed. The rest of the unit had reached the hill. The group reformed the defensive wall as Wallace slid back down. "Are you ok?" he and Yousef asked simultaneously. The CIA agent raced over the moment he saw his friend shot.

"Yeah, I think so. I've never been shot before." Sophia's eyes were filled with pain, and she felt the hot blood seeping through her fingers.

Wallace grabbed her arm and examined it. "Just a graze; you'll live."

"Thanks, Doctor. Your bedside manner is impeccable," Sophia snapped back through clenched teeth.

"Come on. We've got to get on the other side." Wallace pulled Sophia to her feet. "We're moving."

He ascended the hill with the others, sliding down the other side as rounds zipped over their heads. Walsh was doing all he could to cover their ascent. "Ry, fireworks, dammit," Wallace ordered again.

Ryan rolled over, pulling a detonator from his vest pocket. "I suggest everyone cover their ears." The team buried their faces in the dirt. Wallace grabbed Sophia, pushing her head down. Ryan flipped open a clear plastic lid with a small red button, pausing for a second. "Boom time, assholes!" He pressed the button.

The explosives they had set earlier in the ammo depot went off. A loud explosion echoed through the air as the top of the metal building blew off, sending a massive cloud of debris flying out.

The blast wave swept through the bay. Flames roiled over the nearest soldiers, burning them to a crisp. The concussive blast and shrapnel killed any AIA man, unfortunate enough to still be in the shock wave zone. The others were swept off their feet.

Wallace, the first to recover, looked over at Tex, who was keeping a close eye on their prize. "All set?"

"Set." Tex flashed a thumbs-up.

"Alright, everyone, grab your shit. Let's go. Ryan, pick up the shit bag," ordered Wallace stepping over the still-unconscious terrorist leader. Ryan hefted him off the ground, then threw him over his shoulder.

Capturing Amell had proven to be the easiest task on the mission. Now, the team would face the perilous task of escaping the island while being pursued by whatever forces remained.

Recovering their equipment, the team regrouped and headed away from the camp. Marching off, in the background, sounds of secondary explosions rocked the landscape, along with the echo of ammo shells being superheated, cooking off firing indiscriminately. As the sun broke the horizon, a massive black cloud rose over the hill.

CHAPTER SIXTEEN

The ammo depot explosion would only give the team a slight head start, so they had to move fast. Wallace, knowing this, shifted course away from the mountain range they had come over, leading back to their Zodiacs parked in the adjacent bay.

They set the course, moving inland.

"Wallace, we're going in the wrong direction. The boats are over there." Sophia announced, realizing they were headed in the opposite direction.

"I know, but we can't use the boats to escape now. We would never make it a safe distance before they caught up to us. Once we boarded those boats, we would be sitting ducks. So we're moving to extraction point bravo. Get on that sat phone, and call whoever the fuck you need to get authorization to have the Saudi Airforce send us a couple of Blackhawks to evac the team."

Sophia and Yousef exchanged looks. The mission was supposed to be covert. Langley and the DOD didn't want the Saudis to be aware they had a Special Forces team operating in their area. Calling for assistance would create a political schism between the two countries, further exacerbating their already fragile alignment.

"I don't know if they'll go for it," Sophia pronounced.

Wallace whirled on her. "If you don't, there will be ten dead American citizens on foreign soil. And that piece of shit," he said, pointing to the lump slung over Ryan's shoulders. "Will be free to reign unholy terror on our country. Tell them that," the sailor snapped.

Sophia recoiled, eyes engorged, seeing the fury behind Wallace's eyes. "Rog… roger that-"

A second loud explosion boomed. This one was much closer than the encampment, though.

Tex threw his head back in laughter, breaking the tension. "Guess they found my present."

Wallace had ordered Tex to set up a trap for the AIA as they came over the ridge. So Tex had placed two claymore mines on either side of the hill's lip, connected by a string. The first group of soldiers that made it over the top triggered the mines.

****

Fifteen minutes later, Wallace returned the Sat phone to Sophia, stopping the team. He slid out a map. Plotting their location on the map, he traced a direct line to a point in the island's center.

"Ryan, on me." Wallace motioned for his second. Ryan unceremoniously dropped Amell, moving to the front of the line. Sophia also converged on the team leader. "Ok, we're moving two clicks to this location." He pointed to a particular spot on the map. There were several rundown structures located around what appeared to be a runway. "It's an abandoned airstrip, but there are some areas where we can hold up until they arrive. It should be somewhat defensible. We just need to last long enough for the Saudis rescue unit to arrive."

"Roger that, Chief."

"Tell the others." Ryan quickly ran down the line, giving each sailor the information. "Sorry about the outburst earlier," he apologized to Sophia.

"Don't worry about it. I'm a big girl," she said, smiling.

****

The team reached the edge of another ridge that sloped down into a vast valley. A half-finished airport lay in its middle. The runway and the surrounding buildings looked incomplete. There were signs of a large-scale battle. Bomb holes dotted the runway; bullet holes littered the buildings. The largest structures appeared to be some sort of house or possibly barracks, although only the walls remained standing. Even those had sustained heavy damage as there were massive gaps in their façades. The roof had almost completely caved in, no doubt the work of a bomb.

Some ten years before, Sophia and her team had landed on the island. There were plans to use it for a bridge linking Yemen to Djibouti. Survey teams had been dispatched to the island. They began preparing for the project by building the airport. Then, its construction was halted abruptly, and no official reason was given.

Over the years since then, several battles have been fought between Yemeni and Saudi forces on the island. They were now looking directly at the destruction those battles had wrought.

The team slid down into the valley one by one, setting course for the destroyed airport. In the distance, they could hear the screams and shouts from the AIA forces. They were closing in faster than Wallace had thought.

"Over there." Wallace pointed at the house with the blown-out roof. "That's where we'll hold up and make our stand."

Rushing towards the entrance, Wallace kicked down what remained of the door. There was blast debris everywhere, scorch marks on the remaining walls, several overturned cots, and the remains of the unfortunate souls that were inside when the bomb dropped. In the middle of the room, a large crater had been carved out from the explosion, about four feet deep; it must have been the living room.

To the right, half of the main wall had been blown out, revealing a kitchen. A short hallway leading to a bedroom was on the other side of the room. With the front wall primarily intact and the building's layout, it would provide the team with a perfect line of sight at the ridge and sufficient cover.

Formulating his battle plan, Wallace pointed at Sophia and Yousef, motioning them to move into the crater. "You two down there. Ryan, please put the shit bag down there too."

"Sure thing, boss."

The sailor turned to the hole, letting go of Amell.

The fall jarred the terrorist leader awake. Yousef dropped into the hole without protest, putting his gun to Amell's groggy head.

"I'm not going down there. I'm staying up here and fighting with you." Sophia's face and demeanor made it clear that she wanted to stay topside to fight.

"Goddammit, how did I know you were going to give me shit? Just get the fuck down there. Please."

"No. You'll need all the guns you can get up here." Sophia knew the odds were stacked against the elite but small team. Every gun would count.

"Maybe so, but if by some stroke of fucking luck, we do get out of this. I need you alive to get the shit bag back home to face justice."

Sophia thought about it for a second. Then, before she could counter his argument, he shoved her in the hole.

"Asshole!" she screamed as Wallace smirked. "Then, at least, take these." She tossed her spare magazines up, motioning for Yousef to do the same. The Arab tossed his up as well.

"Holy shit, that's the first time I've heard you use that type of language," he joked, handing the spare clips to Ryan to disburse them amongst the team. "Oh, by the way, what was the ETA on the choppers?"

Sophia, in a half pout, checked her watch. "Twenty minutes. And we're going to talk about his later."

"Sure we will." Wallace smiled, throwing up a thumbs up, and backed away from the hole. "Just keep your heads down."

That was all he could hope for. The prospects of his small eight-man team holding out twenty minutes against a much larger hostile force weren't great. Eventually, their pursuers would realize their advantage and overwhelm them with sheer manpower.

Wallace rejoined his team at the front wall, where they were waiting for him. "Ok, guys, not going to lie. We're in a bad spot here. We need to hold them off for twenty minutes. Conserve your ammo; shoot only at what you can hit. We've got this. This is what we've trained for, men. Ryan, Ahmed, and Walsh, I want you in the bedroom. Gut, Tyus, and Johns take the kitchen. Tex, you're on me here in the living room. Try to drive their forces in the middle. Don't let them flank us, or this is over before it begins. Let's give them hell, boys." The sailors moved out to their assigned posts, awaiting the arrival of the AIA.

****

The SEALS waited silently, contemplating the battle ahead of them. Eyes glued to the ridge as they listened to the shouts of the

AIA drawing ever closer. Seconds turned to minutes.

Down in the crater, Sophia's eyes were fixated on Amell and his on hers. While they were locked in an intense staring match, Yousef held his 9mm Beretta to the back of Amell's head. The sight of the terrorist leader made Sophia's stomach churn. But she couldn't turn away.

The man was responsible for many deaths and had orchestrated the most significant attack on American soil since 9/11. Now, he sat only a few feet away from her. Questions raced through her head; she couldn't wait to start interrogating him.

"You and your men will all die here today. And you, you traitor," Amell lisped, shifting his focus to Yousef. "We'll burn you alive for the world to see." He smiled through blood-stained teeth, revealing a recently missing tooth.

"Looks like you're missing something there." Sophia pointed to her slightly open mouth and tapped one of her front teeth.

Amell ran his tongue around the top of his mouth, feeling a gap between his teeth. "INFIDEL!" he shouted, hocking a blood-filled wad of saliva at Sophia.

Yousef smacked him on the back of the head with the handle of his gun. "That's not how you treat a lady."

"Umph," he snorted. "She's no lady; she's an American dog. A bitch." Yousef struck him again.

Sophia raised her hand. "Yousef, stop. If you beat his brains out, I cannot get anything from him."

"You'll get nothing from me anyway," he said, folding his arms across his chest like a child in protest.

****

The crackling boom from Tex's sniper rifle went off. "Contact, contact left."

The first wave of AIA soldiers had arrived, cresting the ridgeline. They were still slightly out of effective range from the rest of the group's weapons.

"Tex, Walsh, drop as many as you can," Wallace shouted. "Everyone else, hold fire."

The two snipers continued to pick off target after target as they came rushing down the hill. The angered mob flooded down into the valley, charging ahead. None fired a single shot as they poured in. "Two, three, four." Tex lined up shot after shot, watching each round explode through their designated targets.

"Why are they not shooting back?" Johns asked.

Probably the same reason we're not. Not within effective range," Ryan surmised.

A few minutes later, the first roars from the oncoming AKs thundered, and muzzle flashes flickered like exploding fireworks. 7.62mm rounds pockmarked the façade, raining flakes of concrete down on the sailors.

The SEALs took cover behind the low wall that separated the inside from the outside.

"Wait, wait, wait for it," Wallace shouted. The first fusillade began to wind down. The few last claps of gunfire crackled.

"NOW."

Wallace finally gave the green light to attack. The SEALS sprang from their cover, opening fire. The oncoming wave of soldiers dropped to the dirt in a hailstorm of bullets. However, the AIA soldiers continue to charge their position. Each time one went down, he was instantly replaced by another.

It was precisely as Wallace had feared. This was a mathematical equation, and whoever was leading the AIA forces was aware of it. Throw enough bodies at the Americans, and they would either be overrun or run out of ammunition.

Which would come first was now the question of the day.

****

Sophia tried blocking out the war, going on two feet above her head. Sensing an opportunity now that Amell was riled up with false confidence that his men would save him, she had to keep him talking.

"Oh, I will get something out of you. You all crack at some point," she said, swelling with bravado and antagonizing the terrorist leader.

"Never, American filth," Amell shouted in defiance. "I'll never betray my cause. Especially to a *woman*." Disdain and disgust filled his voice.

"You say that now, but we will see how you feel later when a *woman* beats you. You think your men will save you?" She laughed practically in his face, igniting a fire in the captured leader. "I have the best-trained elite fighting force up there. You're done. Your cause is over. Ha-ha. That's a joke. You managed one successful attack. We stopped the other, and now we have you captured," she bragged. "Strolled into your home, snatched you right out of it. "Some leader you are," she continued, giving him a dismissive look from head to toe.

Fury and rage burned behind Amell's eyes, anger rising as Sophia mocked.

****

Bullets pounded the dirt and walls in a relentless barrage of gunfire. More men poured into the valley, hell-bent on killing the Americans. However, Wallace's team held the line, shooting and killing the oncoming force with brutal accuracy.

Their years of training were in full effect, making every round count, as opposed to the AIA's lack of training and wildly inaccurate weapons. The SEALS continued to thin out the herd. Bodies littered the valley's ground, soaking the dirt red with blood.

Wallace hoped that at some point, the AIA would be forced to pull back at the risk of losing everyone.

"Sir, I think we've got something," Wallace heard over the radio. It was Gutierrez in the other room. From the corner of his eye, he'd spotted a small dust cloud in the distance. He squinted as something within the cloud began to take solid form. "Holy shit, we've got a technical," he shouted.

Two Toyota pickup trucks emerged from behind the cloud of brown smoke. In the beds of both trucks sat .50cal machine guns that opened fire the second they came into sight. The large-caliber rounds exploded into the wall, tearing through it. Gutierrez, Johns, and Tyus took cover from the barrage, throwing themselves to the ground. Debris fell on top of the sailors, burying them.

"Son of a bitch, we've got to take them out," Wallace ordered.

"I've got it." Tex shifted, dropping back to a prone position, lying flat on his stomach. The bipod legs of his high-powered rifle dug into the dirt. The massive machine gun rounds gnawed away at the wall. Ignoring the chaos around him, Tex peered through his scope, lacing the crosshairs on a driver's forehead. Staring him in the eyes, Tex mumbled, "Today is not my day to go."

*B*oom!

The rifle recoiled, kicking back, sending the deadly projectile rocketing through the air, breaking the sound barrier. It shattered the windshield, piercing the driver's head and blowing out brain matter in a spray of blood.

The truck careened to the left, hitting a rock and sending it airborne. The gunner and passenger were thrown from inside. The vehicle crashed back down on its front end, smashing the gunner beneath two tons of scrap metal. The passenger, seeing the carnage up close, tried crawling to safety as the truck wobbled for a second before gravity took hold, pulling it back to the earth's surface and falling onto the passenger. His legs were pinned under the tailgate, snapping his tibia and fibula in half in a sickening crunch of bones.

"Woooo!" Tex crowed, gawking at what he'd just done.

The second truck's gunner shifted focus, witnessing his friends' deaths, adding more hatred. The .50cal peppered the living room with devastation.

"Goddammit, Gut, take him out!" Wallace ordered.

Gutierrez and the others had the time to dig themselves out from under the debris as the shooters had shifted focus to Tex's more imminent threat. They were now free of the rubble. Gutierrez staggered to a kneeling position, searching for something on his tactical vest.

"Got it," he slid the barrel assembly open of his M203 grenade launcher, finding what he'd been looking for. Removing a small, canister-like object with a domed tip—a 40mm high-explosive round—he dropped it down the launcher barrel attached to the bottom of his M4A1, slapping the breach closed. The second truck came into focus. Judging the distance, anticipated route, and rate of travel, he aimed for a spot in front of the approaching vehicle. And squeezed the trigger.

Whump

He sent the high explosive hurtling through the air. It fell back to earth, landing a few feet in front of the pickup and blowing a small hole in the ground.

A cloud of smoke and dust suddenly blocked the driver's view. He couldn't see the freshly made hole. The truck plowed into it with such force the back end flipped up, causing the entire vehicle to cartwheel, running over several charging AIA troops in the process, and bounding across the plain.

"Technical down," Gutierrez shouted, pumping his fist. The rest of the team whooped it up, seeing the devastation.

"Don't celebrate too early," Wallace warned. "More incoming." Incredibly, the terrorists were still sending more men.

Perhaps their intel on 200 enemy combatants was incorrect?

****

"See, my men will keep coming for you. You're outnumbered. Allah wills your deaths today," Amell ranted.

"You can have three or four hundred men. It wouldn't make a difference. Those sailors up there are the best of the best, trained by the best. Your goat farmers with pitchforks are no match for us," Sophia taunted.

"And what makes you think some of the same haven't trained us? America is a whore, selling itself to whoever pays. Money is your religion. Allah is ours. He wills the death of the West."

"All you care about is sending kids to do your dirty work, asshole," Yousef growled, angered by the comments.

"All you Americans are the same. All you want is war. To you, war is profit. America causes war only to profit from it. I'm a servant of Allah, using your greed against you. To cleanse the world of all infidels."

"'Servant of Allah, using our greed against us.' What does that mean?" The last sentence caught Sophia off guard, triggering a memory of something Tarik had said the day before.

As he was about to answer, a loud whistle flew over their heads, followed by an explosion behind the house, toppling one of the back walls.

****

"RPGs," Ahmed shouted as a second struck near the kitchen.

The explosion was deafening; Wallace's ears rang as he looked over and saw the dust settling from the blast. He could see Tex shaking the dust off, scooping up his rifle, and continuing to shoot back.

Most of the wall that had separated the living room from the kitchen was gone. What was left of the roof in that section had collapsed in. Muffled wails were coming from the other side.

Gutierrez, covered in debris from the roof, threw what he could off him, looking for his rifle. Ears ringing, someone's pained yelps sliced through the drumming. Still dazed, he sifted through the debris, finding his rifle. Staggered, he picked it up. A person dressed in a beleaguered camo uniform appeared, firing his AK blindly into the house. One round struck Gutierrez in the left shoulder, rocking him before he could react to the gunman.

Before the shooter could get off another volley, Wallace swung around the corner, firing, striking the trooper in the head. He looked at Gutierrez, who was slumped against the inner wall.

"You good?"

The SEAL flashed him a thumbs up. Their hearing was returning. "Where's Tyus and Johns?"

"Here." Johns rose from a pile of rubble, holding his head. There was a large laceration across his forehead.

"Tyus?"

"Here! I'm over here," the sailor cried out.

The three sailors found Tyus pinned underneath a wooden beam that had snapped his leg. They quickly shifted the debris off their comrade.

"Holy shit, man, you good?" Asked Gutierrez, looking for other signs of injury as he saw his friend's leg bent in an unnatural position. Luckily, the bone hadn't broken the skin.

"What the fuck do you think? My leg is broken," he answered, wincing in pain as Gutierrez continued his quick examination and then gave Wallace a sign there were no other serious injuries.

"Can you still fight?" Wallace asked.

"I'm still in the fight, boss, yeah."

Looking at Gutierrez and Johns, he inquired, "We're good?" The two responded in the affirmative. "Great, because we're not done yet, boys."

Another RPG struck a few feet in front of the house.

"We need to hold our sectors. The choppers should be here any second."

"Boss, need you over here," Tex shouted.

Wallace raced back out into what was left of the living room area.

****

Yousef used his body to shield Amell as the RPGs exploded above, knowing nothing else mattered but getting him out alive. Walls and debris pummeled them from above, filling in the crater.

Sophia had shielded herself from the rocks raining down. Through the dust, she could see Amell and Yousef struggling. Amell used the RPGs as a distraction to try and escape.

Sophia scrambled through the dirt, picking up her Glock 22 and searching for a clear shot. But, unfortunately, she was too late. Somehow, Amell had broken free from his restraints and wrestled the knife away from Yousef. Gun drawn, on Amell, he was standing behind Yousef, using him as a human shield, with the knife to his throat.

"I wanted to save this traitor from the fires, but I suppose now I will have to do it." He smiled through his gapped-tooth grin, malevolence in his eyes.

"No, don't," Sophia shrieked.

Amell ran the knife across Yousef's throat. Blood squirted, the blade severing the Arab's jugular vein, dowsing Sophia in her friend's blood. Then, with Sophia blinded temporarily, Amell made his break to escape.

211

****

Coming back down the hallway and entering the living room, looking for Tex, Wallace swung around, hearing a blood-curdling scream from the crater in which he'd stashed the CIA agents and their prize. Amell scrambled out, cresting the bowl. "Son of a..." He drew to fire just as another RPG flew by his head, striking the back of the house. The blast threw Amell back into the crater, knocking Wallace and Tex down as well.

****

Sophia recovered, wiping the blood from her face, her heart pounding. She kneeled, hunching over Yousef, staring at his face, his life being drained away right before her. She couldn't believe it; one of her oldest friends was killed right in front of her, and she just stood there, letting it happen.

A few feet away, Amell began to move again, grunting as he held his arm against his ribs. The blast had broken several of them. He stumbled to his feet. Sophia looked up to see him trying to climb back out. Her body trembled with anger, every fiber filled with rage and hatred.

"AMELL!"

She stood up, setting her eyes on Amell's back as he desperately tried again to climb out. She rushed towards him as he reached the top, grabbed his leg, and ripped him back down.

Amell grabbed a fist full of dirt on his way down and slung it in her face, allowing him time to pick up the knife he had used to kill Yousef and slowly scrambled to his feet. Sophia clawed the soil from her eyes.

"Now you die bitch," he lunged forward, the knife flying at her stomach. She dodged, the blow spinning to her right, throwing Amell off-balance. Unable to stop his momentum, it carried him behind her. She quickly unsheathed her knife, all in the same motion, blindly jabbing the blade behind her, driving it into the back of Amell's skull.

She let it go as his body fell, turning to see his corpse hit the dirt. Breathing heavily, she watched the terrorist's leg twitch. The last movement he would ever make.

Amell al-Gharsi, the architect of the Harley Davidson Museum bombing, was dead in a way that served the justice that thirty American families deserved.

Another loud noise entered the fray. Two Apache helicopters rumbled overhead, buzzing past the house, unleashing a fury of machine-gun fire, along with hellfire missiles pounding the area outside the battered house. Another larger chopper came into view seconds later. It was their means of escape from this hell.

As Sophia climbed out of the crater, the SEALs converged on each other. "Let's go. We need to move," Wallace shouted, running up to her.

"Where's Yousef and Amell?"

Sophia stared blankly at him, shaking her head. Wallace peered down into the crater. Both Amell's and Yousef's bodies were lying there.

"Shit!" Jumping down, he lifted Yousef's body out. "We leave no one behind," he told Sophia. "No one."

The Apaches continued to circle the house, making strafing runs to keep what was left of the AIA at bay. At the same time, the SEALs gathered to get to the transport helicopter.

"Gutierrez, help Tyus out."

The sailor slung the comrade's arm over his shoulder. "Sophia, you go with them. We'll cover you," Ryan suggested.

Everyone nodded in agreement.

Sophia, Gutierrez, and Tyus ran out toward the helicopter. Tex followed them, providing fire for Wallace, who was carrying out Yousef's body. Once they made it safely, Ryan, Ahmed, Walsh, and Johns made a beeline for the chopper.

Midway between the house and the chopper, Tex spotted a glint from a rifle scope.

"Sniper!"

A second later, a bullet struck Ahmed in the arm.

Tex grabbed his rifle, searching for the source of the shot. Before he could locate the shooter, he got off another shot. This one tore a chunk of flesh from Ryan's leg. He fell to the ground. Ahmed managed to make it to the chopper on his own. Wallace saw Ryan go down. He leaped from his seat, racing to his buddy.

The shots gave away the sniper's location. Tex picked out a small shape from the top of the ridge.

"Got you fucker." He fired; a spray of pinkish-grey mist bloomed.

More men appeared, getting ready for another charge. "Let's go," Sophia shouted, grabbing an M4 and laying down cover fire for Wallace and Ryan.

The two made it back to the chopper.

"Get us out of here!" the SEAL team leader shouted.

Ahmed quickly translated, and the Blackhawk took off in a windstorm. Several stray rounds binged off the side. Sophia sat out of breath, staring out the side door and watching the Island slowly fade into the distance. As the chopper passed over the blown-out house, she could still see Amell's body lying in a pool of blood. Knife sticking out the back of his head. A fitting end, she thought, spitting. Hoping she'd hit the body.

CHAPTER SEVENTEEN

Sophia was finally shown to her room at the U.S. Embassy in Saudi Arabia's capital city sometime after 10 am. The flight from Perim Island to the Embassy took an hour, and once they arrived, the rest of the day was a whirlwind of events.

The injured SEALs were taken to medical. Wallace was pulled away immediately for a debriefing by a General who appeared from nowhere. That was the last time she laid eyes on any of the men who orchestrated and pulled off the mission that laid down justice on the perpetrator and all of his goons who attacked America. The plan was initially to take him alive.

Dead also worked fine since it saved the country from wasting money on a trial.

Wallace wasn't the only one whisked away for a debriefing. Two men in suits appeared before Sophia seconds after the commander had been taken away. They escorted her to a small conference room, which would become her home away from home for the next twelve hours.

First, it was the CIA station chief, then a DOD official, followed by the Director of the FBI, and then someone else. By that time, she didn't care who was doing the questioning.

It was all the same type of questions.

She had to rehash every detail of the mission. Most of them wanted to know why Amell al-Ghasari was not brought back into custody and how he wound up dead, along with one of their own.

After the grueling marathon of debriefings, she was brought to her room by two uniformed sailors who, thankfully, didn't ask any questions. Had they, she may have screamed in their faces. She was over all the questions, frustrated, and, most of all, tired.

There was only one thing she was looking forward to at this point. A nice hot bath away from anyone who could ask another question.

As the tub filled with water, she stood at the sink, staring blankly at her reflection in the mirror. Her body wanted/needed rest and sleep, if only for an hour or two. Every fiber of her body

215

ached; she craved it. But every time she closed her eyes, nightmarish images flashed.

Amell's featureless face haunted her as he held Yousef hostage. Echoes of her voice pleading with the terrorist leader not to do it reverberated on an endless loop.

Every image was so vivid, as if she'd been transported back to that moment in time. The moment Amell opened Yousef's throat, the feeling of his warm blood splashed across her face. The event played out in excruciating detail, haunting her.

It also didn't help that she had to review the mission details and relive the event repeatedly with each new set of interrogators, which only served to engrain that moment in her brain. It had taken its toll on Sophia, and she finally had the time to break down, sliding into the tub. Unable to hold back the tears, they cascaded down her face, leaving her a shaking and sobbing mess, knees to chest, rocking back and forth in the tub.

That gut feeling at the outset of the mission had unfortunately proved true. Not only had she not brought Amell back alive to face the punishment for his crimes as she had promised, but she had also gotten one of her oldest friends killed in the process.

Sitting in the tub, crying into her hands, it struck her. Yousef's parents would soon be told some lie about how he was killed in a car accident or whatnot. They will never know that he died defending the freedoms his adopted country provided them. How unfair was that?

As Sophia lay on her bed, exhaustion finally catching up, she stared at the plain, eggshell-white ceiling. The fan above spun lazily, its blades creating a hypnotic pattern reminiscent of a helicopter in flight. The physical strain of the day, combined with the emotional weight she carried, began to take its toll on her.

As her body relaxed, her skin wrinkled, revealing the evidence of prolonged exposure to water from her walk around the tennis courts. She felt a deep weariness settle in her bones, each muscle protesting against further movement. She struggled to keep her eyes open, her heavy eyelids fighting against gravity, the battle becoming futile as they succumbed to its pull.

In the silence of her room, the sounds of explosions and

gunfire permeated the air. Men's shouts and screams reverberated from all directions, blending like a surround sound theater system playing a high-intensity action movie. The echoes danced around the room, creating an unsettling symphony of chaos and violence.

The weight of the day's events weighed heavily on her mind as she drifted into a restless slumber. The darkness enveloped her, offering a brief respite from the turmoil that plagued her thoughts. Her body sank into the softness of the mattress and pillow, offering a momentary sense of peace and comfort.

But then, in the depths of her dreams, an explosion shattered the tranquility. Yousef's face flashed before her eyes, his pain and anguish evident in his fading gaze. The memory of his loss surged forward, threatening to consume her peace and pull her back into the harsh reality she sought to escape.

Sophia's body jolted, a reflexive response to the vivid images that invaded her subconscious. Beads of sweat formed on her forehead, a testament to the emotional turmoil that still lingered within her. Slowly, she closed her eyes once more, hoping to find solace in the depths of sleep, even as the memories continued to haunt her, waiting for another chance to resurface, which wouldn't be long.

The moment Sophia began to feel herself drifting off, letting tiredness overtake her weary body. The silent night was shattered once more by a familiar disembodied voice.

"This is your fault," Yousef's voice rang out, distorted demon-like. His eyes now blazed red, his face contorting into a smile. "And you're next," he rasped.

Sophia shot straight up, her hand clutched to her bosom, her heart thudding, and her body glistening, drenched in sweat. Her eyes darted around the room, coming to rest on the clock. Large red blocked numbers signaled she'd managed to sleep for an hour.

Breathing heavily, she walked into the bathroom and filled a glass with water, downing it in a huge gulp.

"Fuck it," she cursed, wiping her arms with a towel.

Throwing on a pair of pants and a shirt that were two sizes too big and undoubtedly provided by the embassy's lost and found department, Sophia exited her room into an empty hallway. Maybe a midnight stroll would ease her mind.

Walking through the silent Embassy hallways, she couldn't help but notice how extravagant the place was. Having spent a fair amount of time traveling abroad for work and staying at several embassies over the years, this one had taken the cake in outright opulence. Several buildings formed a square around a sizeable lavish swimming pool and tennis courts in the center. The place gave off more of a resort hotel vibe than an Embassy filled with diplomats.

Wow, this must be a nice duty station for the CIA chief, she thought.

The CIA utilized the Embassy in Riyadh to conduct all its operations within the country. It made the most sense in terms of security level and embassy size. Plus, it was a hardship station, so the comforts of the Embassy made it a little easier to stomach.

She strolled around the tennis courts, her gaze fixed upon the vast expanse of the night sky above. She felt a growing sense of tranquility with each step, her mind slowly clearing off its clutter. The familiar constellations dotted the darkness, and she silently named them in her head, finding solace in their celestial presence. While the number of visible stars was not as abundant as the previous night, when they shimmered amidst the waves of the Gulf of Aden, they still offered a comforting sight, unobscured by the city's blinding lights.

As she continued her walk, the exercise began to work its magic. The intrusive and troubling thoughts that weighed heavily on her heart gradually dissipated. The peace of the night, coupled with her focus on the stars, allowed her to find respite from the turmoil within. The rhythmic steps and the gentle breeze caressing her face created a soothing rhythm, as if nature itself was aiding in her healing process. The grip of the darkness was loosening, replaced by a renewed sense of calm and clarity.

Amid the vastness above, she found a small but significant refuge. It was a reminder that there were forces greater than the world's troubles and that even in the darkest moments, beauty and serenity could be found. With each step, she drew upon the quiet strength of the night sky, embracing its vastness to find inner peace and renewed hope.

"Hey, Sophia."

She turned to see Wallace striding over.

"Oh, hey, Wallace. What are you doing up still? It's like one in the morning."

"I was just coming from the medical ward, checking on my guys. What are *you* doing up?"

"Can't sleep. Hell, I can barely close my eyes without, you know, seeing-" Sophia couldn't finish the sentence. Instead, her eyes wandered off, searching for another thought to avoid watering up again.

The sailor had seen that look many times and knew exactly what was happening in her head.

At one point, he had experienced it himself. Losing someone in battle, let alone a friend, is one of the most difficult experiences you can have in this line of work.

"Hey, don't take this too personally, but you look like shit," he said, trying to keep her mind from straying too far into dark territory.

"Fuck you," she replied, taking immediate offense to the comment, slugging him on the shoulder.

"I'm kidding; you look fine," Wallace added with a smirk. "I needed to snap you back here. I have seen that thousand-yard stare before."

"What stare?" She was unaware that she had drifted off.

"That thousand-mile stare off into oblivion." He placed a hand on her shoulder, twisted her body around, and guided her back to the building. "Hey, I know a great café. It's called the cafeteria, and they serve coffee 24/7. It might taste like shit at this time of night, but." He shrugged, "So what do you say we do something daring and try it out?"

"No… No, I'm okay." She tried to pull away. "I just want to be alone."

He continued guiding her, face falling flat, implying he wasn't taking no for an answer. "That wasn't meant to be a question. Let's go. I'm not leaving you alone."

****

Wallace poured two cups of coffee and snatched a carousel of condiments from the booth next to theirs on the way back to the table. He placed it all in front of Sophia and pulled out his chair. It scratched against the tile floor, echoing through the empty cafeteria. They winced at the sound before looking around to ensure no one else had entered the room.

Sitting silently across from each other, both parties sipped at their coffee. Sophia's face scrunched up as she struggled to ingest the liquid contents. "This is terrible," she mumbled, setting the cup down and pushing it away with a disgusted face.

Wallace shrugged, taking another drink. "It's not that bad," he said, fighting back the urge to wince himself.

"You know this is getting a little creepy," Sophia stated, folding her hands over each other. "I thought you wanted to talk?"

"No, I wanted you to talk. You need to talk about what happened out there."

"No… No, I really do not. I've been talking about that all day and am tired of it." She shook her head, not wanting to rehash it again, especially to someone who was there.

"You have been *recapping* the details. Not *talking* about it. There is a difference." The sailor leaned back, stirring creamer into his coffee. "And you know exactly what I'm talking about."

Sophia nodded. "I…I just-"

"You don't want to. I get that. I didn't want to talk to anyone the first time I lost a sailor in combat."

"You've lost sailors in combat before?"

"Of course," he responded, his tone carrying a mix of resignation and understanding. With its underlying assumption that he was an exceptional commander, the question itself was a testament to the idealized perception of Special Forces and their supposed immunity to loss. However, he knew all too well the harsh reality of their dangerous work. Not everyone had the privilege of returning home alive. The weight of that truth settled heavily on his shoulders.

"This line of work comes with its inherent dangers," he

continued, his voice tinged with a touch of melancholy. "Sadly, I have lost six brave men out there." He paused briefly to pay his respects to their memories. He mentally recalled each name. "I can tell you everything about each one of them. I carry their stories with me, ensuring that their legacies live on in some form or another. It's a way to honor their sacrifice and keep their spirits alive."

His words carried a mix of reverence and determination. Despite the losses, he remained committed to his duty and to preserving the memory of those who had fallen. He carried a solemn responsibility with him, a reminder of the high cost of their mission and the sacrifices made along the way.

"I know, but this is starting to become a theme. I go somewhere and bring people along with me. Then, at the end of it all, I'm the only one coming back," she sighed, dropping her face into her hands, doing all she could to fight back the tears.

Wallace put his cup down and leaned back, crossing his arms and stroking his beard.

"Yeah, there's a word for that. It's survivor's guilt. You lived; he didn't. You survived Belgrade; the other agents didn't. Back in Orlando, your partner Fred didn't die but could've. You're wondering why. Why are you the lucky one? Why do you get to continue living? Right?"

"I… I guess," she stammered. "Yeah, why me?" Realization hit home, slamming her fist against the table. "I'm no better than they were." His voice cracked with anger peeking through. "Hell, I got them all into the situations that killed them."

"No, you didn't. They knew what could happen when they signed up. That's no one's fault. It just is. You survived. They didn't; those are the facts. You move on. Honor their memories by living in a way that keeps them alive in your heart. That's all you can do. There is no rhyme or reason to these things. They just are."

"That's it. That is your grand advice?" she asked, clearly frustrated that he had forced her emotions out only to give this crappy advice. "Basically, to get over it."

"Hey, what do you want? I'm just a SEAL, not a psychologist, and besides, you're not paying me," he laughed.

To Sophia's shock, though, Wallace's advice took immediate effect. She could almost breathe a little easier, feeling the weight of her decisions lift, and a small smile grew on her face as she was forced to concede to the advice. "Shut up. Have you ever known anyone who tells you you're insufferable?

"Yeah, my ex-wife, about a thousand times. But at least I got you to smile for a second."

"Wait, hold up." She waved a finger. "We're not going to breeze past that nugget. Someone actually married you?"

"Hey, you know I kind of take offense to that," the sailor said mockingly. "I was married. It lasted like two seconds, but yeah."

"Wow, just wow. I'm sort of shocked." The news genuinely took her aback. She figured most Spec Ops sailors lived a bachelor life, making it easier to just up and go at a moment's notice.

"Whatever. So, what are you going to do now?"

For the first time in months, she didn't have an answer to that question. Her entire life had been consumed by the investigation and tracking down Amell. With him dead, there was no mission left. No task or anything else to move on to.

"Come to think of it, I don't really know. I guess I'll return home, probably for another round of debriefing." Sophia again trailed off but with a different look. The word 'debrief' rekindled a thought within her.

"Take a vacation. You earned it," Wallace retorted. Noticing she wasn't listening to him anymore, he snapped his fingers. "Hey, Sophia, I thought we moved past this."

"No, I just thought of something. Amell said some interesting things to me in the hole that, for obvious reasons, didn't click at the time. But now…"

"Like? Besides, he knew his goose was cooked. He would probably say anything to save his life."

"No, it wasn't like that. He never begged for his life. However, it was something he said, combined with something Tarik said during his interrogation.

"Ok, what?"

"Tarik mentioned that this would be his last deal with Amell. He was angry about a perceived slight, believing Amell had betrayed the cause.

She was thinking, mentally putting the puzzle pieces together.

"Amell was talking about this crazy belief that America creates wars for profit and that he and his men were trained by the best, just like you guys," she pointed to the SEAL commander.

"Well, he was not wrong about that. There is a ton of money to be made during wartime. So-"

"So, America profits from war?"

"Not exactly. It does have its advanta-" Wallace stopped as he discovered something. "Holy shit."

"What, what?" Sophia slid to the edge of her seat.

"Fuck, son of a bitch," Wallace sputtered. "You know when we lost communication entering the ammo depot."

"Right, what about it?"

"Planting the bombs, Ryan found a logo on the side of a crate. I've seen it before but couldn't place it at the time. It's a logo for a paramilitary company. Soter Corp, I think. They are a bunch of real douchebags, ex-special forces types. Mercenaries for hire if you ask me," Wallace added.

"Really? Why would a group of Soter Corp crates be in Amell's possession if he obtained all his weapons and supplies from Tarik?" Sophia pondered, running scenarios in her head. Analyzing the facts in real time.

"That is an excellent question. How do we get an answer to that?"

"I think I need to have another chat with Tarik," Sophia said, pushing her chair out—a new mission in her eyes.

"That might not be possible right now, though," Wallace objected.

"Why not?" Sophia asked tersely.

"It's three in the morning, that's why," Wallace said, laughing at the fact that she had seemed so upset when he told her she couldn't go see Tarik right this second.

Sophia's face sank with that realization. "Oh yeah."

"Go back to your room and get some rest. I'll swing by at nine, and we can go together. Sound like a plan?"

Sophia didn't want to wait to talk to Tarik until then. She

wanted to get to the bottom of this new mystery as soon as possible. However, seeing the merits of Wallace's proposition, she could also use the time to prepare a line of questions. Sophia gave in.

"Fine, we'll do it your way. But I expect you at nine a.m. sharp, though, sailor."

"Yes, ma'am," he said, smiling and saluting. "I'll be there, don't worry."

The two returned to the residential building together, parting at the entrance to retire to their rooms. Walking the empty corridors, Sophia started to think about what type of questions she would ask Tarik.

Thankfully, after their earlier conversation, Yousef had arranged for him to be transported to the Embassy.

Their last discussion had gone smoothly partly because she offered the weapons dealer a deal for the information that led to Amell's capture and subsequent death. That deal hadn't been signed yet, to her knowledge. Maybe that could be an inroad to get him to divulge more information in hopes of securing the agreement entirely. Additionally, a few enhancements could be added to sweeten the deal.

****

A knock at the door startled Sophia awake. Sitting straight up in bed, an intense wave of light blasted her in the face, causing her to raise her hand and shield her eyes from the encroaching beams of light that seeped through the cracks in the blinds. Her eyes scrunched up as she peeled away from the brightness like a vampire retreating into the shadows. Sophia pawed around the nightstand, searching for the clock.

Finding it, she gave it an angry yank closer, allowing a second for her embattled eyes to read the time. The numbers blurred together in a patch of red. Unfortunately, she'd taken out her contacts last night and had no idea where she'd put her glasses. The blotch of red slowly began to formulate into something discernible.

Frustratingly waiting for them to become clearer, another knock on the door just as the numbers came into focus.

It was nine am.

"Just a minute," she called out, slipping on her shoes and walking to the door. She opened it to see Wallace standing there, a cup of coffee in each hand.

"Come on, let's go, sleepyhead. I thought you wanted to talk to this guy?" He had a bright smile on his face.

She snatched the cup from his hand and retreated to the bathroom. "Thanks," calling out, closing the bathroom door. "Give me a few minutes."

Wallace sat in a chair in the corner of the room, patiently waiting for Sophia to finish getting dressed. Afterward, they made their way to the detention area, where Tarik was being held. He was still awaiting the final paperwork for his deal to come through. Part of it consisted of being taken to America to serve his sentence instead of being handed over to the Saudi Government for trial.

Sophia spoke to the Captain in charge of the detention center. She had been granted permission to talk to Tarik by the station chief.

Sitting in a small interrogation room, she and Wallace waited for Tarik to be brought in. Minutes later, a guard walked in with Tarik shackled.

The prisoner rolled his eyes at the CIA agent waiting for him. "What else do you want from me? I told you everything I know on how and where you could find Amell," he hissed with disdain as the guard forced him into a seat. He cuffed his hands to a bar built into the table.

Sophia waited for the guard to depart. "I know. Thank you for that," she started after the guard left. "But I wanted to ask you a few more questions. More specifically, the comment about how he betrayed the Jihadi beliefs. What did you mean by that?"

"You will have to ask him that yourself."

Sophia leaned forward with a grin. "I would if I could, but since I stuck a knife in his head, that might prove to be a little tricky. Unless you know of a good psychic or medium," Sophia said in the most badass tone she could muster to prove herself to

Tarik.

Tarik sat back in his chair, analyzing what Sophia had just said. "How did you manage that? How did you get close enough with Hassan near him?"

Sophia looked at Wallace, puzzled. Wallace shrugged, looking back at her just as lost.

"There was no one by his side. We snatched him in the middle of the night."

It hadn't dawned on her until now. Where was Hasan? Ryan said they lost him after he crossed into Yemen, presumably on his way back to the island.

"Hahaha, and I always thought Amell slept with Hassan by his side. No wonder *you* could kill him so easily. *Kis, "* he spat.

Sophia and Wallace were now even more confused by what Tarik was saying. "What does that mean?"

"And why should I help you again?" Tarik asked sharply.

Sophia prepared for the question. "Because I can give Rasheed a somewhat better life. So if not for you, how about doing it for him?"

Tarik thought about the offer silently. Suppose word had gotten out that he and Rasheed were lovers. Leaving the younger man behind in Saudi would be like signing his death warrant.

"I want him to be taken to America."

Sophia nodded.

"Okay, Amell, he was just, how do you say it, a 'face man.' A puppet." He knew nothing of combat or war. Or how to even fight. Hassan was the muscle, kept everyone in line."

"Okay, well, that's interesting; I guess we'll have to track down Hassan at some point," Wallace said.

"That does not answer my question, though, Tarik. What did you mean by betraying the belief?" Sophia pushed harder.

"Amell and his organization had a deal with an American company for supplies and training. So, in essence, he worked for you Americans. That's how he betrayed his brothers. He took your money and supplies."

Hearing that the AIA terrorist group had been funded and trained by an American company hit Sophia like a piano falling from the sky.

Wallace himself moved to the edge of his seat.

"Bullshit. You lie. There is no way an American company would allow some jihadist piece of shit to attack their own country. Fuck you," the American sailor growled.

"Don't believe me; I don't care." The arms dealer shrugged. I only tell you what I know and what I have seen. Here, I draw you their logo."

Sophia slid a piece of paper and pen across the table. Tarik proceeded to draw the logo.

Sliding the paper back to Sophia, she picked it up and showed it to Wallace. He confirmed it was the exact same logo he had seen in the ammo depot of Perim Island the day before.

If Tarik's information was correct, then an American Paramilitary company was working with a terrorist group, actively attacking America.

Sophia thanked Tarik for his help and promised to start working on a deal for Rasheed before leaving the interrogation room.

"Well shit, that was a very illuminating conversation there," Wallace said once they exited the hallway. "So, what are you going to do now?"

"I need to get back home and discuss this with Fred and Tobias and bring them up to speed. If what he just said has any shred of truth to it, we need to find out why and stop them."

"Well then, I think this is where I get off the ride." Sophia looked at Wallace. "I'm a sailor, not an investigator. So, good luck with that. If anyone can do it, it's you." He smiled at her.

"Thanks for the confidence boost. Actually, in all sincerity, thank you very much. You've been here for me throughout this whole trip. I'm truly grateful to have had the opportunity to work with you and your team."

"Hey, the pleasure was all ours. Just promise me, wherever this leads, you'll get your man."

"That, I can promise you for sure. Thanks again, Wallace."

"Listen, if you ever need anything, my boys and I will come running, so don't hesitate."

"I won't. Oh, and tell the boys I miss them. Till next time." Sophia smiled and hugged Wallace when they reached the residential section again. She turned and walked down her hallway. Wallace watched as she disappeared.

Sophia spotted two gentlemen in black suits standing before her door, knocking. She was unsure who they were and why they had come to her door.

"Excuse me, gentleman, that is my room. Can I help you?"

The two men turned, flashing DOD badges. "Agent Sophia Evans?"

"Yes, who are you, and what do you want?"

"I'm Agent Wilks, and this is Agent Roberts. We're from the DOD. We have been asked to escort you to your debriefing."

Sophia gave them a look of confusion. She had just been briefed for the better part of the previous day, and now they were asking for another debriefing. "I was debriefed yesterday; I have no other information to add." The way the two men carried themselves alerted her that something didn't add up.

Their movements were more military than any agency she knew of. Having spent the last few days around a group of SEALs, she could discern the distinction in their stances.

"The CIA debriefed you. This is a DOD debrief for the Senate Intelligence Committee," Agent Wilks responded with a stern demeanor, boarding on abrasive.

"And I had a DOD debrief as well. So, anyone else who wants to know what happened, especially members of the intelligence committee, can read the debriefs."

"Yes, ma'am, and they have, but they have a few follow-up questions."

Sophia got the feeling this was not a situation she could say no to. However, it didn't mean she had to tell the truth.

Listening to her gut feeling, she decided to go with the two men. They escorted her to another room. However, this wasn't an interrogation room; it was an empty office. The two men closed the door behind them. But instead of hearing the echo from their shoes as they walked away. It sounded like they had posted up by the door.

An hour later, Sophia was starting to get antsy and had had enough useless waiting around as no one had even come to talk to her. No offer of refreshments or anything. She'd just been made to sit in an empty office. Then, the door opened just as she contemplated getting up and leaving. An African American man came in, strong-jawed and sharply dressed, with a fresh military fade.

He walked over to the bar and poured himself a drink, silently offering her one. Sophia refused, so he set the bottle down and motioned for her to sit while he took a seat in the chair across from her. She'd been pacing for a bit now, clearly agitated.

"I'm sorry about the wait, Agent Evans. I'm Agent Henry Williams with the Department of Defense. I have a few follow-up questions for you."

At this point, Sophia was on the border of frustration and outright anger. "That's what goon one said. What type of questions?" She was already on the defensive.

Agent Williams opened his folder, reading a highlighted portion of the documents contained inside. "In your debrief, it says that before *you*... stabbed Amell in the back of the head. He was in your custody for a little while. Is that accurate?" He glanced up from the paper, giving her a once-over look, almost astounded that she could kill anyone.

"In a sense, yes. We did have him, but the team and I were a little preoccupied with escaping alive. So yes, we did have him for a bit, but he was mostly unconscious. That was up until the battle at the airport."

"Umm, did you get to interrogate him then?"

"You have the report right in front of you. What does it say?" she snapped, allowing her emotions to get the best of her for a second. But on second thought, she settled back down. "No, I did not get the chance to have a chat in the middle of a gunfight."

By now, Sophia's earlier feelings had been confirmed. Something was off about Agent Williams and his line of questioning. Feeling at ease about her decision to keep what she knew to herself, she continued to lie about the interaction with Amell.

"Well, don't you think that was a little irresponsible on your part? You have America's most wanted terrorist by your side, and you don't ask him any questions. He doesn't say anything to you the whole time?" Agent Williams' tone grew increasingly pointed as the conversation progressed.

"NO! As I said, we were in the middle of a firefight." Sophia got more agitated with him in turn. "You know, staying alive."

"That's not accurate, though, is it? The SEAL team was in the middle of the firefight. From what I read here, you and your partner, Yousef, were hiding out in a bomb crater with the target, correct?"

"No, we were not hiding," Sophia, now furious, raised her voice. "We were ensuring he didn't run in the middle of the fight. It was not a situation conducive to conversation. I figured I would have plenty of time to interrogate him if we made it out alive. Unfortunately, things went a little sideways at the end. I ended up having to kill him. Believe me, it wasn't my first choice, but you know things don't always go according to plan."

"Ok, calm down, Agent Evans. I didn't mean anything by it. We would like to know if he gave any information to any of his networks and/or group activities. Maybe clues about another strike they may have been planning? I understand his right-hand man, Mr. Hasan, is still at large."

"No." Fury had started to take over. "He did NOT say anything. Had he, I think I would've divulged that by now. It was all just gibberish and bluster. Now, can I go? I have to pack and get back stateside." Sophia stood. She didn't really care what the answer was; she was leaving regardless.

Agent Williams held out his hand to shake hers. "You can go."

Sophia dismissed his hand and stormed out of the room. The whole line of questioning was off to her. He seemed only concerned about any possible conversation that may have taken place and nothing else. Why was it so important to know if/and what Amell may have said? It raised more questions, adding to a mounting pile of evidence that something more significant may be at play.

She rushed back to her room to pack. Knowing there would be

plenty of time on the flight to digest everything and determine her next steps.

CHAPTER EIGHTEEN

Sophia disembarked her flight after collecting her carry-on bag. She was slightly disappointed that she had to fly commercial for the return trip to the United States instead of the CIA-sanctioned black flight into Saudi Arabia. The lack of personal space made her yearn for the more spacious seating arrangement of the G5 jet.

Never in a million years would she have contemplated being spoiled by anything as trivial as a plane flight. It was an even bigger shock since most of the flight over had been spent catching up on sleep.

This time around, however, she was up for most of the flight.

Whether it was the haunting images still plaguing her sleep or the massive revelation that an American company was financing terror in the homeland, Sophia didn't care. Instead, she used her time to review transcripts of Tarik's other debriefings while also running everything Amell had said through a new filter. She ran every word and conversation back through her head, searching for and connecting any dots she could find.

There was one thing that the CIA agent was having trouble grasping. Paramilitary Companies, i.e., PCMs, operated a very cutthroat business, getting into bed with anyone who showed them the money. However, Agent William's entire 'interrogation' on behalf of the Senate Intelligence Committee was odd and out of place. It only aroused her suspicion that more was going on than everyone initially thought.

Could there be a connection between Soter Corp and the American government? Maybe? But where was the evidence? The hard evidence? All there was to support the conspiracy theory that America creates wars for profit was the word of an arms dealer, a dead terrorist leader, and a Navy SEAL commander. Only one of those three is considered credible.

Besides, there was one massive order of business to attend to first.

****

She exited the terminal to flag down a taxi to take her home for the first time in two weeks. She was excited to see Carol and worried about what to tell her.

Is this the right time to expose her secret life as a CIA agent, or would it be best for all parties involved—mostly her, to call it quits?

The wind caught and blew her wispy hair as she handed her bag to the wiry old man who clamored out of the cab. She had the next thirty minutes to figure it out.

Sophia ducked into the cab as Vladimir slammed the trunk; that's what his placard said. Then, as she glanced out the window across the street, something or someone caught her eye. He seemed familiar, but she couldn't quite put her finger on him.

He was a tall, blonde-headed man with short-cropped hair and a scruffy beard. There was no mistaking it, though; he was definitely the military sort, which wasn't entirely uncommon for the area, being near several military installations. However, the fact that she couldn't place where she'd seen him before was bothersome. Additionally, the stranger was trying to conceal his presence and avoid being seen. That was a major red flag.

The taxi pulled away; Sophia turned to watch him out the back window when it suddenly popped up where she had seen him— the Embassy!

For a fraction of a second, when Agent Williams entered to question her. She caught a glimpse of one of the men guarding the door. It was definitely the same guy. Am I being followed? *She* thought.

"Driver, can you make a right turn here, please?" she asked, peering out the back.

The first thing was to determine if he was following and, if not, whether it was a random coincidence.

A dark sedan pulled away from the loading lane right after Sophia's cab. The windows were tinted, obscuring her view, but it stopped, and the blonde man hopped in. Possibly a coincidence, but training told her not very likely.

"Ma'am, that's not the way we need to go," Vladimir interjected at the course change.

"I know; I need to make a stop first. Please, can we go right now?" she insisted, keeping a close eye on the sedan.

"Sure thing, lady. It's your dime," he answered. She could see his eyes roll through the rearview mirror.

"Thanks," Sophia said tartly, not impressed with his attitude.

Still keeping watch, the sedan followed, making the same turn. Sophia issued a few more directions to the confused driver. With every new command, the mystery vehicle followed, confirming what Sophia had suspected. She was being tailed by someone connected to the DOD, or possibly Sotor Corp had sent someone to kill her to cover their tracks.

Whatever and whoever was following her, one thing was sure: she needed to lose them.

"Crap," Sophia moaned, facing forward.

"What was that, ma'am?"

"Nothing," she sighed. It was time to dust off some of her CIA training. "Change of plans," she informed the driver. "Take me to the Sheraton Pentagon City Hotel."

There was no going home now. They most likely knew where she lived. They would be waiting there, too, undoubtedly.

She thought about Carol. Would they try to get to her through her lover? No, that would draw too much attention—the murder of a cop. No, the best way to protect Carol now was to stay far away.

****

Vladimir stopped the taxi on the front drive of the Pentagon Hotel. Waiting impatiently for the cabbie to collect her luggage from the back, Sophia moved about like she didn't know someone was tailing her.

Entering the hotel lobby, she headed for the front desk. "Hi," she said, smiling and addressing the young man behind the desk. "I would like to make a reservation for tonight."

"I'm sorry, Ms., but We're all booked for this weekend," the front desk agent responded politely.

Leaning over the counter, Sophia tugged down her shirt, exposing her ample cleavage. Batting her eyes at the poor agent.

"All of your rooms?" she asked in a low, seductive whisper. "Come on. I used to work in a hotel." This was true; she worked at a hotel during her freshmen and sophomore years in college. "I know you have at least one room on standby. I only need it for tonight. I'll even pay the full price."

The clerk hesitated, his eyes fixated on her breasts. "Ok," he said after a long leer. "Only for tonight, right?" Sophia nodded. "I can offer you a Queen Deluxe, but please note that you won't be able to have a late checkout, okay?"

Another nod.

Several minutes later, the clerk handed her a room key. "Thank you, Sergio. I hope to see you again," she added, walking away and giving him a wink.

She shuddered upon boarding the elevator. She hated using sex appeal to get what she needed, but it came in handy in her line of work, no doubt. She had never felt comfortable using her body as a means to an end.

Sliding the key card in the motorized mechanism released the door lock. Sophia tossed her bag into the room and closed the door. Figuring her tail wouldn't be more than a minute or two behind at best, she raced down the hallway, barging through the door to the stairwell, and bounded down the steps two at a time to exit out into a parking garage. Then she circled back to the road, avoiding the front drive, flagging down another taxi.

"Sir, take me to the closest rental car place," she said, panting, looking back. No one in sight. Had she managed to lose her tail? "Please."

The taxi driver sped off.

Sophia had no clue who was following her but did not doubt that he worked for Agent Williams. The question now was who Agent Williams was working for and why they were tailing her. She had to lay low from here on out until she could figure out who was running everything.

Michael Lee Williams

****

After renting a car, Sophia drove out to a public storage place. Years ago, she had stashed a go-bag with money, credit cards, and IDs. Now that she was being followed, the clock had begun to tick. Time was of the essence; every hour that passed could be her last.

Death wasn't far off if Sophia couldn't figure out what was happening. Either at the hand of the blonde-haired stalker or at the end of a sniper rifle, someone properly wanted her dead. She had to work quickly to find out who. And there was only one person out there she knew she could trust with her life, literally.

****

Fred walked back into the house after retrieving the mail. He was still on medical leave from his head injury and a subsequent short stint in a coma. It seemed like a small precursor to retirement life, and he wasn't enjoying it. The days seemed to drag on longer and longer. He had begun to go a little stir-crazy with nothing to do, so the phone rang just in time.

"Hello?" Fred answered.

"Fred, I don't have much time. I need your help," Sophia whispered on the other end of the line.

"Sophia, oh my god, you're back. I've been going crazy waiting for any word of the operation. Does Tobias know you're back?"

"No, I mean maybe."

"I wonder why he didn't say anything. Did you get him? Did you get Amell?"

"Sort of. We had him, but then I had to kill him. But Fred, focus; I don't have long." Something was off. Sophia's generally calm demeanor was gone. Her words almost blended as she tried to talk faster than her mouth could move.

"Ok. What's going on?" Fred asked. "You don't sound like yourself."

"Not over the phone, ok. Do you trust Tobias?"

"Of course I do." The question threw off Fred. "Sophia, what's going on?"

"I need you and Tobias to come to Washington D.C. ASAP. There is something much bigger going on than we thought. I need your help."

"Ok, we can be there by tomorrow." Sherry walked in behind Fred and heard him talk about leaving.

"Great, I'll send the directions to your office. Follow them precisely, ok? I gotta go." Sophia hung up before Fred could answer.

As he turned, Fred came face-to-face with Sherry. Her cold, dead stare told Fred all he needed to know.

"And, sir, just where do you think you're going tomorrow? The doctor said that you need to rest. *A lot* of rest. You still have a concussion," Sherry demanded, arms folded, tapping her right foot.

"I know that dear," Fred drawled, sliding his phone back into a pocket. "But, that was Sophia. She's back in the States and wants me and Tobias to meet her in Washington."

Sherry's demeanor lightened when he told her Sophia was on the other line. "Oh my god, how's she doing? Did they get that animal?"

"Yeah, he's dead. Something happened, though. I could tell it in her voice. It sounds like she's in trouble."

"Well, then get your butt in gear. Get Tobias and go, go, go." Sherry opened the closet door, pulling out his suitcase.

"Wait, what just like that? What about the concussion and the doctor's order?" Fred was somewhat offended that Sherry would push him out the door in a heartbeat to help Sophia, but she was like a protective mother bear over anything else.

"Yeah, of course, just like that. Sophia is *our* girl. If she needs help, you better be there for her."

"Ok. I'm off then."

****

Fred stopped at the FBI office on his way to the airport. He explained as much as he could to Tobias, who did not hesitate to drop everything and go. They picked up the envelope Sophia had delivered to the office and headed to the airport, catching the next flight to Washington, D.C.

Immediately after they landed, the two FBI agents arrived at the Northwest One Neighborhood Library a few minutes before 2 p.m., the time Sophia had specified in her letter.

Fred asked an attendant about the meeting. She was an older brunette with wire-rimmed glasses—the picture-perfect embodiment of a librarian. The irony didn't escape the pair. She helpfully led them to the meeting room where Sophia had already been set up.

Fred and Tobias walked in.

"Sophia, what's going on? Why all this cloak and dagger spy shit," Fred asked. "I mean, you're an amazing spy."

The fact that she *was* actually a spy just now registered in his brain. Despite their time together, he still never saw her as a trained CIA spook.

"I know. Come in, please. Sit down, both of you. I'll explain. First, thank you both so much for dropping everything and coming." Sophia was as apologetic as possible, knowing the inconvenience it caused for two powerful agents to leave their responsibilities based on a phone call.

"I wasn't really doing anything other than sitting around the house recovering," Fred said.

"I'm sorry I wasn't there when you woke up. How are you doing? I've missed you." It dawned on the young woman that she had never actually asked yet.

"I'm doing fine, actually. Still feeling the after-effects of the concussion. Nothing major."

"And you, Tobias? It's nice to see you again."

"Likewise."

All three took their seats. The two agents regarded each other, unsure of their purpose. "Though, I would like to know why you dragged us out here. Fred made it sound like you were in trouble," Tobias added.

"I know. I'm really sorry for keeping you both in the dark for so long. I'm… well, we're in trouble, I think." Sophia shuffled through some papers, looking for something. Her hand shook, and she was talking faster than usual.

"I… I…" she stammered, running a hand through her hair, which looked unkempt as if she'd been sleeping in a car. "I don't yet have everything pieced together, but the attack in Milwaukee is larger than we knew."

Again, the two agents exchanged glances. Fred's face betrayed a worried looked, watching Sophia move around in her chair, unable to stay in one place for more than a few seconds.

"Yeah, we know the attack was the first in a series of attacks which we stopped. The one in Orlando, and now that Amell is dead, the AIA is crippled. Isn't it?" Fred was doing his best to slow her down, trying to understand where she was going.

Sophia took a deep breath. "Yeah, sorry, I forgot. You were probably not authorized to view the debrief of the mission. Ok, where to start." She relaxed a bit but was still clearly agitated.

She opened her laptop.

"How about you start where you left off?" Fred suggested.

"Right, right, yeah, yeah. So… so we managed to track down Tarik and capture him. He led us to Amell's base. We captured him, but only for a few minutes. He tried to get away during the firefight, and I… I sort of had to." Pausing momentarily, she recollected her thoughts. "No, I actually wanted to kill him. So I did. But it was self-defense."

Fred and Tobias looked at each other, satisfied Amell had been killed. Fred, in particular, was impressed that Sophia had done it herself.

"Everything is gravy then, bad guy dead. So why are we huddled up, and why are you in trouble?" Tobias asked.

"Getting there," she snapped. "Long story short," she continued, rattling on. "Talking with Tarik and Amell, I discovered that Amell and the AIA were partially funded and supported by a PMC company called Soter Corp. They run missions all over the Middle East as government contractors." She slid a fist full of documents to the two. "They have their hands in all kinds of shit." Finally, Sophia paused, allowing her companions to absorb what she had just told them.

"Let me get this straight then," Tobias asked, perusing several papers. "You're saying an American PMC company is behind the attacks. Am I correct?" he inquired hesitantly, shaking his head in disbelief.

"No way. I don't believe that." He put down the documents, turning to Fred, who was still reviewing the papers.

"Yes. Only, I do not have hard evidence of this. It blew up. Nor do I even begin to know why. That is what I have got so far. And the 'spy stuff,' Fred, as you so eloquently put it, is because someone followed me on the way home."

The confession piqued Fred's interest and attention.

"I managed to ditch the tail and have been laying low, collecting what I can. However, I need your help. I can't share this with anyone right now without evidence. Additionally, I'm unsure who I can trust outside of the two of you. I'm only eighty-five percent certain I can trust my boss, Owens, but again, with no proof, I'm up the creek without a paddle. I mean, you two, believe me, right?" The question was more directed toward Fred than Tobias.

The two leaned back and folded their arms simultaneously as if they had rehearsed the bit a thousand times before. Neither of them spoke a word, lost in thought.

Sophia waited, tapping her foot and fingers, eager for one of them to speak.

"Sophia, of course, I'm with you, and I believe what you're saying is true," Fred said, breaking the weird silence. Dismissing her disheveled appearance and hyperparanoia, he instinctively knew he could trust her. In the time they had known each other, Sophia had never given the impression she was privy to flights of fancy. When she spoke about things, it was because she *knew* about them.

"It is Fred, I swear it. I swear," Sophia jumped to defend herself.

"I know. I just said I believe you. Now, all we need to do is determine how and why. For that, we follow the money trail." Fred looked at Tobias, who sat with a blank expression, not wholly convinced.

"Tobias, you with us?" Fred asked, nudging his friend.

"I don't know," the older agent confessed. Unlike Fred, he hadn't worked as closely with Sophia. Plus, he had a lot more riding on not believing her. Fred was about to retire. He'd be fine if he went down a rabbit hole of a government conspiracy. Tobias, on the other hand, still had a career he wanted to continue. "What you're saying is a little out there. Why would a company attack its own country?"

"*Money*!" she shouted, practically coming out of her seat, startling both men. "That's what Amell said. He said that all America cares about is money. There are huge dollars to be made in war, especially as the number of conflicts we find ourselves in increases and the military is stretched further the more we rely on PMCs. We earmark *billions* a year for them in our defense budget," Sophia ranted. "Can't you see? It's all about money."

"Fred. A moment." Tobias signaled for the two to step outside, holding a finger up to Sophia. She ignored it, pacing and talking to herself as she tried to put the puzzle pieces together. The two stepped outside, Fred sliding the door closed.

"Do you really believe her?"

"Of course I do," Fred answered. "She has been right about everything else so far."

"Look at her, man," he pointed out, noting that she was still pacing and talking to herself. "Maybe what happened in Saudi Arabia broke her. You said in Orlando that she froze. We don't know her mental state. I don't know. Americans attacking America?" Tobias was still not convinced. More so based on Sophia's mental state than what she was saying.

"I know. She isn't looking or acting like herself right now. However, we don't know how long she has been up. Did you clock the stack of Red Bulls?" Fred had noticed it the moment they walked in. The trash can had been filled with the liquid caffeine drink.

"If she was indeed followed, she's probably terrified of falling asleep. I looked at some of the documents she gave us. It may make sense. The DOD has almost exclusively used Sotor Corp. It can't hurt to look into it."

"Fine. If you believe her."

"I do." Looking through the glass wall at the frantic and disheveled agent. His heart felt pain for not being there for her in Saudi Arabia.

"Alright, let's go back in there." The two re-entered, taking their seats. "Alright, we're in. What do we do next?"

Sophia gave Fred a look he had become familiar with. She knew when she was out of her depth on something, which was the case here.

"That's why you're here," she said.

"We treat this like any other investigation then," Fred said, taking the lead. "As I said, we follow the money, get the evidence, and go from there."

"I've secured this meeting room for the next few days for us to work out of. I booked a room for you at the motel across the street where I'm staying. Thank you both," she added with a smile. "Should we get started then?"

She had little doubt that Fred would help, given their relationship. This would make it easier to win over the Special Agent in Charge, resulting in a powerful ally. At this point, Sophia needed all the allies she could muster.

The plan had worked to perfection. Now, the three of them could start to unravel the mystery behind the second-largest terrorist attack on U.S. soil.

****

The trio would spend the next few days digging into Soter Corp, Amell al-Gharsi, and the AIA, looking for all connections between them. Finally, after extensive research into Soter Corp's dealings, Sophia found the money trail they had been looking for that led back to the AIA.

The evidence began to mount from there as the puzzle pieces fell into place. Finally, they were very close to putting everything together—or at least enough to get them a warrant to search Soter Corp's offices.

The lights in the library dimmed as the door to the meeting

room opened. The librarian poked her head into the room, warning them the library would close in the next few minutes. Packing up and collecting the plethora of documents spread across the table, Sophia came across an article about the rise of the AIA in Yemen.

The report contained a few pieces of information that jumped out at her, recalling what Tarik had said.

"Fred, when did the AIA become a major player on the world scene?" she asked.

"Hold on." He shuffled his stack. "About two and a half years ago. Why?"

Sophia skimmed through another newspaper clipping. The New York Times had done a piece on the AIA and Amell after the Milwaukee attack, where he took the credit, announcing the AIA to the world.

The article mentioned that before the attack and announcement, no one had ever heard of Amell al-Gharsi. He was very young, unlike most of the leaders of major terrorist organizations. So, he wasn't a lifelong warrior who had been fighting since his youth. He appeared overnight and from nowhere. Confirming Tarik's story, he was nothing but a face of the organization and one that Soter Corp could hide behind.

Hearing the timeline piqued Tobias' curiosity.

"Well, that's interesting."

Fred and Sophia turned to face Tobias, waiting for him to elaborate. "That's right about when Soter Corp started seeing their first big bump in government contracts."

"That is not too big of a coincidence. The more terror attacks happen, the greater the need for protection and, thus, weapons. We knew that already, though," Sophia countered, not all that surprised.

"Yeah, but before that, Soter Corp was struggling to stay afloat amidst a wave of blowbacks from a couple of botched operations in Saudi Arabia, along the border with Yemen. They were nearly bankrupt until a sudden influx of cash from a silent partner."

Fred opened his laptop, typing away as Sophia shuffled through a folder. A thought jumped to mind.

"So Soter Corp was in and around Yemen when Amell began

his ascent up the terror ladder. He went from being a nobody that no one had heard of to the leader of a major threat to the U.S. Does that not sound a little unusual to anyone? Sophia pondered aloud.

"Son of a bitch," Fred exclaimed, staring, blinking rapidly at the computer screen in disbelief. "That motherfucker. It makes sense now why he wanted us to kill, not capture, Amell. He never intended for Amell to get caught. How Naseem was discovered and how Amell managed to escape the country after Orlando."

Sophia and Tobias glanced at each other and shouted, "*What?*"

"Soter Corp's silent partner. Fred spun the computer around so the others could see. "Is Josh Freeman." Saying the name, thinking that Sophia and Tobias would automatically make a connection. They stared blankly, not knowing the name.

"Really, guys, haven't we been poring over the same information for the last few days? And you, Tobias." He shook his head. "I thought you'd get this." The other man shrugged. "Josh Freeman, the husband of Megan Freeman, whose maiden name is Megan *Stone*."

Tobias sat up in the chair, eyes widened. It had just struck him the same way it had hit Fred moments earlier. "Motherfucker."

Sophia was still entirely in the dark about what her two partners had just figured out. She waited patiently for either of them to explain what was going on.

Fred saw the lost look in Sophia's eyes.

"Megan is the daughter of Senator Roy Stone, who sits on the intelligence committee that has been convened to oversee this investigation. He also happens to sit on the committee that approves the companies that receive defense contracts." Fred paused when he saw the light go off in Sophia's head.

"Son of a bitch."

Fred and Tobias were shocked to hear Sophia utter a curse.

"So, let me see if I have this right. Soter Corp creates a terrorist group and unleashes them to wreak havoc. Our already stretched-thin military needs aid from Paramilitary groups to help protect American interests. So, the good Senator Stone sits at the head of the committee that doles out these contracts. He finds a way to push said contracts to Sotor Corp. Which, in turn, ensures them billions of dollars in profit. Then, at the year's end, the investors divide those profits. One of them is the son-in-law of the man who secured those profits for the company. And then it is undoubtedly funneled back to the Senator, making him richer. Do I have all that correct?"

Fred nodded his head in agreement. "That's what it looks like. There are millions of dollars in payouts to the silent partner."

"Well, do you think we've got enough here to bring these guys down?" Sophia asked Tobias.

"We will need a little more evidence to make a prosecution stick, but I think we have at least enough to get a warrant to search Soter Corps' private financial records and enough to bring the good Senator in," said Tobias.

"Before we do any of that, though, we must get this to the Attorney General. After all, We're trying to take down a sitting Senator. The AG will be our most powerful asset if we can get her on our side."

"Great, we can do that first thing in the morning then," Sophia said, shoving her files into her backpack.

"Let me reach out to her tonight and get something for early in the morning. She and I go way back. In fact, she owes me a favor."

Tobias' contacts were coming in handy, just as Sophia had hoped.

"Everyone, let's return to our rooms and prepare for tomorrow's big day," Sophia said.

They left the library, crossed the street, and headed back to the motel.

"You two go ahead," Tobias said, breaking off from the two. "I'm going to reach out to Amy. I mean Attorney General Amy Sanchez," He quickly corrected with a sly smile before disappearing around the corner.

Fred and Sophia continued after watching a gleeful Tobias turn the corner. Their years of investigative work had led the pair to believe that their good friend and the AG must have shared something intimate in the past.

The pair stopped at the bottom of the stairs outside of the two-story motel. They exchanged one last laugh before Sophia climbed the first few steps. "Good night, Fred," she said.

"Ahem." He cleared his throat.

The slight-framed blonde turned.

"I just wanted to say good work. I know we didn't start on the best of terms. And that was my fault, but..." Fred looked down, twisting his toe into the ground. "I'm glad you've become a part of my family over the last few months."

Sophia retreated to the bottom, planting a kiss on the weathered agent's face. "Me too, Fred," she said, hugging him before climbing the stairs again.

Fred watched her until she was out of sight. "I'm proud of you he whispered." She wasn't his birth daughter but was now part of his family.

CHAPTER NINETEEN

As soon as Sophia left Fred's sight, he began swelling with pride as he turned. He was amazed by everything the young agent had accomplished since they had met. Shaking his head and grinning ear to ear, he started toward his and Tobias's room, releasing a lion-like yawn. It had been a busy day of research and sifting through thousands of documents—a more exhaustive task than most people would think.

Sophia had booked a room for the FBI pair together before their arrival. Though it wasn't the first time, he and Tobias had shared a room in a dingy roadside motel. He thought fondly about some of their past investigations. However, it had been years since, and they didn't have to go through all this secrecy back then.

But Sophia's instructions to him in Milwaukee were precise. They took every precaution to ensure that they were not followed. Fred found the whole process very intriguing. The lengths she made them go through felt exhilarating, as if he were in some spy movie. Coming to think about it, he pretty much was.

The familiar feelings and excitement of being on a case enveloped him.

His coma and bed rest had given him a small window into the retirement life he had convinced himself he wanted nearly six months ago.

But doubt started to creep into his mind now that he was in the thick of things again. Did he make a rash decision to give it all up? But… he had promised Sherry.

And that was the end of that. There would be no way she'd let him return to the FBI.

Opening the door to his room, Fred contemplated what he could say to convince Sherry to let him stay one, maybe two more years as he entered the pitch-black room. Still unfamiliar with his temporary abode, he ran his hand up and down the wall to his left, searching for the light switch, finding it, and flicking it up.

Nothing happened; no lights came on. Perhaps the bulb burned out, or the lamp switch needs to be turned on first. Whatever the

247

case, Fred slowly entered the room and closed the door, feeling around for the bench at the end of the bed he knew was waiting to trip him. He didn't want to stub his foot or trip over it. A chilling breeze entered through the window as he cautiously navigated the room. The sound of the whistling wind and the gentle flapping of the curtain caught his attention, prompting him to pause for a moment.

Suddenly, he remembered neither he nor Tobias had opened the window before leaving this morning. The hairs on the back of Fred's neck stood on end as an ominous presence enveloped him as if he were in a horror movie—the unnatural feeling that he wasn't alone in the room.

A dark shadow lurched forward. He wasn't alone in the room.

Fred felt the tightening grip of a thin nylon rope clasp around his neck. Instinctively, he stumbled backward to the door, slamming his attacker against it with a thud.

Grasping and clawing at the rope, choking for air. His windpipe rapidly shrunk under the applied pressure.

He had to get free somehow, or he'd die in a minute. He felt his chest start to tighten.

The two struggled violently. Fred leaned forward before throwing himself back, trying to crush his attacker against the door repeatedly, doing what he could to break the hold and get free. He was quickly expending whatever oxygen was left in his body. What he was doing clearly wasn't working.

The tightening noose around his neck dug deeper in the struggle. Whoever this person was had him in a vice-like grip. Mustering what was left of his strength, Fred cocked his elbow to the side before driving it back, hoping to hit some part of the attacker's body.

Pay dirt; his elbow struck the midsection just below the assailant's ribs. A muffled grunt emerged from the dark figure. He'd hurt the person, but not enough to completely release the garrote. Fred repeated the strikes several more times, driving the wind from the man's lungs.

Two could play this game.

The last blow caused the attacker to lose his grip on the

strangulation device, releasing Fred from the death hold. Freed, the agent staggered forward, trying to catch his breath, and gasped to refill his burning lungs. Before he could fully recover, the attacker rushed forward, spearing Fred in the back.

They fell to the bed and rolled to the floor. The assailant landed on top and immediately began a series of strikes aimed at Fred's head. Beleaguered and still winded, Fred managed to shield his face from the oncoming blows, waiting for his opportunity.

An opening in the strikes gave Fred his chance. He parried the oncoming blow, moving his head to let the attacker's fist slam into the ground.

Then, using his momentum against him, they rolled again, putting Fred on top. Snatching an ashtray from the nightstand, Fred swung it, striking the side of the attacker's head with a sickening thud. He pulled back for another strike to finish him off, but a wave of pain stabbed at his kidney.

The attacker landed a direct blow to his side, stinging the agent and throwing Fred off. Then, in a move straight out of a martial arts movie, he kip-upped, landing perfectly on his feet, shaking off the blow to the head, and ready to continue the fight.

The attacker, dressed in all black, charged. This time, Fred was ready. He wrapped his foot around the leg of the bench, yanking it over and kicking it into the attacker's way, hoping he'd trip over it. Instead, the assailant bounded the obstacle like it wasn't even there.

Big mistake, Fred thought, as he caught him in midair. He wrapped his arm around the attacker's head and neck, falling back, driving them both through a coffee table, the man headfirst. Fred landed with a thud, sending a stinging wave of agony down his spine.

Rolling off the unknown assailant, Fred staggered to his feet. He could hear his opponent moaning, staying motionless on the ground, breathing heavily.

Taking the momentary reprieve from action, Fred arched his body, walking off his pain and stumbling around the darkened room, cursing. Then he spotted the dark shape on all fours, trying to get up.

"Oh no, you don't, asshole."

Scooping up a desk chair, he angled it to drive it into the man's back. Fred swung, only for it to be blocked by the ceiling fan. The blades knocked it clear from his hands in a shower of wood. The blade panels sheared from the housing unit, knocking Fred off balance as the chair smashed against the wall, giving the attacker an opening.

He whipped out a silenced 9mm pistol from a shoulder holster. Fred clocked the movement of the gun with its elongated barrel and kicked it from his hand. It skittered several feet away. The two stared at each other for a second. Each was waiting for the other to make a move so that they could counter. The break in the fight seemed to last minutes.

Simultaneously, they both dove for the weapon, wrestling on the ground. The attacker gained control of the gun, but not before Fred could put him in a headlock. Fred tried to hold on, but his grip was slipping due to the sweat of both men from the fray.

In a few seconds, he would lose his grip and thus control over his opponent. There was only one thing left to do. Summoning the last few ounces of strength, Fred shifted positions, giving him enough space and leverage. Rotating both arms in opposite directions, he felt and heard the crunch of the attacker's neck as it snapped. The man's body dropped lifeless to the floor.

Fred fell to the ground, sitting beside the dead person, panting heavily. Every part of his body ached. He definitely felt his age after the fight.

"Let's see who you are," Fred rasped, leaning over to unmask his would-be executioner, revealing a man who appeared to be in his mid-twenties with brown hair styled in a military buzz cut. He couldn't recall ever seeing him before. "Don't know you, but…" he panted, checking the corpse for identification, finding only a few knives and a stick of gum. "Not sure how you found us," Fred said, snapping a photo of him. "And it doesn't look like you'll tell me either. But apparently, we've pissed off somebody who doesn't want to be known."

A thought struck him suddenly, "Oh shit, Sophia."

If someone had just tried to kill him, Sophia was most

assuredly a target, too. Fred raced out the door, shouting, "Sophia!"

****

Sophia stood in front of the door to her room, using one hand to brace herself up and her tired legs ready to give out, while the other hand searched for the key card. Fighting back a yawn, she was exhausted beyond belief.

"Come on, where are you?" Letting out an exasperated sigh upon not finding the key right away, her hand angrily stabbed around in her book bag. Then, frustratingly, she opened the bag, staring blankly into the dark void.

"Fuck."

Her eyes were barely functioning, trying to uncross themselves after hours of staring at page after page of documents and financial records. At one point, the ink had bleared into something like a Rorschach painting. No wonder she couldn't find the keys.

"Finally!"

She retrieved the hard-plastic rectangular object and looked at it as if it were the golden ticket. She slid the key into the reader, a charging wind-up of motors grinding into motion, drawing the bolt back and unlatching the door.

She had only two things on her mind: a nice hot shower and sleep.

The last week of her life had been a marathon. There hadn't been much time for sleep or any kind of rest, for that matter. However, the end was in sight.

Entering the room, Sophia tossed the book bag onto the bed, glancing at the soft mattress wistfully. "In just a minute," she mumbled, caressing the sheet, retrieving a change of clothes from her suitcase, and heading into the bathroom, her thoughts always on her objectives.

Hopefully, Tobias will secure the meeting with the Attorney General in the morning. They would hand over all the evidence gathered and let the justice department take it forward. Of course, she still desired to see it to the end, but once Senator Stone was in custody, her part in this nightmare would be over.

She wanted to become a spectator, just like the rest of the country.

First things first, the shower she so desired was just a few feet away. Undressing, she realized she'd forgotten her toiletry bag. "Oh shit, my kit." She wrapped a towel around her naked body and returned to the bedroom.

The young woman gasped, her eyes widening at the sight of a tall figure standing just in front of the closet door that had been opened. The person had been hiding in there until the opportune moment.

The intruder was dressed in all black, wearing a ski mask, and he had also frozen in place, not expecting his prey to be aware of their presence.

His eyes darted to the edge of the bed, zeroing in on the black book bag Sophia had just thrown there. Hers following his. In that instant, Sophia deciphered that Senator Stone must be onto them, and this was a hit. Her heart palpitated, skipping a beat for a second.

The intruder looked at Sophia, then back to the bag again. Were they there to kill her or collect the evidence? Or maybe both.

Who was going to make the first move?

The CIA agent did have an ace up her sleeve. Her Glock was in the bag's front pocket if she could just reach it in time.

Sophia ran towards the bed. But, before she could reach the bag, the chilling sound of a metallic charging hammer cocked, freezing her. She came to a dead stop, arm outstretched for the strap.

"Stop, back away," the intruder barked. His voice was gruff and gritty. Sophia's eyes looked up from the book bag, fixating on the silvery glint of a Beretta 9mm pistol pointed at her head. "Is that all your research? Who else knows what?" he rasped, jabbing the gun at her.

"I... I have no idea what you're talking about," Sophia answered, hands raised. "What research?"

"Don't play dumb with me, bitch. Who else knows?" the man insisted, waving the gun again.

"Look, okay, okay, no one else knows anything. I'm on my own here. Everything I have is all in that bag." She pointed to the end of the bed. "Here, I'll give it to you. Just don't shoot me. I can forget all about this."

She inched a step closer.

"No, back away."

Sophia retreated, obeying, snatching her hand back. Both hands were now gripping her towel tightly.

"Is everything in the bag?" He took a step closer to the bed but also drew nearer to Sophia.

"Yup, everything. Just one favor, if I may?"

The man signaled that he was consenting to her last request.

"Please, at least let me put on some clothes before you kill me." Sophia pulled at the towel, letting it unfurl, exposing her naked body.

The man, clearly not expecting such a cunning maneuver, gawked. His mouth was agape, gazing upon Sophia's athletically toned physique and nude body. His mind was distracted from his mission. He stared, eyes wide, admiring the view.

Sophia tilted her head to one side, the corner of her mouth twisting into a half-smile, as she seductively took a few steps closer. In a low, sexy whisper, she continued, "Or, if you like what you see, we can-"

She had gotten close enough to make a move. Still holding the towel in one hand, Sophia whipped it forward, cracking it at supersonic speed against the side of his head. The blow to his ear disrupted the intruder's equilibrium, staggering him briefly.

Sophia spun roundhouse, kicking the gun from his hand, watching it slide under the nightstand by the front of the bed. She turned to deliver another swift kick to his chest, knocking him backward as he fell over a desk chair.

She turned and ran for the door. The man alertly stuck out his leg in time to catch Sophia's foot. She tripped over his outstretched booted appendage and fell to the floor with a thud.

"You stupid bitch. I'm going to kill you," he growled. Turning her over, he climbed on top and pinned her to the floor. "Then your girlfriend is next. Just because you pissed me off."

He gripped her head in his hands, slamming it against the ground, trying to crack it like a coconut.

Sophia's vision blurred. Stinging, radiating pain shot out in waves over her skull as he slammed it a second time, further disorienting her.

"Die whore," the intruder shouted, spittle splattering her face. He pulled her head up once more for another blow.

Groggy and disoriented, she still had the willpower to fight back and reached up, digging her thumb into his left eye socket. He drew back, opening the opportunity to grab and twist his thumb, forcing him to release his grip as he wailed in agony. The pause in the attack allowed her to squirm out from underneath him. She pulled both legs back before springing them forward, driving them into his solar plexus and propelling him back.

He teetered before falling over.

Scrambling for the door again, she felt his hand clutch around her ankle, dragging her away from salvation. The searing pain of rug burn over her naked body helped fuel her anger.

Flipping over, she drove her foot into his face. Feeling the cartilage of his nose crumble against the bare skin of her foot brought a little relief.

The book bag was now within reach on the bed; she grabbed the strap and kicked him again in the chest. The blow gave her a few seconds. Fiddling to open the front flap, she drew the gun and whipped it around onto her target.

The man charged, screaming. "Die!"

The door flung open, sending splinters of wood flying in all directions. Followed by a series of shots. The man flailed with each successive strike, rocking backward as his body was riddled with slugs before he fell to the ground.

A dark shadow loomed over the young woman—light at the back of the second shooter.

"Sophia, are you ok?" Fred asked, lowering his weapon; he looked at Sophia lying on the ground. The CIA agent peered up, blinking, and huffed and puffed.

"Whoa, why are you naked?" Fred whipped around, shielding his eyes.

Sophia stood, wrapping herself back up in the towel. "Well, I was about to shower when I found this guy in my room," she said, catching her breath and thumbing to the dead person.

"Ok, get dressed; we've got to go." Still abashedly covering his eyes, Fred hurried into the room, closing the door behind him. "I had a visitor, too," he informed her. "Can I look now?"

"Give me a second, jeez," Sophia answered, annoyed. "I've probably got a concussion." She rubbed the back of her head.

Fred, still shielding his eyes, walked over to the body, pulling off the ski mask. Sophia peered over his shoulder as she finished putting on her shirt.

"Holy crap, that's the blonde guy who had followed me from Saudi Arabia. Quick, take a picture."

Sophia continued to get dressed and pack the contents of her bag, which were spread out across the floor. At the same time, Fred took a few snapshots of the body.

"Come on. We've gotta go."

He shoved Sophia down the steps and left the Motel. Police sirens wailed in the background, but they were drawing closer.

"I think someone called the cops," Fred said sarcastically, rounding the corner. The pair sauntered, heads down, not even glancing at the first police car that rushed by.

"Oh wait, where is Tobias?" Sophia asked, looking back. Fred shoved her head forward and down.

"I don't know. Possibly still setting up the meet. Should I call him?" Fred pulled out his phone.

"No! How did they find us? We took every precaution," Sophia stated, worry turning into suspicion.

Fred could see the wheels turning in her head. "Oh, hell no. Not a chance in hell," he said, cutting her off at the pass. "I know what you're thinking, and *no*. I have known Tobias for a long time. There is absolutely no way that he turned on me."

Sophia picked up the level of conviction in Fred's voice. She thought about the suggested accusation for another two seconds. Fred was completely adamant that Tobias could be trusted, and though she hadn't known the SAC as long, he'd never given her any reason to distrust him.

"No, you're right. I'm sorry, I'm just a bit tired and have a massive headache," Sophia apologized, dismissing the thought entirely.

"Ok, call him. Make sure he's okay and have him meet us at the diner around the block." Fred started to dial.

"Oh, and thank you for saving my life back there. I owe you one," Sophia said, jabbing Fred in the shoulder.

"You don't owe me anything. I'll take a bullet for you. You know that, right? You're like a daughter to me."

"I do, I do," Sophia said, blushing because her new adopted father figure had just seen her naked and because she loved the idea of having a father who loved her no matter what.

"But, still, thanks anyway. Now hurry up and make that call," she nudged the FBI agent. "We need to know if the AG will hear us out. And now we have even more evidence. Senator Stone just tried to have us killed."

CHAPTER TWENTY

Shortly after fleeing the newly minted crime scene, Fred and Sophia met with Tobias at a small, dingy, 24-hour diner several blocks away.

They hoped to gather some respite and determine their next move. Things had escalated rapidly, and a new strategy had to be devised. It isn't every day that you find yourself barely surviving an assassination attempt. But luckily, they had.

Tucked away in a booth in the farthest corner of the old restaurant, sipping on cup after cup of coffee to stay awake, they watched the flashing lights of first responder vehicles rush by. They took a few moments to collect themselves before catching their friend up on their separate ordeals.

It had now become evident. They were on a rapidly ticking clock. The group's supposedly incognito investigation wasn't as secretive as initially thought.

Could the probe and Tobias's use of his security clearance to help gather some of the personal and financial records of either Sotor Corp. or Senator Stone have tipped them off? Maybe that had sent some signal flare-up, suggesting that an unknown entity was snooping around.

No.

That would mean someone would've had to monitor internet traffic and web searches. Only the National Security Agency would have the power to keep track of such inquiries. However, that might not be a significant stretch with Senator Stone's involvement.

At the moment, it hadn't completely registered on Sophia's radar as significant, but while digging into the great Senator from Oklahoma, she'd uncovered that before becoming a member of Congress, Stone had briefly worked for the NSA after a stint in the Marine Corps as a Signals Intelligence Officer. He might suspect that Amell had spilled the beans on their operation. So, he may have used his sway at the NSA to monitor her from the moment she touched back down in the States.

Whether it was Sotor Corps or Senator Stone, it was evident

that they wanted both her and Fred dead. Or, at the very least, they wanted whatever evidence they had found linking the Senator and Sotor Corp to the terrorist attacks and the funding of the AIA. If any of their evidence ever came to light, that would spell the end for both parties.

It was something worth killing over.

Fortunately, Tobias escaped the evening without an attempt on his life. Undisturbed, he had been able to reach his old college friend and brought back some much-needed great news. However, it was not as entertaining as surviving a hit squad.

"Wow, I'm sorry that I wasn't there," Tobias said, gazing at the pair sitting across from him. "I'm glad you both survived because I have great news. Amy agreed to meet us and hear our case against the Senator in the morning. We have to be at her office by seven a.m."

"That's amazing, Toby," Sophia said. "Ugh, I can't wait to sleep in my bed once this is all over." She buried her head in her hands, smelling the aroma of the fresh cup of coffee the waitress placed in front of her.

Picking up a hint of annoyance, the older woman practically slammed the drink. "Maybe we should order some food," Sophia whispered as the woman walked away. They had been occupying the booth for several hours and hadn't ordered a morsel of food, just copious amounts of coffee.

"I guess we should," Fred added, checking his watch. "We have about three hours before our meeting."

"Yeah, and I think we need to find a place to freshen up before we go." The three smelled themselves, their faces scrunching up in disgust. "Yeah, it's been a long-smelly day," Fred confessed.

"I might have a place," Sophia said, remembering one of her old 'Farm' mates lived in the D.C. area.

****

Several hours later, as the sun began to creep over the buildings, bathing the concrete streets of the political jungle known as Washington, D.C., the trio stood in front of the Robert

F. Kennedy Department of Justice building—home to the U.S. Attorney General.

Tobias nervously fidgeted with the sleeves of his suit jacket, trying in vain to pull them lower, looking down at his tight, high-water pants. "I look like a dad wearing his son's suit," he grumbled, looking every bit as uncomfortable as one would be wearing a suit a size too small.

Fred and Sophia had to fight back a chortle physically.

"I'm sorry," Sophia added, covering her mouth. "Leslie's husband isn't as tall as you. But hey, at least he let you guys borrow some clothes. And… that look is apparently in style these days," she said, unable to maintain eye contact for fear of outright laughter.

"Mine fits perfectly," Fred chimed in, adding insult while admiring the lent clothing. 'This thing had to cost at least $1,000. What does Leslie's husband do?"

"He's a *very* high-priced defense lawyer for guys… well, like Senator Stone."

"Let's just get this over with," Tobias said, shaking his head and starting for the doors. Fred and Sophia followed behind, still laughing.

Inside, they were escorted to Amy's office by a burly U.S. Marshal. They waited for several minutes until Attorney General Sanchez entered. The three rose.

"Please sit down," the woman ordered, pausing for a moment to inspect Tobias curiously. "My goodness, Toby, what are you wearing?" she chastised her old friend, laughing.

"I'm told it's in style," he said, turning to Sophia, who smiled back and shrugged.

The pants rose to just under his calves as he sat down.

"Ok," the AG dismissed the fashion faux pas, taking a seat. "By the way, you sounded last night, at one in the morning, I might add, you have something fairly important to discuss." She sounded displeased.

"We do, but I'll let Agent Evans take it from here," Tobias indicated to the CIA agent, who then took the floor. They'd rehearsed the spiel several times while getting ready.

Sophia went on to make their entire case, providing all the supporting evidence they had uncovered over the last few days, up to and including their attempted murders the night before.

A.G. Sanchez leaned back in her seat upon Sophia's conclusion. Her head swirled as she tried to wrap her thoughts around what had just been laid at her feet. A United States Senator is working in concert with his Son-in-law's Private Military Company to not only propagate terrorism but also profit from it.

"Jeez, Toby, how the hell did you stumble into this one? This makes me sick." A wave of displeasure swept over her face as she processed the story. "I can't believe it. I know Senator Stone. I thought he was a patriot through and through."

"Nope, just a sellout. Killing Americans just so he and his family could grow richer," Fred growled.

"Ok," she said, shaking her head, still in disbelief. "You've got your warrants. One is for Senator Stone's arrest, and the other is to be served on Sotor Crops headquarters. Just give me a few hours, and we'll have everything drawn up," she said, standing. The trio, along with her.

"In the meantime," looking at Tobias with a smirk. "Toby, may I suggest you find some clothes that actually fit you," she teased, drawing a laugh from everyone, including Tobias.

****

The sun dipped below the man-made horizon of buildings. City Street lamps flickered on one after another, illuminating the street in a sparkling glow as the beams refracted off puddles of water. The whooshing of wiper blades drowned out the pitter-patter of rain cascading over the Cadillac Escalade as the vehicle lurched to a stop.

Sitting in the passenger seat, Sophia barely registered the cessation of movement. Her eyes never once shifted from the slip of paper—the search warrant and warrant for Senator Stone's arrest twirling in her hands, although she could feel the gaze of her partner leering at her.

"Penny, for your thoughts?" Fred asked.

"Just thinking about Tobias and what he'll find in Oklahoma at Soter Corp's office." That was about as much as she wanted to go into her thoughts.

Fred wasn't buying the young woman's explanation. He knew there was something else at work in that mind of hers. "And?"

She broke eye contact with the warrants, leveling an accusatory stare at him. "What makes you think I'm thinking of anything else right now? Are you a Sophia expert?" she sniped.

She had no genuine desire to tell Fred what she was currently thinking. They were so close to finishing this that she didn't want to curse anything.

"Um, yeah, I kind of am. You're not as impossible to read as you think," Fred replied, pressing the accelerator as the light turned green. "It's also just what you do. You think. Sometimes, a little too much."

Sophia's brow furrowed. "Hey, that is completely uncalled for, sir," she protested, but she knew he was right.

"What are friends for? They tell each other the hard truth, right?" He smiled.

"I suppose so, but it still does not mean it hurts any less." She was playing the offended victim role a bit longer, hoping to delay divulging what was on her mind. The tactic worked. The Escalade rounded the last corner. Senator Stone's house lay just ahead.

"Well, put your game face on. We're about to enter the lion's den," Fred said, pulling the vehicle up into the driveway of the Senator's brownstone.

Fred and Sophia exited the vehicle and walked up the path to the front door. Several more Escalades pulled up behind them, and additional FBI Agents disembarked. Fred waved them off, signaling them to stand by.

He didn't want to startle the Senator and immediately put him on the defensive, which a cadre of law enforcement officers on your doorstep would tend to do. He wanted a little alone time with the man who had attacked his city. Maybe by catching him off guard, he would slip up and accidentally incriminate himself.

Before reaching the door, though, Senator Stone opened it, calmly holding a glass of whiskey. "Good evening, Agent Jones;

it's nice to see you again. I've been waiting," he said smugly, sipping his glass—so much for catching him off guard.

Someone must've gotten wind of the warrants and warned him. "So, what exactly do I owe you for this pleasure?" His arrogant demeanor and posture oozed a level of condescension that infuriated Fred. Every word that dribbled out of his mouth reached the maximum level of fakeness that couldn't fool a five-year-old.

Fred started, "Senator Roy Stone-"

"Oh, and this must be the CIA agent who put an end to Amell al-Gharsi." Cutting Fred off as he reached out to shake Sophia's hand, he exclaimed, "You're a real American hero for ending that terrorist."

Sophia jerked her hand back as Fred stepped closer, pushing the door open. They spotted several suitcases by the stairs. "Oh, planning a vacation, it seems. I didn't know they were calling the session to a close so soon."

"No, those are my wife's. She's flying back home tomorrow. Why don't you guys come in for a second?" Senator Stone stepped aside to allow Fred and Sophia to enter.

"Good, because you shouldn't make plans to leave anytime soon," Fred stated, slipping past the Senator. Sophia slapped the warrants to the Senator's chest so hard he nearly spilled his drink before signaling the other agents to approach as she walked past.

He quickly scanned the warrant.

"You know I'm a United States Senator, right? And these allegations against me are wholly false."

"And which allegations would those be?" Sophia questioned, whipping around, glowering at the older man. "Oh, and you may want to start updating your resume to former Senator and current inmate," she quipped.

From the living room, a voice called out. "Roy dear, who's at the door?"

"No one, honey, they were just leaving," the Senator answered his wife. "You… you can't do this; you're making a huge mistake. " I will have your jobs," he hissed as several agents brushed past him and entered the house.

He finally let his shield of pompous arrogance drop. Whoever had tipped him off about the warrant didn't know what the charges were. The Senator stood slack-jawed. The trio had gathered enough evidence to put him away for three lifetimes.

Fred entered the living room, where he found Ms. Stone sitting and watching TV. She panicked when she turned and saw him standing at the top step of the room, wearing his FBI jacket.

"Roy, what's going on? I thought you said they were leaving. Why is the FBI here?"

Senator Stone rushed in, grabbing his wife. These men are here to search the house. They *think*," he spat scathingly, his supercilious façade returning. "That I have done something wrong." Eyes fixated on Fred, he continued, "Which I have not, and you'll be paying for this tomorrow."

Sophia stood at the top of a staircase leading to the lower floor. "Ha-ha, done nothing wrong. That is the most ridiculous thing I have heard all day. Ma'am, did old Roy here tell you where he gets all his money?"

"Sophia, don't," Fred barked, jabbing a finger in the air at her. "Just search the house."

She sarcastically ran a finger across her lips. The universal sign of zipping up. "Is your office downstairs? Oh, oops, never mind, no need to answer that. I have a piece of paper that says I can just go check for myself."

She sauntered down the staircase, which let out into a small office. Flicking the light on, Sophia half-expected to find a smoking gun. The story Fred had told earlier about his ego made her think he would be dumb enough to believe he was untouchable.

Sadly, nothing was left laying out—no master plan or bank records linking all parties—just your typical run-of-the-mill home office.

Deciding to make her way back upstairs, Sophia knew that the other agents would eventually join her. Besides, staying in the basement would prevent her from witnessing the Senator's impending discomfort as his carefully crafted plans were about to unravel. As she prepared to ascend the stairs, she saw a massive, matte-black safe tucked away in the corner of the room.

Her curiosity was piqued, and Sophia's investigative instincts kicked in. She approached the safe, examining its imposing presence. Thoughts raced through her mind. What secrets could be hidden within? Was there a connection to the Senator's nefarious activities? Determined to uncover the truth, Sophia made a mental note to revisit the safe once the chaos subsided and she had the opportunity to investigate further, or if the Senator would be kind enough to open it for them. He should have no problem being transparent if he had nothing to hide. She crossed her fingers. It'd be that easy to ascend the stairs.

"Oh, Roy," she crooned, re-entering the living room. All decorum had disappeared at this point. In her mind, the Senator was no longer worthy of such a title. "Would you be so kind as to provide us entry into that safe of yours down there?"

"Fuck you," the senator lashed, much to the dismay of his wife.

"Fine, I'm sure we can get in one way or another," she said, turning to see Fred coming down the stairs from the bedroom, shaking his head, having found nothing of note.

"Alright, boys, continue going through the house and pack up everything worth noting." He stopped. "No, wait, pack up everything. I want it all."

"That includes the safe in the downstairs office," Sophia jumped in, watching Stone as she said it. The look behind his eyes revealed a hint of worry. "Actually, how about we start with the safe? Let's get a saw in here," she added.

Fred stared blankly at the CIA agent, who looked back at him almost intuitively, sending her thoughts to him. They really were on the same page.

Fred picked up precisely what Sophia was up to. "You heard her. Let's get a saw. Cut that damn thing open. Unless-" he ordered, facing the Senator. "You're willing to open it for us. Make things easier for you." No witty, sarcastic, or condescending comment was hurled back. Nothing but a shake of Stone's head. "Ok, fine." Retrieving a pair of cuffs, he approached the Senator. "Guess you're coming with us. Turn around."

"Please, no cuffs," the senator begged, his head hanging low as humility overtook him. "Honey, call the lawyer and tell him what's happening," he directed his wife. "You know the number."

Fred seized the man by the arm, putting away the cuffs. Silently agreeing to the request, much to Sophia's unspoken chagrin. The pair led the Senator outside to their Escalade, placing him in the back as news vans poured onto the block. Several agents moved to hold back the frenzied reporters.

The D.C. metro police were called in to assist. They arrived just in time to cordon off the area. Fred and Sophia departed with their prize, heading toward the FBI office with their prisoner in custody.

Pulling into the parking garage, Amy Sanchez stood waiting for their arrival. Two agents flanked the SUV, pulling Stone out and ushering him inside. She approached after watching the Senator being escorted away.

"Agents Jones and Evans, it's nice to see you again." They shook hands. "I trust you have a plan in mind? Because I'm taking a great many calls right now demanding to know why I issued an arrest warrant for a state Senator."

"Sort of," Fred answered. "We have a lot of evidence on him, but he's smart, so I'm not sure what we'll get. But we will hit him with every trick we've got."

"You have until morning to get something substantial out of him, or if Tobias can obtain anything from Soter Corp., that would be great. Just make sure you have him at the courthouse early in the morning. And you better have something to convince the judge to lock him up. Or he is going to go scot-free, and all our careers will be over by the end of tomorrow."

"Twelve hours. I think we can get something."

****

Fred and Sophia allowed the Senator to sit alone in the interrogation room for an hour. They wanted him to feel the weight of the world coming down around him.

Fred was convinced that allowing him to sit and stew in his

worry and doubt would soften him.

Satisfied, they had waited long enough. The pair prepared to enter. "Hey, when we go in there, let's bring up the safe," Sophia said, grabbing Fred's arm before he could open the door.

"But they haven't been able to break into it yet," Fred countered.

"I know that. You know that. He doesn't. You didn't see his face when I mentioned the safe at the house. Something's in there. Something he doesn't want us to see."

"Sof, that's a huge gamble. If we play that card, and he calls our bluff. That's it. We'll never get him to crack before tomorrow morning," Fred countered; the experienced interrogator in him appeared. Knowing it was risky business to bluff someone as smart as the Senator. "I know how bad you want this guy. Believe me; I do, too. We've both lost people close to us in this. But let's not let our emotions cloud our judgment here. We've got careers riding on this," he said, reminding her of Amy's warning. Fred reached for the door handle again. Sophia pawed at him once more.

"But I know it's the right play," Sophia insisted through clenched teeth—a fire behind her eyes.

Fred removed Sophia's hand from around his wrist with a tinge of disappointment. "Ok." He led her to an adjacent door, opened it, and rushed her inside. "I'm going in there alone. You're going to watch from here." They were in the observation room.

"The hell I am," she spat, trying to bulldoze her way past him.

Fred blocked the door.

"Need I remind you that we're currently in an FBI building? I'm an FBI agent. And this is still technically an FBI investigation. So yes, you're staying put."

He pushed her back inside, closing the door behind her.

Sophia had no choice but to obey. Fred, after all, was right. She turned to the viewing window, glaring at Senator Stone, who sat alone on the other side.

"I hope he cracks you like a fucking egg," she hissed, folding her arms across her chest, simmering at being sidelined.

Fred calmed himself before entering the interrogation room.

Heartland Strike

He meandered about, circling the embattled senator, not saying a word, shuffling some papers about in a manila folder before pulling out a chair. He placed the folder on the table and then spread its contents out so his interrogator could see the fruits of the investigation. Fred leaned back in his chair, wearing a smug smile, the kind the Senator had given him earlier.

"So, here's an idea. Why don't you just come clean right now? Save yourself, me, and the country the embarrassment. Maybe we can work out a deal of sorts."

Stone glanced at the documents before him, unwaveringly unresponsive.

"We've got *you* dead to rights. Or we could settle this the way you wanted me to do to Amell all those months ago. That's why you wanted him dead. He knew too much. And you wanted us to help cover your tracks, right?"

The senator didn't budge.

"Fine, have it your way. You'll be tried for treason, and I hope they stick a fucking needle in your arm."

Fred stood up.

"Wait!" Stone shouted before Fred reached the door. "Ok, I'll tell you everything you need to know."

Fred maintained a composed smile as he returned to his seat, unfazed by the Senator's outburst. The Senator, in turn, edged a little closer, his voice lowered, taking a defeated tone. "It all started with," he began, drawing Fred in. "With I want my fucking lawyer now!" His defiant laughter filled the room. "Ha-ha, you thought you could scare me into confessing something I didn't do. You've got nothing, or you wouldn't even be in here. I'm not saying another word until my lawyer gets here."

Fred remained calm, his demeanor unchanged. "Ok, that's how you want to play this fine." He knew the game had just entered a new phase, and the battle was far from over. Fred gathered the evidence files. "I'll just go make sure he's on his way then." He headed towards the door. "Sit tight for the next few hours to years."

Outside, Sophia met Fred in the hallway. "That didn't go well," she said sheepishly.

"No fucking shit," he fired back tartly.

"Maybe I could try. Use the safe."

"No. He's mentally prepared for this. We just have to hope that they crack that thing by morning. Or the judge feels we have enough here."

"Unless," Sophia countered, a thought suddenly occurring to her.

CHAPTER TWENTY-ONE

Time had run out on Fred and Sophia. Once the Senator lawyered up, the abbreviated interrogation came to a close. Fred had underestimated how prepared and savvy Stone was. The bevy of evidence did not affect the man. Almost as if he knew that no matter what they threw at him, he'd beat it.

They stood shoulder to shoulder, arms folded, in the dark and damp underground garage, watching as the object of their ire was escorted to one of the four SUVs waiting. Sophia and Fred felt defeated, their faces twisted in disgust.

"He's going to get away with this, right?" Sophia sniped.

"Not if this works," Fred mumbled, death stare fixed upon his target.

"Yeah, laugh it up," Sophia shouted as the congress member strolled by with a smirk as wide as the Grand Canyon. "Just wait till we crack your safe, asshole." Giving him a cartoonish shake of her fist.

"Really?" Fred quipped, breaking his gaze and turning it to his young cohort with a frown.

"I take it he didn't confess, then?" A.G. Sanchez said, coming up behind the pair.

"Not yet," Fred answered as the Senator was shoved into the back seat of the SUV. "But this isn't over."

"I take it you have a plan?"

"We do. Something I should have listened to my partner about hours ago," Fred said, glancing at Sophia and cracking a smirk of his own.

"Whatever it is, you'd better have a confession by the time you arrive at the courthouse," she said tersely before walking away.

"Here goes everything," Sophia added, breaking toward the vehicle.

The four-car escort pulled out of the FBI garage onto 9th Street, then made a sharp right turn onto East Street. The sun had just risen; light beams flicked in between the buildings.

It was early Sunday morning, and the streets were mostly empty except for a few cars passing by. The light traffic would make the drive to the courthouse relatively quick.

The move had been planned meticulously throughout the night. It was relatively simple, a quick jot of a few miles. They were to travel down East Street, turning right on 3rd Street—fifteen minutes total.

In preparation, a decoy convoy was dispatched approximately twenty minutes before departure. This one had much more fanfare and police escort attached to it. The goal was to throw off the horde of media parasites camped out in front of the FBI building all night. Clamoring for a tiny hint at why the Senator had been arrested. It worked. Not a media member was in sight, and no one followed them. They only had fifteen minutes, and it was now or never.

Time to execute the plan. They just needed to get him talking. It didn't matter what. Just get him going, play to hubris, and hopefully, he will slip up.

"Hey, Sophia, have you ever wondered what it's like to be a traitor to your country?" Fred asked.

"Not really, but I suppose if I did want to know, I could just ask the dirtbag sitting next to you," Sophia goaded, peering into the rearview mirror. "Although I would reckon I would feel like a shitbag." Sophia continued to mock him in a country drawl.

"I don't know. I think it would take some big brass balls to attack your country. Kill the citizens you supposedly love... just to make a few bucks. Wouldn't you?" Fred stared at Stone.

"You know you two can't talk to me," his voice boomed smugly.

"I wasn't. I was asking my good friend Sophia a question. I will have plenty of opportunities with you later."

The Senator smiled; his eyes leered upon Fred longer than they should have, showcasing his penchant for dramatic flair. Sophia watched the creepy exchange through the mirror. The look sent chills down her spine.

"I wouldn't be so sure of that," the senator remarked. A strange level of confidence behind his words. It was as if he secretly knew something no one else did. Almost like he had some magic trick to get out of the hot water he was in.

Fred, for his part, laughed off the arrogance. Chopping it up to false bravado.

The Senator had swelled with overconfidence. There would be no chance of escaping this without facing prison time. "Someone is a little smug this-"

The convoy had been stopped at the red light on 6th Street. It changed; the lead SUV pulled out into the intersection. Speeding up 6th Street, a black Ford F-150 barreled through the red light, smashing into the passenger side of the SUV.

Sophia watched in horror as the large frame of the Escalade flipped over upside down. She could hear the metal frame of the vehicle crunch from the collision. Glass exploded into the air, showering the roadway.

Stunned by what had just happened, the agent stared slack-jawed.

Two Land Cruisers pulled into the middle of the intersection, following the now crumpled F-150, their horns blaring. The driver slumped over, his face planted into the airbag, the windshield missing.

Six men clad in black military uniforms burst out of the Land Cruisers, their movements swift and purposeful. The tranquil street instantly transformed into a chaotic war zone as the men unleashed a barrage of gunfire upon the three remaining SUVs. Adorned with ski masks and bulletproof vests, their ammunition pouches prominently displayed across their chests, they were fully prepared for the assault. Armed with AK47s, their weapons spat fire and lead.

Amidst the mayhem, one of the men retrieved a long, gleaming silver device resembling a rocket launcher from their vehicle. With calculated precision, he aimed it directly at the three functional SUVs that had survived the initial onslaught. The air crackled with tension as the weapon's ominous presence hinted at the impending devastation it could unleash.

As the commando affixed the weapon to his targets, two of his friends rushed to the toppled SUV. Sophia could see the muzzle flashes from their AKs as they emptied their magazines into any would-be collision survivors.

"Wilson, go back, go back!" Sophia shouted at their driver, reaching for the dash radio, breaking from her momentary surprise at what had just happened.

"What's going on? Did they get hit?" Fred asked, peeking around the driver's seat headrest, glimpsing the carnage. "Son of a bitch."

"Hold on," Wilson bellowed, throwing the shifter into reverse, hoping Agent Watts in the rear vehicle would follow suit. The tires spun, kicking up a plume of smoke, and the heavy-bodied SUV jolted backward.

Sophia keyed the mic to the radio. "What the fuck is that? Get down!" she shouted, noticing the object being pointed at them.

The SUV shuddered to a halt, followed by static over the radio. All their vehicles and communications had been disabled. Bullets pinged off the SUV's chassis.

"What the fuck just happened?" shouted Wilson, stomping on the accelerator, not moving, turning the key.

Ching, ching, ching.

The ignition wasn't turning over. "They must have hit us with an EMP. We need to get out," Sophia said, unbuckling her seatbelt.

The three agents in the Second SUV had already jumped out and taken up a defensive position behind their car's doors, returning fire at the six commandos who were advancing. Sophia knew they would not last long without backup. The agents were outgunned, as their Glocks were no match for the AK's heavy firepower and the commandos' bulletproof vests.

"We've gotta move." Fred kicked open his door, sliding out, dragging the Senator with him. "Come on, shit bag." Agent Wilson laid down cover fire as the two scrambled to the rear of the SUV. Fred and Stone were met by Agent Watts and the two agents from vehicle four.

"What do we do, sir?" Watts asked a look of uncertainty on his face, clearly having never been in a gunfight. A situation that Fred would usually have envied, but his previous experiences were now going to come in handy.

"Stay alive," Fred responded. "Sof, get your ass in gear."

Sophia tried to jump out, but the seatbelt caught her holster, pulling her back. Slamming into the doorframe, shoulder-first, she crumpled to the asphalt. Roars from the AKs snapped her back to Perim Island for a second as she scrambled to her feet. "Fuck shit, fuck. Not again!" she cried.

Several rounds dotted the side of the vehicle as they raced to the back of the SUV, tearing holes in the sheet metal—chasing her.

Scrambling to the rear of the SUV, Sophia caught a glimpse of a mother hunched over her child hiding behind a brick column of a nearby building as she ran. Sophia motioned for them to stay put, reaching Fred and the others, who were panting and throwing themselves against the back of the car.

"What are we going to do?"

"Why is everyone asking me that?" Fred complained.

He had already pulled out the tactical gear from the back of the SUV. Handing her a vest and M4. "Here, put this on and take that. We need to help the others."

"What about the Senator?" Sophia asked, although she didn't really need to. Knowing Fred, there would be no way he would ever put her in danger. So she already knew the answer.

"He stays here with you," Fred said, slapping a magazine in, pulling the charging hammer back, and chambering a round.

"And you don't go anywhere. Stay put," he ordered, shoving Stone closer to Sophia, who grabbed their captive's arm. "Wilson, you two on me. Watts, stay here and help cover Sophia."

Fred then slid around the rear of the SUV, disappearing along with Wilson and the other two agents, Chamberlain and Bass.

The quartet moved up the driver's side, keeping low and heads down. Reaching the front, Fred peeked over the frame, looking through the windows, searching for the attackers. The roar of more machine gun fire erupted from behind them, shattering the glass above his head. Fred ducked as the window blew apart, fragments of the safety glass sliced across his cheek. Losing his balance as he went down, Fred slipped on the fallen shards and fell forward, somehow managing to twist his body to face the direction the shots had come from.

Three more identically dressed commandos were quickly closing in on their position from 7ᵗʰ Street, opening fire with another burst.

Fred, Wilson, and the other agents scrambled back to cover between the SUVs. They were trapped inside a perfectly executed kill box. They couldn't move forward and now couldn't move backward.

From his position, Fred could hear one of the agents from the second SUV screaming for help. He watched the masked attackers slaughter the three agents inside the vehicle, slamming his fist into the car door.

"Dammit," he cursed.

Fresh from their slaughter, the soldiers turned to find their next prey. However, instead of advancing their position, they held, adopting a defensive posture, as did the three coming up from 7ᵗʰ Street. The Agents were hemmed in, with nowhere to go.

A voice shouted out. "You know what we want. Hand him over, and I might let you live."

"You have got to be kidding me?" Sophia knew that voice; she had heard it before.

"What?" Fred asked.

"That voice, I know who that is." Fred waited for the answer. "Some guy who introduced himself as Agent Williams. He debriefed me in Saudi. He said he worked for the Department of Defense." She put two and two together. "Which means he probably works for Soter Crops."

"Well, that's great. We now know who's going to kill us today. What do we do now? We're pinned down," Wilson fretted, frantic. "What are we going to do?"

"Ok, people," Williams shouted again, irritation in his voice. "I don't really want to ask again. So please don't make me. I hate repeating myself."

"Over there." Sophia pointed across the street at an alleyway between a building and a parking garage. "If we can make it there, we can make a break for it. Metro police should be here soon."

"None of you are making it out of here unless you hand me over," Stone needled. "You will all die."

"You know the last asshole that said that to me, I put a knife through the back of his head. Would you like me to repeat that?" Sophia snapped back, grabbing the man by the collar and pulling him closer, baring her teeth as spittle misted his face.

"Sof, back away." Fred separated the two.

"Ok," she conceded. "I don't see another way out. So that's the plan then." Checking for confirmation from the group.

"You could hand me over," Stone reiterated. "I don't think he's going to ask again," he said, referring to Williams.

"Shut up," Fred fumed, slapping him in the face. "Just because I pulled her away doesn't mean I won't hit you." Fred drew back for another blow. The man flinched, throwing his hands up in front of his face. "Yeah, that's what I thought." Fred faced his team. "Alright. We go with Sof's idea. Watts, Chamberlain, Bass, and I will lay down cover fire. Sophia, Wilson, you head for the alley. I'll follow with the Senator, then you three follow." Fred pointed at Watts and the others.

"I'm done. You have ten seconds to release the Senator," Williams shouted. "One, Two..."

"Well, that's annoying," said Fred, rolling his eyes. He hated countdowns. Felt like they were overused and cliché. "Anyways, when he gets five, go." Sophia nodded, cricking her ear to hear.

"Four, five..."

Hoping to catch the commandos off guard, Sophia sprung to her feet, slinging her rifle around her back using the sling, before rushing out from behind the SUV and making a beeline across the street. She could feel adrenaline flood her veins like never before. Not even on the Island did it feel so strong as it fueled her now. Running faster than ever.

The mad dash caught Williams and his team off guard, allowing her to make it halfway before they even opened fire. Running in a zig-zag pattern, giving a more elusive target, chunks of pavement spat up, rounds slamming into the ground all around.

After a quick peek behind, Wilson was right on her heels, encouraging her to run faster. "Move, move, now." The taller agent caught up despite getting a later jump.

At full speed, she drew near to the edge of the building. The tip of Wilson's shoe caught Sophia's heel. Sending the agent stumbling forward. If she fell, her body would be riddled with bullets within seconds. Tumbling, her arms waving wildly, she tried to keep her balance, but the ground began to rush toward her face, and she found herself almost horizontal to the concrete. She was going to eat pavement, then a bullet. There was only one option to avoid becoming a bullet sponge.

On the verge of face-planting, Sophia pushed off with her back foot, launching herself through the air. She glided forward in an almost ethereal free fall before crashing back to the hard earth. She drove her shoulder into the ground, letting out a yelp of pain as a burning sensation overtook her. Landing, she rolled head over heels into cover. The force of the impact and subsequent roll had snapped her rifle loose. It skittered down the alley. She snapped back up, waiting to see Wilson barrel into the alley.

However, when she looked back, Wilson's body lay motionless on the ground two feet from the safety of the building. He didn't make it. Blood oozed from a gaping hole in his head. "Fuck," she spat, looking for her rifle.

****

Fred watched helplessly as Sophia and Wilson sprinted for the alleyway, wincing at every impact of the bullets trailing behind them. Praying none would strike true. Every round somehow missed their targets; as the pair approached the alley, Fred became increasingly less concerned with every foot safely traversed, allowing him to relax.

Too soon, however, the respite was short-lived. As Fred's heart raced with the hope of safety, an unforeseen turn of events shattered his relief. His heart sank as he witnessed Wilson's foot accidentally clip Sophia's heel, causing her to stumble. Time seemed to freeze for a fleeting moment as Sophia tumbled towards a fate that spelled certain death. If she were to halt her forward motion, the relentless hail of bullets would inevitably catch up to her.

The weight of the impending tragedy became unbearable for

Fred. Overwhelmed by the prospect of witnessing Sophia being mercilessly torn apart by bullets, he turned away. His eyes snapped shut, his body instinctively turning aside, shielding himself from the heart-wrenching sight that unfolded before him.

For a brief second, the gunfire stopped. Fred was afraid to look. "She made it," Watts shouted. "She made it, sir, but…" Fred opened his eyes to find Sophia safely across, scrambling to find her rifle. Relief swept over him for a second until he saw Wilson's lifeless body lying face down on the sidewalk. Blood pooled around a gaping hole in his head.

Fred whisked around on Stone, grabbing and yanking him by the collar. The two were face to face. "I'm going to add Wilson to your counts of murder, you piece of shit!" His anger was now barely contained. "So help me, god, if you don't run, I will fucking put a bullet in your head if it's the last thing I do," the agent seethed.

Stone stared blankly, unsure of how to respond. "Ye… Yeah," he managed to choke out, primarily out of fear of what Fred would do to him if he said anything else.

Preparing the two for their crossing, Fred scooped Stone up off the ground, forcing the older man to move in front of him. Fred would push the Senator to safety if he had to. Readying to go. The veteran agent steeled himself, preparing to face a similar onslaught of bullets Sophia had just barely escaped. "Ready." Stone nodded. "Go."

With adrenaline pumping through their veins, Fred and Stone charged forward, bracing themselves for a fierce barrage of gunfire. However, to their surprise, no deadly projectiles rained down upon them. Williams swiftly issued a command to his team, instructing them to cease fire. The mercenary understood the importance of protecting their valuable captive from any stray rounds.

In this unexpected moment of respite, the FBI agents seized the opportunity to shift from a defensive stance to an offensive one. They harnessed the momentum, ready to take the fight to their adversaries and regain control.

Agents Watts, Chamberlain, and Bass used the break to their

advantage, as did Sophia, springing up to fire on their attackers, sending them scrambling for cover, shooting back desperately to cover their movements.

Sophia now had a clear shot from the alley at the three commandos approaching from 7th Street. Opening fire at the same time as her cohorts from behind the SUV, Sophia hit two men, with Watts striking the third in the throat, having shifted fire as Chamberlain and Bass had the others covered.

Fred quickly took stock of the switch in action, his side pressing its advantage, and stopped before reaching the alley. It dawned on him that they wouldn't risk hitting the Senator. He now had a human shield. "Change of plans." He grabbed Stone, forcing him in front of him.

Spinning, he fired a fusillade, striking one of the commandos flush between the eyes. Fred wanted to push forward while they had the ability.

"Fred, keep moving," Sophia shouted. He glared over, not wanting to pull back and retreat. The CIA operative could read it on his face. "Now, we've got to go."

Reluctantly, Fred disengaged and met Sophia near the edge of the alley. "Here," he said, pushing Stone into the waiting hands of Sophia. Turning, he signaled for Watts and the other agents to move. "Let's go."

Watts and the other agents made a break for the alley. Williams's team opened fire as the agents broke for the ally, Fred laying down cover fire.

However, the second Watts left the safety of cover from behind the SUV, he was struck in the knee. Fred tracked the shot back to its location, shifting, spraying, and suppressing fire in that direction and sending the shooter back down.

But the damage had already been done. The second Watts went down screaming, clutching his knee, Chamberlain and Bass stopped to help their fellow agent, only to be hit themselves immediately. A round sliced through Bass's neck, tearing a ragged gouge of flesh. He fell limp over Watts, who had taken a second round to the head, killing him instantly.

Chamberlain, seeing the carnage, stopped and retreated to the

SUV. He wouldn't make it, though, as he took a round to the temple, fired by Williams.

"No!" Sophia let out a blood-curdling scream, watching her fellow agents slaughtered. She tried to dart back out onto the street. Having seen the gruesome scene unfold from the corner of his eye, Fred broke off his attack and retreated. He snatched Sophia around the waist, hauling her back into the alley. "Let me go. Come on, Fred, we need to help them." Sophia jerked away from his grasp.

"They're dead," he shouted, hauling her back again. "No one can help them. But listen." He held up a finger in the air. Faint sounds of sirens wailed in the distance. "The cops are almost here." Unfortunately, the wailing sirens didn't have the full calming effect on his partner that he'd hoped for. We won't let them get away with it. But we do need to save ourselves first and secure our cargo." Thumbing to Stone.

Sophia's anger simmered, her gaze burning with fury as she glared at the Senator. Her finger hovered restlessly on the trigger of her rifle, the weight of the decision pressing upon her. At that moment, she entertained a dangerous thought. What if she took matters into her own hands, ending it all right then and there? She contemplated delivering the ultimate justice and exposing the traitor. With Stone dead, Williams could slink back to whatever hole he'd crawled out from. The country would get its retribution, and she and Fred would survive. The barrel of her gun slowly rose, finding its place, pressed firmly against Stone's forehead, her finger tapping on the trigger, each tap resonating with the gravity of choice before her.

"Sophia," Fred sibilated. "That's not justice. That's revenge. You know that," he hissed. "Look at me." She glanced over.

While discussing the merits of putting a bullet in Stone's head, the duo hadn't registered that the gunfire had ceased again. "The offer still stands, but only for thirty more seconds. One, two…" Williams began counting, breaking up the debate.

"Fuck, he's actually going to count. Sof, you know this is wrong. We need to go."

The CIA agent knew deep down she couldn't pull the trigger.

"Damn it," cursing, she lowered her weapon. "You're lucky I actually obey the law," she rasped at Stone, who appeared unfazed by the confrontation. Either knowing she couldn't or that Fred wouldn't allow his prized protégé to commit what would've been tantamount to murder. "Ok, let's go. We can run down the alley. They won't have time to chase us."

Stone laughed. The pair turned their gaze to the Senator. "What's so funny, asshole?" Fred questioned.

The old man's smirk widened as he relished his revelation. "I've been a resident of this area for twenty long years, and let me tell you, this alley is a dead end. Quite literally for the two of you," he taunted.

Unfazed, Fred wasted no time and swiftly dashed down the alley, disappearing for a brief moment. He returned quickly, his expression confirming the old man's claim. At the end of the alley stood nothing but an imposing brick wall blocking any possible escape route.

Relishing the situation, Senator Stone couldn't help but interject, a victorious gleam in his eyes. "Furthermore, those sirens you hear? They're farther off than you think. The response times of the D.C. Metro are severely lacking," he declared, his confidence brimming brightly as if he had already emerged as the winner.

"Sof, He's right."

Taking a moment to soak in their situation, all Sophia could think about was everything they had been through. Every emotion felt. The names of everyone they had lost flooded through her head.

All for nothing. They were being forced to hand over the person responsible for all the death and destruction that had occurred since that July 2nd day. The deaths of all the people at the museum. All the agents who have died. Her friends Naseem and Yousef. Everyone else had been affected by this man's greed.

"Time's up. What's your choice going to be?" Williams shouted.

"Sof, what's it going to be? I'm with you either way till the end."

"Fine," she whispered. "I'm not going to have your death on my conscious, too. Let him go." Sophia collapsed against the brick wall, sliding down it, unable to believe it had come to this.

"For the record, Agent Evans," Stone said, adjusting his clothes. "This is the only option you ever had. You actually thought you could arrest me," he said, laughing as he walked out into the street. "Oh, and I'll see you two later." Winking and blowing Sophia a kiss, he continued his strut to freedom.

"Do you think we can trust him, Fred? He's going to let us live?" Sophia asked, dejected.

"Not a chance in hell, but we should have backup arriving in a few seconds. I just wanted to buy ourselves a little more time," Fred countered. He was pressed against the side of the wall, peering around the corner, watching as Stone approached his mercenary team.

"Ok, so then what do we do now?"

"Wait for it," Fred growled with an intent stare, piercing daggers through Stone's back.

Senator Stone approached Williams, placing his hand on his shoulder. "I want those two dead." He glared back at the alley.

"Sir, the cops will be here in a minute."

"It's two fucking agents. Toss a grenade or some shit. I don't care; I want them dead. And get me out of here."

Williams nodded at two of his men. "You heard him; go end them." The two men moved forward, advancing on Fred and Sophia's position, checking their magazines.

Two cop cars flew around the corner of 7th Street. The two shooters stopped spinning around, unloading full magazines into the vehicle, instantly killing the driver with precise shots through the windshields.

"That's it," Fred shouted.

The distraction provided Fred and Sophia with the perfect opening. The two sprung out from the alley, firing at the two shooters. With simultaneous headshots, both men dropped to the ground.

Williams turned to see the two agents headed straight for him. Unable to get a shot off, Fred and Sophia's rounds sent Williams ducking for cover.

The rounds pounded the side of the Land Cruiser that Stone had just climbed into. The reinforced armor was barely dented from the high-velocity impacts.

"Look, Sof. We still have a chance."

Running full speed ahead, they tried to close the gap. Williams returned fire, forcing Fred and Sophia to split up and dodge the shots. Sophia dove behind the brick column she had seen the mother and child behind earlier. Now, both of their bodies lay on the ground in a pool of blood. The mother shielded the child so the small girl was not hit. The sight of the dead mother protecting her child sparked a newfound hatred in Sophia. One way or another, this man would not live to the end of the day.

Fred ducked behind the SUV where they started the battle. Williams focused his fire on Fred's location. Sophia, using his divided attention, swung around the column, giving her a clear shot at Williams.

She squeezed off a three-round burst from her M4. All three rounds struck Williams, two in the right leg, the other hitting his forearm.

He swiftly descended to the ground, instinctively reaching for his sidearm. Without hesitation, he fired several shots in her direction. Sophia reacted swiftly, evading the incoming bullets by moving and zigzagging toward cover. She desperately sought refuge behind a nearby trash bin positioned strategically outside the entrance of a shop that lined the side of the road.

Sophia's gambit opened the window for Fred. Coming out from his position, he opened fire. Hitting the two remaining commandos before they could return to help their boss.

Williams was slow to recover from his injuries and couldn't shift positions fast enough to get off a shot at Fred. The FBI agent took two more shots. Williams' head snapped back as a round pierced through his skull. His hand and body went limp.

The two agents scanned the area for more threats, realizing no one was moving. Their eyes locked on each other from across the road. Fred gave the signal to move up.

They inched closer to the Land Cruiser. Stone was still inside, looking bewildered. The two converged in the middle of the street, guns drawn. "Freeze, don't move," Fred shouted, seeing one of the commandos crawl into the driver seat of the Land Cruiser. The gunman ignored the warning, turning the key and starting the SUV's engine. "Dammit, I said freeze."

Fred aimed at the engine block. The back window rolled down, and Sophia caught the shimmer of the sunlight glinting off the barrel of a handgun pointed directly at Fred.

Boom.

Sophia dove, tackling Fred to the ground and knocking him out of the way of the oncoming bullet. She landed on top of him with a hard thud, and they lay face to face. With the wind knocked out of him, Fred could hear the SUV's tires squeal as it peeled off.

"Phew, thanks for the save, Sof, but you can get up now." Sophia didn't respond. Sophia, who usually felt very light, as her slight athletic frame would suggest, now felt like a sack of bricks. He looked down at the top of her head.

"Sof?"

No response.

"Sophia?"

He reached around her body, gently rolling them over. Warm liquid oozed onto his fingers. His hand lurched back, and he instantly recognized the substance. Not wanting to peer down at his hand, he forced himself to do it. Fred gaped in horror at his blood-soaked appendage. It was her blood. Sophia's blood.

"Oh my god, no!" Fred shouted, undoing Sophia's vest and looking for the wound. She'd been hit in the back, just below the vest. Fred frantically searched for the exit wound. "No, come on, stay with me," he pleaded. "Where is it?" He began feeling around her abdomen. Several police cars careened around the corner. Officers descended on Fred and Sophia.

"Sir, get your hands up."

"I'm FBI! Call a medic now!" Fred shouted at the closest officer, ripping off his vest and jacket. He lifted Sophia's head, placed it in his lap, and used the coat to cover the wound while cradling her.

"Fr... Fred?" Sophia tried to sit up and look down at her

wound. "I… I… am."

"No, don't worry about that. Just look at me," he said, taking her by the chin and forcing her to look at him. "Ok, your eyes here." He pointed to his own. "Why did you do that?"

Sophia gulped. "Because I owed you one, remember?" She managed a blood-stained smile. "Besides, I told Sherry I would return you to her."

Fred's eyes welled up. "Well, damn you for that. I have a promise to keep, too. I told her I would never let anything bad happen to you."

Choking out a laugh, she said, "I guess I win. Again."

"Oh, no. You're not done just yet." He looked back up at the officers. "Where the fuck is the ambulance."

Sophia's eyes started to roll back.

"Stay with me, dammit. Help's almost here."

Sophia could feel her body growing cold. Her eyelids felt as though bricks weighed them down. Choking back the pooling blood in her throat. "Just promise me you'll get him."

Fred saw two paramedics approaching. "I'm not going anywhere. I'm right here with you."

"No, go get him." She whispered as the paramedics pulled Fred away.

"Sir, we need to get in here," a female paramedic said, grabbing Fred by the shoulder and pulling him back.

Fred shouted, "Stay with me, Sof."

The officers pulled him back to give the medics room to work.

"I'm not going anywhere, and neither are you."

"Fred, get him," Sophia said, her arm outstretched, as Fred's fingers slipped away from hers. Her eyes rolled back as her arm dropped. Then, the rest of her body fell limp.

CHAPTER TWENTY-TWO

Sherry wondered what could be going through her husband's mind at this particular moment as he turned into the hotel's parking lot. Even after fifteen years of marriage, Fred remained an enigmatic puzzle when it came to matters of the heart.

She glanced over at him to see his face as stoic as ever. He hadn't said a word since leaving the house. Stubborn and defiant until the very end, he adamantly refused to have a retirement party. It felt wrong to celebrate, given everything he had lost this last year. Though with most things, he caved in at the eleventh hour, especially given all the work his wife had done to prepare the extravaganza. She used his party as a showcase of her skills and an advertisement for her newest career endeavor as an event coordinator. Part-time, of course. She'd also tried to convince Fred to take up a part-time hobby or career himself.

"Fred, we're here. You coming in?" Sherry asked.

"I have to, don't I?" he answered with a deep sigh. "It's my party, after all, right?" Fred snapped, staring out the window.

"Ok, I'll see you in there then," she said, closing the door. Hoping her husband wouldn't maintain this terse attitude all night. Sherry headed inside the hotel.

"Shit," he groaned, running his hand through his hair. Fred instantly felt terrible for his tone. "Sherry, wait," he called, getting out of the car and running to catch up to her. "I'm sorry," he apologized, holding out his hand. The two embraced, sharing an unspoken acceptance before continuing inside.

The ballroom put Fred in a better mood.

Streamers hung from the ceiling, and a large banner stretched across a small stage at the head of the room. Several high-top tables had been strategically placed in the middle of the room. Along the far wall, a mobile bar stood, with a bartender serving drinks to the attendees. Next to him was a table stretched along the wall, topped with an assortment of appetizer-style foods.

The room was full of agents from the office and several of Fred's retired friends. Sherry also invited some of her closest

285

friends to attend. She didn't want to feel too left out when Fred went to mingle. Looking around the room, he lit up.

He leaned over to peck his wife on the cheek. "Thank you, honey."

"Do you like it?" She waited for an answer.

"I do," he said. "I think you have a real knack for this stuff."

"Really, Fred, you think so?"

"Judging by this setup, I would say yeah. I think you'll do fine as an event planner," he said reassuringly, knowing she'd been having doubts.

"Well, time to do something you hate," she said, shoving her husband forward. "Go mingle." Taking her leave, he grumbled, waving to a friend across the room.

Tobias stepped forward, seemingly out of nowhere, and handed Fred a champagne flute. "Welcome, a little late," he said, shaking his friend's hand. "That's unlike you, Fred. Already settling into retirement mode," he ribbed, drawing a scowl.

"Har-dee har," Fred managed as he took a sip. Never one to indulge in alcoholic beverages, but this was a celebration—his, after all. "You know me and events," he commented, smiling sarcastically.

"This place looks great." The two took in the surroundings. "Sherry really has an eye for this stuff."

"She does," Fred added, his voice filled with pride. "So, what's the latest on the Senator's whereabouts?" He changed the subject quickly. "Please tell me there's been an update?" He was fishing for information from his former boss. Fred had been out of the information loop for weeks now. The question had been burning a hole in his psyche since D.C.

Tobias shot him a look of apprehension. "Fred, you know I can't discuss an open case. You're officially retired as of this morning, remember?"

"Dammit, Tobias, how long have we been friends? I can't just walk away without knowing something. It feels like I'm leaving the job unfinished. It's been two months."

Tobias inhaled deeply, thinking. They had been friends for a decade, and he knew that not catching Stone had been eating at his friend. Making sure no one was within earshot.

"Look, between you and me, the last word I got was an unconfirmed sighting somewhere in Europe. However, with his wealth and connections, it will take time. Besides, it's now out of my hands. When he's caught, you'll be my first call." He placed a comforting hand on Fred's shoulder. "For now, enjoy your party. Your wife worked hard to set this up. Speaking of." He smiled at Sherry as she approached. "He's *all* yours now. Good luck."

Tobias slinked away, leaving the couple standing next to the dance floor. An eight-by-ten section of the carpet had been covered with a hardwood portable dance floor. Fred took his wife's hand and led her out onto the floor.

"Not what you wanted to hear, I take it," Sherry opined, seeing the disappointed look on Fred's face.

"What, no, we were just-"

"Just talking about whether they've caught the Senator yet. I figured," she responded as the two embraced, swaying about

"Please don't be mad." He spun his wife around mid-stride as the two glided across the dance floor.

"I'm not mad, honey," Sherry said, laying her head on her husband's chest. "On the contrary, I want that bastard brought down just as much as you do. However, it's no longer your fight. I want my husband back. Can you do that for me?"

Sherry had always been an understanding wife. She sacrificed their entire married life by sharing him with the FBI. Now, she just wanted her husband to be with her full-time. And Fred knew that. "Yeah, I can do that, I suppose," he whispered, looking down at her.

"Good," she said, smiling. "Then it's time for your speech." Peeling away from his chest, she took her husband by the hand as if he were a small child and led him to the stage, pushing him up onto it and shoving him in front of the mic stand. Before quickly rushing back, she left her husband alone at the microphone in front of the room and assembled the gathering. Sherry joined the crowd that slowly migrated to the front upon seeing the guest of honor take the dais wearing a mischievous smile.

Fred hated being the center of attention, and now Sherry had

287

just pushed him up on stage with everyone looking at him. He gave her a stern look that shouted out 'How dare you' without having to say it. All eyes turned to him.

"Um, most of you in this room are familiar with me," he began, his voice filled with emotion and sincerity. "And you know that I'm not one for speeches. So, I'll keep this brief. I wanted to express that it has been the greatest honor of my life to serve my country for over twenty years. An honor that is second only to being a husband to my incredible wife, Sherry, who has made just as many sacrifices as I have. It's no secret that this past year has been the most challenging of them all. I'm profoundly grateful to each of you who have been there for me throughout my career for the unwavering support and camaraderie that I have experienced. And to my dear friend Tobias, thank you for always being there. To all the agents gathered here and those who are unfortunately absent." He paused for a moment, his voice tinged with solemnity. "We have lost many valued coworkers and dear friends this year, and I would be remiss if I did not take a moment to mention them. So, let us remember Agents Wilson and Watts..."

Fred recited the names, each one carrying a weight of significance. Then, he came to a name that struck a deeply personal chord. "Agent William Finch, whom I personally took under my wing." Fred's voice faltered as he uttered William's name, and he swiftly wiped away a tear before gathering himself to continue. "And..."

"Naseem Girgrah and Yousef Ali," a voice shouted from the back of the room.

The crowd turned their heads at the interruption to find a woman standing at the back of the room.

Sophia Evans, blonde hair pulled back into a ponytail, wearing a form-fitting black sequence dress. Complete with her signature black wireframe glasses. "Don't forget Yousef Ali," she said again.

Fred smiled widely upon seeing the CIA agent. He continued. "Yes, and Yousef Ali. These agents made the ultimate sacrifice for their country. We will miss all of them. I want to thank you all for attending, and I encourage you to continue serving this country with the same pride that I have. Thank you." Fred stepped off stage, confronted by Sherry.

"I told you she would come. Now go talk to her," Sherry said, pushing her husband forward.

"Fred, it's nice to see you." The two embraced, lingering longer than usual.

"Sophia, I'm glad you made it," he said, squeezing her as tight as he could, forgetting she was still recovering.

"Can't... breathe," she whispered. Fred released his grasp. "I wouldn't have missed this for anything, old man."

"And, wow, look at you. You look like a million bucks in that dress, all done up. WOW." Fred admired her new look. "I should have called you, but I didn't think you'd want to talk to me."

"What?" Sophia exclaimed. "Why would you ever think that?"

"Because I let you down. I didn't catch the Senator. He got away and is still on the run."

Sophia scoffed, head tilted. "Come on now; I love you. You're like a father to me. I could never hate you." The pair made their way to a table.

"First off, I should have protected you better. And I didn't, and then I let him get away." He hung his head.

"We did our jobs. We both came out of it alive." Sophia subconsciously clutched her side, where the bullet had struck. "In my book, that's a win. Besides, he only got away because you refused to leave my side. It was your voice that pulled me back in the ambulance. I was a goner. So yeah."

"You really mean that? I have been beating myself up for weeks over that day."

"Of course, I mean that. I would have told you the same if you had come by during my recovery." She punched him in the shoulder.

"I'm sorry for that. I just cou-"

"Oh, shut up. We're family. I forgive you for bailing during my recovery. Now take me to that wife of yours." Fred led Sophia to their table, where they spent the rest of the night talking.

Sophia followed them back to Fred's place after the party. They spent the rest of the night catching up before she had to catch her flight back to Virginia.

****

Finally, back home, Sophia lumbered into her now half-empty apartment. Carol had left her after discovering she had lied to her their entire relationship. Never did she divulge that she worked for the CIA.

Sophia plopped down on the bed, exhausted.

Her phone rang.

"Sophia, I've just received your paperwork. You've been cleared for duty again." It was Director Owens on the phone. Her boss.

"Yes, sir," she said, silently pumping her fist. "I'm ready to go."

"Great. I need you in the office immediately."

****

As Sophia stepped out of the elevator, she was greeted by a group of agents who had congregated, applauding her arrival and creating a path for her to navigate the room. With a warm smile, she expressed her gratitude to everyone she passed along the way, acknowledging their support and well wishes. It had been weeks since she received the prestigious Intelligence Star Award in a ceremony, and this was her first time returning to the office since then. The recognition and applause reminded her of her achievements and the esteem she held within the agency.

"Sir," Sophia said, poking her head into Owens' office, red-faced with embarrassment, suffering from the same infliction as Fred. They hated being the center of attention.

"Sophia, great, come in. Sit. That wasn't my idea, by the way." He made sure she knew he hadn't put the office up to the idea. She took her seat, acknowledging he wasn't complicit in the impromptu parade. "As I mentioned over the phone, your paperwork has been processed. You're cleared for duty. I also received your request to return to field operations. Is that correct?"

"Yes, sir. That is correct. I want to go back out there," Sophia answered enthusiastically. "Ready to jump back in the saddle." She had been through so much over the last year and felt it was time to get back out there. She knew she was ready, having learned valuable lessons and drawn motivation from Fred and Wallace.

"Are you sure you're ready?"

"One hundred percent sure, sir."

Director Owens pulled a folder from his desk drawer and handed it to her. "Well then, I have the perfect assignment for you."

Sophia took the folder, unsure why it was separated from everything else. "What is it, and why is it perfect for me?"

"It's perfect for you because a) you can pull this off better than most agents and b) partly because you were requested."

"Requested by whom?" Sophia asked, puzzled as she opened the folder.

"Requested by eight other people. Apparently, you made a great impression."

The folder contained dossiers on Wallace's entire SEAL team, as well as pictures of the Senator and Hasan Althani, Amell's former enforcer and bodyguard.

Director Owens continued. "I want you to head up a new black ops team. You will take your directives straight from me and answer only to me. You will be in charge of the SEAL team and can handpick your support staff. Your first mission is to hunt down and take out Senator Stone and this Hasan Althani guy by any means necessary. Can you handle that?"

Sophia sat stunned and speechless, her mind reeling from what Director Owens had just handed her. "By any means necessary? Like assassination? This isn't a capture mission, is it?"

"Capture if you can. If not, the powers that be want us to ensure that Stone never sets foot in the United States again. So, can you handle this?"

Sophia tensed, clearly uncomfortable but understanding, as she'd wanted to shoot the man a few months earlier without a trial. "I want to be sure I have this correct. You want me to head up a black ops squad of SEALs to take these men out, right?"

"Yes. That's your first mission. After that, you work only on the missions I authorize. You will have anything you need at your disposal. Just one phone call to me, and you'll have it."

"I… I say yes. I want in." Sophia was shocked at herself for accepting the appointment.

"I was hoping you would say yes. Tonight, there is a flight leaving for Istanbul. You will be met by the CIA station chief there. Given the rest of the information, and meet Commander Wallace's team. Happy hunting, Sophia."

Sophia rose from her seat and extended her hand to Director Owens, a mixture of excitement and trepidation coursing through her. While she had taken charge of the team in Saudi Arabia, this new assignment felt distinctively different. The lifestyle awaiting her would starkly contrast with what she had grown accustomed to in the past three years. Although she had expressed her desire to return to the field, she hadn't expected it to materialize so quickly, let alone being entrusted with leading a black ops squad.

Returning home, she packed to leave and embark on her new life. One thing made her smile. After everything that had happened, she was still going to be the one to catch Senator Stone once and for all. She couldn't wait to tell Fred that she would be the one to close his last case.

Catching a glimpse of her reflection, she smiled back at herself, imagining it would be the same look on Fred's face. Slinging her go bag over her shoulder, she gave her empty apartment one last look. The ending of one chapter and the beginning of another. She closed the door.

THE END

EPILOGUE

With a thunderous roar, a rugged black Land Cruiser tore through the open gates at Jet Linx Private Terminal at Dulles International Airport, steam spewing from its powerful engine.

The driver grunted in pain, swinging the heavy vehicle around a sharp corner and tossing Senator Stone around in the back seat.

"Will you slow down, goddammit?" he barked, punching the back seat. "Where are we going?"

"Sorry, sir," the injured driver said, clutching the bullet hole in his leg, wincing. "I don't know."

"Where's my wife?"

"I don't know, sir,"

"Well, son, what the fuck do you know?" Stone demanded, holding on to the handle above the back window.

The vehicle lurched around another bend.

A stunning, immaculate white Gulfstream G700 blazed into view on the tarmac, its powerful engines roaring at full throttle and ready to take flight into the unknown.

"Is that my ride?"

"Yes, sir," the driver answered in the affirmative for the first time.

"Jeez, the kid finally knows something. Is my wife aboard?"

"I believe so; a team was also sent to pick her up."

The Land Cruiser came to a screeching halt. The injured driver dragged himself out of the battered vehicle, hobbling to the rear, opening the senator's door. "Right this way, sir," he said, guiding the disgraced politician around the back of the SUV.

A man and woman met Senator Stone near the steps that led up to the private jet. The tall, dark-haired man reached out to shake the former Senator's hand with a smile. "It's nice to meet you finally, sir. I'm Captain Rick Smith," he said, flashing a set of pearly white teeth. "And this is Amanda." He gestured to the svelte redhead beside him. "She'll be your attendant for the flight."

Impatiently, the senator responded, "Yes, let's proceed. We

293

likely have a schedule to follow." He brushed past the welcoming committee members, forcefully ascending the steel steps with resounding thuds.

"Yes, sir. And your wife is already safely aboard."

Next, the captain turned to the injured driver, who was, in fact, a soldier, to say, "You know what to do, right?"

"Yeah, yeah, get rid of the fucking car, and throw the police and feds off the trail. Got it, flyboy," the soldier mumbled, limping back to the steaming SUV.

A few moments later, he was driving away from the Jetstream's vantage point.

The pilot and attendant safely boarded the plane and closed the hatch as a grounds crew wheeled the staircase away.

"Do you know where we're going?" Stone asked the pilot.

"Male, in the Maldives. We're to meet Mr. West there," Rick stated, starting the take-off procedure. "I would suggest taking a seat now, sir. Amanda?" The young redhead promptly escorted the Senator to his seat.

"Roy, what's going on? How did you get out of jail so fast? And why are we going to the Maldives to meet Rebecca's husband there? The senator's wife bombarded him with questions as he buckled in.

"I'll explain everything later. When we're safely away from this place," he replied curtly.

"Did… did you do everything the FBI agents said?"

"I'll explain everything later." He raised his voice. "I've had a pretty shitty day so far. So if you could just *shut up* for a second."

His wife recoiled at the outburst and remained quiet for the rest of the flight.

****

The next day, Senator Stone was sitting in a bar overlooking the Arabian Sea, sweating profusely. The hot tropical air was much too humid for the Oklahoma native. He nervously looked around every few minutes, feeling the eyes of the world on him.

On the other side of the table, Rick had thrown his feet up, lounging back in the chair, sipping a beverage. He'd been eyeballing a table of three local women across the bar.

"Will you stop that?" the Oklahoman politician snapped. "You're drawing attention to us. And get your feet off the table." He pushed the pilot's feet from the top of the table, causing the younger man to spill some of his drink. The women chuckled and snickered at the scene.

"Relax, sir," the captain said, wiping liquid from his chin with a napkin. "No one is looking for you here. We made sure no one could trace the plane."

"Where is Jonathan then, hmm? He was supposed to be here ten minutes ago." He checked his watch. Then, he took a deep breath and scanned his surroundings. "I can't believe I'm on the fucking run. That damned CIA bitch."

His companion gave him a look of bewilderment.

"Oh, never mind. Ah, here he comes." The senator stopped the puzzled pilot before he could inquire further.

Jonathan West entered the bar and took off his sunglasses as he spotted the two men. Two other men with beards flanked him— all three wearing Hawaiian shirts and cargo shorts.

Jonathan was the owner of Sotor Corp and Senator Stone's son-in-law. He was of average height, physically fit, and had a six-pack of abs that played peek-a-boo from behind his fluttering shirt. The former Marine Force Recon soldier-turned-corporate owner cut a formidable figure.

"Roy,' he said, sitting at the table. It seemed as if he didn't have a care in the world.

"How could you be so calm at a time like this? Everything we worked for is blown," Senator Stone fumed. "Where is Rebecca?"

"She's okay; I just left her with Martha in your room. And yes, I know things are fucked right now. But we've covered our tracks, so this shouldn't take too long to blow over."

"The hell we did," shouted the Senator, pounding the table. The patrons started looking over. "If we had covered our tracks, I wouldn't be sitting here in the Maldives. The FBI wouldn't have raided Sotor Corp and come to my fucking house."

"Look, I've got a plan. Americans have a short attention span.

295

So…"

"They don't forget terrorist attacks on their country, though," Stone retorted fiercely. "For fucks sake, you should know that, being a former soldier."

"I know that, but all we have to do is give them a reason to see why you did what you did. We can spin this."

"I ran away. There's no way we can spin that," Stone fumed.

"But did you run? Or were you kidnapped by the very terrorist that someone wanted the American people to believe you were funding?"

"What?" Stone finally calmed down enough to listen to his son-in-law. "Who would do something like that?"

"The Russians. They planted evidence to make it look like you were funding a terrorist group."

"Why would they do that?"

"To help destabilize the country. What better way to take down America than to have it fight itself?"

The Senator started to grasp Johnathan's intentions. "Ah, I see. The Russians aim to undermine our reputation and sow doubt among Americans about their government. They've already interfered in our elections, so this wouldn't be too far-fetched. I understand. But how do we make this narrative believable? We would have to discredit all the evidence presented by that CIA agent. Then, we need to identify someone to shoulder the blame, the scapegoat. The kidnapper, perhaps."

"Let me worry about that first part. As for the second, here he comes now." An Arab man pulled out the chair next to Senator Stone and took a seat.

His cold, dead eyes made the Oklahoman shiver.

"Glad you could make it, Hasan. Hope the flight wasn't too rough," said Jonathan, forever the voice of reason.

Hasan Althani stared at the Americans through an intense gaze. He had disappeared after crossing the Yemen border and wasn't on Perim Island during the assault. And yet, here he was.

"It was fine," he growled. Not the type of man who had time for niceties.

"Hopefully, my men weren't too forceful bringing you to this meeting?" Jonathan continued.

"No."

Stone couldn't take his eyes off the Arab.

"This is the man that's to be the kidnapper?" Stone asked with a gulp.

Hasan's reputation had always preceded him. He had a penchant for ruthless violence and notoriety for beheading dozens of American and NATO soldiers.

"Yup, tracking him down after Amell's death took a bit. Tsk, tsk. Why would you leave your boss all alone like that?" Jonathan said, mocking the Arab.

In an instant, the situation escalated into a display of raw aggression. Fueled by anger, the man attempted to leap out of his seat, but his actions were promptly thwarted as the two accompanying individuals forcefully pushed him back down.

"Now, we have a few things to discuss here," Jonathan continued, unfazed by the outburst.

"Do I get to kill Americans?" came his sneering reply as he eyeballed one of the two guards.

"You do," Jonathan said with a sardonic grin, leaning in, mouth twisting into a cartoonish smirk.

"One in particular," Stone fervently interjected. "A CIA woman. The bitch that brought this whole thing down," he growled, angrily clutching his fist. "Got my whole damn family on the run like some common criminals."

"The one who killed Amell?" Somehow, Hasan's glare intensified as he glowered from behind the dark coals of his eyes.

"The very one," Jonathan answered.

"That's all I needed to hear. I'm in."

AUTHOR'S NOTES

I want to thank all who have taken the chance leap into purchasing a book from an unknown author. I sincerely hope that you've thoroughly enjoyed reading the story that has unfolded on the pages before this. As HEARTLAND STRIKE was a leap for me to write, having never thought of myself as much of a writer before embarking on this journey years ago.

Creating HEARTLAND STRIKE was a blast, as I have always loved to create things in my head. However, creating in your head for your enjoyment differs from putting it down and out for the enjoyment of others. Being an author had not been something I had thought of being until about eight years ago.

If you'd bear with me for a few moments to take a quick trip down memory lane, I promise that I'll get back to the book and its genesis.

Never in a million years would I have thought that I, of all people, could sit down (and be still enough) and be able to focus and channel my scatter-brained thoughts into a cohesive story. Growing up as an only child in California surrounded by friends who all had siblings, I found myself going home at night with nothing but my imagination to keep me occupied until I could spend the next day playing outside again with my friends.

Using that imagination, I would create games, stories, and scenarios that I could preoccupy myself with until bed. So, I guess I always knew deep down that I had a knack for creativity, as I loved creating. However, being able to focus and foster that creative side was never something I had ever thought of doing.

Though I should've known there was a writer somewhere inside of me when in tenth grade English, I was nearly expelled from school because the teacher believed I had plagiarized a story. It was a mid-term assignment in which we had to write a ten-page short story. Me being me, of course, found schoolwork as secondary in life to being outside with my friends playing sports. I procrastinated writing it until a few days before the assignment

298

was due. Another problem that still plagues me today, as I am sure it does for many people. (Procrastination, that is.) I remember sitting at the table, pencil in hand, notebook in front of me, hurriedly scribbling my story down two days before I had to turn it in.

I waited until the last minute to put it down on paper. However, the entire story had already been concocted in my head during the week prior, a tactic I still use to this day. I got everything down on paper and eleven pages later turned it in. Only to receive the assignment back a few days later with a giant red 'F' and a note to stay after class. My heart sank. I'd never had an F before on anything, and couldn't fathom how I failed the assignment. I knew at the time (and still) that I am not the best at grammar, but I felt the story itself was good. Grammar aside, and I shouldn't have failed because of that, as he'd stated that on this assignment, grammar would make up, I think, twenty percent of the grade.

Class ends, and I walk up to the teacher, paper in hand, and shakily ask why I got an F. He confidently stated he'd given me an F because he believed I plagiarized the story. To my shock and anger, I told him I did not steal the story, and that I did, in fact, write every word on my own. He refused to believe me and said he'd recommended to the principal that I be expelled because he would not tolerate literary thievery. After a parent/teacher/principal meeting days later, I am totally vindicated because the teacher had zero proof I plagiarized, because there would never be any, because I did not.

Needless to say, that was my last venture into writing for several years. It scared me away from writing honestly, and I had other things I enjoyed doing far more.

Fast forward four years (stay with me here, almost to the book), I am in Afghanistan shooting the breeze with a buddy of mine. Out of nowhere, I am struck with a sudden desire to write again as he and I are brainstorming crazy ideas. I bought a notebook and pencil from the base PX and began writing what would be the blueprint start of HEARTLAND STRIKE. For various reasons, one being my penmanship is absolutely atrocious: sometimes I can't read what I write, and since I am in a combat zone, I stop.

Skip ahead about ten years, and I am working at a job that I no longer enjoy doing, and in fact, I just want to work for myself. That writer's itch creeps back in. I look into how to become a writer. Finally.

A few months and dozens of read articles later, I officially begin my writer's journey with some short stories, which can be read on my website. I know what I write about, history. I love history and mythology, so I wanted to write a series of books, something like Indiana Jones, Tomb Raider, or the Uncharted video game series. However, I still don't know if I can write an entire novel. I needed proof of concept that I could sit down and write an entire book.

This is where HEARTLAND STRIKE officially comes about. One night, driving to work, I am struck with the memory of the conversation my buddy and I had all them years ago in Afghanistan—the plot that I had come up with. That night, I smoothed out the details, and the next day, I started writing.

The most interesting thing about the book you've just read is…it was never supposed to see the light of day. HEARTLAND STRIKE was supposed to be for me, and me only. To prove that I could write something from start to finish that was coherent and a good story.

After finishing the first draft, I put it away. I had done it; I'd written an entire book. On to the next challenge, writing the one that I really wanted to. I started work on the AEGIS ORDER that will hopefully one day be something that you all can enjoy reading.

While writing it, I learned a little more about the industry. I learned I needed to build a platform if I wanted to be successful, because most people's first books don't do well. I didn't want that to happen to my pet project, no, I couldn't let that happen.

That's where HEARTLAND STRIKE truly comes into play. I already had a book that could help launch my platform. It was rough, well, very rough. I needed to refine it, but I could use it as my first book, then pick back up with the series that the AEGIS ORDER kicks off. I spent the next several months reworking

HEARTLAND STRIKE, and it was during this process that I started to really fall in love with what I had created. The characters, the story, the genre, and everything else about it.

The book morphed into something entirely different from its original self. I started to see another path for it—from something that was never supposed to be seen to a one-off book that would hopefully launch my author's platform, to now, what will be the start of a whole other series of novels.

The process that this book has been through has, in a way, become a metaphor for my life. A series of twists and turns that have culminated in what I hope will be the start of something new, something joyful, and something which I hope all of you have enjoyed reading, as much as I have bringing it to you.

Oh, and don't worry—Sophia and the team will be back on a brand-new adventure. America will have its RETRIBUTION.